ADVANCE PRAISE for
The Legend of Leanna Page

"If you are looking for an epic fantasy flavored with mythical lore, adventure, a splash of drama and romance, plot twists, and suspense, **The Legend of Leanna Page by Cedar Flyte is a perfect pick**. ... The poetic prose unfolds at a deliberate pace, allowing readers to connect with the well-crafted cast. ... The cinematic depictions vividly captured the medieval setting and made me feel as if I were next to the cast, experiencing every moment. ... **This page turner is an amazing debut** in the Elenvian Adventures series, and I can't wait to read the next installment."
– Keith Mbuya for *Readers' Favorite* (FIVE STARS)

"Flyte's well-paced story is full of creative worldbuilding concepts and intriguing characters, and it features some thoughtfully timed twists and turns along the way. ... The narrative as a whole—in which Leanna and Kennedy grow and explore their world and work to encourage peace and understanding among their respective peoples and kingdoms—is **exciting and skillfully delivered**, and it's sure to keep aficionados of the genre invested. **An immersive and well-constructed adventure tale**."
– *Kirkus Reviews*

"The Legend of Leanna Page blends epic fantasy, political themes, and moral challenges in a single connected story. ... **Flyte's captivating writing sounds like a tale handed down through generations**, giving it a lasting sense of history ... Family, loyalty, and bridging divides are central themes, and the story shows how understanding and cooperation matter in a divided world."
– David Jaggart for *Readers' Favorite* (FIVE STARS)

"Cedar Flyte builds a secondary world whose most arresting feature is not its marvels but its moral weight ... Flyte writes with patience for the process and consequences, showing how borders are strengthened by ink and ceremony before a stone is ever laid. ... **A spectacular entry into the series**."

– Jamie Michele for *Readers' Favorite* (FIVE STARS)

"Everyone who knows me dearly now knows about this book, and anyone who will get to know me will eventually get to know it too. **I genuinely did not want this book to end once I started it.** ... This book has everything for everyone; romance, betrayal, found family — and in my opinion the most important part, a courageous, compelling heroine in Leanna. As the author has said, she is the kind of character that stays with you even after you close the book, and I find that to be true. **I loved both the poetry and the prose in this book, it was such a fun time throughout**."

– Terezija Meštrović, Reviewer on NetGalley (FIVE STARS)

Art by Tobin Pratt
Oil on canvas

The Legend of Leanna Page

or

The Elenvian Adventures

A tale hidden in time

as remembered and retold by
Cedar Flyte

VOLUME ONE
A BEGINNING

FOR ELENVIA PUBLICATIONS
Martinez, California.

The Legend of Leanna Page - Volume One: A Beginning
Copyright © 2026 by Cedar Flyte.

All rights reserved. No part of this book may be used or reproduced in any manner whatsoever without written permission from the Publisher except in the case of brief quotations embodied in critical articles and reviews.

Creatives are encouraged to allow this work to inspire work of their own but are here warned that all characters and settings are covered under this copyright and may not be included in any other work without written permission.

Visit ForElenvia.org for information on contacting the Publisher.

Library of Congress Control Number: 2026931527

Cover Artist: Tobin Pratt
Editor: Addam Ledamyen

ISBN: 979-8-9932767-0-0

About the Publisher

For Elenvia: Publications and Productions

We are 501(c)3 non-profit, interdisciplinary arts organization focused on using theatre and literature to collectively imagine a better world and consider how we might make it real.

Our Mission

With a focus on theatre and literature, we use the arts to unite people under a common philosophy of limitless respect, empathy, and curiosity. We believe in the possibility of a better world and work towards its creation through artistic education and active community organizing.

Our Vision

We imagine a future where people can unite across all borders: psychological, socioeconomic, or geographical. This future we see is one of peace, safety, and liberty, and we call it Elenvia. We believe Elenvia is achievable through philosophical questioning and artistic joy. We see ourselves as the bridge between our current era and the next. We will find and generate an abundance of Elenvian art through promoting and developing an abundance of Elenvian artists who will help us find ourselves, at last, in a great Elenvian day.

About the Publisher

Our Values

For Elenvia adheres to the following values in every aspect of our organization, from internal affairs to our works of art.

- All life forms have dignity and shall be treated with the reverent respect that is due to them by nature of their existence.

- There is nothing and no one that is above critique. Anyone should feel free to respectfully disagree with anyone else.

- We define hatred as a lack of respect for another's basic dignity, and this will not be tolerated in any circumstance.

- The world is full of philosophical mysteries. We will ask questions and delight in the investigations but never pretend we are certain of the absolute truth about anything.

- We find it evident that when peace and safety are combined with joyousness, something has gone right, and that thing is good. Everything we do and every project we support will work towards creating more of this good for as much of the world as possible.

Thank you for supporting our efforts!

For all those who would help build our own Elenvia.

CONTENTS

Dedicatory Epistle	1
Map of the World Within the Woods	5
CHAPTER I. Masor	6
The Favorite of the Sky	15
CHAPTER II. Pavoline	19
CHAPTER III. Far Off Love	35
CHAPTER IV. The Cave of Dreams	49
Love Will Find	49
CHAPTER V. Discovering Destiny	55
Lady Sundar-Khar	61
CHAPTER VI. Finding Family	67
CHAPTER VII. The Birth of a Legend	75
CHAPTER VIII. The Adventure Begins	83
Dramatis Personae	97
CHAPTER IX. Kennedy Meets Alquoria	100
CHAPTER X. Stepping Into the Light	116
Lines of Ivy No. 1	129
Lines of Ivy No. 2	132
CHAPTER XI. Stablehands and Pages	134
Lines of Ivy No. 3	136
Lines of Ivy No. 4	138
Lines of Ivy No. 5	144
CHAPTER XII. Nebulous Is Stolen	145
CHAPTER XIII. A Drought's First Days	156

CHAPTER XIV. Byrdon, The Father 167
CHAPTER XV. Guiomar, The King 172
CHAPTER XVI. The Aldorian Waterfall 186
CHAPTER XVII. Love and Loyalty 199
CHAPTER XVIII. Friends, Enemies 214
CHAPTER XIX. Another Home 225
    Sketch Our Souls 227
CHAPTER XX. Maddening Truth 232
CHAPTER XXI. An Alliance 241
CHAPTER XXII. The Wingless One 247
CHAPTER XXIII. Defending Love 260
CHAPTER XXIV. The Woodbound Players 279
CHAPTER XXV. Philosophy's Art 290
CHAPTER XXVI. One Last Mural 301
CHAPTER XXVII. Nebulous Rises 309

The Legend of Leanna Page
Volume One - A Beginning

DEDICATORY EPISTLE

A Letter from the Author

To my dear Reader,

The pages before you are filled with a world of legend. I want to assure you before beginning that every character, setting, and event portrayed within this volume, and the volume forthcoming, is entirely true, although how much is factual, I cannot say. With the time that has passed between their happening and their telling, there can be no doubt that some details will have shifted. I ask simply that you look beyond them and hold within you what we all might recognize as truth.

The second incident of these pages I shall ask you to oblige is the very fashion with which I have written them. I make no apologies for my archaic parlance; still, if you are to spend such time amongst my paragraphs, I suppose you may be due an explanation of their form. Thus, I shall offer you the following. This tale was not told to me quite so elegantly as it is here. Instead, it was spoken to me night after night by my grandfather, same as it had been sung to him by his own, in an ill-advised attempt at using adventure to lure a child to sleep. Within the confines of my small familial unit, the stories of Elenvia and Leanna Page were held and remembered alongside those of Robin Hood and King Arthur. It was not until I bravely quoted the royal fairy, Kennedy, to an early school instructor that I discovered with dismay the tales were entirely unknown. I do not blame the world for this, though at first I tried, for my grandfather at last sat me down and explained the truth: There are many magnificent legends the world rudely disremembers, but it happens that this one they have truly never been told.

It was then I learned of a tie to Elenvia I would never have dreamed. It was my own grandfather, Jemison Flyte, who, as a young Elenvian himself, had ventured deep into the Infinite Wood and, at long last, discovered us at the end of his journey! The moment he stepped beyond the Woods, into our own land, they vanished behind him and, despite his efforts, he was never to discover that infinite Forest, nor the world that hid within it, again.

But my family is not the subject of this story, merely its teller, and the telling of it has been the inspiration for my life's work. I have read through many publications in preparation for it, from various depictions of the Arthurian tales and the Merry Men of Sherwood Forest to the novels of Ann Radcliffe and Walter Scott. It was, in fact, Scott's "Dedicatory Epistle" preceding his *Ivanhoe* that gave me cause to consider composing one of my own. He, in his own antiquity, set out as I do to tell a tale of a different time, and his thoughts on the endeavor, which I copy in part for you here, mirror very much my own:

"*The painter must introduce no ornament inconsistent with the climate or country of his landscape; he must not paint cypress trees upon Inch-Merrin, or Scottish firs among the ruins of Persepolis; and the author lies under a corresponding restraint. However far he may venture in a more full detail of passions and feelings, than is to be found in the ancient compositions which he imitates, he must introduce nothing inconsistent with the manners of the age; his knights, squires, grooms, and yeomen, may be more fully drawn than in the hard, dry delineations of an ancient illuminated manuscript, but the character and costume of the age must remain inviolate; they must be the same figures, drawn by a better pencil, or, to speak more modestly, executed in an age when the principles of art were better understood. His language must not be exclusively obsolete and unintelligible; but he should admit, if possible, no word or turn of phraseology betraying an origin directly modern.*"—Walter Scott, 1817.

There is the occasional poem contained within which, memorized by generations, finds you in all but its original form. The rest, however, required recomposing, and I thought it an injustice to the legend to allow its introduction to our contemporary world to take place in any manner that failed by its form to entirely respect the nature of its subject. Our own literary history is filled with legends that were told in the same manner as this one, and they have held a rigid grasp on our societal unconscious for centuries. The heroes of this tale are vastly dissimilar to those the centuries have known, and I hope that mirroring the style of old legends to tell this own anew will prevent their differences from delineating these to a lesser status.

Furthermore, I know this style of prose will seem antiquated to the modern ear, for I too once had to read my first volume written in it, but upon engrossing myself in the language I grew to adore it as I would an old friend.

Now I maintain a love for these words, and their distinct ability to convey the most haughty humor or describe the perfect sunrise, and I hope that fondness will seep through the holes in these letters and replicate itself in your soul. I assure you, had the words of Radcliffe not made me burn to look through the windows of Udolpho, I would not have accepted them as my mentors.

My grandfather always told me that the legend of Leanna Page was an important one. I never cared much for his deliberation on its meaning as a child, but as I grew and witnessed more of the world around me, I came to better understand. Leanna's story tells of a broken world, kept apart by hatred, despondency, and pride, that at last was brought together by a simple serving girl who, of course, was always so much more. It is the origination of a state for humanity that feels, in our own time, impossible to attain; however, Elenvia is not a perfect place. It is not free of grief or anger or cruelty. It is only the combined efforts of most people living within the land environed by the Infinite Wood, regardless of their status or nationality, collaborating towards a world that serves them all. Perhaps their stories can be a lesson in their world's attainability, but if you rather not consider it so then consider it only as thus: It is a tale, magical and romantic and filled with adventure at every turn. It is my dream that telling it in the way I do will cause it to infiltrate your heart, same as it did my own. If you find the legend herein enticing but the words unrelatable, I entreat you to consider this only the original text and accept my heartfelt invitation for you to tell it again in a new way.

Elenvia may be lost to us now, but perhaps through the rebirth of their stories, we can create one anew. Furthermore, the volumes you now hold contain only what my family's memories were able to impart. While writing, further details came to me in dreams and, knowing Leanna, that they did so should be no surprise. Once you open your mind to it, more Elenvian history may reveal itself to your imagination. I implore you to release it from concealment and share it with the world as I do now; for, if we are ever to find Elenvia, we must know what we are searching for.

Esteemed Reader,
I am, here on forth, your devoted servant,

Cedar Flyte

May 27th, 2021.

P.S. —

After he passed, I discovered many notes and drawings amongst my grandfather's belongings. Among them were dozens of drafted maps, speculative and historical, outlining the world through its many eras. I have gathered them together and utilized them to create what I hope to be an accurate representation of how the world appeared during this early part of our story. I present it for you here.

Map of The World Within The Woods

CHAPTER I

Masor

It was still early in Spring, and the chill left behind by Winter nipped at the air, but only enough to make one shiver with excitement and forget any idea of wrapping themselves in a shawl. The castle at Masor stretched its towers of elegant gray stone into the bluing Sky and relaxed its base into the ground beneath, content to never see the sunrise from behind the gargantuan Trees of the Infinite Wood—a forest seemingly infinite in both height and area, for none have returned from attempting to discover otherwise—upon whose edge the castle resided. Masor's queen, the good Fionella Oxbien, stood atop the tallest bastion of her castle taking in the magnificent sight of the Wood. A northwestward wind blew from the Forest and seduced her with the scent of sweet herbs and fresh mystery. She tilted her head back, lifting her gaze to its furthest extent, and sighed at the impossible task of discovering the Treetops, even from the great height of the bastion. Turning to look beneath her toward the north, she studied the topmost leaves of the Masorian woods within her borders. These, miniature in comparison, were known for their game and adventurers; yet they held none of the mysterious magic that danced constantly around each of the infinite Trees.

Fionella had never traversed a step beyond Masor into the Infinite Wood, for it was well understood in both kingdoms that no royal was ever to attempt it. Still, on this day in particular, the aged queen could not help but remember her wedding night when the king, Madrick, had whispered to her one especially sweet story of the Wood.

"Are you thinking of the Forest?" His voice rose from behind her as he joined her on the landing. She turned and smiled at the spark in his eye.

"So you recall it as well?" she teased, returning her gaze to the Wood.

"The grove at Lufian is said to be charmed with the most endearing of magics, making an act of love underneath it unbearably divine." He stepped to her, encircling her waist within his arms and resting his chin on her shoulder. Whispering, he confessed, "I remember tales of it every year on this day."

Fionella chuckled, disengaging slightly from her husband and facing him. "How did you hear of it in the first, oh careful King?"

Madrick shrugged. "Rumors come and go. Moreover, I was not always a wise king but once a reckless prince, prone to fraternizing with the local charlatans who would venture into the Wood against better advice."

"'Tis a shame our son takes after your younger half," Fionella thought aloud.

"He shall grow."

"I suppose."

King Madrick took hold of his beloved's hands and returned to their romantic musings. "Come, Queen, what say you? I think our fortieth anniversary of betrothment is a splendid time for an adventure."

"To the Wood? Oh, think truthfully, love, we cannot enter it. What would the Ranzentines say?"

"The Ranzentines need never know! There has been so little communication between our castles this past decade, how would they ever discover it?"

"Rumors come and go," she reminded him.

Madrick stepped back in a playful huff. "So, if we were discovered by the royals of Pavoline, what of it? We will have committed no crime."

"You know the Ranzentines are more superstitious about the Woods than we are. They may view our entering it as a risk to the truce."

"King Petrenair is gentle. He never leads with the sword. We would send him a small billet of good intent, he would invite us to share a weekend in his castle, and we would share a laugh over it all."

The queen smirked as he removed her arguments but could not yet accept he would have an answer to them all. "And what of the fairies who give the Woods their magic and protect it from invasion with violent force?"

"I do not pretend the journey is free of risk; therein lies half the fun! Still, I cannot imagine fairies, even, are so cruel as to prevent the entrance of two old fools looking to share an evening of bliss."

Fionella smiled. The two royals watched each other's eyes deeply and found agreement in their glance.

"Isolda will be furious," Fionella remarked with a knowing grin.

"Then upon our return she shall observe our joy and take a much-needed lesson in the acquisition of gaiety."

The king and queen laughed until Fionella's countenance began to fall somber.

"Is it not unwise to venture so, aging as we are?"

Madrick tucked a wisp of gray behind the queen's ear and held a finger under her chin. "What better decade to fulfill your fantasies than one which might be your last?"

"Have they gone mad?" Princess Isolda, daughter to the king and queen, was indeed in a bewildered frenzy at the news of her parents' flight. She stood at her writing desk, fists upon the face of it, and focused her fury at Fionella's young maid, Esta, who had come with the message.

"Mad in love, it might be," Esta explained with a contained giggle. "It seems the arrival of their anniversary has rekindled certain flames."

"Dost thou find this funny?"

Straight-lipped, Esta replied, "No, Your Highness."

"What if they perish? What do they expect my brother to do, become King?" Isolda scowled at the thought of it.

"O dear, I daren't think on their demise," said the maid.

"Well, someone must!"

"I am certain the prince would sober for his coronation."

Isolda huffed, fell back into her chair, and shook her head. "Send me instant word upon their return."

"Of course, Your Highness." Esta congeed and took her leave.

The princess' gaze returned to the book of Masorian histories which lay open atop her desk, holding tales of their kingdom's heroes and records of every lagif who had helped govern in service of the crown. What had been but a light morning's pleasure read now turned her thoughts to ones of a more severe gravity. She sat forward in an instant and flipped to a familiar chapter early in the volume, offering particular care to the extremely well-read pages. The story of the first Oxbien to rule over Masor had especially interested her as a child, her being second born just as Emmrand Oxbien was. She scanned the paragraphs, recalling every sentence without needing to read them in full, angering at the thought that her extensive adolescent efforts to bound ahead in her education had done naught to change her older sibling's birthright to the crown, and calming as she found herself at the climax of the old tale.

In the days before kingdoms, Emmrand was nothing more than the second child of Lagif Admist Oxbien who presided over a small hamlet just half a day north of the Gwahanu River. It was the first province to carry the name Masor. As dictated by family tradition, Emmrand's oldest sister, Rouge, was set to inherit their father's lagifship. Tradition dictated further that, while his younger siblings might lead lives as varied as merchants to nobility by marriage, Emmrand would serve his life as vice-lagif to his sister so long as she lived, a position holding more letters in half its title than responsibilities of import. Such was the duty of the second-born; it was a great honor, the book said.

The Ranzentines across the River held the city of Pavoline. With its sandstone architecture and vast natural reserves of precious metals, the southern city soared high above the flat farmlands of Masor. Emmrand made frequent visits to the city, crossing the wide Gwahanu at the strait at Its center where was constructed the only bridge between North and South. The book stated his motive was always to obtain stronger material for new farm tools, but Isolda thought a certain silent interest might have been a much stronger motivation. In Pavoline, he would have been witness to a different way of life. There they had no lagifs, but lords and ladies, each with a stated purpose designated by sex. If he had been born in Pavoline, then that Emmrand was the second child would have been incidental, for being the First-Born Son would have granted him rights to his father's title. The histories spoke of this with disdain, and Isolda naturally thought it absurd; still, she understood the desire to circumvent the rule of birth order and even admired the first ancient Pavols who managed to do so through whatever means they could.

At the time, the city of Pavoline had been ruled by Lord Drume Ranzentine, a title set to be inherited by his son Percy. However, there was an unusually small age difference between father and son, and the lord's strong figure and sprightly demeanor meant Percy was likely not to see his inheritance until he himself was an old man.

None of the writings were clear on how or wherefore the war began, the implication in Masor always being that Pavoline had attacked unprovoked. What was known was that, within a year, Pavol forces—led by Percy Ranzentine—had left their city, traveled north, and overtaken Masor, leaving Pavoline undefended against the near simultaneous movement of Masorian forces—led by Emmrand Oxbien—into Pavoline.

What intrigued Isolda was how long Oxbien and Ranzentine spent fighting, and yet how little they really fought one another. The battling continued for many a year past the conquering of each city with most so-called battles consisting of nothing more than each army traveling further north or south respectively and overtaking unprepared villages in their wake, ever increasing their stronghold. When all land encircled by the Wood belonged to one family or the other, and in order to conquer more they would either have to fight each other or the fairies of the Forest, the fighting ceased. Instead of battling across the River, the sovereignties of Masor and Pavoline were simply bordered and agreed upon, everything north of the Gwahanu becoming the Kingdom of Pavoline, and all to the south Isolda's homeland of Masor.

Under the chaos of war, both Lord Drume Ranzentine and Lagif-Heir Rouge Oxbien separately fell ill and died. They were grieved and counted among the lost, and when the Truce of the Two Kingdoms was struck and the war was ended, it was Percy Ranzentine and Emmrand Oxbien who were set to rule. Of these two mythic kings, the stories tell of lifelong enemies who found peace and respect through matched military might. Still, between the lines, Isolda could not help but read of two young allies who desired more than they were promised and found a way to achieve it.

Isolda closed the volume and sat back in her chair. She considered her parents, by now sure to be frolicking in uncharted Forest, and she examined possibilities of what royal life might be after the sudden disappearance of the king and queen. If her brother, Prince Madrick Oxbien II, was unprepared to govern—as surely he was—would she, as vice-crown, be able to assume every right and responsibility of the throne in his stead? A smile crept up her countenance, but a wave of guilt washed it away; for, although the idea interested her, she could not covet in earnest the early loss of parents who, though ridiculous at times and childish, had loved her too dearly. She shook all thought of it from her mind and wished her parents a speedy return.

Alas, the day passed into night and morning rose again, and still the king and queen remained unseen by the palace guards keeping watch. Days passed and all in the castle grew increasingly uneasy, no one more so than Princess Isolda who desperately wished her musings had not led her to so accurate a prediction. As the sun began its descent on the fourth day of their absence, Isolda battled contradicting senses of excitement, shame, grief, and determination until she at last accepted the inevitable responsibility she felt hovering over her shoulders. She approached her brother in his bed chambers.

"Madrick," she called, rapping the tall door with the back of her fist, cream-colored against the dark wood. There was no answer. She tried again. "Brother, we must speak, I implore you." After a moment, a sloppy voice finally came booming from the chamber.

"Hark! I am king hither, and I decree thou shalt not pass."

"You are not king of Masor yet," Isolda rejoined.

"You misunderstand. I mean not of Masor, but of these bed chambers. I am king here, and I am dressed not, and I desirous not to speak to thee."

"Nor I to thee, Brother, but alas, Mother and Father are gone now four days and the kingdom may well fall upon our shoulders within the four following. It is an issue, as she who'll be thy vice-crown, I beg thee to grant the utmost importance and urgency, so please pull up a pair of trousers and open this forsaken door." After her speech, Isolda knew she had won, so she waited silently, listening to her brother rummage about in search of trousers. At length, the door unclosed, revealing her brother, the prince, hair knotted, trousers backward, and chest lacking a shirt. The siblings each stared into the other's disapproving gaze.

"May I enter?" Isolda inquired. Madrick responded with a sly smirk as he side-stepped, bowing low, allowing the princess to pass. Once she had entered sufficiently, he retired to his desk where he kept his wine. Propping his heels on the edge of the wood, he leaned back and sipped from the bottle.

"How may I assist thee, Your Highness?" the prince jested.

Holding her breath against the stench of alcohol, Isolda responded, "We must discuss thy kingship."

Madrick whined, "I cannot be king. I am but of two and twenty. Is there no fairness? Father had twelve years more, at least!, to make himself ready."

"If thou hadst studied, like I, thou might feelest differently. For years now I have felt I could assume the duties of the crown."

"Then be crown, Isolda."

She sucked in a breath. "As much as it pains me, you know—as the younger of us—I cannot."

Madrick sighed at her formality. "Then why come here to flaunt your intelligence when you know it can be of no use?"

"I mean not to flaunt, for I believe it can be of great use. As your vice-crown, I am bound to serve, and while the title of crown may be required to fall upon you, the duties could, in theory, be appointed elsewhere." Madrick stared at his sister with understanding while she awaited his response.

"You want them, Isolda, the duties of the crown?"

"I would be honored to hold them." She chose her words with care.

Madrick closed his eyes and pressed a hand against the ache in the space between them. "I fear you are trying to take something from me that I should hesitate to release," he said.

Isolda pushed, "I mean only to ensure the prosperity of Masor."

Unclosing his eyes, he looked to her a moment and saw a determination—a passion—in her glare that he wondered if his heart would ever have the capacity to grant him. He took another swig of wine.

"Very well," he decided. Then he rose the bottle in a toast and nodded. "For Masor," he said sincerely.

"Well chosen, Brother." Isolda, having achieved her aim, began to exit.

"It will matter not," the prince blurted. "Mother and Father will return. The knights will find them."

With an honest sympathy for the drunken, optimistic fool, Isolda responded, "I am afraid it will lessen the ultimate pain if we begin the grieving now."

"Then you believe they are dead true?" Madrick held back a sob. Isolda nodded and quit the chamber, leaving the prince to let his tears fall in peace.

The young knight, Kn. Grilliot, whose weary heart and fatigued legs had led the royal search of the surrounding Woods for now seven days, began to give in to his fear that the king and queen were not to be found. Even after a week, neither he nor his fellow knights had quite overcome their apprehension at walking and sleeping amidst the infinite Trees, and all were ever on edge in anxious wait of their first encounter with a fairy. Grilliot knew from the tales that the creatures were far too skilled to have let even their small military contingent go unnoticed. The fairy warriors—known for visages as verdant as the leaves—would surely be hidden and observing from the Trees. Though they spoke not of it, all in the group were aware of the circumstance. Morale amongst them was dreadfully low.

Grilliot lifted his canteen, hoping to revive his spent strength, but stilled at the sudden call of Kn. Pouray. Racing past the others, he strode to Kn. Pouray's side, hope refilling his chest, but he deflated again as he witnessed the unpleasant cause of her call. The once fearless king lay lifeless on the Forest floor. The Oxbien family's Golden Oleander, which was once sewn into the king's elegant purple cloak, was torn off and thrown across his chest, all of it now ensanguined, stained in red. Beside him lay the queen in a no more delightful position.

The next morning, cries were heard throughout Masor as the knights returned to the castle, the king and queen stiff in their arms. Isolda received them in the Great Hall, standing proud in the face of tragedy. Madrick stood beside her until the doors unclosed, for upon seeing a hint of the bodies he gripped Isolda's shoulder, steadying himself, then stumbled out of the room. Isolda did not once remove her glance from her mother's hair, matted and unclean like she had never seen it before. Upon Madrick's exit, the new vice-crown merely stood taller as her parents' bodies were laid atop death tables in the center of the hall. She stepped down from the raised throne to stand beside them, staring expressionless for a time at one and then the other, the surrounding knights growing uneasy with every passing breath, unsure how to read the princess's thoughts. At long last, she spoke softly:

"This was no accident of the Woods."

Kn. Pouray, after a glance to her other knights, took it upon herself to respond for the group. "Their wounds do not appear to be made by any animal or weapon known to exist in the kingdoms. Shall we conduct an investigation into the cause of death?"

"When a king and queen are found dead in the heart of fairy territory, the question of the cause begs no answer."

"Shall we prepare a retaliation, Your Highness?"

Isolda shook her head. "The Fairy Nation is too powerful, and Masor now far too weak in spirit to risk waging a fruitless attack. We cannot retaliate with military force but retaliate still we must. Spread word amongst the civilry: Fairies have proven a menace to our kingdom. Any brave Masorian with the courage to enter the Infinite Wood shall be greatly rewarded if they can destroy a member of the Fairy Nation and gift their severed wings to this castle. They may have pretended friendship with us long ago, but there is no returning from this. I shall have it known, forever forth, the fairy folk will find no friend in the House of Oxbien." Isolda stormed from the Great Hall, purple cloak waving royally being her, leaving a chill in her wake.

The coronation of King Madrick II took place the same afternoon, as with the swearing-in of Vice-Crown Isolda Oxbien. Only slightly worse than was to be expected, the new king spent the evening wasting away in the castle wine cellar. None dared enter to see the young man turned in on himself, crouching in a corner, nursing a strong bottle to completion, though several servants who passed by could hear his sorrowful singing. The old cook stood by to hear the song. It was muddled through the king's tears, but could still be recognized as the favorite tune the recently lost monarchs used to sing with their children. Even the cook could not help but cry now at its final verse.

THE FAVORITE OF THE SKY

Take heed, for I shall tell a tale
Which peeves the people that fly.
It tells of how we humans were made,
And made the favorite of the Sky.

At first, our world was naught but Trees;
Just trees and dirt and Sky.
The Trees grew tall, grew very tall—
Became the meaning of "high."

Although the Trees were beauteous,
They were also dull and dry.
The Sky desired more than them,
So the Sky began to cry.

The tears that fell were many and
The tears that fell were strong.
So strong a massive pool remained
Aft' the Sky's saddened song.

Numerous years the pool stayed full,
Encircled by Trees around,
But then the pool began to sink;
The tears embraced into the ground.

When last the water ran all but dry,
The Sky saw what It had done.
Where once was only massive Trees,
Now a new terrain had won.

There were deserts, valleys, grasses,
And mountains made of stone.
Some forests did remain, but so much smaller
Than those the Sky had known.

Across the center of this new clearing,
The strongest tears refused to sink.
There the great Gwahanu River emerged,
Beginning, on Its own, to think.

The Sky paid the River no heed,
Only gloried in Its new world.
The River simply simmered below,
As Its waves rippled and curled.

The Sky thought Its new world beauteous,
But thought It too was a sight to see.
It wished for one who could admire It,
Someone like you and me.

It first made fish, then deer and ram,
And best of all, the bird,
But none of them admired the Sky,
Such as the Sky would have preferred.

A human, last, bore from tear-soaked ground,
And looked up to the Sky.
"Oh, what a beauty there is!" said they,
And It gave a contented sigh.

More of us were born from earth,
Then more from our own powers.
Without long, the World Within the Woods
Had become completely ours.

The River, though, grew jealous,
And wanted one Its own.
It tossed and tossed earth above Its waves,
Until it sparked, shimmered, and shown.

Thus It made the fairies of the Wood,
Much like us, if we could fly.
These beasts contested our right to home,
And angered, much, the Sky.

The Sky used Its wind to hold them back,
Trapping them in the Wood
Until they conceded the World Within,
Letting alone, as they should.

Children, now, fear not the fairy folk.
Leave them to their Woods to cry.
Their River powers can harm us not,
For we are the favorite of the Sky.

During this time, Vice-Crown Isolda took charge of sorting the king's affairs. She gave orders to the knights, dictated official notices to be sent to Masor's lagifs, and informed the collectors to report to her directly. No one raised any argument to her assumption of the post. The one action she was incapable of was to sign the crown's papers, for it had to be done with the royal seal and, despite her wishes, the ring on which it was engraved remained on the hand of the king.

At last, night fell on this, Isolda's longest day, and she sat somber at her chamber window, pondering. There was a soft knock at the door and she bid the person enter. Isolda was at once surprised and relieved to see Esta, her mother's maid, standing in the doorway.

Esta spoke. "Your Highness, as you know, my family has been in the service of yours for longer than either can remember. With the queen gone, I request to be maintained in your service, if you will have me."

"Of course, Esta. Gramercy." Isolda smiled sadly. The maid bowed and watched the princess's smile fade from her lips.

"Is there anything I can do for you now, Your Highness?"

Isolda paused in thought and, at length, said, "Dost thou recall the color of my mother's eyes?"

"Green, Your Grace."

With a sigh, she said, "Yes. My thanks, I had forgotten. That will be all."

Esta made to depart, but the moon's glare betrayed a wetness in the vice-crown's eye. She approached and knelt before Isolda. "You needn't always wear a mask of strength, Princess. To cry can do good for the spirit."

Isolda looked into the eyes of the wise maid, just barely younger than herself, and within them found a comforting sanctuary. She thought to throw her arms around her and release the tears of her grief into the maid's shoulder, but she sat taller and feigned a content smile. "That will be all, Esta," she said. The maid nodded, congeed, and took leave of the chamber, catching one final glance at Isolda as the stoic vice-crown returned her faraway gaze to the window.

CHAPTER II

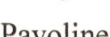

Pavoline

Past the plains of Masor, across the Gwahanu River, and deep in the heart of the kingdom of Pavoline, King Petrenair gazed into his looking glass and pushed aside a gray curl that had fallen across his eye. A month had now passed since the death of his friends in the House of Oxbien, and the old king felt his own reaper drawing near; still, as the eldest member of the House of Ranzentine, his will to survive kept strong his rule of Pavoline throughout every ailment and attack which had threatened him thus far. He thought of his son, the lone Ranzentine descendant. The young Guiomar, now but a few years off from his thirtieth, had grown strong-willed and stubborn like his mother, Queen Helena. Petrenair smiled, remembering the days his Helena swore there existed no force capable of severing her from his side. Until the fatal night of Guiomar's birth, nothing could have dissuaded him from this perfect notion. Alas, he sighed, once again entreating his heart to forgive the world its cruelty.

He eased his pain with thought of his son, his beloved wife's spirit blazing with life behind the prince's eyes. It was this spirit that was one day to lift the kingdom of Pavoline from his shoulders, trading its own as support. Guiomar was sure to lead Pavoline towards its greatest prosperity, but the king felt his son had still more to learn. He could see within the boy an excellent warrior and a brilliant statesman, but there was some ineffable side to the prince that gave his father pause. Guiomar's fearlessness and pride perhaps lacked an anchor in benevolence and patience. His one wish for the eventual day of his departure from Earth was to feel no trepidation at his son's reign. He sighed once more, bidding his disquietude to take its leave, and shifted his gaze to the chamber window. He looked out over the castle courtyard, the citadel, and the farm country beyond, and saw the small cloud of dust which had grown over the road to the south. He watched the flags of the Masorian procession making their way along it toward the castle gate. From where he stood, he could see his own family banners hung on his castle walls, adorned with the chartreuse sundew plant, its carnivorous tentacles wrapping over and consuming a silver sun, centered within a field of dark green. This was Percy Ranzentine's choice for their house, a change from the image of the sun peaking over Ancient Pavoline's mountaintops made during the Great War. Looking again at the Oxbien flags as they neared his gate, Petrenair realized the Oleander and Sundew had not both been within his sight for some time. To prepare, he called upon his servant, Byrdon, who proceeded to lay the king's emerald cape across his broad shoulders. With a final glance in his looking glass, King Petrenair quit the chamber and strode to the grand entrance to greet his guest upon her arrival.

Guiomar joined his father on the magnificent stairway which connected the outer court to the interior of the castle. The royal Masorian carriage was making its final turn and, together, the prince and king waited in anticipation for Princess Isolda to emerge. Petrenair had hoped to speak to the new King Madrick II but was informed that the king had been taken ill and the princess would visit in his stead. Neither Guiomar nor his father had entertained their Masorian allies in many a year, and both were eager to see how the princess had grown. When the carriage came to a halt, the driver, jumping from his post, opened the coach door and offered his hand to the vice-crown who soon stepped onto the cobblestone. The servant, Esta, stepped out from the far side of the carriage and ran to the back of it where she picked up the large vase of yellow roses that was to be a gift to the king. Vase in hand, she followed Isolda up the steps.

The princess walked slow and proud, her thin hair falling in front of her chest and framing an already stern visage. Prince Guiomar privately noted the self-satisfaction she carried in her raised chin and thrown back shoulders. King Petrenair noticed only that she appeared polite and had grown significantly taller.

"Welcome to Pavoline, my friend," the king said, taking Isolda's hand. "I offer you my deepest condolences. One moment with you assures me that the Oxbiens were magnificent parents, just as they were friends."

Isolda graciously smiled and replied in kind. "Masor is grateful for the friendship of Pavoline, and I am grateful for the gentleness of your soul."

Guiomar cleared his throat. The king turned. "Isolda, you remember my son."

"Guiomar, yes; it is a pleasure," she offered her hand.

Remaining still, hands clasped at his front, he responded slowly, "Isolda, Princess of Masor, the pleasure is mine."

Isolda allowed her hand to fall, curiously staring toward the prince, wondering at his attitude. "Vice-Crown is perhaps the more proper of my titles to use if we are engaging in official introductions," she replied.

Guiomar smirked in condescension and stared at her until they were locked in a silent challenge of wits. At length, she turned back to the king, breaking the tension.

"Please accept these yellow roses, grown only in the royal Masorian courts, as a token of our long-living alliance."

"We shall cherish them," the king bowed. "Byrdon, take these from the maid and bring them to the main hall. They will decorate our table tonight at the feast!" He gave his arm jovially to Isolda, who accepted it kindly, and the royal three strode into the palace.

Esta climbed the steps to meet Byrdon, who descended toward the maid. As he reached out to collect the flowers, the fingertips of both servants happened upon each other at the side of the vase. Esta and Byrdon both stood still, their eyes holding each other in a trance.

"Byrdon, was it not?" Esta asked.

"Indeed, and what be thy name?"

"Esta, handmaiden to the princess."

For thy beauty, my mind might have confused thee for the princess herself. Byrdon's thoughts betrayed him in a small smile, though he said no word of his feelings.

"Welcome to Pavoline," he said, as the vase completed its journey into his grasp. Esta smiled shyly and, together, they followed their sovereigns inside.

"And for moons after that day, my Helena would not speak but to relish in the memory of your father catching her from that bucking horse." Petrenair laughed as Byrdon filled the final glass of wine. At a wave from the king, Byrdon bowed and quitted the hall, leaving the royals to their private convivialities. "In truth, there were times I wondered if, but for Fionella, he might have been capable of stealing my queen for his own kingdom, but I knew he would never dream of it. Your father was a good man."

"He was a good king," Isolda agreed, and King Petrenair nodded. He then looked down.

"I would that he had not traveled into the Forest," he said.

"As would we all," the vice-crown replied.

"Indeed. Perhaps his son will be more cautious."

Isolda raised her glass to that and sipped at its edge.

"I regret to hear of his illness," the king continued. "I hope he recovers swiftly."

Isolda took a breath. "Unfortunately, my brother is prone to fall prey to illness such as this quite often. In fact, the majority of the crown's duties have been delegated to myself, for precaution's sake."

The king's brow rose with his understanding. "Then it is perhaps for the best we are meeting with the princess instead of the king."

Isolda smiled politely, taking another sip of her wine. She looked toward Guiomar who returned a scornful gaze. No longer willing to suffer his behavior by naming it as simply odd, the princess spoke.

"Guiomar, enlighten me," she began, "by what misfortune do I happen upon you in a time of such despondency?" 'Til now the prince had yet to speak so much as a sentence. "If my memory serves, last we met you were spry and delightful. I'faith, after the visit my mother jested our kingdoms might one day align through marriage 'twixt you and me. I laughed her off, and have not agreed with myself so much then as I do now, but can one's disposition truly change so drastically over the years, despite how many they may be?"

Guiomar prepared to speak, and his father interrupted. "Forgive him, Isolda. It is true, he acts not as himself tonight, but I surely expect it has naught to do with you." He shot his son a cautionary glance.

"Yes, I beg you to forgive me," Guiomar responded. "I am afraid the occasion of the newly departed has begot me to think of my own memories with my departed parent; or, the memories that would have been had she not been taken from me."

Isolda nodded. "It is a difficult time for us all. Though I must inquire as to your harsh inflection in the phrase 'taken'. You would not suggest foul play? I understood your mother's death to be a tragedy of nature, unlike the murder of mine."

"Perhaps their deaths were not so different."

"Son, hold your tongue," Petrenair whispered through gritted teeth.

Isolda ignored the king. "How can you say this? Did not Queen Helena die giving birth to you?"

"Yes, under the failed aid of a Masorian midwife."

"Guiomar! Silence!"

Isolda scoffed. "Albain is known throughout both our kingdoms for her skills as a physician as well as a midwife. She was a gift to ease the labor, you surely cannot blame her for what was out of her power to control."

"'Tis not her I blame, but the Oxbiens who sent her."

King Petrenair stood. "Prince Guiomar, do not disgrace yourself this way."

Isolda held up a forgiving hand to the king. "No, sit, my friend. I wish to hear the full accusation. Pray, Guiomar, elaborate. Explain to me the way in which my recently deceased parents, your longtime allies, facilitated your mother's death."

"Isolda, I beg you—" the king tried, but the princess's determined glare seated him into silence.

Guiomar offered a hesitant glance to his father, then turned his attention to Isolda. "I hardly believe you are ignorant, Isolda Oxbien, but perhaps the telling will remind you, Father, of our true plight. Many years ago, I discovered a journal authored by Viridian, my mother's maid, in which she kept in full detail the story of my mother's fall. It was she, you see, who had been beside the queen throughout the entirety of her birthing journey, and she witnessed first-hand her postpartum decline."

"Surely you will not make such accusations on the word of a servant," Isolda said.

Guiomar rejoined, "A servant who never faltered in her loyalty and whose condition at the time of writing offered naught in reasons to lie. She tells of how the babe, still unborn in Helena's womb, was prone to violent jolting bursts—"

"The child, of course, being yourself, Guiomar. Do you not find the rightfully accused in your looking glass each morning?"

Petrenair turned to the princess. "Dear Isolda, I beg, do not aggravate him. I would that the subject be dropped, but if you wish to hear of it, let my son speak."

"Thank you, Father," Guiomar said, and he turned back to Isolda. "I believed for so long that I held the blame, but I know now it was not so. The truth is swallowed with daggers, Isolda, and you have already lifted the cup. You must accept my words."

After a breath, she said, "Accept I will not, but I concede I have now sacrificed my ear. Do continue but, by the River and Sky, do so with caution."

King Petrenair flinched at the princess's oath, but it only served to strengthen Guiomar's smile of contempt.

"Indeed, Princess, I shall," he said. "The queen was in pain from the child's kicks and, though strong in the face of it, even she could not wholly withstand the effects. Gaxon, our loyal physician, was brought in to ensure the safety of the queen and the babe, and after an examination, he deemed it best for the queen to remain bedridden for the remainder of the gestation. Her pains would continue, but with rest, they would do no harm. A week after this treatment was thus prescribed, the dear Oxbiens sent Albain." The sounds of the woman's name dripped from his lips with tangible disgust. "The midwife came with her Masorian medicines and traditions. She brushed aside Viridian and Gaxon, insisting that she alone be allowed access to the queen, and you, Father, granted her such luxuries, despite the impossibility of her loyalty—"

The king shook his head, fury raging within him. "I maintain that our full trust was rightfully placed with the Oxbiens. They meant us no harm," he insisted.

"I was made to believe we were finished with interruptions." Guiomar remained calm.

"You cannot sit at my table with the princess of Masor and spit upon our alliance!"

"An alliance with the foundation of betrayal is no alliance at all."

"To your chambers!" Petrenair boomed. "Guiomar, retire at once."

The prince smirked. "You would deny our guest her wish?"

He sighed. "Isolda, for the memory of your good father, for your mother, I beg you do not request he continue."

"For their memory, I must," she said. "No one can be defended against an accusation left unheard."

The table fell silent and, after a respectful nod to Isolda, Guiomar went on, leaving the king to simmer in his seat. "With only her queen's interest at heart, Viridian defied the woman physician and followed my mother everywhere, hidden out of Albain's sight. The first day of her appointment to the queen's side, Viridian notes that the Masorian had the queen walking about, pains in full, expressly denying the virtues of Gaxon's prescription of bed rest. The maid watched, helpless, as her beloved sovereign was paraded around the castle, Albain at her arm, as her pain increased by the day. She braved the king's reprimand and found Gaxon to tell him of the atrocities—a mother in such stage of expectancy walking about!—and he maintained his method was tested, tried, and true, and what a needless risk the Masorian physician was taking with the life of the queen and her heir. Alas, our king would not hear of it, insisting our friends in Masor could do us no harm, and the midwife was allowed to go about her ways. Under the watch of the Masorian, the queen ate foreign food with foreign potions. They sat together and sang foreign songs to the fetus. Albain would emerge from the queen's apartment with well-told lies of improvement, but Viridian could see the truth. At night, she would listen to the cries of her queen who felt only more pain than before.

"Finally, the day of birth came. Thankfully I emerged in full health, surely in spite of Albain's efforts; but alas, my mother was not so lucky. The pains in her abdomen increased tenfold and she fell into a dreadful fever. Albain claimed full ignorance as to the cause and Gaxon was brought in again for examination. In accordance with years of experience, he prescribed an urgent bleeding treatment, essential to saving my mother's life, but as he readied his equipment Albain stopped him. Father, you listened to her appeal as she claimed mad dangers of the treatment, denying its usefulness. You must understand, she manipulated your affected state, causing you to order your own physician against a life-saving treatment for your wife, your queen!, and in doing so achieved the Masorian's goal. Days after the birth, she put her bags together and quit the castle, leaving you to put together funeral arrangements.

"In your grief, you were unable to take control of newly occurring outbursts in the orchard villages beside the River, so our 'friends' in the castle of Masor graciously offered their services once more. They sent their condolences and took our land, extending their border across the water and around the troubled towns. Pavoline has grown strong once again, but the land has not been returned; no, it is left as a gift in thanks of the Oxbiens' friendship. Petrenair, I swear, if you were not my father and king, I would be tempted to name you a fool."

Isolda nearly laughed in surprise as she saw the king look furiously down at his plate.

"As for you, Isolda," Guiomar concluded, "you must know by what trickery your parents hatched the wicked plot; by what betrayal they planted my mother's pains; by what provocation they sparked the town outburst; by what greed they took my mother's life in exchange for some measly villages. You claim a friendship with Pavoline but act only for yourselves. Viridian went mad with grief after the loss of our queen but, thankfully, wrote her testimony before she followed my mother to the grave so that I would be able to later discover it and make known the truth."

There was silence. Isolda examined Guiomar as he watched her in return. Petrenair looked to his son then slowly dared to observe the princess's face. It offered him nothing as to the state of her mind.

"A powerful speech, Prince Guiomar. Rehearse it long, did you?" she finally said.

"Do not mock me," the prince scowled.

"I do not mock you, Guiomar, you mock yourself. I can speak nothing of the physician's art, but I am without doubt that Albain performed only the treatments she thought to bring wellness, and prevented only those which she thought were sure to cause harm. Have you not considered that Albain's skill and experience may be superior to that of your 'Gaxon'? As for the foreign food and potions, I expect you speak of traditional Masorian dishes and medicines derived from native herbs and spices, which perhaps it may benefit you to taste. If not, then I simply beseech you not to speak harshly of that which you have no knowledge. You say your mother's mad maid knew better than no other, but she knew nothing of the gracious and charitable heart which led my king and queen to their every decision. I regret your grief, Guiomar, but I regret more so that it was your birth which made Queen Helena incapable of providing Pavoline a more fitting heir."

"You see this, Father! She insults us even now."

"No, Guiomar, she insults you." Petrenair shifted in his seat, directing himself to the vice-crown. "Isolda, I do not dream to beg your favor toward my insolent son, but I pray the alliance of kingdoms may hold true in spite of his unforgivable transgressions against your honor. Long have I known his opinions of the past. I ignored them in hopes time would present a day when his opinions would more mirror my own, and I maintain those hopes. All I desire is a continuance of peace between us all."

Although she maintained a countenance of repressed scorn, within Isolda the flames of anger sank into embers as she took in the kind and penitent manner of the king. She responded dutifully. "King Petrenair, you have proven a loyal ally to Masor." She considered her next words as she folded her napkin, placed it beside her half-cleaned plate, and stood beside her chair. She spoke only to Petrenair. "Out of respect for the deceased, the friendship between us does not die on this day. I am sure our alliance will live as long as you, but I regret what may occur beyond that. Your Majesty." She bowed and quitted the hall without one glance toward Guiomar.

Petrenair stood to see her go. He steadied himself on the dining table and stared towards his fists, waiting for the heavy door to hide the last crack of light from the hall. Suddenly, he sprang up and smacked the prince across his cheek.

"If ever thou dost dare to endanger our alliance again, I will not hesitate to revoke thy crown."

Guiomar felt the sting on his face but dared not nurse it. "You have no other heir," he said.

"Then the Ranzentine dynasty shall die with me."

The prince's face fell into submission; but beneath, his heart betrayed the once gentle king, and a canker of hatred slowly encased his soul.

Outside the ominous scene of the feast, the servants had an adventure all their own. After having departed from the great hall in which the royals dined, Byrdon saw the shape of Esta passing the corridor and the sight filled him with an eagerness he dared not explain. Retiring his pitcher to the nearest windowsill, the servant of Pavoline set off after the Masorian maid, his eyes catching her once more as he rounded the bend, breathing to speak, tongue stayed by the sight of her beauteous obsidian hair in a multitude of braids, cascading around a graceful ebony neck. At length, he found his voice.

"Good evening, dear lady."

Esta stopped and turned, her heart forcing a smile upon her lips at the sight of the wooing man. "I but serve the ladies, good sir," she said. "I am not one myself, you need not call me such."

"Admittedly, I might have been fooled. But as both our occupiers occupy themselves tonight, perhaps I could entreat thee with a guided walk about the castle?"

Esta assented, hardly daring to glance in Byrdon's eyes, as she placed her hand in that of the Pavol, his russet skin appearing golden against the silver tones of her own, foretelling a notion of the splendors that would grow from their affections. Together, the two servants strolled through palace hallways, forgetting throne rooms and royal chambers, passing portraits and tapestries, conversing in so tender a discourse that would raise envy in the bosoms of the Sky's own stars, each step further securing the knot that was to bind their hearts in everlasting care. Time flew, the servants knew not how long, until they found themselves encircled by the romantic glow of the starlit night, strolling out upon the outstretched balcony that capped the palace's southern wing.

Byrdon, caught in the ocean of Esta's eyes, fell silent and pensive. He turned, walking to the edge and resting himself on the parapet, its ivy-strewn stones so familiar. He looked upon the deep green leaves with their bright veins running to and fro, ever connected yet ever each in search of their own path, twisting sharp with pangs of indecision, weakening with each sudden turn. On his first night in service of King Petrenair those years ago, he had discovered the peaceful solemnity of this parapet and had seen wisdom in the same leaves which so troubled him now. Surely a young boy of fifteen able to so impress the king as to obtain a service role by his side could believe he was set on the right path. He then set out to follow on straight, keeping to the center vein, the strongest by its sheer width, so as not to risk a destiny marked by the weak mangled turns on the leaf's edge. But with him now stood a turn so tempting. There was nothing in all the world greater than her beauty save for her own wisdom, and that wisdom was matched by naught but her own kindness. He already knew of her devotion to Masor and would not dream to bid her betray it, but in thinking of his own loyalties, he surprised himself to find that they endeavored more to follow this maid than they did his king. Looking back to the ivy leaf he noticed the four other veins born at the stem alongside that of the center, all leading to their own point. Though true, the others grew not as tall, they appeared no less content. Could he turn so drastically towards a cause so sentimental? His heart laughed at the question, for it long knew the answer. Decisive glee filled his chest and he turned from his leaves to gaze upon the face of his conclusion.

Just as he would have declared his affections, Esta's expression turned to one of utter fright! Byrdon hurried to her side, soliciting an explanation, but in following her gaze one was no longer needed, for hovering just behind the parapet was none but a fairy: the very image used to warn every child in the two kingdoms away from the dangers of the Infinite Wood and, now, the very beings charged with the assassination of King Madrick I and Queen Fionella of Masor. Esta and Byrdon made for the inner hall, but the fairy spoke.

"Wait! Run not, I pray, I mean you no harm." The look of terror in the small being's eyes, perhaps more extreme than that of Esta and Byrdon together, stayed the servants' feet as they slowly ventured to listen.

"State thy business here, sprite," Byrdon said. "Thy kind is not welcome within the borders of the kingdoms."

"I beg your trust," the fairy said. "My name is Stoman. I serve in the forces of Queen Okalani of Alquoria— or, 'The Fairy Nation', as you call it." The servants could see the truth of this by the being's green skin, informed by tales of the fairies which spoke of warriors like the foliage of their Wood, peasants with countenances like the noon-day Sky, and nobility with cheeks like dark orchids. "I have been sent with an urgent message for Princess Isolda of Masor. She is visiting the castle of Pavoline today, is she not?"

Esta came forward. "She is, for I am her maid, but she shall not speak with thee. Grief for the losses thy people have caused her has raised hatred in her like she hath for no other, and unless thy word can exonerate thee, thou wouldst be better to get hence."

"It is precisely those losses I come in regard of; but, her maid, you say?" The fairy thought. "Forgive me to dream, but you alone may save me from a fate most dreaded. It is no accident I am sent to one who would have my life extinguished; it is punishment for the deeds I come to confess. But if you would suffer me to relay to you my message, so that you may then relay it to her, I may indeed get hence without at all enduring an encounter with the princess herself."

"To relay the details of how our king and queen were murdered by fairy hands may only cause the princess to increase her anger," Esta said. "Your kind would only reap more hatred. Why would you risk such a cost?"

"Though I come to confess a small part I played in the event, it is the true hand responsible I come to reveal; for 'twas neither I nor any of my kind. The fairies have been unjustly accused of acts we do not own and already suffer the undue effects. Masorians now enter our Wood to hunt and return with no stag head but fairy wings to mount. Queen Okalani risks my presence here in hope that the truth will bring about our protection."

Esta and Byrdon stood a moment in shock.

Esta spoke. "Their wounds appeared seared yet slashed, simultaneously cut and burned as though with lightning directed. Weapons of such power exist only in rumors of the Fairy Nation; how can we believe otherwise?"

"Suffer me to tell my tale, and all will be made clear."

At length, Esta assented. "Make haste and speak true."

Stoman began. "I had been sent to patrol the southeast Woods, a near insult for the ease of the task, and yet forever the most envied of posts. The area is known for naught but the Forest of Lufian, a destination for none but young fairies in passion. I thought it harmless to bring another, so my beloved Alizren, stationed just north and finding a similar lack of danger in her post as in mine, flew to accompany me in the Forest. When we arrived, the Forest's serenity nearly overcame us, but we soon felt an odd stillness in the air, and our soldier sensibilities took control. In all the Infinite Wood, there is a hum of liveliness from the beating of wings or the songs of swallows; a buzzing stilled only by the footsteps of one from your two kingdoms. I reached for my bolt-spear, the same one rumored, a fairy warrior's sacred weapon, capable of harnessing the power of lightning itself towards the wielder's purpose, but Alizren stayed my hand.

"It was then we saw your king gambol under the long billowing threads of leaves, your queen in tow, exuberant with bright love and cheerfulness. I caught his eye and they stopped.

"He said earnestly, 'Pardon us, we mean not to intrude, only to share in the delights of such a beauteous Wood.'

"Understand, we in the order of the Fairy Queen are charged with blanketing protection over all life in the Infinite Wood and are under no direction to deny its glories to harmless visitors. We bid the royal couple well and they graciously returned the tidings before turning away happily to their private endeavors.

"I looked upon my Alizren and she drew me close, our wings ashine with jubilance, as a flood of youth invaded our hearts, unabashedly anticipating the approaching passion, oblivious of this moment being our last of peace. I gazed in horror upon my love, now bright, and now bleeding, as she fell beneath my grasp upon the Forest floor. I felt the Trees weeping as the mystical branches above us descended like rapids, cocooning Alizren, raising her into the bosom of the Trees and holding her above the dreadful scene, protecting her from further pain. In the vines' retreat, it was revealed to me the visage of he who caused our grief: a predator with eyes squinting toward his prey. I put up my bolt-spear but, now recognizing the man, held my attack lest I risk bringing war, for now the attention of the Oxbiens had been brought upon us as well. In my moment's hesitation, I gazed upon the man's poignard, dripping in Alizren's blood, and felt all my strength fly hence. He demanded my spear and, in fear for my own life, I relinquished it. I cannot deny my crime of cowardice, but I implore you to trust it was not I, nor any of mine, who brought death to your king and queen; it was he! I witnessed it! I watched only a sufficient time to see him wield the spear's power upon them. I fled, trusting the Lufian Trees to heal and protect Alizren so she could return to me, and reported all to my queen. The fairies maintain to wish no harm upon the kingdoms so long as the kingdoms wish no harm upon us. Do you hear me? By the River and Sky, it is he who is villain to Masor! Not we of the Wood."

"I hardly believe you lie," said Esta, "but pray tell who is 'he' you speak of?"

"I must have your word that you will believe, for the truth will not come easily to your ears." Esta gave her word and Byrdon agreed in kind. Stoman took a breath and revealed: "He is the prince, Guiomar of Pavoline."

"The prince!" Esta exclaimed. "How can it be?" She looked to Byrdon expecting to find shock and confusion in his countenance to mirror her own but instead found a stoic understanding. He explained his thoughts.

"The prince had been traveling during the time of their death; a hunting trip. Alone, as he prefers it. He returned only a week before word arrived that the king and queen had passed."

"But what cause would bring him to act so? The Oxbiens were friends of the Ranzentines," Esta said.

"I have heard Petrenair speak of his son's resentment toward the court of Masor," Byrdon said. "I know not the cause, but perhaps it indeed had the strength, when aligned with opportunity, to bring about the worst." The servants fell pensive and, by their silence, Stoman knew they believed the truth.

Addressing Esta, he said, "Share my story, speak for my kind, and know I will be forever in your debt," and he hastily flew for the Wood.

Just then they heard Isolda calling from inside for Esta to immediately gather herself and the princess's belongings, for they were to stay in Pavoline not a moment longer. Byrdon began to address Esta, ever fervent now in his intention to follow her away from Pavoline, but she interrupted before he could spell out his purpose.

"You must keep a close watch on the prince," she said, and Byrdon's heart sank. "We know not his full designs, and as a trusted presence in his father's court, your knowledge will be invaluable in the coming times. All of Masor and Pavoline—indeed all within and of the Wood—rely on us now. Prince Guiomar cannot be trusted."

Byrdon spoke. "If you reveal Guiomar to your princess, she would be sure to seek vengeance. Our kingdoms at war, would I see thee no more? I could bear it not."

Esta sighed sadly. "I cannot speak for the future, nor is my mind quite decided upon what to reveal, but I know my heart, and it sings for thee alone. Stay true to thy post, and I assure thee this will not be our final meeting." She began to hurry for the vice-crown, but Byrdon stayed her a moment longer, running to the parapet and tearing a leaf of ivy from the vine. Upon returning to Esta, he placed the leaf in her palm as he kissed her hand affectionately.

"I pray, let this direct thee hither, to me," he said, and with a final moment of longing the two servants ran to find their royal counterparts.

As she sat in the Masor-bound carriage with Isolda, Esta was fully acquainted with the events of the feast, as Isolda's ranting spared no detail. In light of the dreadful circumstances, Esta marveled at the vice-crown ability to maintain both her composure as well as the peace. She wondered if perhaps Byrdon was mistaken. Could she inform Isolda of the truth without bringing war? The maid, treading carefully, inquired on the strength of the alliance.

Isolda rejoined, "The alliance holds out of kindness for Petrenair alone and out of honor for the friendship he held with my parents. Nothing more."

"Surely, Your Highness, you do not wish for war?"

"No fair ruler would. As of yet, only our honor has been bruised, and though there is temptation in vengeance, I know better than to yield for such a cause; however, if appropriate cause arose, no friendship could stay my sword."

The wisdom that balanced on Esta's tongue tore at her mind. She held her ivy leaf and peered out of the carriage toward the castle of Pavoline, thinking first of those whom she knew to lie within—a king, a murderer, a love—then at once of the fairies, innocents misjudged. Her thoughts continued on in a maze until at last she looked down and her gaze landed on the central vein of the ivy leaf her new love had bestowed upon her. Though she was consciously concerned with issues of state, her heart, like that of Byrdon, wept at the notion of infinite separation. Still, she found her central vein pointed not to him, but rather to honor and truth. Fairy cries filled her imagination. She tried to quiet them. She wanted to turn to the next vein; she wanted to turn towards love. She closed her eyes tight and saw the good face of Byrdon, then held them tighter to wish the sight away.

"He killed them," she blurted.

"Pardon?" Isolda inquired.

Esta unclosed her eyes and sighed. "There is no doubt that he despised our king and queen and now they are gone, killed at a time when no one can account for Prince Guiomar's whereabouts. While you learned of his true ideas, Your Highness, I learned of his true actions. Forgive me for entertaining it in the first, but while you were inside a warrior of the fairies approached me and told me the truth. It was the prince. He killed them."

The vice-crown watched the maid. "Their scars were magical. Only the fairies would have access to such a weapon."

"But it was only they whom Guiomar stole it from, not they who shot the blow."

"Careful what thou sayest, maid."

Esta looked her in the eye. "Would I risk saying so if I did not believe it?"

The princess flinched at the servant's tone but let it rest, searching and yet finding no sign of dishonesty. "I know thou dost believe, and I thank thee for it, but see the truth. The fairy lied, Esta. They are beings of wickedness."

"And, your highness, Prince Guiomar is not?" she replied.

"There is no reliable witness. With only this, I must assume thou art mistaken."

"I know what I am," the servant said. "I know you cannot attack based on my word. Still, Your Highness, I have been loyal all my life and would never lead you astray. Will you not at least begin an inquiry?"

"An inquiry into a false accusation would be an insult. In that realm, the court of Pavoline owes Masor a debt, and I will not risk making us even on that footing before they have paid it."

"But if the fairies are innocent—!"

"They are not," the vice-crown held fast. "Thou shalt speak no more of this, to me or to anyone. Dost thou understand?"

Esta, shocked at the princess's unwillingness to question her own presumptions, replied "Yes, your highness," and dropped her gaze into submission. She looked now upon the ivy in her hand and lost all certainty as to which of the leaf's strong veins pointed in the direction of loyalty and which to love. In the next instant, the two seemed blended into one. If the sovereigns would not listen to reason, the entirety of the World Within the Woods might depend upon two servants and a fairy to defend it against treachery. Riding alone with Isolda, Esta was helpless and weak, but she looked into the ivy leaf and, seeing Byrdon within, now felt strong. She wanted to shout to the world the truth, make them believe, make them act, but if war did come she knew this source of her strength would be gone from her forever. The cries of fairies filled her thoughts again as she considered the many who would die at the hands of Masorians she failed to convince. Still, she knew with an ineffable certainty now that she could make no impact if not attempting so with Byrdon by her side. This chance at love which crossed the River, that was her path to loyalty. She studied the dark outdoors beyond the candlelit carriage and wondered how much of the truth she could reveal before Isolda silenced her with force. Shaking the thought from her head, she swore by the River and Sky that, come what may, she would find herself with Byrdon again. For as long as was necessary, she determined to hold her peace.

CHAPTER III

Far Off Love

Guiomar sat in his chambers one morning a fortnight following the disastrous dinner, leaning on his desk, remembering his bruised cheek, and nursing his bruised pride. He had spoken barely a word to the king throughout the weeks since then. What right had his father to threaten him as he had? The throne of Pavoline was Guiomar's birthright, and he should rule as he saw fit. Despite his silent anguish, the prince thought better than to attempt further confrontation, as he knew well there would be no reasoning with the king. Though genial to all others of the human race, King Petrenair made no secret of his disappointment to Guiomar. He coated his mortification in a dream of improvement, saying always he looked forward to the day his son—the hopeful, future iteration—would lift the kingdom of Pavoline from his old, fatigued shoulders. The prince looked forward to this day as well; however, it could never be as the son his father preferred. The king expected him to assume the qualities of his late Queen Helena, but instead found a darker soul, more attuned to militancy than music, and destitute of all gentler inclinations. Guiomar recognized this in himself and saw strength. Once he became King, no longer would Pavoline fall prey to treachery, for he would distribute no trust that could be betrayed.

His blood curdled with remembrance of the Masorians, each one surely ruled by the same greed and cruelty that took his mother. His only regret in his method of revenge was that he would garner none of the credit due to him from the feat, for he knew to acquire it presently would lose him his heirship. When his father was no more, and after altering the opinions of the Pavol lords and ladies, he would shout his victory over the royal Masorians from the tops of the Infinite Trees. He thought with fondness on the time his reign could begin. He would purify Pavoline of all its Masorian ties; better yet, superstition be damned, he would conquer the surrounding Woods, keeping all of Masor trapped within itself, bound to obey his law. What could stop him now?

He turned his gaze toward the nearby corner of his room and took in the sight of the wrapped artifact he kept there, maintained from his secret excursion to the Woods. For the first time since his return, he stood up to it, taking it in his hands and placing it upon his desk. Untying the twine and unfolding the wrappings, he revealed the instrument of his crime: the fairy bolt-spear. Its wooden shaft measured nearly as long as Guiomar's wingspan, and the mysterious swirling grain of the wood from an Infinite Tree naturally decorated the smoothly sanded length. The head of the weapon appeared solid blue, like a sharpened precious stone, and yet too seemed constructed from nothing but light and energy itself. It shimmered with power, and small sparks of lightning flickered around it with anticipation. Could he unleash its powers again to cause his coronation to fall closer at hand? He jumped at the sound of a servant's footsteps passing in the corridor beside his chambers and, turning away from the object of his musings, leaned against the open casement, suffering the wind to clear his mind.

Byrdon likewise leaned out a casement of the Pavoline castle, but from the chamber of King Petrenair as he listened to another of his sovereign's jeremiads on his son's transgression. If he had made any attempt at attentiveness, the servant may have found opportune moments to reveal the true depths to which the prince had sunk; however, his mind was entirely occupied with fantasies and curiosities surrounding his new lover somewhere across the River, lost to the vastness of the Sky. He yearned for even a whisper of her in the wind but knew the only course which would result in his contentment would be a journey to Masor where he might set his eyes on her once again. He remembered his promise to look after Guiomar but, in the end, what could a lowly servant of the king do to prevent the evil doings of the prince? He thought not of deserting his post indefinitely, only the double fortnight it would take to again hold the hand of she whom he most desired and to say a proper farewell, one untainted by the grave issues of state which circumstanced their first meeting. Settled, he stood taller and spun towards the king, determined to request a month's leave.

"Didst thou hear me, Byrdon?" the king asked.

The love-sick servant stared blankly, having heard not one word. "Forgive me, Your Majesty, my thoughts were... entertaining other notions."

"Other notions? What of thy notions could be of more importance than what we discuss?"

Byrdon's bravery nearly retreated, but his determination held strong. "I do not claim a grander importance to the kingdom, but I beg your pardon to admit these notions hold a vast importance to myself."

Petrenair softened. "What dost thou speak of?"

"I wish to travel to the Masor citadel," the servant admitted.

"Dost thou have family there?" The king would have been surprised to hear so but could suppose no other cause for the long journey.

"Not as of yet." Byrdon looked to the floor, and Petrenair laughed with his growing understanding.

"The serving girl who attended Isolda; this is thy reason to travel?" His smile tore at Byrdon's pride.

"I beg you not to laugh, Your Highness," he said, and the good king fell somber.

"Thy feelings are true then?"

The servant looked in his king's eyes to report, "They are truer than I've known them to be for anything."

"Anything?"

"Your Highness..."

"Thy feelings to Pavoline, Byrdon. Are they truer than those?"

Byrdon thought of the truth, then he thought of Esta and what she would have him say. "I have served you long and well. Must I answer such a thing, My King?"

Petrenair considered it, then moved on. "If I granted this leave, how long would be thy stay?"

"Only a day in the citadel. Even considering travel, I would be gone but a single moon."

Nodding, the king asked, "And how could I be assured of thy return?"

"I am a servant of Pavoline, My King, in title and heart. I will return." Byrdon was sincere; still, the king could hardly believe a meeting with love would not alter his sentiments.

"A dutiful response," King Petrenair said. "It is true. Thou hast not only served Pavoline, but served its king for many a year, and served him well. This service has been so satisfactory that it has granted thee access to hours of my mind. I have spoken to thee of my fears, of my hopes, and of my plans in case hopes go awry. I would like to grant thee a wish, Byrdon, and if it were any other I would, but I cannot have a trusted servant of mine roaming the citadel of Masor."

"Please, Your Highness, I would never betray you, I swear it," the lover begged.

Petrenair smiled. "What thou art devoted to today can mean nothing tomorrow when put against the callings of love. My answer remains, and there shall be no changing it. I am sorry."

Byrdon stood tall against the sinking of his heart and nodded his acceptance of the king's decision.

"Good man." Petrenair sighed away the tension and shifted to earlier thoughts. "Now, I am taking thee out of my service."

"But Your Highness—!"

"This has naught to do with thee and Masor. This is what I told thee a moment ago when thou wert not listening."

"Oh."

Petrenair smirked at the servant's embarrassment. "Can I now count on thine attention?"

Byrdon nodded. "Of course, sire."

"Gramercy. I have decided to place thee in the service of my son."

"Prince Guiomar?"

"My only," said the king. "His hatred of the Masorians has gone farther than I dreamed, and I fear nothing from his father will yet change his mind. Of course, in addition, he now refuses to speak with me. Still, I have seen his mother in him. He has her eyes, he must have her goodness somewhere deep down, I know it." Petrenair smiled at Byrdon. "And thou shalt be the one to bring it out." The confidence in the king's grin made Byrdon tremble.

"A daunting task," he replied, and the king's smile fell away in an instant.

"I may speak of him that way; thou cannot." Petrenair glared at him with an intensity that assured Byrdon the king would hear nothing of his son's crimes.

"My apologies, sire. I intend no insult; still, if you have been incapable of changing him, then how do you intend me to succeed?"

The king shrugged. "Thou art a young man. A good man, with no history the prince can exploit. I know my son well enough to be sure he shall never trust thee, but neither will he deign to despise thee. Offer friendship. Offer advisement. Tell him of thy dalliance at love with a Masorian! Perhaps he shall open his mind. If thou dost succeed, perhaps, under his rule, thou shalt win a higher station and a better king. It must be attempted."

Images of the night the Masorians visited filled Byrdon's mind. If the fairy had spoken true, then the prince was beyond hope.

"May I be permitted to speak freely, My King?"

With a slight chuckle, Petrenair asked, "Hadst thou been restraining until now?"

Byrdon did not share in the mirth and the king offered assent for him to speak his mind.

"What if you are too late and the prince is too far gone? I fear for myself in his service, Your Highness."

"His politics are crude, but I do not see how that would cause danger to befall thee. In truth, if war did come, thou wouldst be most protected in the service of a king."

Byrdon hesitated to speak in full but hesitated more to hold back entirely.

"I do not fear from others, Your Majesty, I fear from him. I fear what he may ask of me."

The king looked sternly at Byrdon.

"Wherefore?"

"Your Majesty..."

Petrenair stepped toward the servant. "I said to speak freely and yet thou dost not. What is it?"

Byrdon held his breath. "I swear I did not think of it myself, Your Highness, but you would never believe me if I told you the source."

"The source of what?"

"Think on it, Sire. The day the Masorians were killed, where was Prince Guiomar?"

"The Forest of Beasts, where he always does his hunting."

"Can you truly be certain he was not much further south?"

There was silence.

"Where didst thou hear this?" There was fury behind the king's calm.

"I told you, Your Highness, you would not believe."

"That Masorian girl? Is this her lie?"

"No, Your Highness!"

"Then where!"

"The parapet!" the servant spouted. "When you dined with Masor, a warrior of the Fairy Queen came to us on the parapet. He told how it happened."

Petrenair's fury settled back beneath the surface of his countenance.

"Now I know thou dost lie," the king said. "No fairy would dare to enter my kingdom, just as no Pavol would dare enter theirs. I've made certain of that. Most especially in my own son."

Byrdon fell to his knees. "I do not lie, Your Majesty, I swear it. I did say you would not believe."

"Good. Thou shouldst well know thy king is discerning enough to know when he is told a lie."

Byrdon shook his head but could find no words.

"What am I to do with thee? Thou hast served so well until this moment; but Byrdon, this! Hast thou spread this through my kingdom?"

"I have spoken of it to no one but Your Grace."

"Good."

"But, Your Majesty, if it is true, if he killed them—!"

"My son is not a murderer!" The king strode close and spoke down upon the cowering servant. "I raised a better man than that. If ever thou darest to tell my people otherwise, I could name thee traitor."

Byrdon controlled his pride. "Forgive me, Your Highness, perhaps I am but a mistaken, gullible man. Still, I swear by the River and Sky—"

"Don't," commanded the king.

"My apologies. On my life then, on my freedom; I swear I mean no harm to Pavoline."

"Then speak no shame upon it."

"You will never hear of it again."

"Thou shalt not think of it again."

Byrdon nodded, and the king sighed, pulling the servant to his feet.

"For thy own sake, Byrdon, I shall choose to believe that Masorian girl played some trick upon thee and these wild accusations shall fade into the distance as doth she. Serve my son well, and we may forget this incident has passed."

The servant could not speak for his racing breath.

"Thou art spared. What troubles thee now?"

"I may be a gullible coward and a fool, Your Majesty, and yet I find I might prefer to live my life in a cell than spend a day serving your son."

All gentleness fell from the king's expression.

He spoke. "Then thou shalt be bound by decree to spend each day serving him until thy very last."

Byrdon watched in terror as the king strode to his writing desk and penned a billet spelling out the servant's sentence.

He held the note out to Byrdon but held on when the servant went to take it.

"If I hear thee, or any other Pavol, speaking of the same thou hast spoke of hither, the sentence that befalls thee shall be far less merciful." The king waited until Byrdon indicated his understanding, then let go and sent him out to report to Guiomar.

Byrdon walked through the palace corridors in a daze. Was the king right? Could he have acted such a fool? Surely the prince would never have entered the Infinite Wood to begin with; a man could spend a month wandering just the Forest of Beasts alone. Furthermore, a royal of Pavoline had not entered fairy territory since the first Lord Ranzentine discovered the creatures somewhere past the end of the River. Even Guiomar would not break that ancient truce. But that fairy, that damned fairy. Stoman had looked so sincere, so frightened. Perhaps he had indeed been the true murderer.

All these thoughts bombarded Byrdon's mind as he turned to face the doors at the end of the hall, opening them into Guiomar's chambers, and standing suddenly face to face with the prince who, resting at the window, had spun round with a look of scorn.

"Have the servants forgotten how to knock?"

Byrdon's gaze fell to the desk on which he saw the spear whose head of a deep blue hue contained sparks of white light swimming beneath its surface. The image of the fairy weapon seared into his imagination and tore away all doubts of the prince's guilt, replacing them with utter terror.

In the courts of Masor, Esta stood at attention for Isolda who, incessantly frustrated, sat rifling through papers at the table in the great hall. The tax collector had completed his quarter-annual duties a day late, and now the farmers of Wesfair and the fishers of Northlake, who were to distribute their goods amongst the cities and to the castle, in itself a week-long project, had yet to be paid and thus had yet to begin, and in order to put this quarter's revenues to proper use, the paperwork required the royal seal which resided on the hand of the king. Isolda had requested Madrick's presence early that morning, but he had yet to make an appearance.

"Esta, do go fetch that blasted king of ours," Isolda sighed. The maid, cringing softly at the disparagement of the crown, left the great hall in search of him. She exited by the small door behind the throne, and, in the same moment, the grand entryway which Isolda faced was unclosed, and a guard stepped inside.

"Your Majesty," he said, bowing. "Lagif Greenwood of Ritahest has come to call."

Isolda, puzzled, glanced sideways across the room to where stood an elaborate floor-length mirror whose glass and carved wood stood silent with muted colors. She returned her glance to the guard.

"He hath traveled to the castle?" she clarified, and the guard nodded. "Goodness. See him in."

He congeed and stepped out, returning a moment later with the Lagif of Ritahest trailing behind. Isolda stood to greet him, offering her hand as he knelt at her feet.

"Vice-Crown," he said, placing a respectful kiss upon her fingers. "It is an honor to have your hand in mine."

"Likewise, my lagif. I cannot recall the last time you came within our walls."

He stood and retreated a step, standing tall as he might with his arms behind him. The princess had never before realized the lagif was shorter than she.

"Forgive me, if my presence is an intrusion, Your Highness," he said, and Isolda attempted to conjure a more genial air.

"Nonsense," she replied. "I only wonder at your cause for the journey. We do possess more efficient methods of communication."

"Indeed; however, while I naturally wished to offer my most sincere condolences on our recent tragedy, it is also, primarily, those very communication methods I have come to discuss with you." Lagif Greenwood made every attempt to maintain his gaze toward the vice-crown, but he could not resist a short glance to the mirror beside them. No matter how often he utilized his own version of the same, the mystical properties of the glass never failed to frighten him.

Isolda did not follow his glance, for she knew too well on what item it fell.

"It is the mirrors that concern you?" she asked.

"Yes, Your Highness, and most importantly whether we are to continue their use," he said.

"Whyever would we not?"

"Your Majesty..." he started. "Their source."

The princess spoke coldly. "Do you fear the fairies, Greenwood?"

The lagif's pride made him retreat from his true answer. "I bring this query to Your Highness not on my lone behalf. It is I, with Lagif Bathleret of Kiefston, Lagif Rosin of Agoshany, Lagif Morische of Charit, and Lagif Diris of Fairiton—"

"So, it is all the First Lagifs, I understand."

"We only fear it would be an insult to your house, indeed to all the kingdom, if we were to make use of something gifted us by the fairies after what they have done."

"Your concern is kindly taken, my lagif," said Isolda. "I assume then this is the last of many a discussion on the matter?"

"The First Lagifs have discussed and debated and at length decided it was not our decision to make. I have been sent to receive the crown's opinion on the matter." At a slanted look from the princess, he added, "Or the vice-crown, as the case may be."

"I see. And how were these lengthy discussions, nay debates, conducted?"

Lagif Greenwood's chest inflated with pride. "I took it upon myself to mediate between us."

Isolda rose a brow. "So, it was your messengers who ran between the cities carrying every lagif's little notes?"

"Oh, no Your Highness," he said, sinking, "Not as such."

"You used the mirrors, then?"

"Your Majesty, as no verdict had yet been reached, and the issue required such back and forth—"

"You used the mirrors because they are a faster, more comprehensive method of communication which leave no trace of their use while enforcing a level of honesty in identity and circumstance that cannot be achieved through wax seal and handwriting alone. They are an invaluable tool of our governance."

"Of course, Your Highness. Still, I fear to utilize them would admit, on our part, some weakness unable to be overcome except through the aid of an enemy."

Isolda sighed and made her way to stand before the mirror. The lagif thought to follow but failed to execute the steps.

"It was a different time when these were gifted us," the princess said, remembering her history books. "The Truce of the Two Kingdoms had not yet been struck, and the fairies were on their knees begging Oxbien not to invade the Wood. The Ranzentines never dared, but we have always been mightier than they. The fairies were honoring the Sky when they did goodness to Masor, placing the only six of these magnificent pieces in our kingdom; for, at the time, they would not dare battle with the Sky's chosen people, and yet we agreed to let them keep their Wood regardless. It wasn't until many a year after that that they turned sour, betraying the Sky and pointing their spears at any Masorians who entered the Forest. These mirrors are a gift from the Sky, not the fairies who betray It now. Furthermore, they are the heartbeat of our governance, and we will not be frightened out of their use."

Lagif Greenwood at length found his steps and stood in front of the mirror with Isolda, realizing the vice-crown must be correct. He turned to face her.

"Forgive me my doubts, Your Highness. They will not be spoken of again."

"Wonderful. Now go, use our gifts, and assure the other First Lagifs we shall all council soon." The princess returned to her seat at the paper-strewn table as Greenwood bowed and headed toward the door. He stopped and looked to her.

"Will the king be attending council?" he asked.

After a moment's stare, she responded, "I wouldn't count on it," and the lagif bowed again before exiting the hall.

Isolda turned to her work. With a huff, she sat exasperated in her chair, remembering her inability to continue her tasks alone.

Esta arrived at King Madrick's apartment shortly after exiting the hall and lightly knocked, opening the door when he bid her enter. She found him, as with so many others that day, gazing pensively out the window.

"My Liege, the vice-crown requests your presence in the great hall."

He did not respond for a moment. Finally, Esta, who had taken notice of the flask in his right hand, looked up from it quickly as he began to speak.

"Are they happy?" the king inquired.

"Pardon, Your Majesty?" Esta replied.

He gestured out the window. "The people, down there, milling about in the city. Are they happy?"

The maid smiled. "Being often one of them, Your Highness, I have on good authority that some are, and some are not."

"Of which are thee?" he asked, turning to the maid.

"I am content," she replied.

"Ah, but I asked if thou art happy. It is easier to be content than to be happy."

"I'm afraid you've chosen an inopportune moment to ask, My Liege."

"Thou art unhappy, then."

Esta hesitated to respond, remembering the hurry of the princess, but she could not resist the sincerity of the king. "I long for something I cannot have," she admitted.

Immediately the king's spirits brightened as he responded, "Tell me what it is; I shall acquire it for thee!"

Esta chuckled. "'Tis not that simple, Your Highness."

"Am I not king?"

"You are, Your Highness, and thus could perhaps provide your royal seal in the great hall?" She tried.

"No, I wish to speak more with thee."

Esta sighed and, taking notice, the king rejoined, "Is it not of my sovereign duties to respond to the needs of my people?"

"Indeed, My Liege; however, to my understanding, it is also of your duties to sign paperwork."

"Dear maid, I pray, indulge thy king. For what dost thou long?"

Looking down at her hands, Esta whispered. "'Tis a man, My Liege."

King Madrick excitedly motioned Esta to the window, exclaiming, "Come hither, do tell, which be he?" and Esta laughed.

"You will not find him out your window, My Liege. I am afraid he is not of Masor." The king turned back to Esta, interest piqued, and implored her to go on. She obliged. "In fact, he serves King Petrenair in Pavoline."

"I see. Well, it is fortunate Pavoline and Masor are friends. Perhaps our castles could visit one another more often, for thy sake."

Esta smiled sadly. "I don't think Isolda would have it."

"Perhaps not. But thou couldst relocate to Pavoline, if that was thy wish."

"I couldn't, My Liege."

"Wherefore? Thou art bound to service here by no law, and I could provide thee with every helpful supply for the journey."

Esta examined the king, whose kindness she was discovering anew, and decided for certain, "I am bound to service here by duty."

"Thy duty would overcome thy love?"

"Wouldn't yours?"

He turned from her gaze. "My duty has been 'delegated elsewhere'. I am bound to naught but my flask."

With true surprise, Esta asked, "Do you feel no honor for your kingdom?"

Madrick took in his kingdom living below his window and, with a sincerity Esta had not before seen in his eyes, he responded, "I feel immense honor for my kingdom. It seems it is my kingdom which feels no honor towards me. Although,—" he looked at his flask "—it is not as though I have given them much to respect."

Esta knew not what to say, so stood in silence. At length, the king removed the royal seal from his finger and held it out to her.

"Here, take the seal to Isolda, she may keep it. It will save both of us much time," but Esta stood still.

"Might I speak plainly, Your Highness?" With his permission, she continued. "I believe there is great goodness in you, King Madrick. You hide behind your drink, but you are capable of much more. I hold our vice-crown in great regard, but I can only imagine the love your people would bestow upon a king of the nature buried within you. Your sister holds your power, but you are Crown, and you need not let her forget it. I think it best the seal remain with you, so that one day you may fulfill the breadth of duties it bestows upon you, My King."

"I know not how to be king."

"No one is king unaided."

"I never wanted to be the crown."

"For that reason alone, you could be the best crown Masor has yet to know."

For a moment, both king and maid stood silent, each further deciphering the mind of the other through their eyes. At length, the king spoke softly.

"What is thy name, maid?"

"I am Esta, My Liege."

In a sudden change of demeanor, King Madrick took a breath and said, "Come, Esta, thou hast been very patient. Let us go to Isolda."

Smiling, Esta nodded. "Thank you, Your Highness."

Returning to sincerity, he responded, "Thank *you*," and after a moment, the two walked out of his chamber and towards the great hall.

Byrdon remained frozen in fear at the sight of Prince Guiomar with the fairy weapon. He thought to run to the king but knew Guiomar could tell any false tale as to how he acquired the weapon, and it would be believed over the ramblings of a poor servant. Guiomar saw him recognize the object but made no effort to conceal it within its wrappings. He beckoned the servant to draw near and smirked as Byrdon's poor trembling legs obliged against their strongest wishes.

"What brings thee hither?" the prince inquired.

Unable to speak for the anxious ramblings of his thoughts, Byrdon silently handed the prince the billet from the king. Having read it, the prince laughed.

"A dishonest young man, called Byrdon, doomed to serve me for all his life." He smiled. "Dear Father does know how to give a gift."

Byrdon hardly heard the prince speak as he was unable to lift his gaze or his thoughts from the weapon on the desk. At a sudden, thinking of his final hope, he found his voice and looked to the prince.

"Your Highness, before beginning my service with you, the king promised me a month's leave to visit the citadel of Masor. I beg you will honor it."

Guiomar scoffed, "No he didn't," and all hope floated from Byrdon's heart. "Still I thank thee for that demonstration of how thou speakest untruths. Tell me, what was the content of the dishonesty that won thy place here in my service?"

Byrdon's gaze fell again to the bolt-spear. "It was what I understand now to be a baseless allegation against your highness."

Guiomar watched intently as the servant's anxiety grew unendingly in the presence of the spear. The prince knew the full content of the allegation, and the true beliefs of the servant on the matter.

"Who else is aware of these allegations?"

"No one, My Liege. It is only myself." He looked directly at the prince in a moment of bravery to say, "and the fairy who told it to me."

Guiomar nodded. "To make accusations of royalty on the basis of baseless rumors must have taken courage."

Byrdon dropped his gaze. "Do believe, Your Highness, how I would now that the momentary courage had never come upon me."

"Yes," Guiomar said. "For thou must now fully comprehend that any allegation made by one of thy status, unless backed by insurmountable evidence—evidence which even then may hardly be enough to usurp the word of one such as myself—would be inherently baseless."

"Yes, My Liege."

"And if thou wert to ever repeat—or, goodness forbid, invent—any such baseless allegations again, why, the punishment could be..."

"Treason, Your Highness. I could be executed for treason."

Prince Guiomar smiled. "In that case, perhaps I could use a man of your nature. I believe the two of us are going to get along handsomely."

The servant shivered as he watched the prince wrap the bolt-spear in its cloth, tenderly tie the twine, and lean it, unassumingly, against the corner wall.

"Will there be anything now, Your Highness?"

Guiomar paced out from behind his desk for a moment's thought before deciding, "I'll have a bath, with a fruit platter and glass of wine placed beside. I've never had a dedicated servant before—in truth, I never wanted one—but I think this calls for celebration." The prince put a hand on Byrdon's shoulder and walked him to the door.

"Of course, My Liege." He tried to bow but the prince's firm hand kept him still.

"Byrdon, I consider myself a rather talented hunter. Do not force me to go in search of thee."

The servant nodded and allowed himself to be pushed from the chamber. Standing a moment in the hall, Byrdon willed his fears and despair to restrain their effect until they were subtle enough that he could pretend he felt nothing. When he found himself capable of movement, he marched on to obey the prince's commands.

CHAPTER IV

The Cave of Dreams

A weary sun was setting on the day that marked a full moon since Esta and Byrdon's first, and only, meeting. Esta sat atop her small bed in her cottage in the Masor citadel and lit her bedside candle. Despite thinking better of it, she indulged her heart and removed her diary from its place beneath her pillow, turning to the specially marked page that held, pressed, the ivy leaf Byrdon had offered her. She gazed warmly at the portrait of him she had adorned the adjacent page with. While she looked, a brave tear dared to creep down her cheek until she sniffed and brushed it away, imploring the world to be kinder and grant her wishes; or else, to lessen her longing. Snapping the pages shut, Esta held the book to her breast and looked out upon her small cottage; an iron oven and stove, weary with age, a pantry of grains and fruit, and her royal maid apron laying atop her simple dresser crafted from oak for her grandmother by her grandfather on their anniversary. She felt the embroidered edge of the comforter beneath her and remembered when her mother had sat in her place and little Esta would snuggle into the opposite corner of the room, wrapped in blankets. Every night while her mother was alive, they would lie in the dark singing to each other until they both drifted off into repose. The finale of their little concert was always sung by her mother—a family melody passed down through the years. This tune had played in Esta's mind every night since the death of her mother, and tonight was no exception; however, on this night, as she snuffed out the light and lay down to rest, the tune began in her ear and the lyrics brought remembrances of new love, bringing up images of Byrdon across her closing eyes. On this night, her heart sang the song to him.

LOVE WILL FIND

My dear who drifts into the night,
Thy dreams may have no bound nor fright,

For I'll protect thee with my heart.
My love will find thee where thou art.

Sleep sound and roam our world unbound.
Adventure waits beyond the ground.
Fear not to roam to realms unchart'
For I will find thee where thou art.

Thou wilt wake in the morning
to have me by thy side.
I'll hear of thine adventures
and swell with love and pride.

The day may come when I must go;
Still, don't despair for even though
They build a wall to keep us 'part,
My love will find thee where thou art.

My love will find thee, she thought once more, and the darkness of sleep washed over her.

My love will find thee. The words rang in Byrdon's ears as his mind left a nightmare and he walked into a new dream. He found himself in the courtyard of the Pavoline castle. From the sound of it, it seemed the whole citadel was deserted. Although, looking up behind him at the tower he could see the light burning in Guiomar's chambers, and he turned back straightaway. Despite the emptiness of the court, Byrdon still heard the sweet music that brought him to this dream; *My love...* Staring through the haze of the dream-night, his eyes fell upon the full moon which hovered just beyond the gates of the palace courtyard. With the formation of the clouds, it seemed to smile, and the pulsing reflection of the great Gwahanu River on the moon's surface beckoned him to follow thither. His feet passed over the cobblestone and the wind pushed open the gates for him to pass through, revealing to his eyes a glorious sunset, radiating thrice its usual size and glowing a fiery red, creating a gradient with magnificent oranges and yellows, mixing in the dark blue Sky and coloring it a deep violet hue. The sun touched the horizon at precisely the point at which Pavoline became Masor and Byrdon knew his love lay just beyond. *My love will find thee...*

His heart tethered to the sun, Byrdon followed the warm moon as it brought him past deserted merchant huts, beyond the eastern side of the citadel, and down below on a path, sided on one hand by the thick greenery of the Forest of Beasts, and on the other, for a time, the short sandstone of the city wall. The path descended with a stoop in the landscape, bringing him a story below the stones. He watched the forest, passing by its numerous small winding footpaths that had been tread into creation by centuries of adventurers, until the moon turned him to face toward the citadel and halted him hither in front of a tall briar. It seemed to beckon him on but he stood still, unsure how to proceed. The air then coagulated and pushed him into the briar, which dissolved as he passed through, and he found himself in the mouth of a deep cave.

My love will find thee where thou art.

Unbeknownst to him, Esta, once her breath slowed into slumber, found herself in a similar dream. The moon had called her from her cottage and led her to an abandoned alley deep in the town in which stood an old forgotten well. A water bucket still hung from the wound-up rope, and moonlight glinted from the bucket's metal casing, drawing Esta closer. She climbed onto the stone rim and stepped one foot in the water bucket, using it to lower herself down the odd, dry, earthen well. There was no water at the bottom. Instead, stepping out of the bucket, she found she had landed at the end of an immense cavern. It was the same of which Byrdon now stood at the opposite mouth. Although separate, their two dreams began to be one. The moon's pull drew them both deeper into the cave, leading them safely as they traveled alone through the darkness. At length, they each halted at a mysterious rustling sound some dozen paces ahead and dared not step further. Suddenly, a light grew from within the cavern walls and enveloped the central chamber of the cave in a clear blue glow, though neither traveler could discern the source of the light nor the cause of its sudden appearance. They thought not long on these questions, for just then they saw their love standing before them and, as though the light grew from within their very hearts and their feet had no need for the ground, the two lovers ran to each other in ineffable elation.

Just as they reached each other, the dream ended, and Esta and Byrdon both awoke alone in their separate kingdoms, but they wasted not a single breath. There was no doubt in either of their minds that the place they had dreamt existed in reality. With capes around their shoulders and minds and memories sharp, the lovers began their adventure. They quit their cottages and set out to follow the paths their dreams had lain.

Sure enough, the moon in their dreams had not led them astray, and without long they had again found the cavern and were running into each other's arms.

"Esta! Thou art no dream; how can this be? Hast thou traveled this far from Masor?" Byrdon could hardly believe his eyes and he kept a soft hand around the beautiful maid to assure himself of her reality. Esta caressed his cheek in equal disbelief.

"I have traveled nowhere but down a dark well in the Masor citadel. Didst thou not journey from Pavoline?"

"Only but perhaps a quarter-hour from the beginning of a cave behind the castle."

"I do not understand it," she said. "But I care not now either. Thou art beside me, I have wished for nothing more." They fell into each other's arms, embracing tighter than the wick clings to the flame. Stepping back to absorb her lover's countenance, Esta was alarmed by wounds she now noticed on his brow. Byrdon tried to calm her worry, but she persisted.

"Do not leave me in suspense. Tell me what harmed thee!"

"It was nothing, do believe me," he tried, but she would not accept such an answer. Finally, he resigned his truth, embarrassed to say: "I jumped into a thicket."

Esta hesitated, then broke into laughter. "And wherefore?" she mustered.

"My dream misled me. I thought I would pass through, and yet, the bush required cutting."

As they stood and laughed, their minds bemused, their feelings found comfort in mingling with the other's and soon it was as though multicolored mists of emotion emerged from their hearts, unable to contain themselves in the chest of their host, and wrapped around the lovers tightly, encircling the pair in a cocoon of light and love.

Perhaps the same magic that enchanted the Forest of Lufian held power over this cave, or perhaps the longing of two lovers, once afeared that they may never meet again, now together in solace and seclusion, was more than their rational minds could overcome. They remained in that cave until sunrise, spending the night in the service of passion.

After falling asleep in each other's arms, Byrdon was the first to unclose his eyes and gaze upon the peaceful countenance of his beloved. His chest glowed with affection but now burned with fear as he remembered his prince's threats, and then his prejudices. If it were discovered that he had left the castle, and if he were to be found with Esta—not only a Masorian but the maidservant to the princess herself!—he wished not to imagine the fate that could befall them at Guiomar's hand. With deep regret, he shifted out from Esta's embrace and began to dress.

Esta awoke at the soft sounds and smiled at the remembrance that the night had indeed not all been dreamt up by her longing heart. Thinking what must be the hour, she followed Byrdon's example and slipped into her clothes. Realizing she'd awoken, Byrdon returned his gaze to her. Esta watched as Byrdon's smile faded and, though he made attempts to conceal it, fear crept into the corners of his eye. Having finished dressing, she approached him, who now sat pensive on a boulder, and knelt by his side.

"Thou art troubled," she began, "but I know not the cause. Yesterday, I had thought our love an impossible dream, but it seems the great River itself hath endorsed us with its magic. How else might we have found each other hither?" She smiled with care, concealing an apprehension to hear his next words.

He stood and paced away from her in anguish. "Esta, my life is not what it was when we met."

"It has been but one moon," she said.

"Yes," he replied, spinning to face her, "and in such time I have been removed from my position and forced into the personal service of Prince Guiomar as punishment for revealing the truth of his crimes to the king. I have been threatened, humiliated, and made to swear on my life I shall be ever loyal to a brutish assassin, one who looks not well upon thy people." He saw the tragedy encroach upon her countenance and attempted to soften. "Our love indeed is championed by the River and Sky. Any force of nature would be a fool to deny us, and we are lucky that nature is no fool. The royal forces of our kingdoms, however, are another matter. This magic that endorses us, if our small comprehension of it is correct, is the same that gives power to the fairies, a race my monarch shall have naught to do with out of fear and thine will have naught to do with out of hate. How are we to rely on such a magic?"

"What else are we to do?" Esta replied. "This is what matters to me now, I will not forsake it, not for fear. Of course, there will be danger. I tremble to think of thy position now especially. Thought of magic aside, Isolda and Guiomar would be likely to slit each other's throats if occasion arose. Either one discovering our meeting would mean our ruin. Still, I don't intend to let that prevent me from meeting thee again now that we have uncovered a way."

"Esta, Guiomar has use for me now, and royal decree to hold me to his service no matter how terrible it becomes. I fear it is only thee he would destroy if he discovered us."

"Then let us not be discovered!"

"I cannot risk thy life so! If any harm were to befall thee on account of my foolishness, I could never forgive myself."

"My life is mine own to risk," quoth she. "If tragedy were to come upon me, the fault will be mine to bear. I think it is far from foolish to follow where thy passion leads. Mine leads to thee, does thine to me?"

Taking her hands, holding them close, he confessed, "My passion for thee burns brightest of all the stars. Still, if submitted to, I fear its light could blind us to inevitable doom. We are from separate kingdoms, separate worlds, now connected by another world entire! How are the likes of us to become one?" His words twisted in her chest.

"I do not wish our love to be a burden," she muttered, turning to the ground. "If thy fear surpasses thy feelings for me, I accept that measures to ensure safety must be taken. If thou dost truly believe we cannot meet without severe risk of capture, I would not wish it either. However—" she looked to him. "—hear me, Byrdon. I deeply believe that, in this, the world, united, is on our side, and meeting in this magical cavern, which itself drew us hither from whence we could only be apart, and whose light appeared only when the likes of us entered it, hither we will be safe to pursue a life by one another's side. I see thou art hesitant, and I would not that thou decidest rashly. Take time to compose thy thoughts, and in one moon, when it is again full, I will be here in this cave waiting for thee. Come, if thou wilt; if not, thou wilt not hear from me again."

Byrdon's heart was overwhelmed so that he could not entreat his tongue to compose words. He took hold of the maid and kissed her tenderly. Stepping back, he looked to her with a passionate determination, and then ran off towards Pavoline, leaving Esta with a full heart; weary, but with an air of hope.

CHAPTER V

Discovering Destiny

Byrdon hurried through the royal halls of Pavoline, keeping a close watch on the prince's morning meal so as to see it did not spill, endeavoring to have the breakfast laid out just as Guiomar preferred before he quitted his repose. With a racing heart and a steady hand, Byrdon leaned against the door to Guiomar's chambers, opening it quietly to cause the least disturbance, and went scurrying about to put all in place for when the prince awoke. Having completed his purpose, Byrdon took a deep breath to calm his pulse. The prince then stirred, and Byrdon stood at attention.

"Good morning, My Liege," he announced.

Guiomar pulled open his eyes and winced at the sun that poured through the windows, one beside the bed and one behind the desk, whose curtains Byrdon had made sure to pull open with perfect symmetry and tie back to their posts with elaborate knots.

"Byrdon," the prince began, supporting himself on his elbows, "for the past couple of weeks, thou hast done naught but entirely amaze me with thine extensive commitment to perfection in the most menial tasks."

"I only wish to serve you with the best of quality, Your Highness."

"Right," Guiomar squinted at the servant. "Due to the rich history of respect we share, I am sure."

"You are the prince, My Liege."

"Yes, but, Byrdon, hear me true; I know I have threatened thy life to protect certain intelligences, and while that understanding of course remains intact, I want to assure thee that I am, on most other accounts, a relatively reasonable man. I would not have thee executed if, say, once or twice, thou wert less than punctual with breakfast." Guiomar smirked with a slight air of apology as he noticed the uncanny cleanliness of his chamber flooring.

Byrdon swallowed a note of spite and told the prince, "I no longer rely on fear as a motivation to serve you, Your Highness. I recognize now that I needed to refocus my loyalties, and they rightly belong to the future of Pavoline; they rightly belong to you, Prince Guiomar."

Guiomar smiled and let out a chortle. "Ha! Very well," said he. "Be this true, then I am much pleased. Thou wouldst be more useful as an honest ally."

Byrdon dreaded to think against whom Guiomar would have him allied, but he knew if he was to see Esta again, he needed the veil of Guiomar's trust to prevent the prince from noticing his after-dark exploits to the magical cave. He stood tall, looked the prince straight in the eye and swore, "I am at your service, in all things, My Liege." Guiomar smiled and allowed the servant to retire.

Once Byrdon quitted the apartment, he stood out in the hall to collect his thoughts. A calmness washed over him. Perhaps it would not be so difficult to align politically with the prince. It had now been two and a half weeks since he met his dear Esta in the cave, and there was no doubt now within him that his personal loyalties belonged to her; still, would she not also be safer if he were to be in the prince's good graces? Thinking of Guiomar's crimes, part of Byrdon was disgusted and afeared with his growing willingness to selfishly abet Guiomar in any of his further doings, but as he compared the calm he felt now with the previous terror that held his heart, he bid those worrying voices to quiet, and they obeyed. An image of the forthcoming full moon flashed in his mind, and he smiled in anticipation. He went about his other duties with a new spring in his step.

At the same time, a vision of the moon—and the tryst she hoped it would portend—gave Esta a giddy air as she carried a basket of bedding from the Masor castle's washroom up the hall to Princess Isolda's apartment. As she turned into a hall that opened on one side, revealing the courtyard, she slowed to a stop at the sight of King Madrick leaning over the parapet. He did not look well. At a sudden, he stepped back and curled as he unleashed his breakfast upon the tile in front of his feet. Esta inhaled sharply, holding her breath, as she watched the king's head fall to rest on his forearms which returned to the banister. He rose at the sound of Esta's footsteps as she approached and, upon recognizing her, shame entered his visage.

"Forgive me, Esta," he implored. "I would offer to clean it, but I know not whither we store the wash buckets."

"Do not worry, Your Highness," she spoke with care. "I shall manage it."

The king nodded and returned his solemn gaze to the courtyard below. Esta stood still a moment then, sighing, rested her basket on the parapet.

"Difficult night?" she asked. Madrick shook his head.

"Difficult morn," he replied, and they smiled.

"I am sorry," she told him.

"'Tis not thy doing."

The king and maid stood side by side, looking out at the courtyard, in silent companionship. Suddenly, Esta's forehead crumpled at the notice of nausea in her own body. At the realization that it was far too authentic, she looked round for an escape but found none in time. As a last effort, her hand flew to her mouth. She looked to Madrick with a mixture of embarrassment and terror, and she saw him return a countenance of curious concern. At last, she held onto her stomach, bent in half, and closed her eyes as her morning porridge cascaded to the floor, mingling with whatever the king had likewise failed to digest. Esta dared not rise as she stared with horror at the ground before her. Madrick laughed.

"I had not seen thee at the tavern last night. Did I simply fail to be observant?"

"No! My Liege, I swear," said Esta, swiftly rising to her defense.

"Be calm, Esta, I believe thee. Art thou ill?"

"I had felt well, and frankly I feel far less horrid now than I did just a moment before. I am not sure what came over me."

"Then let it be forgotten. Thou shouldst get gone, I am certain Isolda would like her sheets. I shall find someone to clean, no one need know thou wert involved here."

"Your Highness, are you certain?"

"Of course! What good is a drunken king if he cannot take credit for excess upheaval on the palace floor? Go, get thee gone, I command it," he said with a kind smile. Esta curtsied gratefully and, taking up her basket, followed his command with haste. As she crossed the hall, her polite smile fell to concern as her thoughts sifted through ideas of what the trouble inside her might be.

As the next weeks went by, and Esta's cycle failed to mirror that of the moon, it became abundantly clear to the woman what was causing her sickness. Though the question of the issue begged no further pondering, the issue in question required much discussion and inspired grave concern within her, particularly as it related to the coming moonlit meeting with Byrdon, should she even find him there at all.

The full moon that had held the lovers' thoughts for the last few weeks, at last, rose into the starry Sky. At first sight of it, Esta and Byrdon, both, picked up their feet and made out for the caves, a swift wind propelling them along in their purpose. When they reached the inner chamber, it again was filled with the mysterious crystal blue light, and the lovers again found each other in one another's arms, any trace of worry fading far into the background. Byrdon assured Esta that he had been a fool to suggest their separation and that he was determined to protect their bond with all his strength. At his words, Esta nearly cried in relief and gratefulness, and, with deliberate diction and steady breaths, she revealed to him the result of their previous meeting.

"A child," Byrdon repeated, breathless.

"There are bound to be countless complications," Esta began. "To begin with, where will it live? We cannot very well have a half-Masorian child running rampant in a castle with Prince Guiomar; and it would be fatherless in Masor, for thou cannot risk the prince thinking thou wert within our borders; and what am I to tell the princess? Surely—"

At a sudden, Byrdon pulled Esta close and kissed her softly, interrupting her racing worries.

"We shall find the right path," he assured her. "I am not afeared as I was last moon. Thou wert right, the deepest magics of the River and Sky are drawing us together, and They will protect our love—" Byrdon placed his hand around Esta's waist, his thumb stroking her abdomen, "—and everything that comes of it. Damn what the royals would say."

Esta let go of her strength and fell into her lover's arms. Stepping back, she looked into his eyes, a hand upon his cheek. "When first we parted, I knew it would be us who were charged with closing the cavern between our people. In this child, there will be no separation. The Gwahanu itself deems it so. In us, the whole of the human kingdoms are one!"

Byrdon smiled. "I only care of us," he said, and they kissed tenderly.

They agreed, for the safety of themselves and the child, that it was best the babe be kept hidden from all royal eyes. Each night, Esta suggested, the couple would meet in their cave, bringing one furnishing with each visit, slowly adorning the cavern with all the necessities of a comfortable abode. Esta decided she would continue her service in the castle until such time as she was unable to comfortably conceal her condition when she would then complain of illness and take leave, residing in the cave until the birth. Meanwhile, Byrdon conspired to dedicate himself more completely towards becoming a trusted member of Prince Guiomar's inner court in the hope of earning protection for his family should the prince's baser instincts overcome the king's goodwill; however, he told Esta nothing of his designs. Byrdon would that she at once left behind her Masorian life and turned Pavol in becoming his bride, but he only dared suggest it meekly, for he expected what was her response: "I cannot leave my home. I have duty there." Indeed, events passed according to Esta's plans.

Moons passed. The cave was now decorated with a stone fire circle, two cots placed beside each other, a basket of cooking utensils, and a water bucket. The day had come when Esta would take her leave, and she sent notice to Princess Isolda with the morning messenger, begging her apologies and promising to return to service as soon as she was able, although without expecting her recovery to come about with great speed.

That afternoon, as she rummaged through her cottage packing a few final belongings for her extended stay in the cave, such as the blanket from her own infancy, comfortable sleep dresses, and some grains and fruits, she heard a rapping at the door. Esta froze, curious at who could be calling.

"Esta!" came a familiar voice. "It is I, Madrick. I asked for thee today and was informed thou hast fallen ill."

"Indeed, My Liege," she replied through the wood. "Please accept my apology for my absence. Is there something you need from me now?"

"No," the king said with a slight whimper. "I had only been unentertained and find I tend to enjoy thy conversation. I come not now for myself, but for thee; to see how thou dost fare."

"That is gracious, Your Highness."

"Art thou gravely ill? I was told not to expect thee for some time."

"Indeed, it is a lengthy illness," she said, "and quite debilitating, for I am unable to be of service, but it is not to cause grave concern, I assure you."

"How can that be?" he remarked. "Any debilitating illness is sure to warrant concern! Shan't thou seest our royal physician? There must be some potion Albain could provide to quicken thy recovery."

"I am afraid not, Your Highness. I am familiar with the illness, and I promise it will fade in its own time. Typically, in several moons."

"Several moons! But Esta—"

"Please, Your Majesty, I beg you not to press the issue further!" Esta waited after the outburst as silence permeated through her door. Fearing she had upset the king, she inquired, "My Liege?"

He spoke. "A thought has occurred to me, Esta, and as I sit with it further, I think myself a fool for not having thought of it before. With the sickness, the new wardrobe, now the absence, I suppose it is not unclear. Fool as I am, though, I suppose I should not be surprised at the slow pace of my intuition."

"Your Highness—"

"Esta, thou needest not reveal to me anything that would be better kept hidden. As a king, I would not dare command it. But if thou wouldst honor me with thy friendship, I would that thou knowest, there would be no shame put upon thee for thy circumstance. If my idea of the occasion is correct, it is a happy one." He paused a breath. "I cannot resist in asking, is it the man from Pavoline?"

Esta gasped, forgetting all she had once revealed to the drunken king. He heard her through the door and endeavored to calm her concern.

"Worry not! If secret it be, secret it shall remain. I wish thee well, Esta."

Sighing, she replied, "Thank you, Your Highness."

"Might I bring thee things from the castle? Help, in some way?"

"I will not be in my cottage for some time."

"Then I will turn others away from seeking thee here, assure them thou art likely asleep," he suggested, excited to be of any service.

"I would be grateful for that, Your Highness."

"And thou wilt send me correspondence if there is more I can provide?"

"If you wish."

"I do. Take care, Esta," and Madrick went off, back to the castle.

"Thank you, My King," she whispered, releasing her tension into the chair at her table and resting her head in her hands. She smiled.

After a breath, the young Esta bounded out of her chair and took up her belongings. Draping her cloak around her shoulders, she took a last look at her little home and said a silent farewell. Then, she unclosed her door and stepped out, making her way to the cave.

The first week of Esta's stay in the cave was filled with much happiness. She spent her days etching old tales and illustrations into the cavern walls and further furnishing the place as she was able. In the evenings, Byrdon, being released at the end of his duties, would join her in their underground abode, which daily resembled more and more a home inspired of love. Indeed, the mystical light, and the inescapable sense of magical awe, only grew stronger with each passing day, and the couple doubted not that their love made it so.

One midweek eve, passing much like the others, Esta rested on her cot while Byrdon prepared a supper over the fire. Byrdon hummed an old Pavol song to the rhythm of his work and Esta, watching him with such care, sang the words he had taught to her.

LADY SUNDER-KHAR

Once lived a lad, a man of great esteem,
Who suffered dear at th'hand of Lord Bascal.
His heart so wide, he dared as yet to dream
One day he'd love the fairest of them all:
The brave, the kind, the Lady Sundar-Khar.

He'd watcheth as she pranced through meadow yon,
And thinketh how one face could be so grand.
He swore himself would marry her anon,
And sought the perfect way to ask her hand;
The fair, the sweet, the Lady Sundar-Khar.

In yonder meadow he bid her to meet,
And led her to its highest peak whereat
He knelt down at her lady's timid feet,
And asked if one day he may well have sat
Beside "his wife", the Lady Sundar-Khar?

Her visage made no answer need be said,
For next, the two were happily embraced.
Two months from hence the lad and lady'd wed;
If only Lord Bascal had not encased
The lad so far from Lady Sundar-Khar.

Indeed, the Lord was jealous of the lad,
Despising all the traits the lady loved.
The boy was hid away with iron-clad
With only mem'ries of his dear belov'd:
The far, the sad, the Lady Sundar-Khar.

The lad who liveth there in tower tall,
So guarded by a beast of horrid strength,
Would beat against his hard and captive walls
With grief in thinking of the distant length
From which he was his love, his Sundar-Khar.

The lady spoke to Lord Bascal in plea,
But he would not release the lad her for.
No, not until she swore to always be
The wife of Lord Bascal forever more:
The hushed, the rich, the Lady Sundar-Khar.

Disgusted by the lord's proposal such,
The lady ran afar from Lord Bascal's.
She leapt upon her steed with mighty touch,
And rode to find her love behind his walls.
The fearless hero: Lady Sundar-Khar.

She found the tower deep in forests dark,
And called to he whom she'd bequeathed her heart.
But fell she sudden from her steed, and hark!
The beast was reared to tear her thus apart.
Afeared, alone, was Lady Sundar-Khar.

The beast confined her there beneath its claws,
And snarled at her heart which pounded so.
But at the lady's smirk the beast did pause,
And wondered at her strange triumphant glow,
The trapped, the captive, Lady Sundar-Khar.

She smiled, for the beast had launched her trap
By pinning her so near his fragile breast,
And sneaking out her poignard from its strap,
She plunged it deep into the monster's chest.
The strong, the great, the Lady Sundar-Khar.

> The lad was freed from walls that kept him feared,
> And reunited with his hero-love.
> At last, the two were wed, and townsmen cheered:
> "Hooray! The happy Lady Sundar-Khar!"
> "Hooray! The happy Lady Sunda—

Esta stopped her singing at once as her jaw hung in surprise and her hands flew to the babe inside her. Byrdon dropped his spoon and ran to her side, terribly worried as to the cause of her alarm. His fear abated when she looked to him with a countenance of glee.

"It moved, my love. I could feel it," she said. Byrdon released the extent of his anxiety and put his arms around the mother of his child, laying a gentle kiss above her womb.

The following morn, after she again bid Byrdon adieu to tend to his prince, Esta sat up in her bed and gazed around, examining each crevice of the cavern walls. Having now endless bounds of time to give over to contemplation, she began to be nagged by the questions they had left unanswered about the cave. As she sat now, her back was rested against the straight wall which conjoined the two passageways leading to the kingdoms, Pavoline to her left and Masor to her right. Before her was the wide indentation that turned these simple tunnels into a grand cavern. Thither, the light shone brighter, slight, bringing Esta to wonder if the shine indeed had some source and to think, if it were so, the source must lay deeper within the hollow. She rose from the left side of her cot and continued across the way to where the tunneled passage from Pavoline opened into the bright expanse. She placed her palm against the dark, rough texture of the initial passage and glid her fingertips round the corner, finding the brighter adjacent face of the hollow to be smooth to the touch. The baby kicked as her hand moved from one wall face to the next and she placed her right hand upon her abdomen to steady it, her left continuing its exploration of the curious stone. She followed its natural crevices, walking the semicircle of the hollow, furrowing her brow as she felt some inexplicable energy seeming to transfer from the wall, through her fingertips, up her arm, and into her very soul. Entranced, she followed it such to the near three-quarter point of the arc. Here, she ceased her exploration a moment, though without withdrawing her hand from the stone, in order to attend to her babe who was shifting about now like never before. With eyes now toward her babe, and now straight before her, she felt as though the small heart in her belly endeavored to go further. She let loose a small laugh, assuming the sense was only a projection of her own curiosity, but her countenance darkened as she took new notice of a break in the cavern wall.

Thither, indeed, was a sliver of space where the light shone brighter still, and, creeping herself towards it, she found a small tunnel. Lowering slightly to fit through the opening, she ventured forward with a cautious step. The passage, she now saw, would be layered with many sharp turns, and she was entirely incapable of guessing whither it would lead. She turned to exit the tunnel, but upon doing so her babe kicked so suddenly that she retreated further into the tight passage in shock. Trying once more to return to the main chamber, she felt the babe kick so violently and continuously, ceasing only when she again spun towards the mysterious path, that she could scarcely doubt the babe had its own intention in the matter. At once, she felt so strongly that whatever the source of this strange illumination, it was somehow deeply entwined in the web of her child's destiny.

With this understanding, no fear could stay her stride, and the young mother strode defiantly on. Each turn in the small tunnel brought a new strength to the mystic blue hue of the light until, in the final stretch, it gave more the impression of existing deep under the currents of the great River. As Esta made a final turn and emerged beyond the passage, she looked up to discover herself in the most terrific chamber upon whose domed walls one could detect reflections of a watery current, and, leaning against them in awe, Esta could feel the pulsing of the current's heart, for indeed it was deep under the center of the great Gwahanu River that this hidden chamber directly resided. At the midpoint of the circular room stood an ominous growth of black basalt, and surrounding it, decorating the walls, were drawn grand, vibrant murals. Strangely, they appeared not drawn by any hand, but rather as though they were designed into the creation of the rock itself. Noticing a narrative thread between the pictures, Esta spun towards the chamber entrance to read them from their start.

The first panel, adjoining the rocky archway through which she'd come, displayed a tall pillar of the same hue as the cavern's light, and just above the pillar hovered a lavish oval Jewel. The gem and pillar stood on their own, and Esta walked on, seeing the mural expand to illustrate a lush river, current strong, with primrose, lily, and other greenery flowing from its beds. The river ran down and out of sight, giving way to the trunk of a sturdy tree with four large outgrowths of branches. The nearest growth had, as in Winter, only bare branches, gently blanketed with a covering of snow, and above them was shown the cloud from which the flakes were falling. The next was an illustration of the tree in Spring and it boasted lovely blossoms of a rosy pink, a few petals of which had fallen upon the noses of squirrels and fawns who scurried about the springward side of the tree trunk. The third growth of branches showed Summer, with verdant leaves shining beneath a nutritious sun. The fourth was Fall, with crimson and amber leaves adorning more the ground beneath the branches than the branches themselves. Esta thought it all quite a delightful approximation of the year.

An image of lightning harshly ended the panel, directing Esta to the next. At the foot of the bolt stood a person's silhouette whose features were all obscured save for their piercing, maddened eyes that seemed to glow with greed and rage. Their right hand, palm outstretched, held the floating Jewel from the initial panel, and their left hand pointed direct to the scene that followed. A red sun burned above the pointed hand, and the sun's visible rays were directed with unusual strength to the ground below. There the river returned but it had dried entirely, all signs of life beside it being shown withered. A barren forest followed the river and, in the distance, a fire could be seen blazing toward the foreground, but the viewer was not permitted to see the fire reach them, for an enormous wave came, erupting from the air, and blocked all sight of the forest. Walking on, Esta traced the wave as it was shown to dissipate and stopped suddenly at the sight of what was left in its wake. Townhomes were shown decimated, crops destroyed, and the ensanguine color of the earth was explained well by the countless villagers who lay dead atop it. Knights and laymen were defeated the same, and any left alive were left weeping. Above the sight there floated the moon, whose thin crescent was warped and withered. The moon's strength could be traced through the sky as a shimmer that trailed off, sucked away towards... that Jewel. The Jewel rested in the sky across from the moon, above the scene, itself a formidable force of nature. All the destruction, the death, Esta realized; the Jewel was its cause. Could such a power be part of this world? Her soul ached at the question.

There was space for one final panel before the circle was complete, but this portion of the wall was covered by a thick layer of basalt that had grown across it. Esta took hold of its edge and pulled, hoping, with morbid wonder, to see what lay underneath. She sighed at her unsuccessful excavation and tried no further, assuming it may be better left unseen. She dreaded to think what terror was hid there.

Esta turned now to the fearful tower of basalt that commanded the center of the chamber. She looked to it curiously, thinking she had heard a crack, and her eyes then widened as she was sure she heard another, then another, then another!, until now for certain the tower began to quake, its force knocking Esta to the ground. She managed to pull herself half up as the ground shook beneath her, and she sat, pushed against the wall, watching the rock crumble around itself as its black dust filled the chamber. Esta clamped her eyes shut, bringing her forearm across her face to shield herself from the horror.

At long last, the quaking ceased, and the dust began to settle. When, at length, Esta unclosed her eyes, she remained frozen in terrific awe of the sight before her. For thither, revealed from underneath the dark stone, stood tall the bright pillar of sky blue from the murals, adorned at its crown with the terrible Jewel. Esta rose, with all her strength, and advanced toward the mythic gem. As in the paintings, an inexplicable force kept it airborne, resting inches above the stone pillar below. The Jewel was unlike any Esta had seen, in life or in dreams. It was flooded with deep yellow and red, and across it were pink and purple streaks, making it appear as though the sunset itself resided in the gem. Were it not for the frightful knowledge of the Jewel's power, Esta would have thought it the most beautiful artifact to have ever graced her vision. She circled it to examine closer and, on the pedestal, she saw was engraved the name:

THE JEWEL OF NEBULOUS.

Esta's focus turned to her babe who was shifting again within her. Strange, however, it seemed, for the movement did not feel as before. It felt now as though the babe was reaching; reaching for the Jewel! Esta's eyes darted at once to the foreboding silhouette on the wall as she was flooded with the horrible presentiment that, one day, her child would grow to wield the wicked stone. Excited suddenly by infinite inquiries, Esta studied again the wall's images and noticed anew that, scattered about them all, were small pictures of fairies. With suspicions confirmed that they were involved in the magic of the caves, she knew in the fairies alone might she find some answers.

CHAPTER VI

Finding Family

Esta ran from the Jewel, back through the tight winding tunnel, and again into the familiarity of her own cavern apartment. Though her feet bid her rest, she wasted not a moment. Taking up a satchel, she filled it with necessary provisions and bounded down the passage headed for Masor, keeping both a tender hand and a cautious thought always over her babe. She placed her foot in the well bucket she left dangling from above and pulled the opposite side of the rope to hoist herself up out of the cave. Once on the surface, she took care to avoid the frequent haunts of those she worked with in the castle and made her way straight to the Infinite Wood, forgetting the long-told dangers of the place in her thirst for more information. She kept her thoughts focused and her eyes ahead, even as the infinite height of the Trees and the awe-inspiring magical power which viscerally swam between them called for her attention. When she thought she had run sufficiently deep into the Forest, she called out to her old acquaintance, having no better idea of how to contact one of the Fairy Nation—or, what had he called it? Alquoria?

"Stoman! Good fellow, I beg you for a word," she cried out, aiming her call in all directions.

"Who art thou?" boomed a voice from the Trees. Esta looked all round but could not discern its source. It was not the voice of Stoman, of that she was certain. At once, she remembered the many tales of the amoral violence of the fairy breed and prayed Stoman had not led her astray in believing they were fiction.

"I am called Esta," she said. "I come in hope of knowledge, nothing more."

"Esta?" It was the same voice now but from a different Tree, and Esta now thought she could see a small green spot, not quite the Tree's hue, hanging onto a leaf. It spoke, "Thou wouldst not be the handmaiden to the Masorian princess?"

"I would," Esta said.

In a flash, the spot from whence the voice had emanated transformed into a ferocious fairy, tall as Esta, emerald in tone, and with sharp wings like translucent, shimmering leaves growing from her spine. With a look of fury, and bolt-spear in hand, she dove towards Esta, attacking from above, pinning the maid to the Forest floor.

"Thou wouldst dare enter these Woods when thy sovereigns have set a price for our wings? And, lo, thou comest seeking knowledge—was not the knowledge of our innocence enough for thee? Stoman told of how thou listened; dost thou still not believe? Perhaps the wound in my side could serve as evidence to thee!"

Esta remembered the fairy's story and at a sudden knew with whom she spoke.

"Alizren. Are you Alizren?" she asked.

"Alizren, Fairy Warrior, and Defender of the Infinite Woods. We warriors do not take kindly to betrayal," she answered.

"I have never meant you harm. I know your innocence for fact; I would never encourage pain to be inflicted upon your kind."

"But it is within thy power to prevent it and thou hast done nothing!"

Esta's eyes widened as she made to defend herself. "I risked my station, I risked war!, to tell her highness the truth. She would not believe me!"

"And why should I believe thee?" Alizren scowled.

At a loss, Esta simply asked, "What would you have me do?"

"Tell her again! Tell your monstrous princess the truth, again and again, until she must believe you."

"I would be in a cell before I finished saying it a second time!"

"You can still speak the truth from a cell."

Esta struggled beneath the warrior's grasp. "You would have me rot beneath the castle when I mean to be a friend to your people?"

The fairy scoffed in condescension. "My people need nothing from you except to make the princess believe."

"She would believe me no more from a cell than she did when I sat beside her in her own carriage. It would do no good! I would be destroyed, and your people would be none the better for it. What's more, I am now with child!" At this news, Alizren started and flew back, releasing Esta from her grasp. The maid slowly rose as she concluded, "I can no longer take such risks. Please understand."

Alizren stood in silence, her fiery, heartbroken, glare saying more than her words could dream to convey.

"Are many of your warriors dying?" Esta inquired.

"No, but a few. The unlucky ones. We are up against no army, only human peasants with knives and arrows. They are not much match for our soldiers unless they can effectively levy the power of surprise. It is the commoners and the children who are most at risk. They have been advised not to travel beyond Anwansi," at Esta's confusion, she added, "the hidden pool which is the capital of Alquoria; however, it seems children would so often rather be brave than safe, and, yes, many of them are dying."

"I am so sorry," Esta said, her hand unwittingly resting on her abdomen. "And Stoman?"

"Alive," the fairy answered, the fire in her eyes diminishing as she spoke. "He was discharged from service. At the lack of change, he was forced to confess he had never spoken to the princess, the condition upon which he would be permitted to return to his post."

Esta, a look of terrible guilt upon her, began to apologize for the circumstance, but Alizren held up her hand to halt the apology.

"He would appreciate your concern. I, however, must admit, I am not wholly unsatisfied with that particular turn of events. He is safer at home, and, while there, he has been able to prepare things. A nursery, especially."

"You too?" Esta smiled, and the fairy nodded, at last offering a small smile in return. "How far along?" Esta asked, and the two learned they were both five months into their pregnancy. "Must you continue to stand guard during it all?"

"Not by decree, but, Esta, we are at war. Not only that, but we are the victims of purposeless mutilation. If my being here could spare some poor fairy's wings, nothing for myself could persuade me to forsake them." At Alizren's words, Esta bowed her head in shame. "Esta, do not think that I am blind to the issue of rank. We fairies are all too familiar with it, I'm afraid. To expect a serving girl to consistently challenge royalty on nothing but the word of an enemy soldier, especially at such risk to herself, is, perhaps, not entirely reasonable. It was simpler to blame you before I had met you, the issue seemed not so complicated. I do not blame you now, Esta."

The maid fell to her knees before the kind warrior and kissed her hand, grateful tears rising to her eyes. Alizren took her by the arm and bid her stand.

"My friend, rise, and tell me, you came to the Wood for knowledge. What is it you wish to know?"

Esta told her of how she came to love a man from Pavoline, the magic cave that brought them together, and the evil treasure she found that it enshrined. Upon learning that Alizren had heard faint whispers of such a Jewel in fairy legend but knew none of the particulars, Esta pleaded with her to travel to the cave, look upon the murals, and try at a further explanation. Alizren refused to quit her post until Esta, in such extreme distress, outlined her fear that her babe would one day wield the Jewel and again implored the fairy to aid her in discovering what the future may hold. If her fear indeed came to pass, Alizren considered, the poor mother's plight would be of import to them all in coming times; thus, with the safety of her own coming child in mind and a deep curiosity in this artifact of legend undeniably forcing her hand, Alizren consented to the journey. Having sent word with a fairy messenger that urgent business required she quit her post, Alizren saluted the fellow warrior who flew in to assume her place and followed Esta to the caves.

As they traveled, the fairy warrior and human maid found their way to converse on pleasantries. They spoke of their employment, their respective queen and princess; they spoke of family that once was and of family that was soon to be. Along the way, each found that they rather enjoyed the other's company far more than they would have expected. At a hint from Alizren that the nursery Stoman cultivated might fail to be utilized, Esta attempted an assurance, thinking her reason was a fear the child would be born without life, but Alizren corrected her assumption.

"While we have the same risk as you, it is not a dead birth that frightens me. What fears me is such an uncommon occurrence it hardly bothers pondering, but there are occasions on which a parent may be compelled to relinquish their babe on account of its color not being in their image. Indeed, it is known to happen, for a fairy's visage is but a reflection of their inner person and, though the demeanor of a fairy child so often mirrors their parents, nature does not decree it be so always. And, by order of the Council of Elders, which even our great Queen Okalani hath not the power to contradict, fairies are to be brought up by those in their own rank, ascertained by color of skin. But again, the chances are so slim, I do but only waste my time in worry."

"Oh, but how terrible the suspense!" cried Esta, "and not to know 'til you hold the child in your arms."

"Not quite so," Alizren said. "Every fairy mother, the night before she is to give birth, has a vision in her dream of how the babe is to appear. I will know then." Alizren showed a smile to Esta but, on turning towards the path ahead, the fairy's countenance faded to one of such gravity that Esta was struck dearly. She could not but imagine herself in the unfortunate situation and, in sympathy, she replied, "If such a commandment were made upon me, I do not know that my heart would allow it."

At length, the warrior whispered her response. "Nor mine, dear Esta. Nor mine."

When, at last, they stepped into Masor, Alizren condensed her size and sat hidden within Esta's hair until they reached the secluded well. Thither, Alizren flew above Esta's shoulders as the maid lowered herself in the water bucket. They then walked together through the passage, Esta always a pace ahead in growing eagerness to discover more about the Jewel. Reaching the hollow, Esta made haste for the hidden tunnel but was forced to pause as Alizren lagged her pace, smiling at the sweet apartment the couple had created out of the cave. At a hint from Esta, Alizren remembered their purpose and followed her new friend through the small opening, along the winding walkway, and into the tomb of the Nebulous Jewel.

Immediately upon entering the tunnels, Alizren had felt an impressive magical strength, but as yet nothing had affected her so fully as the power emanating from within the smaller chamber in which they now stood. She remained speechless in awe. Esta, halting in the entryway, watched Alizren intently as she drew near the walls, placing her hand upon them, feeling the Gwahanu's waves course from her fingers through her wings. Esta gasped as the fairy's wings shined with such exuberance, returning to their typical state only once Alizren had drawn her hand from the wall.

"There is power here like I have known in no other place," Alizren proclaimed. "The Nation of Alquoria, and each of us within, source our magic from the Anwansi Pool, and even it draws magic power from the elemental Gwahanu River which spreads Its veins all throughout the Forest. But it seems to me that this place must draw upon no external source. It is a heart of magic itself, sibling to the River and Sky, not child of either. And this Jewel... it is as though all the power of the vast Gwahanu and Anwansi combined is concentrated into its deceivingly modest size."

"It is a danger, then?" Esta asked.

Alizren looked at the murals. "Quite so," she replied, and turned her gaze back to the gem. "I hardly dare approach it. Its power near overwhelms me already from this few feet's distance."

"Is it wicked?"

"Of that, I cannot unequivocally say. Magic is; it is neither wicked nor benevolent. And yet, I know not of a soul who would seek out such power as lies here with the intent to use its means toward benevolent ends."

Esta let out a groan and leaned against the cavern's opening archway for support, her free hand grasping her pregnant stomach.

"I cannot be birthing a villain," she told herself.

Alizren flew to her side and reassured her that, even from their short acquaintance, it was evident that within her beat a strong and tender heart, more than capable of raising a kind and compassionate child.

"Think not on what may be in years to come, but on the beauty that will arrive shortly. Raise the child well, and it will not wish the world ill," Alizren advised. She took Esta's hand and the expecting mothers looked to each other for a time, a thousand words of kinship passing silently between them. At length, Alizren explained she had to return to the Forest, and the new friends parted with a compassionate smile, the fairy flying out as swiftly as she had first appeared. Esta, now alone in the cavern, took a final glance at the Jewel of Nebulous, then turned and quit the place, leaving it all behind her.

That night, when Byrdon returned, Esta told him what had passed. He marveled at her telling of the Jewel's powers and the pictures that foretold its evil purpose, and he immediately wished that she lead him thither so he could look upon them. A tremor ran deep through Esta's soul at his request, and she refused to approach the Jewel's vault. Byrdon did not understand her apprehension entirely, for she had kept secret the connection she felt between the Jewel and their babe in hopes that, if ignored, it would not come to pass. He let the issue alone at her request.

They did not speak of the Jewel again. Months passed, and the little cavern home returned to its state of happiness, with ever-increasing excitement at the growth of the baby. Often Byrdon would return with a bag of grains or legumes or dried fruits from the castle and, over time, they built up a comfortable supply. During the day, Esta made sure to store the food from Pavoline, together with baskets of Masorian spices and vegetables she had gathered, in front of the opening of the small tunnel to the Jewel of Nebulous, the full supply hiding it entirely from view. By the time the lovers fell asleep under their ninth moon, even Esta had all but forgotten the nefarious magic weapon that adjoined their sweet apartment.

While Esta slept on the eve before the twenty-first of March, she was visited by such a dream as yet she had never known. Every vibrant color appeared to flash and spiral before her eyes, leaving her in utter awe. The colors balanced themselves as though resting on a horizon and shifted hues until, for a moment, soft lines of light and dark magenta held their place against a field of yellow and red, instantly returning Esta's imagination to thoughts of the Jewel of Nebulous, until a wave of rippling turquoise cooled the fiery image and put Esta at peace. As the pulse of an underwater current beat steadily in her ear, it seemed to repeat a sound; a word... a name:

Leanna.

Esta awoke with a start, placing her palm on Byrdon's chest, shaking him 'til he woke. He quickly readied to be of assistance, holding still for Esta's word, an inquisitive eye controlling his expression.

"I think our child has just told me her name," Esta uttered.

"Her?" Byrdon repeated, his inquisitive countenance cautiously turning to glee.

Nodding, Esta's expression mirrored the happiness of Byrdon's as she explained, "Her name is Leanna." The parents kissed in delight. Esta detailed her dream, leaving unspoken any guesses at its magical cause, but offering no doubt as to the vision's legitimacy. The two agreed, with an occupational surname to honor her heritage, the child would henceforth be known as Leanna Page.

In the morning, when Esta again awoke, she unclosed her eyes to see Byrdon huddled over a small fire, stirring a pot, the delectable aroma of perfectly spiced porridge filling the cave. She watched him a moment, imagining her head resting on his kind shoulders. She watched his soft hand wipe the tip of his perspiring nose and felt her heart gleam in adoration. All would be well, she could feel it.

The porridge being ready, Byrdon looked up to Esta and saw that she lay awake. Carefully, he filled a bowl with the breakfast and, sitting half of himself on the bed beside her, he placed his pillow on her lap and rested the bowl atop it. Kissing her forehead, he held her as she thanked him and devoured the delicious meal. When she finished, Byrdon restored the plateware and sat again beside her. He told her that he sent early word to

Guiomar this morning of his feeling ill, followed by an assurance that he would return to service as soon as he was able. The baby being so near, he dared not be away another moment.

Suddenly, the couple heard a distant patter at the end of the tunnel to Masor. Byrdon rose to investigate.

"Is someone there?" he cried. "Announce yourself!"

It was then that they came into view; Stoman and Alizren, full height, floated into the light. Stoman held a basket in one hand and Alizren's arm in the other. Both their countenances portrayed a slight fear, and they appeared disheveled. The patter of their wings ceased as they halted at the beginning of the hollow. Esta rose to greet them.

"Alizren! My friend, what a joy. And Stoman, I hope you are well. What brings you here?" she asked.

"I beg you will forgive the intrusion, Esta. I knew not to whom I could turn; I thought only of you," Alizren said.

"Forgiveness is unneeded, you are always welcome. Are you well?"

"We have a favor to ask." Alizren looked grave. "I had the dream last night; our little fairy girl will be born today." Esta smiled wide and Alizren's countenance thanked her briefly, but she continued grave as before. "She will be of the royal orchid color, not of ours." Esta understood immediately. "I imagined tomorrow when she would no longer be mine, and I could bear it not. We are warriors to the depths of our souls, and we serve our people, but we serve our own hearts as well. So, with great deliberation, we packed up our belongings and flew. I thought of your home here, the beauty and comfort combined elegantly with seclusion and safety. I know what it is to ask, but still, I must: Might we join you here, and raise our secret children side by side?"

Esta smiled, overjoyed to add her friend to their family and she looked eagerly to Byrdon for an agreeing glance. He had sought her gaze in the same moment, likewise expecting agreement, but expecting to agree to precisely the opposite. Both their expressions faltered as they came to understand they yet had no agreement at all.

CHAPTER VII

The Birth of a Legend

Esta gestured for Alizren and Stoman to wait a moment while she took Byrdon's arm and pulled him across the hollow into the relative privacy of the opposite tunnel leading to Pavoline.

"My love, thou canst not mean to agree to this," he whispered, flickering an involuntary glace toward the fairy warriors as he spoke.

"We must! Imagine if we were in their circumstance," Esta tried.

"I hardly understand their circumstance!"

She sighed, remembering all she had chosen not to tell, and relayed what she had learned of the fairies from Alizren during her day in the Woods.

"Thou wert in the Woods?" Byrdon put all his effort into maintaining a low voice.

"Please, love, that is not the purpose now. They are friends to us, and they need our aid."

"How can they be friends? They are fairies."

Esta's countenance twisted and she stepped back, astonished at the difference in their thoughts.

At the opposite end of the hollow, Stoman began to pace, inching back toward Masor with every turn.

"Patience, dear one," Alizren whispered to him. "We have asked of them something great indeed."

"Yes, and the last time we did so I lost my place as a warrior."

"That was different, Stoman."

They met gazes and understood one another in silence.

"How can we trust them?" He finally asked.

"They are our friends."

"We have friends in Alquoria, yet we are not trusting them."

Alizren scoffed. "Which Alquorian warrior shall we trust to protect the secret of our crime?"

Stoman sank. "Perhaps there is reason this is not done."

Alizren's gaze floated toward the ground then landed on the human couple as they continued to converse.

"Dost thou not see how similar they are?"

Byrdon nodded facetiously. "Indeed, with their wings and verdant hue? Dost thou not see the difference?"

"The exact hues of thee and I are not the same," Esta said. "There is no knowing what our child will be. What if she emerged a bright blue? Wouldst thou love her?"

He rose one of his eyebrows. "Our child will not be blue."

"Thou dost not know these things!"

"How would she be blue?" He nearly laughed.

Esta remained stoic. "That is beside the point. Wouldst thou love her?"

Byrdon realized she was sincere and mirrored her. "Of course I would."

Relief overcoming her, Esta gestured to Stoman and Alizren. "Then thou seest how they are the same?"

Byrdon looked toward their guests.

"Stoman, art thou uncertain of this? Regardless of Esta and Byrdon, we two need to be certain."

Stoman took Alizren's hands and held them tight. "We put ourselves in grave danger with this."

"Yes," she agreed, having already given it great consideration.

"They would lock us under the pool for this."

"Yes," she agreed again. "That is why we must not be discovered."

"If what they say is true, then the child will be different from us. We know nothing of raising a royal."

"She will not only be royal. She will be ours."

Stoman held back a torrent of concern. "What if she does not see it as such? What if, upon understanding what we have done, she resents us? What if she returns to Anwansi and turns us in?"

Alizren was silent. Her expression made it clear that this she had not considered in the slightest.

Stoman deflated, hoping she would have prepared some wisdom that would calm this particular concern, but she remained silent still longer.

With a hand over her abdomen, the fairy mother looked across the hollow to Esta. Suddenly, she smiled and returned to Stoman.

"Our child will not hurt us," she said. "We will raise her well, and she will not wish us ill."

Stoman wanted to smile but faltered. "Canst thou be certain? We need to be certain."

"I am certain," she nodded, stroking Stoman's cheek. "Our love will guide her. She may have the mind of a royal, but she will have the heart of a warrior. Perhaps—" Alizren glanced again to Esta and Byrdon. "—she will also have the friendship of humans! She will be like no one in our world."

At last, Stoman smiled, encouraged by the loveliness of Alizren's confident eyes.

"And she will be ours," he said. He brought her close and they kissed, sparks of tenderness flying from each their wings.

"Their love is the same as ours, isn't it?" Byrdon said, bashfully turning away from the fairy couple's embrace.

Esta nodded, taking Byrdon's hands. "We cannot forsake them."

"I do not wish to, truly. It frightens me, I admit, but that is not really any change from our life at present, I suppose." Esta chuckled. "Still, my love, we reside not even in a single room, but the single hollow of an odd cave. I have wondered if it will be sufficient space for three to live and grow, but six? We would be more tightly knit than I care to imagine."

"There will be small difficulties in abundance, I am sure, but I cannot see that as reason enough to turn them away."

Byrdon sighed and kissed her hands.

"Very well," he said.

In that moment, both couples looked to each other and, as the humans smiled, met again in the center of the hollow.

"Welcome home," Esta told them, and all broke into smiles, thanks, and embraces, soon setting to work adorning the space for its new inhabitants.

Stoman and Alizren would sleep in their shrunken form and thus required only a pillow, but their babe, too young yet to understand the mechanisms of her magic, would not be able to transform to her smaller size for a few years and would therefore need to sleep in her larger form. This they had considered and, instructing Esta and Byrdon to stand some feet back, Stoman placed their basket on the floor, decreased to the miniature with Alizren, and together they flew into the basket, emerging again holding a tiny bassinet between them. When they grew again to full height, holding the object, the bassinet grew with them to its useful size. The humans laughed at the clever sight.

"It can stand right beside Leanna's," Esta said, and Byrdon set about helping Stoman move it to its place while the expecting mothers sat aside on the beds.

"You have named it then?" Alizren inquired excitedly.

"Not I," Esta whispered. Seeing that Byrdon and Stoman were beginning to engage in their own conversation, she elaborated for Alizren all that she would not share with Byrdon. "She told me her name last night. I had a dream, much like you had described. I cannot understand how, and I have not suffered Byrdon to know all, but I know the vision came from her. I can explain it no other way."

"You had the dream! Incredible. Only magical beings have such visions before birth," Alizren replied. "Perhaps I too quickly dismissed the connection between your child and the Jewel." She said this involuntarily looking toward the store of provisions where she knew the tunnel to be hidden beneath. Esta interrupted her ideas.

"I dread to think of that horrid gem. All I wish is for it to be lost and forgotten. Please, refrain from its mention."

"But Esta, it is an elemental source of magic. What if your proximity to the Jewel has allowed your baby to be born of its power? A magical human, unlike any being known in our world!" She smiled, thinking of her own child.

Esta tried to pacify Alizren's spiraling thoughts with the remembrance that Byrdon and herself were devoid of magic, thus their child could not be otherwise, but it only spurred Alizren on.

"Remember, Esta, magic does not operate under the same assumptions as human genealogy. The same magic that allows two green fairies to birth a purple one, assuming the child's essence demands it, and the circumstances fall in perfect order, perhaps could indeed allow a magical human to arise from two of the standard variety!"

"But then what kind of creature would she be?"

"I cannot even begin to speculate." Alizren smiled in wonder but saw that Esta grew keenly concerned and at once regretted the eagerness with which she had conjectured. "All I have said before remains true," she assured her. "You are good and kind. Leanna will be also." Esta thanked her friend and, releasing her anguish, rested her head upon the fairy's shoulder.

Alizren shifted with a sudden remembrance, speaking straight to Esta with renewed excitement. "You do realize, of course, that a magical child is born the day following the mother's dream. Our children shall be born together!"

Esta smiled and took Alizren's hand, replying, "Then it is fitting they shall be raised as friends."

Indeed, before long, both mothers began to feel their birthing pains and the fathers began to run about, preparing the home for the double event. Esta and Alizren comforted one another while Stoman and Byrdon pulled the larger cots apart and brought one to the opening of each of the tunnels. Byrdon then helped Esta lie down on the cot in the Masor tunnel and Alizren in the other while Stoman flew out towards Pavoline to fill buckets with water from the Woods to aid with cooling and cleaning. He marveled aloud at the magic of the tunnels when he returned again within minutes, then was brought back to his purpose by the howls of the mothers whose pains continued.

Stoman, with Alizren's unvocalized approval, offered the human pair a variety of magic salves and potions they had brought with them which were used in Alquoria to ease births, but Esta and Byrdon politely refused, both still wary of magic. Their effectiveness, however, was quickly evident for, in a couple of hours, Alizren was flying above the cot in a final effort, at last releasing the baby into Stoman's arms, wrapped in a blood-soaked cocoon of her own little wings. Alizren floated down and closed her eyes, exhausted, while Stoman disconnected the mother and child and cleaned the babe with a damp towel. A smile crept further and further up his cheeks as he peeled open the drying wings and first laid sight upon the lids of his daughter's purple eyes. The tiny wings began to flutter and release their first lavender sparks as the child started to cry. Alizren opened her eyes and held out her arms, taking hold of her dear babe and turning the whole room to smiles.

Stoman stepped away from Alizren's side to begin cleaning from the mess, beginning with the bloody towel.

Byrdon noticed the towel and said, "Your blood is red."

The fairy looked up to him, curious. "Indeed. What is yours?"

Byrdon smiled. "It is the same."

They held one another's gaze for a moment with increasing appreciation and understanding until it was broken by Esta's renewed cries which returned all Byrdon's attention to her.

"Thou art a marvel, my love," he told her. "Hold onto thy strength."

She grasped his hand, shaking her head. "Something is wrong, Byrdon. Feel the baby, something isn't right."

He let go of her hand and felt her womb, turning to her a moment later, trying to maintain a lightness over his concern.

"She's spun around the wrong way, Esta." Esta groaned. "Do not worry, my love. Surely, we can turn her."

Over the next several hours, Byrdon made many attempts to turn the baby, but she would not be moved. All the while, Esta's pains and worries continued increasing.

"I do not understand," Byrdon said after another try. "I have followed every instruction; still, I cannot make her move even an inch."

Esta bellowed again and fell against him in grief and frustration. Holding her a moment, he suddenly shrieked in joy.

"Oh! She moved! Only slightly, and in the unhelpful direction, but she moved all the same. Return to where thou wert, let us see if she moves again."

Esta was confounded but too exhausted to argue so she returned to her original place in the bed. Byrdon laughed in relieved amusement.

"She acts like a compass!" He cried. "Her head will only point in that direction." He gestured behind him, and Esta followed the line of his hand with her gaze, knowing through the wall her child was pointing directly to the Jewel of Nebulous. A tremor ran through her as Byrdon gleefully continued. "Let us simply spin thee around, and inside thee she will turn accordingly!"

"No!"

Byrdon was startled but attempted sensitivity. "I know it will be painful to move now, but I am here to assist thee."

"I will not move," Esta declared. "Thou must turn the baby."

"She is stubborn," he complained.

"So am I."

"But, dear, it does not seem that she wants to point away from her current direction."

"She knows nothing! Wilt thou bend to her every whim when she is born? Turn her!"

Byrdon's brow rose in distress. "I do not know that I'll be able to, love."

"Byrdon, please!" Esta cried.

At a push from Alizren, Stoman approached them with one of their special balms.

"May I offer this?" He said. "It is known to calm the inside child when it is stubborn."

Esta nodded. "Anything. Yes. Just—" She took a breath to calm herself. "Just turn her."

Byrdon wordlessly assented as well and Stoman stood by Esta's bedside, covering the skin above her womb with the cool, clear ointment. It was some hours still before they reached full success, but soon enough Byrdon was able to begin turning the child's head toward the center of their home. Although her pains persisted, Esta noticeably calmed and, with the assistance of another fairy potion, managed to push the child into the world, and into her father's arms, before the end of the night.

"Show her to me," Esta begged when Byrdon was cleaning her.

"She's perfect," he said, but the mother did not yet smile.

"Show me," she said again.

Byrdon gently handed Esta the child, who was newly wrapped in a soft blanket. Her dark brown skin was smooth and faultless, and her little nose wrinkled with a sniffle and a cry. Esta brushed a tight black curl away from the child's brow and gazed upon her sweet chestnut eyes. There was nothing unusual about her. She was a baby like any other. At last, with a sigh, Esta smiled.

"As I said," Byrdon repeated. "She is perfect."

Esta wholeheartedly agreed.

After restoring the home to its usual state, Byrdon built a small fire and Stoman made a light stew. The four parents stayed awake late into the night in awe of their children, their friends, and their abode. Now, the family sat as if in tableau; Leanna in the arms of Esta, Esta embraced by Byrdon, Stoman with his arms around Alizren, and Alizren with their daughter in her arms. They named her Kennedy. With deep feeling, Stoman bowed his head and kissed Kennedy's violet brow. No one spoke. They only watched peacefully as the fire burnt down, the embers glowing and shedding a warmth throughout the cavern, a warmth which would carry on in love for years to come.

CHAPTER VIII

The Adventure Begins

For many years, the family in the cave lived together in comfort. Esta returned to her post under Princess Isolda, much to the glee of King Madrick who further employed her as his chief conversation partner when she was not otherwise occupied. Byrdon continued to serve Prince Guiomar, relaxing into his duties, as of yet finding them sufficiently lacking in the assistance of wicked plots. Alizren resumed her warrior station, informing her friends and superiors alike, with feigned sadness, that Stoman and she had found a secluded hovel in the Forest to live and grieve in after the loss of their babe who had not lived more than a few moments before the fates cut her strings. Stoman, still excluded from the Fairy Queen's army, assumed the post which all the other three secretly envied: he remained in the cavern to look after Leanna and Kennedy.

In the early years, he would feed them each bottles of their mother's milk, read and sing to them, and rock them to midday sleeps. As they grew, his duties as entertainer quickly dissolved as the two girls spent all their time entertaining one another. They acted out scenes from plots of their creation and used mud to paint warrior marks on each other's cheeks. Stoman taught them to use a paintbrush and soon after the long tunnel walls were covered with their commendable—if juvenile—works.

In the evenings, all the adults would return. Together they would make a meal, and the six of them would sit around the fire for hours, telling tales, singing songs, and explaining to the children how their world was structured, and why it would be such a danger for Kennedy in particular to leave the caves. Understanding the fear of separation, Leanna swore never to leave Kennedy's side. Stoman and Alizren, having been taught to read as children in Alquoria, instructed Kennedy and Leanna, and Esta and Byrdon by proximity, on the ways of literature and philosophy, and the children were taught their history. Every night, as they were being put to sleep, Esta would sit by the children's beds and sing to them softly her mother's old lullaby.

'My dear who drifts into the night,
Thy dreams may have no bound nor fright,
For I'll protect thee with my heart.
My love will find thee where thou art...'

Eleven years passed thus, and all were quite content. Then, one Spring afternoon, as Stoman was out collecting firewood in the Forest of Beasts, Leanna woke from a nap at a sudden and shook Kennedy awake beside her.

"Kennedy, I have just had the most beautiful dream in the world!" she said. Leanna told her friend of a path she had found herself on, surrounded by tall green hedges, which were decorated with vibrant yellow flowers in full bloom. At the end of the path was a magnificent castle and, at its base, she saw her own mother entering a small door. "I cannot explain how I know it," she continued, "but I am almost certain I have seen the very castle in which my mother serves."

"How can that be? We have never seen its image," Kennedy replied, and Leanna shrugged. Kennedy thought a moment then, staring Leanna in the eyes, said determinedly, "We should go to it."

"Do not be silly," Leanna rejoined.

"But if thou hast truly visited the castle of Masor in thy sleep, then thou must have been aided by magic, and if thou art capable of magical dreaming then we may be even more alike than we knew! Dost thou not burn for the truth?" Kennedy argued.

"I do, but what if we were found? What if thou wert taken!"

"I shall shrink to the size of thy very palm and conceal myself in thy pocket," she explained. "I will not be seen, and who art thou to attract eyes amongst a city of humans?"

Leanna sighed. "We are not supposed to leave the caves."

"Nor can we stay in them forever."

They paused, looking towards each other. Leanna's logic tried to restrain her imagination as it went off to explore the unknown streets of Masor, but even her most rational fear was incapable of it, and she knew, without long, she would agree to the inadvisable expedition. When Kennedy spoke to her, her very soul gave her no power to ignore. She considered, and then spoke.

"Thy father did fly toward Pavoline in search of wood. It would not be of great difficulty to escape toward Masor."

Kennedy smiled, and Leanna's countenance responded in kind. In the next minute, once Leanna had put on her pocketed coat, the two were racing down the Masor-bound tunnel, giggling, running farther from the hollow than they ever had.

Arriving at the bottom of the well, Leanna wondered at how her mother reached the surface each morn. Kennedy flew up and discovered the long rope, wound and secured, at the top. She lowered the bucket to Leanna and dropped her the remaining rope, which she utilized then, stepping in the bucket, to hoist herself up until she could take Kennedy's hand and clumsily tumble onto the land. The earth was warmed by the sun as she had never felt before. Pulses racing in their clever success, the girls made sure to tie the rope up again, hiding that it had been tampered with.

They heard voices outside the alley, making Kennedy instantly condense and dive into the outer pocket of Leanna's coat, observing the world through an unclosed buttonhole. Leanna stepped toward the bustling street, full of shouting merchants and a torrential current of villagers, all of a significantly taller height than she, passing to and fro. She hardly dared to enter it. Gazing all around, her eyes caught on the peak tower of the Masorian castle, and she realized, in her vision, she had seen the same exactly. Upon this, her determination increased tenfold. She bounded out into the market, racing like a guppy up the wild stream, eyes and mind set on her destination: the castle. She found herself, at last, before the palace gates. But, wary to enter the courtyard, she walked around to the unpopulated side and, to her astonishment, saw, in the distance, a large hedge of yellow roses. She moved towards its beginning and knew not that she was running until she stopped suddenly on a path environed by parallel thickets of flowers.

"It is just as thou hadst said," Kennedy marveled, peeking her head out of the pocket.

"It is just as I saw," Leanna replied in even greater amazement. "Kennedy, how can this be?"

The fairy jumped up and, ensuring they were out of sight, flew to sit upon her friend's shoulder. "Remember my father told us of the visions fairy mothers have before birth," Kennedy began. "The same magic must be at play here. There is only one explanation, Leanna. Thou art part fairy!"

Leanna was speechless in marveling at the thought; then, suddenly inquisitive, she asked, "Dost thou think I may grow wings?"

Kennedy turned her head. "No," she rejoined. "Fairies do not have visions of anything except their baby before giving birth. Thou dost not have wings. 'Tis only fair. Thou cannot have everything, Leanna."

Leanna laughed, and Kennedy soon followed in kind.

"Come, let us go further," Kennedy urged, pointing to the servants' entrance door.

"Hast thou gone mad?" asked Leanna in earnest.

"We have come this far," Kennedy pleaded.

"We cannot go inside the castle!"

"Art thou not curious? Hast thou never wished to know how the crowns live? I certainly have."

Leanna stared at her friend with bitter adoration, then shook her head with a slight smile. "Thou really art a royal, aren't thee?"

Kennedy smiled in response and sparks of eagerness flew from her wings.

"Very well, Thy Majesty," Leanna submitted, and Kennedy clapped with joy.

"But restore thyself to thy pocket," Leanna ordered. Kennedy hastened to obey.

Leanna crept to the end of the rose bush and examined the terrain before her. When the way was clear of spying eyes, Leanna darted to the door, catching it just as it was closing from its last use. Immediately upon entrance, they found themselves in a musty washroom where royal sheets hung on wires and gossiping maids sat laundering the king's clothes. Further down the hall was a kitchenette with furnaces and fruit baskets. There was suddenly a jab at Leanna's abdomen and she looked down, with furrowed brow, to Kennedy who pointed to the far corner, adjacent to the kitchenette, where Leanna now saw her own mother standing and preparing a plate of biscuits and berries for the princess's lunch. She dove behind a nearby crate, watching from below as Esta turned away and carried the plate through another door. In the brief moment of the door's opening, Leanna and Kennedy both could see it led to a hallway far more exquisitely decorated than the servant's hall they now occupied. Leanna's coat moved as Kennedy flew forward in the pocket, and, knowing it would be worse to argue aloud lest they be heard, Leanna submitted to her own inevitable curiosities and followed the fairy friend's lead. She crawled along, unseen, and when no barricade continued to hide her from view, she straightened her shoulders, lifted her chin, and sauntered through the door, undisturbed.

Leanna looked round for her mother, but she was no longer to be seen, and, her attention being now caught by walls of such smooth shine, hung with such tapestries, her feet strolled on aimlessly as she craned her neck to absorb it all. She wandered so for some time, occasionally turning a corner or hesitating before a display of armor at Kennedy's silent request. Finally, they turned onto a walkway whose inner wall was replaced by an open parapet. Turning towards and standing before the banister, Leanna's eyes reached just underneath the wall's height, and she rose to her toes in hope of seeing what lay beyond. From her vantage, she could see a hint of the perfectly clear Sky, the vivid cerulean mesmerizing her. Kennedy slumped further into her pocket as, from her buttonhole, she could see nothing. The movement in her coat tugged Leanna's focus from the Sky and she realized that sounds of the citadel could be heard from below. In an attempt to witness their sources, Leanna held onto the parapet and leapt up, seeing hints of villagers, but falling back again much too soon.

King Madrick wandered onto the balcony to gaze out at his world when he saw the small jumping child. He paused and sought round for to whom she might belong but, finding no one near who was claiming her, approached her gently.

He asked, "Might I help thee with a lift?"

She was startled and looked to him a moment in silence.

"Be not afraid, I will harm thee not," he comforted. "My name is Madrick."

"The king!" she exclaimed, eyes widening.

"Only by title, thou needest not think of it. And thy name?" he inquired.

She paused with caution. "My mother says it is not safe for us here."

"Oh! Us? Is there more of you?"

"No," she said quickly, correcting herself.

"With all my kingly power, I swear, I shall allow no harm to come to thee. I pray, trust me with thy name."

Meekly, she responded. "My name is Leanna."

"Leanna," he smiled. "Would thou likest me to lift thee onto the parapet?"

She nodded and he did so, keeping a close watch as she leaned outward to see more of the view.

"There is so much of the world!" she cried now, having in her sight the whole of the palace courtyard, much of the market, and miles of green Masorian hills and forests past the citadel walls, the Infinite Trees looming all around. "It is so beautiful. I didn't know," she whispered. Kennedy too now could see what appeared as all the world laid bare before them and had much the same sentiments as Leanna.

"Thou dost reside deep in the city then?" Madrick asked her. She looked to him a moment speechless, then simply nodded, returning her gaze to the land beyond the walls.

"Thou wert born here?"

Again, a nod. Invariably curious as to the child's origins, he pressed further. "Dost thou have a relative in the castle?"

Unthinking, Leanna revealed, "My mother serves Princess Isolda."

The king's eyes widened as he clarified, "Art thou Esta's child?"

She flinched, realizing her error, but remembered her mother's better sentiments about the Masorian king and decided to trust him. She nodded again.

"Of course! All those years ago, I thought—" he stopped himself. "Well, no matter now, this is splendid. Thou shouldst know, I am quite fond of thy mother."

Leanna looked at him daringly. "She says thou art a drunken fool."

The king's laugh erupted from his chest and billowed through the halls at both the child's sentiment and speech.

"And in doing so, she, likewise to thyself, hath earned my further respect." Madrick took on a more didactic tone. "Although, if thou art to spend time amongst the prissy nobles who haunt the castle, it will be to thy benefit to avoid speaking to the king as though he were of an equally low status as thyself."

Leanna, fully conscious of her disrespect, replied, "Sorry, Your Highness. She says *you* are a drunken fool."

He smiled, restraining another laugh. "A drastic improvement. Come, if thou wilt allow, I will show thee through the castle; reveal all thy mother's haunts."

Leanna thought this quite a wonderful idea and, with a nudge from within her coat, she knew Kennedy agreed. She thus consented and Madrick lifted her from the parapet, returning her to the ground. He brought them first to the nearest place of excitement, the armory, and boasted of their glistening shields and sharp battle swords. Leanna wondered aloud as to their purpose, and he told her of famous battles for land and honor that had been won by Masorian knights of the past. Leanna's nose wrinkled, with furrowed brow, at the thought of any estimable person utilizing these weapons to strike another. She knew of such things from stories, and Kennedy and herself had passed many an hour pretending it with long spoons in innocent fun; still, when confronted with instruments that had been used for true harm, her sadness cast a dark shadow over her adventurous soul.

Going on, Madrick explained, "We have not fought such a war for some time. Now, Isolda holds the knights ready to defend us from a fairy invasion."

"The fairies have no intention to attack," Leanna said sharply.

"So we may hope. Their wickedness has already taken too much from my family—from our kingdom. I have no faith in their passivity."

"But it was not—" Leanna tried.

"This is not a pleasant subject, let us move on." Madrick turned to exit the armory, and, out of his sight, Leanna looked down to Kennedy, her sympathetic eyes slightly calming the fairy's anger.

Next, they toured the full royal kitchen, housed in a wing opposite the washroom the two children had initially entered, and Madrick told Leanna of his childhood when he would sneak around the cook, stealing extra sweets and pastries against his parent's demand.

"The secret, of course, is my behavior never changed," he said, guiding Leanna along his stealthy route and obtaining a small, delicious cake for her, which she shared pieces of with Kennedy when Madrick was concentrated elsewhere. They all giggled as they ran from the cook, who saw them now and chased them away with a rag.

"Come, I shall take thee to Isolda's chambers so thou canst see thy mother's most frequent place. We shan't enter upon her highness however for, if she is occupied, we will only be scolded, and if not, she will likely bore thee with superfluous motivational histories. Regardless, we will run outside again either at her command or else to escape the tedium."

Leanna laughed.

As they walked, Leanna opened up to the conversation and, though telling nothing of her family or circumstances, told much of her love for stories, music, and painting. For her youth, Madrick was impressed by her conversation and rather taken by her childlike wisdom and charm. Leanna noticed in the king the lack of assertiveness her mother spoke of; but, like Esta, she even more recognized the good—if misguided—man whose mind and passion lay hidden beneath the heart of a frightened fool. As the two furthered their acquaintance, Kennedy let her focus wander over the castle walls, her wings often sparking in excitement as they passed regal portraits or lavish landscape tapestries of the Masorian woods. The light in her wings darkened, however, as they started up a grand staircase. Centered upon the wall of the landing was a large, framed case, inside of which was pinned a pair of grand fairy wings, once vibrant, now dulled, showing only hints of the emerald veins that once pulsed with energy. Leanna, engrossed in talk, failed to notice and continued to follow Madrick down the hall, past the display, but Kennedy was struck so strongly, she flew from Leanna's pocket and hovered in terrific awe before the cruelly trophied wings. Without thought, she grew to full height, standing now on the ground, staring, still, and silent.

"Halt! Thou winged beast!"

Leanna spun at the guard's call to see Kennedy frozen at the top of the stairs. Checking her pocket in confusion, and now again surveying the scene, she looked to Kennedy in fear but tried to hold her strength when she perceived her friend's complex countenance of grief, anger, apology, and desperation. The guards, now three, rushed upon the violet child and Leanna thought with such vehemence, *Fly, Kennedy, Fly!*, that she felt as though her friend heard her silent plea. Indeed, as the guards reached out for her, Kennedy constricted her size and flew down the hall, past Leanna. Madrick pulled Leanna to the side just in time for the guards to come stampeding past in pursuit of the young fairy.

Leanna stood stupefied in such extreme distress and, misinterpreting its cause, Madrick placed a sturdy hand on her shoulder, promising, "Worry not, for Masor's knights are the best in all the land. They will catch it."

At this, Leanna's small heart could bear no more and, leaning against the wall, she fell to the floor, curled her knees to her chest, and cried into her self-embracing arms. Esta rounded the corner now, concerned at the commotion.

"What has happened?" she asked Madrick, not yet noticing Leanna.

"There was a fairy in the castle," he informed her. The shock in her following countenance was true, but the fear she combined it with was feigned. She looked down to the crying child.

"And who is—Leanna!" she realized, immediately kneeling beside her. "What art thou doing in this place?" Though when Leanna looked to her with such grief, she thought of the escaping fairy and understood the worst of it. Asking no more, she took her daughter in her arms.

"I was merely offering her a tour of the castle," He said into their embrace.

Drying Leanna's tears, Esta responded, "Thank you, My Liege, that is gracious. I suppose an introduction is then no longer necessary."

"We have been well introduced," Madrick assured her with a kind smile. "In fact, so well introduced I would like to offer her thy place as my chief conversationalist, if she is not already employed. She is a bright child. Isolda has been begging me to acquire a servant for myself; I can think of no one I would rather appease her with. Leanna could become a page in the castle just as thyself!"

"We shall consider it, Your Highness. Thank you, again." All of the mother's focus was on her crying child. The king did not entirely understand their preoccupation.

"Is it no longer considered quite an honor to serve the king? I hope the position would maintain its respectability despite who sits on the throne."

Esta turned to him now in deep apology, keeping a hand on Leanna's knee. "Oh, it does, Your Majesty, it is an immense honor and it is well appreciated. I am simply afraid neither of us are in the mind to decide it just now, please forgive me."

It was now Madrick's turn for apology. "No, forgive me, Esta. I should have chosen a more opportune moment to ask. The little one has seen an ordeal, I suppose."

"Yes," Esta said, with more meaning than Madrick understood.

"Why dost thou not take her home? I shall cover for thee with Isolda."

"I should not ask that of you, King."

"I do not recall any asking. Please, allow me to help."

Esta met her daughter's swelling eyes and knew there was truly no other choice. Grateful, she nodded to the king. "Thank you. Sincerely, thank you," then graciously bowed and, taking Leanna's hand, led her from the castle.

Stoman, finding the children missing upon his return, had gone out again in a frenzy, first back to Pavoline then finally to Masor, frantically searching for the children. When Esta and Leanna returned to the caves, they found them empty, save for a new pile of firewood abandoned in the middle of the cavern floor. Leanna told her mother what had all occurred as they journeyed home, crying and apologizing profusely before describing each event. On arriving in their hollow, Leanna, exhausted, fell upon her cot and, after a few more tears, sank directly into sleep.

When Stoman, at length, returned again to the caves, he fell to his knees in relief to see Leanna safe. Esta approached him with delicacy, but he prevented her from revealing the loss of his own child. For his last discovery had been to watch from above as Kennedy, wounded, was lifted from the edge of the Infinite Wood by warriors of the Fairy Queen and taken to their nation's capital on the Anwansi Pool. Once all events were detailed to him, Stoman merely sat stupefied in terror and shock. Esta wanted to comfort him but could imagine no words that would suffice. Instead, she made a fire and, together, they silently awaited the return of their partners, both watching over the lone resting child.

Deep in a tumultuous repose, Leanna's mind scoured through infinities of dense forestry, dreaming tree after identical tree, searching, though she knew not what for; she knew only to lose it would be to lose a vital chamber of her heart. She found herself suddenly in a brightly lit grove and lifted her eyes to find a spot of aquamarine light breaking the cast over clouds of a leaden sky. As she stared upwards, a grand wind blew beneath her feet and, as though her spirit willed it, lifted her up through the vibrant clearing. Thither, all the clouds melted away, erasing the remaining world as they dissolved, leaving Leanna standing in an unknowable expanse of light blue, crystalline sky. More unending than even the Infinite Woods, Leanna thought her new quiet hideaway to be one of simple peace. She remembered then for whom she sought as she now discovered a violet form in the distance.

"Kennedy," she said, now taking restrained steps, and now running to the figure before her. The figure smiled as she came further into view and, wings emitting sparks of glee, rushed towards Leanna with haste. In mere moments, the two friends, reunited, were locked in each other's embrace. Remembering all the events now that led to their separation, Leanna stood away from Kennedy with a somber countenance. At Kennedy's curiosity, she explained, "Thou art but only a vision. I miss thee so, and I lost thee I know not to whither, nor do I know if I shall ever see thee more."

"Thou seest me now, Leanna," Kennedy said. "I am no vision; but a moment past I thought thou to be a vision of mine."

"I don't understand." Leanna eyed her strangely.

"If thou thinkest thyself the owner of this dream, and I think myself the same, then perhaps both and neither are the case, but instead we own the dream together." An idea came to her. "For thy mind alone could not inform thee that I, the far Kennedy, now lay in a medicine bed amidst the Anwansi Pool, surrounded by healers of the Alquorian royal court, and yet such is the truth."

Forgetting a moment all her doubts as fear overcame her, Leanna asked, "For what dost thou require healers?"

"We will come to it," the fairy assured. "Tell me now of thyself so I may know thou art not mine own imaginings. Whither art thou?"

Mind still reeling from the possibility, she answered slowly, "The cavern. My mother found me in the castle and we returned together."

"Then thou art safe?"

Leanna nodded, and Kennedy let loose a held breath in relief.

"Astounding. To think that we have found each other through dream at such a length," Kennedy marveled.

"I still understand it not. How can this be?"

"It must be thy magic, Leanna! If thou canst travel through mental prowess alone to places thine eyes have never seen, perhaps the minds of others lay similarly within thy reach. I am real, Leanna. I swear to thee."

Her words soaked into Leanna's heart and, indeed, she realized, Kennedy and herself shared an essence of realism not found in her usual dreamscape. She looked now to Kennedy, whose wings shone nearly as bright as her exuberant smile. Her eyes, Leanna saw, sparkled as brightly as she remembered, and the hints of lilac which floated in her irises gave them all the beauty of the last time Leanna had gazed upon them. Leanna's smile grew as she allowed herself to believe Kennedy's assertions and, at her sudden initiation, the two were once again caught in a caring embrace.

"What happened to thee?" Leanna begged, holding Kennedy at a short distance. "Thou wert able to escape the castle?"

Kennedy nodded and began to tell her tale. "The guards were swift, but in my small size I managed to evade both their grasp and their weapons." Leanna's eyes widened at this, remembering the extent of danger in which she had left her friend. She continued, "I flew out the casement of a turret and kept straight on. I wanted so to halt and seek the well from which I could return home, but flying weapons were set upon me and I feared to slow. I wished so for speed that would hasten me from danger and, in hoping so, I grew to my larger height so my wider wings might carry me more swiftly. This, however, was in grave error for though greater in speed, I became also a target of a larger size and within a moment I felt the head of a Masorian arrow drive through my side. Leanna, calm thyself, I am safe. For though I shall say the pain was piercing, I still kept a great alertness; or, so I tried. Though my mind was sharp, I could feel my consciousness slipping. Forgive me, Leanna, but I forgot my search for the well and flew straight for what I saw to be my nearest place of physical safety which, now, was the Infinite Woods. Falling upon the Forest floor, I both feared discovery—for I knew it meant my separation from thee and failing my parents who always kept me from Anwansi—and I feared not to be discovered, for I had nothing but to hope for the aid of healers, and I knew I had not the strength to carry myself from the Woods. Before long, I saw two warriors of the Fairy Queen fly toward me, and I let my consciousness fade. When I next awoke, I was lying in a healer's bed, the arrow was gone from my side, the wound cleaned, and leaf bandages were wrapped securely around my waist. Though I grieved at our distance, I will admit, in the moment, I felt nothing but relief."

"Feel no shame at thy relief," Leanna said. "I am so thankful for thy safety, for certainly I did nothing to ensure it." She averted her gaze in self-disappointment. "Still, Kennedy, I worry. What hast thou told them of thy origins? Thy parents could be sent to the dreaded prison under the pool if their crime of raising thee were to be known."

Kennedy turned from Leanna, explaining, "I know all too well the dangers, and I have spoken of my parents to no one."

"They have not asked thee?"

"No, they have asked. They have asked nothing but from whence I came. More, due to my color, the questions come from all the highest places. From fear of saying too much, I have said nothing at all. They ceased their questioning on the assumption that I am mute."

Despite herself, Leanna laughed. "Dost thou mean to say the royal Kennedy, whose endless chatter has kept me from repose of numberless nights, is now thought of by all of Alquoria as being unable to speak at all?"

Kennedy shrugged, and with a bemused smile revealed, "They know not even my name."

Leanna laughed again. "Then as soon as thou art well, thou shalt fly again home and we shall be safe and happy once more."

Her smile fading into anticipatory pensiveness, Kennedy's eyes drifted downward. Leanna immediately noticed the change in countenance and inquired as to its cause.

"Thou dost intend to return to us; or do thee not?" She realized the truth as she spoke but refused to believe it until Kennedy affirmed her fear.

"I will not pretend to feel at home in this place, nor would I dream to ever feel so at peace, so loved, as I do in our family's arms. I dread to think of how lonely I shall be when night falls and I have thee not beside me, nor my brow warm with the kisses of my mother and father, nor thine own mother singing us to sleep, but in this place I feel a new sense of belonging, a calling, as though I am needed here. I have found my adventure here, Leanna, and I cannot dream to let it go."

Leanna breathed back a tear, her grief now overcome with both an understanding and a fear of what was to come.

"What am I to do without thee?" she asked.

Kennedy smiled and took her hand. "Thou art to find thine own adventure. I may be some type of royalty, but, Leanna, thou art something special beyond what we can imagine. Today we found only part of the Skies, and already it has proven so grand, and more vast than we had dared to dream! I hope thou wilt not simply return to the caves, now that thou hast seen the world."

Thinking a moment, Leanna replied, "The king of Masor offered me the position of his servant. Perhaps my adventure begins there."

Kennedy smiled and joyfully kissed Leanna on the cheek.

"I shall miss thee so," Leanna said, but Kennedy rejected her lamentation.

"There will be no need," she said. "I have no doubt our adventures will be much intertwined, and until that comes to be we shall meet every night in our dreams as we do now. This is not goodbye, Leanna. I swear to thee, there will never be a goodbye."

Leanna suddenly awoke in her cot as her father's hand felt her forehead for illness. As her mind slowly came out of sleep, she heard Kennedy's voice whisper in her ears.

I love thee, it said.

Leanna smiled.

The family gathered round the young dreamer as she told them all of her earlier vision and her recent dream. All were amazed, none more so than Byrdon who had yet never been told of Esta's suspicion of the child's mystical nature. Esta was indeed amazed at her daughter's magical abilities, but her surprise was exaggerated for Byrdon and Leanna's benefit. However, despite this, the four adults were unable to maintain this subject long, for thoughts of Kennedy overpowered their imaginations. Alizren and Stoman grieved at both the gulf that stood between them and their daughter, and that she would choose it. Leanna exerted all efforts towards relating Kennedy's love for her parents and her conflicting passion which kept her afar. She told of how their familial tie was not yet known outside the confines of their family and emphasized that none of them were in danger. The fairy parents appreciated Leanna's attempts, but they knew there would be no peace for them now that their only child had been thrust into the system of rank that they had so desperately tried to keep her from. They felt the only way to regain what little peace they could was to return to their cottage on the Anwansi Pool and, though at a distance, keep watch as their daughter grew.

    That night, Stoman and Alizren took up the bags they had long stowed away and packed their belongings. Embraces and tears were shared between all and, with a final look at the cavern walls, which were covered in the girls' childhood paintings, the couple took hands and flew out through the tunnels, into the open air, towards Anwansi.

DRAMATIS PERSONAE

A Brief Interruption

Dear Reader,

At this time in our journey, you have now been introduced to most all the historically significant figures of our tale. If you will permit my interruption, I would like to so graciously thank you for joining me in this adventure. You see, I am the last surviving member of my Elenvian lineage and, as such, my mind has been the lone conduit through which all these great Elenvian figures have sought to be heard. As extraordinary as it may sound, I swear it is true that in some way these magnificent spirits continue to reach me, sending their stories across the Wood, nearly haunting me with their persistence. Of late, however, those from this 'Beginning' which you now read have begun to quiet in my ear, and I have no doubt this is only the case because they have found yours to whisper into in my place.

This being the case, I feel it pertinent to pause the tale so I might remember each of its main actors to you, familiarizing you more completely so that you will be sure to recognize them whenever—and wherever—they appear, whether it be here in your further reading, or in your dreams.

With gratitude, I am yours,

Cedar Flyte

(in order of appearance)

ISOLDA OXBIEN—Royal of Masor; second child of Madrick I and Fionella, now passed; younger sibling to Madrick II. She is extremely well-read, talented in tact, and brilliantly bright. Still, Reader, I caution you, it is worthy to be wary of her word.

ESTA—Servant to Isolda in Masor; partner to Byrdon; mother of Leanna. She is deeply loving and passionately stubborn. I think of her in times when secrets must be held and wonder how it was she kept them.

MADRICK OXBIEN II—Royal of Masor; first child of Madrick I and Fionella, now passed; older sibling to Isolda. He is emotional, caring, and kind, and has difficulty claiming his inner worth. I thought of him often during my not-so-well-handled teenage years. Admittedly, his influence both helped and hindered.

PETRENAIR RANZENTINE—Royal of Pavoline; father of Guiomar. He strives for what is best but is tired, fatigued, and blinded by grief. Sometimes, when I am confounded by the actions of even the better people in power, this particular king comes to my mind.

BYRDON—Servant to Guiomar in Pavoline; partner to Esta; father of Leanna. He is guided equally by love and by fear. I am forever fascinated by the combination of determination and desperation which led to his actions.

GUIOMAR RANZENTINE—Royal of Pavoline; child of Petrenair. He is cunning and thoughtful. His thoughts, however, never waver from their presumptions. His vengeful eyes haunted me when I was a child.

KENNEDY—Child of Kesk Fairy Warriors Stoman and Alizren, but herself one of the purple-skinned royal Nachovy. She is the closest friend of Leanna Page, and a personal childhood hero of mine.

LEANNA PAGE—Ah, what to say of the legend herself? To begin simply, she is the child of Esta and Byrdon, dearest friend of Kennedy, and (soon) the servant of Crown Madrick in Masor. She walks in and out of dreams and travels the world in her mind. She is small and yet reaches so far. I have always found it fitting that the first words we know her to have said are "Kennedy, I have just had the most beautiful dream in the world!" May we all find it within us to dream as grandly as she does.

Reader, I will keep you no moment longer, for there is much to unveil. Before returning to Leanna, however, we must first follow the adventures of the little fairy. In the next pages, you shall fly alongside Kennedy as, at long last, she meets the nation of Alquoria.

Dear Reader, read on.

CHAPTER IX

Kennedy Meets Alquoria

There was no place in the world, Kennedy thought, that felt more alive than the Anwansi Pool. Her early home caves had always pulsated with power, but thither the energy was dormant, silent, and not yet awoken. Anwansi, in contrast, never slept. It consisted of a massive circular hollow, connected at its rim to the eastern end of the Gwahanu River and open to all the stars; yet, even on a cloudless night, only a small patch of the stars could be seen due to the infinite Trees which environed the area above. Around the upper rim of the hollow, Tree roots jutted from the high cliffside, intertwining in a brilliant mosaic, and casting a beauteous array of shadows on the mid-level rockface below. This interior stone facing was entirely smooth and provided a sparkling surface for rays of the sun to dance upon. It also prevented the designs of any wingless ones who would think of climbing it to reach the bottom.

At its base, the hollow was wider than at its rim. From wall to wall, the floor of the hollow was filled with calm, pristine water, creating a decently deep pool which appeared indefinitely undisturbed. The serenity of the pool was, however, inexplicable when one took into account the great waterfall which cascaded into the hollow from the River above. The torrent was massive and powerful and shimmered with every hue imaginable. Where the fall hit the pool, any waves that might have arisen became gentle ripples, and the mist that erupted from the collision reflected a vibrant rainbow. Being a hand of the River, the fall had long ago taken hold of this colored light and solidified it into a rainbow bridge that would contain its cascading mist and aid travelers in walking around the fall.

Most pleasant to Kennedy were the sweet cottages, shopfronts, and wooden walkways all floating atop the still water of the pool, and the ever-present breeze that arose from the constant fluttering of wings as fairies passed to and fro. It was this consistent commotion of wings in the day and the protective thundering of the Anwansi Fall in the night that imbued the young Kennedy with the impression of sensational liveliness which she felt certain could nowhere be replicated.

It had been a fortnight now since her arrival in Anwansi and, as yet, she had never been permitted to leave the Healing House. It was a structure, like many others, carefully built upon the lower rockface just above the level of those on the pool, adding a lovely—and practical—second story to the city. She was constantly attended to by healers who would dress her wound and utilize all their most recently discovered magics that might aid in the healing. Everyone she met in the Healing House had countenances of one or another shade of blue and, in her first week especially, they treated her with a distance and deference she had never before experienced and didn't much care for. Remembering her parents' teachings about Alquorian culture, she knew the attitude was due to her own hue of purple and thus made every effort, albeit through silent means, to put everyone she encountered at ease.

Now, at the end of her second week, the odd quiet child who evidently cared not for her natural status had become a favorite of the healers and their staff, and she was always met with smiles and pleasant salutations. She was also now allowed to wander about the Healing House and was shown what would become her favorite room in the place, the library. Whenever her wound was not being attended to, she would amble through shelves of volumes, picking out tales of Alquorian heroes she had never yet been told of and sitting within the cushioned sill of a circular window, looking intermittently at the page she held and at the fairies down on the pool below, taking pleasure equally in both.

On this day, she found herself incapable of maintaining attention on her book. She held a volume open on her lap, leaned against the side of the casement, and looked only out the window, her wing on one side relaxing against the glass and the other falling down towards the open room. She sat and took in all of Anwansi. Blue fairies flew between the floating storefronts and cottages, their children diving into the pool, playing games in the water that reflected their aqua hue. Around the high edges of the cliffside, small green fairylings weaved and swung between the branches and roots, training for their warrior destiny, overseen by an instructor of their own color who wore a distinct uniform, dark green and designed sharply with a belt of tools which, for the warriors, included a bolt-spear. In all her time observing from above, she had rarely seen anyone of her own purple color, and when they did appear, they were bowed to and moved away from. They also tended to seem particularly disagreeable. The few purple fairies she had seen wore the same style of uniform as the warriors' instructor she saw in the branches, although it was altered to match their royal color. Despite the assumption these would be instructors for the purple fairylings like herself, Kennedy had never once seen a single fairy her own age who was also her own hue.

On the previous night, when her most frequent healer, an older fairy named Yareth, had come to place new dressings on her wound before she went to sleep, they had remained a moment beside her cot in clear indecision.

Kennedy had looked at them expectantly, inviting them to speak.

Taking a breath, Yareth at last spoke on how clear it was Kennedy was enjoying her time in the Healing House.

She smiled and gave several quick nods.

Yareth could not help but give a slight smile in return, but it soon fell to sincerity. They explained regretfully that it could not last. Kennedy was healing well and would not be able to remain here much longer.

Kennedy would not feign surprise, but her disappointment was evident.

In particular, Yareth went on, her friendliness and good nature towards the azure-toned staff of the Healing House would be viewed unkindly by those who would soon come for her.

At this, Kennedy displayed her confusion.

Yareth was not supposed to speak of it but felt too terrible leaving Kennedy unprepared. The very next day, they had found out, a royal instructor would be arriving to bring Kennedy to whither she belonged.

The fairyling's confusion heightened and she burned to ask to whither it was she would be taken, but she merely allowed herself to forcibly twist her countenance and hoped Yareth would understand.

The old healer understood well, but they would not speak more of it, for such was not their place. They assured Kennedy how dearly she would be missed, then quit the sleeping hall, extinguishing the mystical lights that wound along the edge of the room, and left Kennedy on her cot in the dark.

She wondered now, as she sat in the library casement with her book, if she would recognize the instructor after all her watching from above. She hoped not, as none of them had seemed particularly pleasant. Investigating every crevice she could see from her place, she tried in vain to determine what part of the pool housed those with her type of visage. Upon giving up her search, she turned at last to the volume in her lap. It was a brief examination of every fairy who had once served as Queen of Alquoria. There were not a great many as the naturally long lifespan of a fairy was enhanced by the particular magic Anwansi gave to its queen, thus making for incredibly lengthy reigns. Still, the tradition of the fairy queen was ancient, and a few had ended short of their due time, so there were a sufficient number of histories that might fill a book.

Kennedy flipped to the end to see a line about the current Queen Okalani. She was chosen to be heir at the age of seventeen, the book said, but her coronation had not taken place until many years later when the older queen had naturally passed.

It was then that he arrived. The royal instructor was not one Kennedy had before spied upon from the window, but he was dressed the same as the others. A lavender suit with a deep indigo lapel came to a point at his waist where lay a belt of the same shade with attachments to hold a scroll and a small, pointed twig, presumably meant to write with. His countenance held the same prideful contempt as the other royal instructors she had seen. He entered the library without a word or nod to the healer's assistant who held the door for him, and only gave pause to see Kennedy offer the assistant a concerned smile, and even a wave, as she closed the door. Silently disdaining the child's unknown upbringing, he returned focus to his purpose.

Without delay or nicety, he introduced himself as Instructor Nichym, said he was well aware of her choice to remain silent and that it would be dealt with at a later date, and told Kennedy he would explain more about her present circumstances as they made way to their destination.

Kennedy remained in the sill of her window. She only offered him a confused and unhappy glance before looking upon her open book.

He assured her books would be abundant in the House of Nachovy, and surely all of them a distinctly higher quality than any she could find in this small healers' library.

A scowl overcame Kennedy's brow, and she pointed it at the instructor.

He sighed and approached the little window. She did not understand, he told her. He bore no ill will upon the Zils. They served their purpose, and it was time a child of her hue served hers as well.

Unhappiness left her gaze, and only confusion remained.

He asked her if she knew the history of their creation.

She thought back and realized she did not.

He stood with renewed disdain and, pacing, began to lecture. Kennedy started to look out the window again, wishing she could shut out the condescension, but her ears could not resist a new story.

Instructor Nichym told the tale just as it was told to him, and to his own instructors, and theirs, and the same for a great many centuries:

When the world awoke for the first time, he explained, there was nothing upon its surface but Trees. Naught occurred but the Trees growing immensely tall. The Sky appeared as it does now, with its beauteous colors, clouds, and stars, but It was unhappy for It had no one who could admire It. One day, the Sky grew so sorrowful that It began to cry. It cried and cried and cried; cried with such force that Its tears created a dent in the earth and a massive pool remained there for many years. As the years passed, the Sky's tears were slowly absorbed into the land, and as the pool receded it revealed new kinds of earth, with treeless mountains, valleys, and some forests still, but of much shorter height. The water receded further and further until it stopped, leaving behind the great Gwahanu River running through the center of the new World Within the Woods.

Fertilized with Its tears, this new ground began to grow creatures which might admire the Sky. The first of them found they preferred the water, such as the fish and reptiles, and thus spent their lives largely unable to see the Sky. The next were the deer, lions, horses, and bears, and while these preferred the land and could clearly see the Sky at any whim, they did not sufficiently admire It. The birds, who came next, found home in the Sky and offered It much entertainment, but still they did not admire Its beauty. At long last, when the first humans dug their way out of the earth, they looked instantly to the Sky and said "Oh, what a beauty!" and the Sky was content.

The young Gwahanu, however, still stirred. Built from the Sky's own tears, It shivered with emotion and bubbled with a power It knew not how—nor wished not—to contain. It continued to push against the earth on Its far edges, eager to introduce Itself to the Woods that lay beyond. Towards the West, It pushed slowly, trickling many different smaller veins in every Woodward direction, rooting Itself to each of the infinite Trees. Towards the East, It was less patient, splashing a great amount of Itself forward, carving a grand hollow in Its descent. Thinking the hollow quite lovely, It continued to pour Itself over the crest as a pool began forming below It. With Its power, It kept the pool level and at peace, taking the fallen water back up through the earth so that It might fall into the peaceful pool indefinitely. This pool, and all the original Woods, became the River's prime joy.

Years went by, and the River watched as the humans of the earth, many kind but many selfish and cruel, would traverse through the near edges of the Infinite Wood and cut down the largest Trees as competition or slay its many woodland creatures as sport. This made the Gwahanu very unhappy but, being made of tears, It had no way to cry. Instead, It reached into Its greatest power to create a creature that could befriend the human as well as destroy it, and who would act as the defender of the Wood. It took earth from Its riverbeds and rolled it in Its waves, repeatedly tossing it above to mix it as much with the air as with the water from the Sky. Imbuing it with elements of Its own power, the River finally cast the creature into the Anwansi hollow and, at last, there hovered the first of the fairies. These first, numbered at fifty, were all Zils, with skin and wings reflecting various shades of blue. They spent their days frolicking about the Woods and, though they populated it quickly, they did naught to prevent the humans from destroying their homeland. Discontent, the River tried again, resulting now in the creation of the Kesks with their green countenances. Each of these first fifty—now a smaller amount of the fairies in all—erupted from the waterfall with a bolt-spear in hand and the intrinsic knowledge of how to forge more. These Kesks were highly effective at clearing the humans from the Woods, but their violent nature soon turned them against one another and much of the fairy population was extinguished, either directly or indirectly, due to their battles.

Kennedy realized instantly that the violent Kesks her tutor spoke of would include the gentle warriors who raised her and she suddenly was swimming in questions and disagreements, but remembering her vow to protect those same parents with her silence, she said nothing and listened as the instructor went on.

Discontent yet again, the instructor said, the Gwahanu made a final effort, creating the Nachovy, their purple visage setting them apart from all but the most elegant in nature, who dispersed throughout the fairy population and led them all to order and peace. It was thus that the creation of the World Within the Woods was complete.

So now she must see, he went on, why it was vital she leave this place and come to live with her own kind. They would teach her the Nachovy practices necessary to maintaining the peace.

They both remained silent a moment, Instructor Nichym waiting for Kennedy to rise, but she did not.

Impatient, he spoke again. It was not only a matter of their physical creation, but the creation of their society was evidence of this necessity as well. He asked her if she knew how their nation of Alquoria was born.

Although she despised the thought of him telling it, Kennedy was also unhappy to learn how many Alquorian tales had been kept from her. She indicated she was unaware of the story.

He remarked on how horrid an upbringing she must have received to have arrived at her age without these early essentials of an education. Regaining his didactic air, he then told the abridged tale of how the first Elders had come together, one from each of the largest clans of fairies which were all spread about the Wood, and, meeting in the Gwahanu's hollow, named it Anwansi. Not long before, the first of the Fairy Queens had been mystically chosen, distinguished through the power of Anwansi by her changed wings, but while she commanded all the respect necessary to maintain order, she was far too reckless to lead the nation philosophically. The Elders invited her to Anwansi and, together, she and they agreed it was best the Council of Elders would design the society and write its ordinances, and the queen would carry it out. They made Anwansi the capital, having all in the nation live within it, while only the queen's warriors traveled the larger Woods to protect it.

Now, really, she must see, he said, since any young Nachovy girl might be chosen by Anwansi to serve as their next queen, it was vital she go through as much proper instruction as was possible in preparation, should the heir turn out to be she.

This piqued Kennedy's interest, and she was unable to prevent a spark of eagerness from flying off her wing.

A prideful smile found the corner of Instructor Nichym's lip as he became aware he had found the key to the child's curiosity. Indeed, he confirmed, even she might one day become queen; however, such would only be possible if she accompanied him to the House of Nachovy, for Anwansi would never place its highest distinction upon a fairy of such low education.

Kennedy gave pause, investigating the instructor's countenance with her eyes. At length, she set down her book and permitted him to lead her away.

She was led out of the Healing House and, for the first time, witnessed the Anwansi Pool from up close and saw an extent of detail that she had yet to even imagine. Every tailor, cobbler, magician, or carpenter seemed so perfectly marvelous that each and every one she passed received her most convivial smile and wave. Once the instructor she followed looked elsewhere, few could resist returning a pleasant acknowledgment to the strange happy fairyling. Craning upward, she watched again the small warriors—now known to her as Kesks—as they flew amidst the high branches of the Trees above the hollow. She thought what fun she could have on those branches, or how delectable it might be to learn to make whatever stunningly scented cake just now passed her by on a baker's tray, but as she thought this she was led away from these sights and towards the bottom of the magnificent waterfall that fell from the River. She paused in front of it, standing upon the solidified rainbow bridge that held back the immense splash, and allowed its mist to envelope her in its cool energy. She closed her eyes, and the mist seemed to kiss her with its magic until she was led away again, Instructor Nichym pulling her arm, to the mouth of a cave that lay within the cliffside, just hidden by the waterfall.

The entrance to the cave was a marvel, with large multicolored gemstones encrusted in its massive arch, and the inside of the cavern was no less impressive. Although there were no windows to offer exposure to the sun, the cave was alive and brilliantly bright. Kennedy looked round and was certain she saw not a single shadow. She realized this cave must be lit by the same natural magic that gave light to the cavern in which she had resided previously, though the magic was immensely stronger here at Anwansi. As she was led past the doors of chambers and through passageways, she came to understand that carved into the cave was the interior of a magnificent castle, that this would be whither hid the rest of her type of fairy, and that it was here, in this beauty, she would spend most of her days.

As she imagined, she was shown to a bedchamber which she was to make her own, and, over the next few weeks, she was entirely incorporated into the learning cohort of Nachovy fairylings her own age who spent all their time in the castle. Despite the castle's size and beauty, it did not escape the young fairy that her wings had again been clipped by her being hidden inside a cavern; still, so long as it lasted, she determined to make of it the best she could. Though she still spoke not, she quickly became a favorite of her seven classmates who all adored the games she made up for them, drawing pictographic instructions on the classroom walls. Best of all was her laugh—the only sounds they heard from her—which had the contagious quality of instantly delighting those all around in a way few of them had yet experienced.

The instructors—for there were many—grew to hold different opinions of the new fairyling. Contrary to that of her classmates, but developing just as swiftly, they looked upon her with distrust, frustration, and befuddlement. Her peccadillos were such that they offered no opportunity to rightfully prevent her behavior, for she played her games only during the time allotted for their freedom, and, though without speech or written word, in which both she refused to participate, she had proven a rather vast intelligence through the specialized assignments they designed to test her knowledge. Still, it was all entirely unconventional, creating a playful atmosphere much more akin to the common Zils than the refined royal attitude reserved for them of higher rank.

Instructor Nichym, having known her the longest, even if only slightly, took personal issue with her behavior. He had explained perfectly well the reason the Nachovy should be separate in attitude from the rest, and he was not to be disregarded. Taking audience with the queen, he requested permission to check Kennedy's behavior and offered numerous recommendations for responses he felt would be fitting to the offence.

Queen Okalani only laughed, insisting no offense had been made.

Nichym wondered aloud if the Elders would feel the same were they to hear of it.

The Elders did not have time for children, she told him. She insisted he let the issue rest.

He had nodded, taken leave of her, and reported the same to the other instructors who, like himself, were greatly disappointed.

Furthering their discontent, as time went on, healers were brought in to examine Kennedy and confirmed there was no medical cause for her muteness or certainly any reason preventing her from utilizing the written word. The instructors all agreed she was likely to be concealing information regarding her first eleven years of life, but they were under order from the queen not to force upon the child any frightful interrogation, and their suspicions were yet too weak to risk wasting time at the Council of Elders with its mention.

Two years continued thus and, as the adults held their misgivings quietly, Kennedy grew to contentedness.

One day, at the conclusion of their morning studies, Kennedy urged her friends with drawings and playful tugs to traverse outside the cave with her, just to the waterfall, to attempt a new game. They were hesitant, but, trusting her near completely, they agreed, and the cheerful sparks that flew from her wings at their concurrence showered them all in such contagious delight that they were all outside in the next moment.

Flying near the fall's peak, Kennedy picked up her legs, curled her wings around her, and fell into the raging water, sliding down, down, until she thrust her wings out again and flew up into the open air just before reaching the rainbow bridge. Her friends eagerly joined her, repeatedly engaging in the fun adventure. Hovering again above the peak, preparing for another descent, Kennedy noticed a small Zil fairyling, a few years younger than herself, watching them from a branch on the cliffside.

She motioned for him to join them in their fun.

His wings turned down and he shook his head vigorously.

Nodding, she motioned again.

He looked around, nervous, then smiled shyly and, his wings sparking with timid bright blue energy, he darted to her side.

She kindly took his azure palm into her orchid hand and together they jumped into the fall, laughing as they emerged at the bottom. Soon they noticed all Kennedy's classmates had turned somber and were watching them silently from afar, none falling again into the water. Some of them gazed beyond her and she followed their eyes, turning round to see Instructor Nichym glaring down at her, dark sparks emerging from his wings in fury. He took hold of the blue boy's arm and flung him behind, out towards the center of the pool as he flew to Kennedy, cornering her into standing on the rainbow bridge. The boy caught his balance in the air and hovered there, watching as Kennedy faced the angry instructor.

Nichym fumed at her about culture and tradition. He quoted ordinances that prevented the socialization of children from different ranks and defended it as a vital precaution taken to protect their way of life. He looked to her for an indication that she understood but received nothing of the sort in her stubborn glare. He demanded she provide affirmation that she would not involve herself with those types of children again, and, at long last, with passion sparking from her young wings, she could no longer stay silent.

"That is not right," she said.

Her classmates gasped and whispered amongst themselves, but Instructor Nichym only nodded and smirked in contempt, his suspicions confirmed.

"So at last she speaketh," he proclaimed. "Why did you take such time?"

"Until now I had more to hide than I had to say; now, I have more to say."

"Ha! What could you say?" Nichym retorted. "Look at this boy. What right has he to fraternize with a Nachov? Zil, get thee hither..." but the boy had flown off, hidden amongst the cottages.

"These customs you protect are absurd," Kennedy said as the instructor turned back to face her. "More than absurd, they are false. You assume a difference in the natural value between myself and—"

"The difference is vast! He is a commoner, you are a royal."

"Then perhaps you should treat me as one and not interrupt," Kennedy rejoined. "With all due respect, Instructor, you are as royal as you will ever be, yet I may one day become Queen."

"You will never be Queen," he snarled.

"That is for Anwansi to decide, is it not?"

Nichym flew close and looked down upon her in disdain. "And what do you know of Anwansi, child? You have lived within it for two short years, I have lived here a lifetime, and I know how its queens are meant to behave. You are hardly fit to live in its castle, much less to rule it."

Kennedy stood a moment, staring into his glare. She then decided upon a course of action which would either ruin her in Alquoria or save her, and as yet she was not wholly certain which she might prefer.

"Take me to the queen, then," she said. "I have here, at last, committed a crime, as you well know. Is it not to her, then, to decide my fate?"

He scowled. "So it is," he said, and taking her by the arm, dragged her around the fall and again through the shining entrance to the caves. Kennedy stood tall as she was able while she followed him silently back through the castle, this time traveling down passages she had never yet seen. At last, deeper into the caves than the young fairyling had ever been permitted, they found themselves at the entrance to the Alquorian throne room. Instructor Nichym announced them and their purpose to the posted warriors standing guard, bolt-spears in hand, and one stepped inside to report their arrival before they were permitted. Once both grand stone doors were unclosed, Nichym lurched Kennedy forward, knocking her off-balance, and dropped her at the foot of the throne.

The instructor launched into a philippic, detailing all he had seen of Kennedy's recent offense to their nation, but she heard not a word of his lamentation. The little royal was entirely entranced by her first sight of the queen. From where she first landed after being tossed to the floor, Kennedy lifted her gaze slightly and saw only the feet of Queen Okalani, planted firmly on the platform of her throne, the chair built of elegantly woven vines and branches and her lavender skin enwrapped by golden sandals. The queen wore an amber gown that appeared almost in motion, cascading down like the Anwansi Fall to her ankles, and as Kennedy lifted her eyes further, she gasped to take in the queen's magnificent, bright wings, unlike any she had seen before; for, the wings of the queen were white. Mesmerized, Kennedy's gaze drove deeper into the wings and, as her eyes adjusted to the light, she saw now they were not white at all, but instead were part purple, part green, and part blue, all the colors mystically cooperating as one. In rapt examination, she did not notice the queen hold up her hand to silence Instructor Nichym, nor did she perceive the reality that the wings were coming closer, closer, closer, as did the queen, who had noticed the child's fascination.

"When a Fairy Queen is chosen," quoth Queen Okalani, "Anwansi makes its choice known by gifting the fairy with a pair of wings unlike any other. The Elders tell us it is to set her apart and remind all her subjects of her authority."

Kennedy's eyes squinted, and her head tilted slightly, but she was yet unable to retrieve her glance from the wings.

The queen smiled and sat back into her throne. "I see now in your furrowed brow, little one, that you believe differently."

Startled by her majesty's acute perception, Kennedy found control of her sight and pointed it to the queen, expecting her countenance would reveal frustration and disappointment, surprised then to see one of kindness that put her directly at peace.

She spoke softly, but with a curious surety. "Forgive me, Your Highness, but I think I believe the Elders are wrong."

Instructor Nichym burst out in exclamations. "How dare you speak of the Elders in such a way! Your Majesty, you see now the insolence of this child."

"Leave us," Okalani told him with perfect calm. He floundered a moment, then left the throne room in a huff. When he was gone, and the doors again closed, the queen leaned forward to be closer to the kneeling Kennedy.

"Tell me what you believe," she said.

Kennedy looked to her own orchid palms in deep consideration, then, looking again to Queen Okalani, she permitted her notions to take shape aloud.

"I believe the wings are not a decorative gift, no, not a gift at all, but a declaration of a queen's responsibility to her people. The combination of all three of our colors is to remind the queen, and her subjects, that although there are differences between us, in appearance, interests, and attitudes, the heart of Anwansi is shared by all fairies in equal parts, and it is harmed the same by the degradation of a commoner as it is by that of a warrior or a royal. The wings of the queen herself are evidence that the separation, and ranking!, of the fairy types comes not from Anwansi, nor surely the Gwahanu, but from generations of Nachov Elders imposing their power upon us all!"

A lengthy silence followed. The queen stared at Kennedy, but the child only looked down again, engrossed in her own new understandings.

"You are eloquent for a child who does not speak," the queen said at last, returning Kennedy from her considerations.

"When one speaks not," she replied, "there is time aplenty to listen, and to learn."

Okalani smiled. "I no longer have any confusion at why the instructors dislike you. Neither would the Elders care to hear you speak in such a fashion." Her smile fell as she finished her words.

"I must again beg your forgiveness, Your Majesty, but it appears I am not much concerned with what they would care about."

The queen shook her head. "You must act with caution. The Elders have much power that even I cannot protect you from, regardless of your birthright station."

"I should not have a birthright station!"

"Say that too near the wrong ears and it may well be taken from you."

Kennedy paused, realizing what the queen had said. "You would protect me?" she asked.

"I believe you are right," the queen said with a sigh. "When Anwansi chooses its ruler, by decorating her so, I believe she is chosen for having a heart much like yours. When I was young, I felt as you do now, though, in the face of conflict, I was far less brave. As queen, I am given the power to lead our warriors and protect our Woods, and in times of crisis I stand to raise the hope of our people, holding us together through the fear; however, despite the call of Anwansi, all inner affairs and ordinances are held under the power of the Council of Elders. Those who break the Elder's ordinances are brought to me so I may execute the penalty for their crimes, and I have severely limited capacity to grant forgiveness, but I am going to reach into that capacity today. You are lucky that, in his rage at you, Instructor Nichym forgot the Zil boy, for it is far more difficult to be lenient with a commoner than it is with a royal."

"That is not right either," Kennedy scowled.

"I understand your passion, little one, but it must be controlled or you will lead an impossibly difficult life."

Kennedy thought, then responded, "I would rather lead a difficult life if it is in pursuit of one that is just."

"You would relinquish your own happiness, your own peace?"

"How can there be peace before there is justice? Permit me to ask, Your Highness, I beg, do you truly wish to continue silently presiding over a nation where children are barred from finding playfellows in fairies of other colors? Or, are you comfortable in the knowledge that there are children torn from their parents due simply to the fact that their visages do not match? If that is the foundation of our culture, how can we claim our culture to be one of any good?" As emotion crept up in her throat, Kennedy halted her speech, fearing she had said too much. Assuredly the queen had understood.

"So that is your secret," quoth she. "Your parents were no royals, and yet they raised you."

Kennedy returned to a bitter silence.

"Fear not. So long as I do not know their identity, I am not compelled to act. Furthermore, I swear I shall instigate no investigation, nor speak what I know to anyone."

Anxiety swept away, Kennedy offered the queen a small grateful smile. "Thank you, Your Highness."

The queen nodded and went on. "It has given you strength, you know; your childhood. There is bravery in you I have only seen in our warriors."

"Perhaps that is because only the warriors had been taught to find their bravery. Until me."

"Perhaps."

The little fairyling waited for more, but the queen said nothing.

"Have you tried to change it?" Kennedy asked.

"Pardon?"

"Our lives need not always stay this way. We could change the ordinances."

"I do not have such power."

Kennedy shook her head and stood to level herself with the queen. "You must have more power than you know, Your Majesty. You have the trust of the people. If you made a public appeal to the Elders, they could not ignore you."

"It is not being ignored that fears me."

"What could they do that would not blatantly contradict the direct wishes of Anwansi? They would not dare!"

"You do not know them as I do."

"I could help you."

"You are a child."

"A brave one, you said yourself."

"It requires more than bravery to survive the Elders."

Kennedy's countenance twisted in curiosity. "Survive them, Your Highness?"

Okalani rose from the throne and paced away from the girl's stare. "There is much you do not understand."

"Tell me."

"No one should understand what I understand." The queen turned back to see Kennedy now framed by the branches of the throne. "Especially one so young," she whispered.

"Please. I cannot do nothing."

"Then fly. Disappear. Return to whence you came."

"You must know that I cannot."

"I adore your steadfast will, little one. You are everything I wish I had been."

"Then help me."

"I will. I will beg Anwansi, nay, the River itself, even the Sky if it will hear me, to not allow you to be chosen as the next queen. You do not deserve it."

Queen Okalani returned to her seat, placing herself within it for near fear, if left empty, the branches would come alive and take hold of the child. Kennedy could only watch.

"Your Majesty," she said at last, "I know I am but a child, and I have much to learn. Still, there is some that I already know. I know I can make people smile, and that I can put other children at ease. I know I could have great influence over a generation that will soon grow into our prime. All I ask of you now is to help me play with the other children. Surely the Elders would not deny you that."

"I cannot be certain."

"But would you be willing to try?"

The queen looked to the child whose wide eyes now beckoned the passion she had buried beneath years of duties. Despite herself, a spark flew off of the queen's magisterial wings, and Kennedy smiled.

"There will be danger, little one. Do you accept this?"

Solemnly, she swore, "I do."

At length, Queen Okalani nodded and sent Kennedy from the throne room. As she flew out the large stone doors, her wings sparked like never before, and she smiled, knowing her adventure had truly begun.

CHAPTER X

Stepping Into the Light

"King Madrick has invited me to become his page," Leanna said to her parents the very evening that Kennedy was lost. She could instantly feel their trepidation, enhanced by the already great emotion of the night, but she continued.

"I would like to accept the position. May I?"

The discussion which followed was lengthy and not unencumbered by fears. Byrdon, for one, was not entirely fond of the thought that his familial connection to Masor might be made known to Prince Guiomar through his daughter's presence in the Masorian courts, and Esta, for another, knowing the king's habits, was uncertain the position was quite fit for one of only eleven years, as Leanna was. Furthermore, if the magic of their adobe, or their close friendship with fairies!, were ever to be made known, the Masorian royals would surely have both mother and child removed from their positions, if not also from their heads, for treason. Beyond even this concern, Esta still fretted on the inarguably magical nature of the child and dreaded to think that anything might release a yearning for the Jewel that lay so near them, but of this she said nothing to Leanna or her father, both of whom remained unaware of the child's prepartum interests.

Nevertheless, Leanna pleaded, and assured them both she would remain ever cautious to maintain the secrecy of all that required concealment, and, as far as the king's habits, Leanna reminded her mother, while they encouraged him towards lethargy and indifference, he remained a good-hearted man of humility who would never dream to do her harm.

"There is still but more, Leanna," Esta continued. "Thou art awake to knowledge that could set our kingdoms aflame. It is true," she looked to Byrdon, "that royals do not often believe accusations on the word of one of our station, but," returning to Leanna, "of all of them, King Madrick might. If thou wert to imply an awareness of the real events that led to his parents' death, it could change everything." Fear made the mother's voice unsteady, but the child shared none of her concern.

"Would that not be splendid?" Leanna asked with amazement. "The goodness of the fairies could be made known!"

Byrdon knelt down and took his daughter's hand. "Such is what we all would wish for if it were not at such danger to ourselves."

"Danger?"

The father nodded. "Masor's king would have all the needed authority to begin a war with Pavoline, and I can hardly believe his nature is so forgiving that he would restrain himself upon believing the truth."

Esta agreed. "I am not certain our family could withstand the fighting that would follow; not when we serve so close to the crown."

"But we live within magic's walls," Leanna reminded them. "Neither kingdom could touch us so long as we always return home."

Esta looked only upon Leanna, not daring to glance at the walls as she spoke low. "These caves have been our veil and protector for many years, but we have no way to be certain they will remain the haven of safety we have come to love." Leanna understood that her mother thought of the Jewel, but the child had learned long ago not to inquire on it. Esta went on. "If one day the cave were to decide we were no longer welcome, or if it asked of us an offering we could not provide, I dread to think we would have no recourse but to return to a world divided by violence. Leanna, hold thy objection and understand. I too once believed the truth was the only path to peace, but I no longer see it as such. This family is the most vivid beacon of hope I see for this world, and I care for nothing now but to protect it."

"As do I," Leanna whispered in meek reply.

Byrdon drew her attention. "It is vital that thou realize, if the Oxbiens were to seek retribution for Guiomar's crime, everyone would wonder how Madrick came to suspect that Guiomar was the killer." Esta nodded in vigorous agreement. "Violence would not only fall around us, but terrible investigations would be directed straight upon thee, and soon inevitably to thy mother."

"It would then take only small remembrances for Isolda to think back to the night thy father and I met and she could well deduce from thence who thy paternal relation might be, and if that were made known to Guiomar..." Esta dared not finish the idea.

Leanna's imagination conjured images of the caring faces before her locked behind dungeon bars, crying out in pain, and she could bear it no more.

"I understand! I do, I swear it. Already I have lost half a family, I will take such extreme care not to destroy the rest of it. I swear it, upon everything, upon the River and Sky, I will not betray us!"

"But still thou wishest to serve the king?" Esta bemoaned.

"Please, Mother," at a sudden Kennedy's words returned to her ear and, though saddened at the pain it might give them, she dared to echo the sentiments. "I cannot live my whole life in a cave."

Mother and father looked to one another and sighed.

The next day, Leanna accompanied her mother up the well, through the bustling market streets, and into the castle, now through the grand front entrance. Leanna held her breath, holding tight to her mother's hand, as they passed easily between the guards without being troubled. Esta took Leanna to the king's apartment and optimistically rapped on the door. Upon receiving no answer, she deduced that the king still slept and allowed Leanna to accompany her through her morning duties until the king would awake.

Following her mother from room to room, Leanna assisted the launderers, peeled fruit for the cook, polished a helmet, and blew off dust from a hanging tapestry. As she now trotted through the hall alongside her mother, who was carrying new ink to the princess's chambers, King Madrick appeared before them, a smile immediately brightening his eyes upon his notice of them.

"Good morn, Esta!" he barked. "May I assume the reappearance of the little one means I have at last fulfilled my sister's request that I acquire a servant?"

Esta smiled and turned to Leanna who nodded joyfully. The young child stepped toward the king and bowed too low for one pretending to be practiced, declaring, "It is my honor to be of service, Your Majesty," in the fashion her parents had taught her the night previously.

Madrick shook his head. "Stand, I implore thee. There is no need for such things. As I have asked of thy mother, I hope thou wilt be willing to consider me a friend."

The maids smiled, both, one with the excitement of ignorance, the other with the pity of wisdom.

"Your Majesty," Esta began. "Leanna's placement in the castle comes not without its risk to our family. If you wish us well, I pray, speak not the name of her mother to Isolda, and speak to no one anything you may suspect of her father."

"Worry not. I indeed wish thee well, and so thy wishes I shall respect. No one ever shall sense a hint of it from me," the king said in earnest.

"Thank you, Your Majesty." Esta curtsied in further thanks. "I must now to Isolda."

"Indeed," Madrick nodded. Esta held Leanna's shoulder, smiled, then walked on, and the king continued. "In fact, Leanna, follow me thence, and I shall now introduce thee to my sister, Her Royal Highness."

When Leanna and Madrick reached Isolda's chamber, they held back in the hall a moment, allowing a minute between their entrance and that of Esta just before, keeping their laughter silent as they counted the seconds. At length, Madrick approached and pounded upon the door.

"Isolda! The king requests an audience," he bellowed in exaggerated jest.

"Can it not wait, Madrick?" came her familiar snarl. He laughed.

"Please, Princess. Grant your brother just a moment of your day."

They could hear her deep sigh from without the door.

"Enter," she reluctantly allowed, and they did so. Without looking up from her papers, she urged, "What is it?" and, looking up now, seeing Leanna, added, "Who is this?"

"Your Highness had requested I acquire a servant. Such is done."

"A child," she confirmed.

"Verily."

"And from whence did you find a mother willing to lend her child to one such as yourself?"

"I discovered the youth wandering about the castle, so eager to serve she was."

"From whither doth she hail, Madrick?"

Leanna met eyes a moment with her mother, who tended to the bedclothes, before the king responded in perfect calm.

"She haileth from directly within the city. A pure-bred Masorian."

Isolda nodded, then shook her head in fatigue. "I had hoped you would find a servant capable of performing duties."

"I am, Your Majesty!" Leanna interrupted.

Isolda stared at her. "I see," she said. Then to Madrick, "and you are comfortable requiring a child to pick your filthy socks off the floor?"

Leanna laughed. "I may instead persuade him to put them in a basket."

Isolda took a sharp intake of breath and, to Madrick, declared, "She speaks out of turn."

"Indeed," Madrick smiled. "I find it rather charming."

"Oh!" Isolda scowled. "Perhaps a child servant suits you, being as you are one yourself."

"Sister, do you think so little of me?"

"In earnest, Madrick, I care not. Prithee, at minimum, have her tend to your horse. We happen to employ a very capable stablehand, and their talents are wasted caring for the old sentimental animal you make no use of."

"That was Father's horse, Isolda."

"And will Father be riding?"

Isolda regretted her quip as soon she saw the joy fade from her brother's visage, but she made her apology merely by continuing on.

"The child shall care for the horse. Beyond that, do what you will. Only know, if her insolence disturbs my peace, I shall have her removed," the princess said, and, raising her quill, she returned to her work.

"Upon such a time, would not the power of my removal reside with the king?" Leanna asked.

Isolda halted her quill mid-stroke and, remaining still, lifted her gaze slowly to Madrick who, smiling again, desperately held back a snort.

"Come, Leanna," he said, breaking some tension. "I shall show thee to the stables."

Isolda watched them, fuming silently, until her chamber door had latched shut. She sat back and looked to Esta.

"What Masorian household managed to raise such a creature?" the princess conjectured.

The secret mother honestly laughed and shook her head in disbelief.

Leanna followed the king through familiar passages of the castle's eastern wing until they stepped out onto a wooden deck overlooking the royal garden with its paths wandering through yellow rose bushes. Surveying the area, Leanna could see that the servants' entrance she snuck into the day before lay not far from where they stood. Madrick led her through the garden until they reached its opposite side, now discovering the stables before them.

The royal stables were well attended to, and the frontmost stalls housed mighty steeds, all trained for use in battle. Leanna, though having heard many tales of the animals, had never been in one's presence and was both intimidated and inspired by their height, strength, and beauty. Madrick, however, looked to none of them and led Leanna straight to the back of the stables where, in the final stall, stood a dark brown thoroughbred stallion, a white diamond adorning his brow. Madrick stopped before it, unlatching the stall door, then stepped back to allow Leanna inside.

The child approached the horse and looked up, her brow just peeking above the point of the animal's shoulder. Madrick circled to the opposite side and placed a hand on his withers.

"His name is Dawn," he explained. "He carried my father to many victories in both combat as well as friendly competition."

Leanna smiled and raised her hand to Dawn's cheek as he lowered his muzzle to greet her. "He's beautiful," she said. Her intimidation at his size faded as his gentle nature was made clear.

"Ho! Who goes there?"

Leanna backstepped outside the open stall to see who had bellowed. She had no recollection of the stern countenance that now marched toward her, so she merely looked to Madrick for how to respond. He knew the deep voice of the stablehand well and, at its steely tone, came round the animal swiftly to explain the presence of the strange girl.

"'Tis only I, Leif. Forgive the intrusion."

At sight of the king, all severe shadows on the stablehand's visage melted away and the worker turned to the floor in obeisance, concealing the gladness that had encroached upon their countenance at the sight of Madrick Oxbien II. "No, forgive me, Your Majesty," they said and, rising to look at the king, added, "You could never intrude."

Madrick found himself caught in a glance with eyes he had not seen for several a year, and at a sudden, he recalled the vague feeling of fondness which, in the past, had consistently arisen in him around the stablehand. Maintaining their glance, and stumbling over syllables, Madrick uttered, "That is very kind. It has been quite long since I visited Dawn. I regret my absence."

"Certainly you were missed, Your Majesty, by Dawn," Leif replied. "Though I swear to you, I take great care of your father's steed. He wants for nothing."

Both of them smiled. "My many thanks," Madrick said.

Leanna stood between the two waiting to be introduced. They both, for the moment, seemed not to remember she was present. Leanna followed the king's gaze and looked up at the stablehand, presuming to memorize the figure lest she be forced by circumstance to introduce herself on her own some time hence. Leif wore fine, well-built boots, of a polished light auburn, with pointed toes and a thin, highly raised heel. Light-colored stitching on the boot shafts twisted up like vines up to where the shoe ended just below the knee, and was a distinct contrast at the top to the dark brown trousers which were tucked inside the shoe. They had on a long light green tunic which draped down just above their knee, and at their waist was cinched a wide decorative belt that also served to hold a variety of tools. Leanna noticed the cut of the garment and the style and placement of the belt created more the fit of one of her mother's tunics than one of her father's, which seemed unusual to her given the stablehand's overall masculine frame, not to mention the neatly groomed stubble that adorned their chin and lip. Too, the top of their hair was pulled taut and tied in the back, accentuating a sharp hairline that squared off at the temples while the remainder fell in light feminine curls down around their neck, one side touching their collarbone as it draped over their shoulder. Although she had never seen someone dressed in such a fashion before, Leanna quickly remembered that she had yet to see much of anything before and thus presumed that this style must be nothing particularly remarkable to one who lived in the town. Furthermore, the incongruent attire, when viewed as a whole, created a rather pleasing portrait of a strong and kind figure.

Madrick cleared his throat. "It's been so long since I have seen..." Hesitating over the best way to convey his meaning, he started again. "...since I have seen anything in the stables; or anyone. Pardon me, I was of course informed those years back when the directive was altered on how to refer to... 'Leif' in the third. Since then, I had not heard... appearance had changed."

Leif tucked a curl behind their ear. "I hope I have not displeased you, Your Majesty."

"No! By the River, I quite mean the contrary. The hair is a splendid fit for... I mean, the way it frames..."

"Do you simply mean his hair looks nice, Sire?" Leanna chirped.

Madrick broke from Lief's gaze to direct an instructive eye to Leanna. "I speak of *their* hair," he corrected. Returning his gaze to Leif, a cheerful countenance crept into his features. "And, well, yes, I mean to say it looks lovely."

"Thank you, Your Majesty." Leif smiled.

A moment passed before the king finally cleared his throat and gestured toward the small page. "This is Leanna. As of this morn, she has agreed to work as my first servant."

"Hello!" Leanna said, extending her hand. Leif generously participated in the respectful greeting, disregarding the peculiarity of her youth.

"A pleasure to make your acquaintance," they replied with a slight chuckle.

"I was introducing her to Dawn," Madrick explained.

"A beauty, is he not?" Leif stepped towards the inside of the stall and beckoned Leanna. She followed them and, at their encouragement, placed her hand where theirs had been on the horse's nose. She nodded, breath caught at the excellence of the creature.

"Dawn was my father's most prized steed." Madrick went on, remaining at a distance. "I think part of him believed the horse was charmed, and so long as they rode together they could never be harmed. Even I, for a time, began to trust that Dawn was incapable of losing a rider."

"What changed, Your Majesty?" Leanna asked in innocent forgetfulness. Madrick feigned having failed to hear the inquiry. Noting the somber glint in the king's eye, Leif took it upon themself to respond.

"It was Dawn who finally carried the previous Crown Oxbiens into the Infinite Woods, and returned alone."

"They died," Leanna remembered.

"Murdered by fairies," Madrick said, regaining his voice. "My parents nearly brought our kingdom peace, and the fairies destroyed it."

"You haven't visited the stables since that day," Leif realized.

"Could anyone blame me?"

"No, Your Highness. I understand entirely."

Leanna looked away from the humans and into the horse's eye as she stroked his muzzle. Pain blazed in her chest as she restrained a cry, burning to explain to the king the true story of his parents' demise, but was halted by the oath she had sworn the night previous. Still, while her parents had found peace in their decision to put the harmony of their family over the exoneration of the fairies, Leanna—especially with loss so fresh—had certainly not.

Without looking up from Dawn, she inquired, "You are entirely certain the fairies are to blame, Your Highness?"

The king nodded. "Their wounds were undoubtedly caused by fairy weaponry," he said, "but forgive me, thou hast recently suffered a fright from a fairy, let us speak of kinder things."

Leanna took a breath and glanced at Leif who returned a kind, curious look. Then, with one hand on Dawn, she slowly lifted her gaze to meet the king's.

"Your Majesty, the fairy did not frighten me," she said.

Madrick laughed. "Thy manner suggested otherwise."

"I do not mean to say I was free of fear, only that she looked no older than myself and it was the fear in her own eyes, followed by the attack of the knights, that caused my concern, not the fairy herself."

"Thou didst feel for her?"

"Yes, Your Majesty."

Madrick shook his head. "Thou art still young."

"Yes, but Sire—" Leanna did not dare to reveal all she knew and break her oath, still she now vowed in the same to do all else in her power toward the fairies' vindication. She returned her gaze to the horse's comforting eyes and, speaking cautiously, said, "—many of the fairies are still young as I am, I would guess. They have no guilt for the crime you put upon them, and yet they are harmed by the Masorian's hatred all the same."

Madrick's grief brought contempt into his countenance. "If only their youth brought them innocence," he said. "The fairy species can think in one of three ways depending on breed, be it foolishness, cruelty, or pride. They are doomed to calamity by their nature; it does naught to reduce their guilt."

"That isn't their nature," Leanna said sternly.

"Whatever stories thou hast told thyself of 'friendly fairies', it is a lie."

"It isn't!" she barked.

"What wouldst thou know of it, Leanna?" the king rejoined.

The young page scowled, unable to respond, and quietly returned her gaze to Dawn. In the silence, Leif spoke.

"If I could, My King, I once came upon a fairy while wandering a Masorian wood. It was one of their warriors, I believe. We saw one another and I chose to remain still and silent. Upon my wishing her no ill will, she nodded appreciatively and passed me by. It is only a moment, next to meaning nothing, I know; more, certainly little Leanna knows no more than her heart has found in dreams, but I would be willing to wonder if she had found the truth nonetheless."

Leanna gave Leif a slight smile of thanks then bravely returned her gaze to King Madrick, expecting his anger. He displayed only pensive sadness.

"Perhaps," he said at last.

Dawn nickered, shaking his mane, and prodded Leanna lightly in her chin. It swiftly returned the stable to smiles; even Madrick laughed.

"He likes thee," he said, and Leanna's smile grew. Madrick turned to the stablehand. "Leif, Isolda has requested that Dawn's care be transferred to Leanna so that... professional talents could be prioritized elsewhere."

Leif made no effort to conceal their solemn surprise. "Oh, Your Majesty, tending to Dawn has been a personal joy. I would be happy for the little page's company, but if it please you I would not abandon his care."

Madrick smiled and sighed. "It would please me greatly, but I can't be certain Isolda would approve pay for time spent with an animal she considers useless."

"Then I would care for him before my paid hour of day."

"For certain? I could never request it."

"I am certain, and if ever there is a day I could not, Leanna could take my place." Leif scratched the horse's chin then looked to Madrick to add, "No one should be considered useless."

"This is extremely generous, Leif," Madrick said, with the utmost genuine of feelings. He turned to Leanna. "Would this suit thee, working here with Leif in the early morn?"

She smiled and gave several quick nods.

"Thank thee, Leanna." Madrick looked from page back to stablehand and was caught again in the latter's glance. "And my sincerest thanks to..." the king cleared his throat once again and spoke more firmly. "Greatest thanks to you, good Leif."

Their brow shot high at the king's deference. "Your Majesty," they began. "Surely I do not deserve such language. My position affords me no greater status than Leanna's."

"Verily!" the page remarked, playing wounded.

"Come, think seriously," Madrick explained. "Knights are afforded such respect, even by royals, yet what knight could rise to greatness without the service of one who cares for their steed? Your work, Leif, is no less vital than theirs and thus I shall refer to you with no less respect."

The stablehand laughed. "I appreciate the stretch of your logic, My Liege, though I must note you have utilized no such thinking before."

"I have thought it before. I was only too much a coward to act upon it."

"I see," Leif began with a coy grin. "And the cowardice has dissipated then?"

Madrick blushed. "Perhaps not entirely, but in this matter, I am content to stand my ground." King and stablehand shared an endearing look.

"So will you also refer to me with respect, Your Highness?" Leanna asked.

"Nonsense," he replied. "Thy service is far less vital than theirs."

"I serve the king!" she remarked.

"Precisely," said he.

"I find this entirely unfair."

"Isolda was right, thou dost speak far too easily out of turn."

"You said you found that charming, Sire."

Leif erupted in laughter and the remaining two could not but follow suit.

Over time, Dawn's care flourished into a beloved meeting ground for the odd company of three. Leif instructed Leanna in all the particulars of equine caretaking, and without long she grew to quite adore the work, and even later gained skill in it. Madrick jested early on it would be an insult to his kingliness to have both his page and stablehand able to enjoy the splendors of the royal steeds without his being able to join them; yet, however much Leanna encouraged him to dirty his hands in the work, for the first six-month he was unsuccessful in answering the early sun's beckon. This eventually saddened him so that he took to forsaking his evening drink so he might repose sooner and thus spring into alacrity with the morn. His first several attempts at this left him weary, stomach sick, and possessed with a certain fury and desperation that Leanna was wholly incapable of managing. She meekly raised the topic to Leif and though they said little by way of explanation, their smile and reassurances were enough to convince Leanna that all might soon be well.

She discovered the next day that Leif had taken it upon themself to tend to the king in the last hours of night, as well as the first of the day, so that when Leanna entered his chambers to begin her work, Madrick maintained a reasonable enough manner to thank her and make of her no requests that required she indulge his sickness. At long last, Madrick attained a state of health that none had seen from him since his childhood, and every childlike ambition and pleasure returned in kind to his spirit.

Over the next many months, despite emerging from her cavern home before the rising of the sun, there were many days that by the time Leanna reached the stables, she found the king and stablehand already within, engaging in charming discourse over the well-attended Dawn. Occasionally, her presence appeared to startle the pair out of a closer, private moment, and she would apologize for making them jump away from nearly touching one another; regardless, they always played at ignorance, insisting nothing of the sort had occurred. She smiled every time.

"It seems as though you two are taking sufficient care of the stables, so I think I shall return to the castle and be king," Leanna once jested.

"And take Isolda's company over ours?" Madrick countered. "I hardly believe even thou art so selfless."

Leanna laughed, admitting her bluff, then caught an apple Leif tossed to her, took a bite, and fed Dawn the remainder, joining the adults in their care of the horses.

In Alquoria, once Kennedy had begun to speak after those first two years of silence, she set herself eagerly upon her mission to befriend fellow fairylings of varying hues. Although she introduced herself to a great many with proactive enthusiasm, those who were to become her best of friends came into her acquaintance entirely by accident.

"Don't step just there!"

Kennedy contracted her falling foot back towards her chest and suddenly fluttered her wings to keep from tumbling down upon the cluttered market pier. An azure hand gripped her own and yanked her behind a cart of berries from whence the voice had first erupted.

"Forgive me, your royalness," the small blue Zil fairyling uttered, though it was without any hint of regret or apology. "but I simply could not allow you to ruin it, not when I have worked so very hard."

In all confusion, Kennedy followed the Zil girl's gaze towards the center of the pier, whither she herself had earlier meant to step, and then saw the stealthy smile that was pulling at the girl's cheeks as an older Zil man began to cross the same path. He stepped directly in the place Kennedy had evaded, and in the same instant a brief cloudless rainfall erupted above him, soaking him straight through.

"Nientz!! When I find thee…" He bellowed, and Kennedy saw the girl condense to her miniature form to be fully hidden by the cart. As the man stormed off, she grew again, holding back her prideful mirth to thank Kennedy for her quiet.

"It is only my father," Nientz explained. "His anger shall dry up in due time, as does his tunic." She giggled. "He despises my little tricks."

"You caused that?" Kennedy marveled.

"I did indeed. Do not be too surprised, your royalness. Zils have more spark in us than we are credited for."

"I had no doubt," Kennedy affirmed, "and now I am all amazement. Can you show me more of your tricks?"

The Zil's night-blue lips stretched into an eager grin.

It was a similar afternoon when Kennedy, on a day's recess from schooling, decided she wished to find the top of the Infinite Trees. She knew it was not truly to be done, but the quest quite suited her wandering spirits. Some leagues up, she was halted suddenly by a flash of lightning shot to the side of her. Looking down, she found a Kesk fairyling her own age flying up at her with a rageful stare.

"You are not permitted to fly this high, young royal," the verdant girl said, rising to Kennedy's level. "This is a warrior's place."

Kennedy smiled slyly, noting an opportunity for fun. "What is your name?"

"Phidia."

"Are you a warrior, young Phidia?"

"Naturally!"

"Yet?" Kennedy clarified, and the girl made all attempts to maintain her sinking pride. She evaded the inquiry, turning back to Kennedy's offense.

"You are breaking the rules."

"Which rule is that?"

"Only a warrior may journey to this height among the Trees," Phidia quoted from her memory of lessons.

"Then are you not breaking the rules as well, fairyling?"

Phidia floundered. "I only have journeyed this high to bring you down!"

"Why not instead allow me to bring you up?"

The green girl's countenance twisted in confusion.

"Journey with me," Kennedy implored.

"Ha! I think not."

"Very well," Kennedy shrugged. "I shall continue on my own then."

"No!"

Phidia's shout was drowned by Kennedy's laughter as the someday-warrior rushed to follow the royal further and further into the Treetops, reaching a nearly breathless height before the latter finally managed to make the other smile with her twirls and airborne tricks. At last, she stopped rising and the two floated down beside one another, returning to Anwansi and sharing some of the details of their lives.

Kennedy found supreme difficulty in her efforts to further befriend those of her own color until she finally conceded it was not to be. Many of her fellow Nachovy were uninterested in maintaining too close a relationship with the rebellious one. Their similarly purple-skinned parents had influence on her classmates beyond what Kennedy could persuade; however, there was a notable exception. Amicus, who had been born of Zils, never knew their parents and so, beside the overly pompous and unyielding Nachovy instructors, they had only Kennedy in their ear. Their rebellion was a quieter one than Kennedy's, for Amicus had not quite the spirit of a mass befriender as did she, still, they felt their spirit was not so neatly categorized as the other Nachovy. Many varied interests pulled at their heart through the years. As a young fairyling, the first rebellion that appealed to them was the writing of poetry, thought to be too low of an activity for a Nachov to spend their time with. To Amicus, poetry was another way of dreaming.

"Teach it to me," Kennedy begged when Amicus told her of it. They were more than pleased to oblige.

After a few attempts scratched into the bottom of writing desks under Amicus's advisement, Kennedy took a copy of her scribbles into the Forest. As often occurred when Kennedy discovered a new pastime, or thought of a well-crafted jest, her thoughts now turned to Leanna as she wished at once to share with her in the fun. Wandering the Woods, saddened at the length she was from her friend, Kennedy found a piece of ivy and, taking a writing stick, scratched a new poem onto the leaf.

LINES OF IVY No.1

A leaf alone has
none such joy as when with more.
Be glad for a tree!

When it was completed, she smiled and held it up to see it against the light of the Sky. A wind blew and tore it from her hand. Devastated, she ran forth and leapt into the air, chasing the leaf with all the speed her wings could muster, but it evaded her. When it passed out of the Woods and into the border of Masor, Kennedy stopped and turned back, empty-handed, to Anwansi, hoping someone out there might discover her words and take a breath to enjoy them.

In their dream that night, Leanna mentioned to Kennedy with a chuckle this little poem that the wind had dropped on her head that day, and Kennedy squealed with delight. The wind, it seemed, favored them, Kennedy conjectured, and she meant to make good use of it.

After the passing of three-dozen moons since she began her royal work, Madrick thought it good to celebrate Leanna's long employment with a day away from the castle. Leif took over the planning of an outing, filling a basket with sweets from the kitchens, and saddling three strong horses who would appreciate some exercise. They turned out Dawn and spent an additional moment cleaning his coat, but would not risk the old horse's back with a rider. Meanwhile, Madrick spent the prior evening tidying his chambers, laundering his riding clothes, and completing as many of Leanna's chores as he could recall. Even he would admit it was done a bit clumsily, but it would be sufficient enough that nothing would be too far harmed by Leanna accepting his offer of a day off.

The little page could do nothing but smile when congratulations for her third service anniversary were bellowed to her from the back of the stables as she entered that morning.

"A lovely day for riding," Madrick offered, and Leanna was happy to go along.

The king and stablehand had taught Leanna everything there was to know about riding. She was no master, but she adored the connection it brought between herself and the animal, and always now yearned for the feeling of the wind roaring past her ears. Today, as soon as they were a suitable distance from the stables, Leanna turned a conniving smile towards her adult company then instantly lurched her steed into a gallop. Madrick and Leif looked to one another with shocked amusement then, with chortles, sped after her into the surrounding

Masorian wood. None of the three could be certain whither they were headed but it became quickly evident they were in a battle of speed. At the same time that Leif and Madrick shouted intentions to get ahead of the page, if only either were able, the stablehand and king exchanged playfully knowing glances as they alternately slowed and sped to ensure Leanna remained in the lead.

She halted at last in a sudden clearing where short grass intermingled with wildflowers and the sun shone bright through the break in the treetops. Leanna had not one idea as to how she found the place, but she was nevertheless certain she had been seeking it all along. When Madrick and Leif joined her, she turned to them and smiled, proud. Both chuckled and exaggeratedly bowed to her skill as a rider.

All three dismounted. Leif and Leanna fed and watered the horses while Madrick took the basket and set out the preparations for a picnic. Madrick laughed upon seeing with what Leif had filled the basket.

"Her mother may be more appreciative if we give Leanna the horse feed, being that she is a growing child with more need of nutrients than pure sweets," he jested. Leanna jumped and ran to kneel before the basket, instantly devouring one of the little cakes. Leif merely held Madrick's gaze with a happily guilty smile.

Before long, the basket was emptied and all three of the company were filled to the brim and under the sleepy spell of a warm sun. Leanna turned away from the others to look out at their little meadow then fell back into the grass, allowing the warmth of the earth to fill her with peace. As they had grown accustomed to do, Madrick and Leif shared a glance, then followed her lead until they all lay in a circle of perfect contentedness.

"I could remain here 'till the end of time," Leanna said. "Couldn't you?"

"Easily," Leif agreed.

Madrick hesitated in his reply. "I think I want to be king," he said at last. Leif offered him their open gaze.

"You are the king, Sire," Leanna said frankly.

"No, I am the brother of the vice-crown. As far as my duties, I am hardly other than a stablehand. Not that it is something lesser to be a stablehand, it is only that—"

"Of course, you should act as king, Madrick. There is no need to explain," Leif interjected to cease the royal's racing thoughts.

"Do you imagine I would be any good at it, Leif?"

Leanna answered in their place. "You will only ever be as good as you try to be, Your Majesty."

"I think you would be marvelous," Leif added. Madrick drank in their kind eyes as well as their words and found the corners of his lips sneaking up into a smile.

"What would you say to Isolda?" Leanna asked.

"Perhaps I'll say nothing and just have thee report to her the good news."

Leif shook their head at the king's cruel jest.

Leanna shrugged. "If you wish it, Sire."

He scoffed. "No, no, it would not be right. Although, in truth, I don't know that much need change with Isolda. I have no interest in handling the gentry, and she deals with them well enough. I want to put effort toward improving the life of the peasant."

"That's incredibly good of you, Your Highness," Leif said.

"Only I don't know how," the king admitted.

"Then ask them," Leanna suggested. "Hold court and invite forth any peasant who wishes to bring you their troubles, then you can do all in your power to aid them."

"Can it be that simple?"

"It could certainly be a start," Leif offered.

Madrick let out a satisfied huff. "Perhaps I shall do just that. Thank thee, Leanna."

"Took you long enough, Sire," she said.

He laughed, then nodded, slight. "Indeed."

The three remained lying in silence for a time and Leanna drifted off into her own contemplations. As the wind softly drifted by, Leanna caught sight of an ivy leaf floating through the air and falling gently toward her. It landed upon her heart. Seeing the hand writ upon it, she smiled.

LINES OF IVY No.2

Let the wind fly these lines to thee and
End the dreary boredom of thy day,
As surely any day without me must be dreadfully drab.
No fear! A fairy's song is here.
No climb! This fairy's gift will find thee when it's time.
And its very lines shall spell thy name!

Leanna reread the poem several a time, holding back her giggles and tucking the leaf safely away in her pocket. Eventually, Leanna returned her consciousness to the present company and tilted her head back so she might see them behind her. Directly centered in her line of sight, she saw the fingers of the king and the stablehand hovering beside each other as though the hands were resisting some incredible force endeavoring to pull them together. As she looked on, the backs of two complementary fingers grazed each other, then melted into the touch. She squinted at it, then turned her gaze back to the Sky, and smiled.

CHAPTER XI

Stablehands and Pages

"I received thy poem," Leanna said with a coy grin as Kennedy entered their dreamscape the night after the meadow.

"I knew thou wouldst." Kennedy's confidence in the wind had blossomed considerably since the first time it stole her poem, and she was now taken to letting leaves fly away whenever she wanted them delivered to her dear friend.

Leanna chuckled. "It certainly added the final touch of wondrousness to the day."

"Dost thou dare imply there was any wondrousness in the day prior to it?"

"I must confess there was."

Kennedy smiled, forgetting her feigned offense. "I wish to hear of everything."

Leanna rejoiced in detailing the day for her faraway friend. When all had been outlined, she commented further, "I never imagined I would hold sway over a king, but in truth, I believe he hath come to respect me, at least so much as to take my advice. Leif hath, of course, has always been an aid in that regard as well. Kennedy, I shall say to thee alone, I have begun to feel that Madrick and Leif are as much a pillar of my life as my own parents. It feels as though they two are no less my family than my mother and father, or thine own of the same, or even thee. I love you all so dearly, and I think Madrick and Leif feel the same way for me! I must assume this is why King Madrick considers the advice of a child." She laughed slight at the thought of it. "It is a great pleasant thing, Kennedy, having such extensions of family. I only wish we were all nearer one another."

"I wish so too. Oh, Leanna, thou dost know how I wish it. I am dreadfully jealous of this king and stablehand who are permitted to spend these days with thee, but, more, I wish to meet them, for thou dost care for them so."

"I am determined that one day such a meeting shall occur. It must. You are all too wonderful, and all too dear to me, to never know one another."

"One day, Leanna, thou must the same meet my Queen Okalani. We cannot spend such time together as thou dost with thy king, but her highness has ordered that whenever an instructor becomes cross with me, they are to march me directly to her throne, forbidding any other punitive measures." She smiled. "I regret to say these occurrences are only becoming more frequent." Leanna laughed. "Okalani doth make pretense at bitterness, but once the instructor is gone, she turns to joviality and even expresses pride in my success at rebellion. More and more I see the spark of a warrior's spirit taking shape in her eye, and with it I feel a certain familial connection grow, same as thou didst speak of. The inclusion of Okalani in my life even now does some to ease the pain of crossing my parents in the castle and not being able to share a loving word. Moreover, she would adore thee, I am certain of it."

"It is decided then," Leanna said. "As soon as we are certain it shall not lead to death and gloom, we shall have a large feast at the edge of the Wood and unite our complete family at last."

Kennedy's smile glowed and a spark flew from her wings. "Indeed, it is decided."

"Perhaps by that time, Madrick and Leif will have admitted they love one another," Leanna said with impatient disbelief.

"Still they pretend?" Kennedy was aghast. She had heard from Leanna many a story that made it plain how the king and stablehand cared for one another, and she had become rather invested in the outcome of their supposed non-courtship.

Leanna nodded and told her how they brushed against each other's fingers in the meadow and yet refused to embrace when they parted that eve. Kennedy fell to the dream floor in exaggerated anguish and Leanna met her there in jest until they were on their knees before one another, grasping hands. When laughter began to fade, they made every attempt to extend it until there was no more jest left within them, and both of their gazes fell to their hands whose colors now mingled together in a careful web.

Kennedy took a breath.

"It is a terrible thing they are doing," she said, "putting off their happiness when it is so nearby."

"It is," Leanna agreed.

Each held tight to the other's hand, but, in the dream, they could not feel the full texture and warmth they remembered from reality. The dreamers separated and went on with an altered subject of discourse.

As Leanna emerged from the well of the cave the next morning, she caught an ivy leaf that had fluttered down around her.

LINES OF IVY No.3

If one doth require a shove
In something thou hast knowledge of,
Keep it not concealed.
Perhaps they'll be healed
If thou dost advise them to love.

Leanna carefully folded Kennedy's limerick and stored it away in her pocket.

After the conversation in the meadow, King Madrick was suddenly full of excitement and energy, planning an increasing number of events and tactics to aid his less fortunate subjects. The people were eager to accept his support. Several months passed by in a frenzy with hardly a moment of rest. The exertion of the king and his staff—consisting truly of only Leanna and Leif— did not go unappreciated, for soon all the common folk in the kingdom knew him as King Madrick, Crown for the Commoner.

In all the activity, Leanna did not think to push the issue of a love between Madrick and Leif. She continued to notice each time they smiled to one another, but she said nothing of it. One day, however, after some months had passed and a new routine had been comfortably established for them all, Leanna stumbled upon Kennedy's limerick that she long ago had tucked away. For several days, she could think of nothing else. After nearly four full years, the king and stablehand had refused to so much as state their feelings for the other, despite how evident they had become, even to those other than Leanna. At last, she could no longer suffer it.

It was no extraordinary day. A slight chill; a few lonely clouds. Madrick sat at his desk, writing letters and conferring with records in preparation for his afternoon meetings, the sequel to those with villagers who had approached the crown the week prior and whose needs took slightly longer to address. Leanna sat in a corner cleaning dirt off the king's boots.

"Tell me, Sire," she said. "You and Leif. Thoughts?"

He set down his papers. "Whatever art thou speaking of, Leanna?"

"You know very well. Must I spell it plain?"

"I'm afraid I must deny this immense comprehension thou dost attribute to me."

"You are obviously in love with them, and they with you. When will you acknowledge it?"

Of course she had seen it; still, before now Madrick had convinced himself it might have passed her notice. He sighed. "It cannot be," he said.

"But wherefore, Sire?"

"They are a servant. I am a king. People would take too great an issue with it."

"How can you be certain?"

"It has never been done!"

"Has it then been done that a fourteen-year-old page could be the closest advisor of the king?"

"Thou art nothing so official as that, I think."

"Your Highness, please. You are the king. Who is there to limit the possibilities of your life but yourself?"

"What if Leif does not want me the way I want them?"

"Have you asked them?"

"No."

"It seems the answer to such a simple question would quite resolve the issue."

Madrick paused and looked to her. "I do sometimes despise the simplicity of thy well-reasoned logic, Leanna."

"So you'll think on it?"

"Of course, I will."

Indeed, within the week, the ideas Leanna planted in the king had compounded into beliefs. At the end of a tiring day, when the duties of both king and stablehand had been sufficiently rendered, Madrick and Leif leaned back against the wall of the tall bastion to view the stars. The two stood close, warming each other against the night's easy breeze. Without looking away from the majesty of the Sky, Leif brought their hand to Madrick's arm and gently brought him closer. The king's heart sighed as he brought his own hand to cover that of the stablehand. At last, both looked at the other, foreheads leaning inwards, eyes glancing at the other's lips though not daring to linger there, eyes at last meeting and not daring to look away. Speech was soft.

"I have been thinking of language today," Madrick whispered against the new heavy pounding of his heart.

"Do tell," Leif implored.

"How we refer to one another; people in general, I mean."

"I understand."

"Why is it we refer to some with the formal 'you' and others the informal 'thee'?"

"Status," Leif reminded him.

"Yes, but other times…"

"To show respect; or, in the other way, lack of; or familiarity."

"Or love?"

"Yes. Love."

"Might I use 'thee' with you, Leif?"

"Such was always your right, Your Highness."

"I do not wish this for the first reason, but the last." Leif smiled as Madrick spoke. "I also would that you used 'thee' with myself, if you feel as I do, that is."

"I do love thee, Madrick, if that is the question."

Smiles, unhindered by fear, flew to both pairs of lips, and the same were soon locked in a kiss fueled with such care that neither had yet had the privilege to feel for anyone. All sense of the outdoor chill disappeared as the sensation of the other filled each of their chests with the warmth of passion. Even as they thought themselves invincible to cold, a chilled wind nudged Madrick in the back and caused the kiss to stumble into laughter and charm. Hand in hand, the couple returned indoors and found their way under the warm comforter of the king's royal bedchamber.

When Leanna found no one to greet her the next morning in the stables, she went to find Madrick and ensure all was well. Upon hearing the two hushed voices behind his chamber door, she stifled a gasp and dashed away giggling to perform every chore happily on her own.

LINES OF IVY No.4

We know with every little spark
That we must only question more
What love will find us in the dark.

On our adventures, we embark
And think of what may lie in store:
'We know with every little spark.'

Yet something saddens our inner lark,
And brings us crying to the floor:
'What love will find us in the dark?'

We aim to make a separate mark.
We feign to question what we most adore.
We know with every little spark.

Still, we do not dare remark
That we know how we hope for
What love will find us in the dark.

We wait alone for time to arc
Toward what within us doth roar.
We know with every little spark
What love will find us in the dark.

As months went by, Madrick and Leif became increasingly open about their affections. Soon, the only person in the castle to have failed to take notice of the nature of their relationship was Isolda, so little did she concern herself with her brother's unimportant peasant projects.

One day, Vice-Crown Isolda stood in her regal costume in front of the throne room's mystical mirror. As she always did at the end of a conference with the first lagifs, she waited stoically until each of their visages had faded from their space in the depth of the glass and the frame's vibrancy had deadened before stepping back and relaxing into her solitude. It was swiftly interrupted.

"Have they all gone?" Madrick peeked from behind the small door behind the throne, hoping to entirely avoid interaction with the lagifs.

"Yes, Madrick. They've gone."

"Splendid!" He said, and he burst forth fully into the room, papers sprouting from the pile in his arms. "Forgive my barging in early, Isolda, but I must take extra time to prepare the space today. I'm expecting a great many visitors, and I wish to be sure I can aid them all."

Isolda shook her head carelessly. "It hardly bothers me, Brother, I was leaving."

He smiled at her briefly and set to work, but something about him today made Isolda pause. He was happy. She didn't want to leave him just yet.

"You know, it would do you well to join the next conference of the lagifs," she said.

He did not turn away from his work. Absently, he replied, "Would it?"

She stepped closer. "If you offer them even the slightest hint of effort, the whole gentry may in time grow to respect you."

"I don't honestly care what the gentry thinks of me, Isolda."

"You must know that is foolish."

Now he looked to her. "More foolish than you, spending your every royal thought on a handful of people."

"That 'handful' and I maintain the order of our kingdom."

"And I maintain the happiness of its individuals, which matters more?"

"One cannot exist without the other."

"I agree, but which comes first?"

Isolda scowled. "You are mad, you know. You cannot rule a kingdom with peasants."

"Oh, I disagree. If it were entirely up to me, I would that stablehands and pages ruled the kingdom."

There was a pause.

"Stablehands?" Isolda repeated.

"Just an example, Sister. Would you leave me to my work?"

"Of course. Well wishes, Madrick."

"And to you."

As she left the room, Isolda could not stop pondering his phrase. Her countenance contorted as she paced down the many halls until, in all her confusion, she realized there must be something she did not know. Her wanderings brought her to the armory whence she found a young knight polishing a shield.

"Knight." The vice-crown barked, and she was instantly given attention.

"Yes, Your Highness?" She sat up straight and wide-eyed. Isolda remained expressionless.

"What is your name?"

"Degora," was the quick reply.

"Kn. Degora, what do you know about the goings on of the castle?"

She shrugged apologetically. "As much as anyone, I'd suppose."

"Leif, the stablehand. What do you know of them?"

Degora smiled. "Only that they and King Madrick are very happy."

Isolda allowed the slightest expression to emerge on her countenance, just enough for Degora to realize: "You didn't know."

"Don't be absurd." Isolda returned to her stoicism. "And the page..."

"Leanna? A sweet child; good servant. Some say she's brilliant even, and advises the king in everything. They say the page is so much like a daughter to him that he has lost any interest in conceiving an heir."

Then Isolda understood. It had been no mere turn of phrase when her brother wished for pages to rule. He had every intention of giving away her crown to a commoner.

"Your loyalties are to Masor alone, is that correct?" The princess demanded of the knight.

Kn. Degora stood in swift concurrence. "Of course, Your Highness."

Isolda nodded. "I have come into some intelligence about the king's intentions that has the power to destroy the future of Masor if gone unchecked. I require your assistance."

"Anything, Your Majesty."

"Discover everything there is to know about this page, Leanna, and report every finding instantly, and only, to me. Is that understood?"

Degora was not the type to question royalty. She nodded, "For Masor," and Isolda turned, exiting in a wind.

A wind from the other direction brought the sound of footsteps running down the hall. When they halted very suddenly, Degora began to listen, and she nearly stopped her own breath in order to hear as the sound of a young girl's whispers floated towards her ear.

"Kennedy?" It said, barely louder than an exhale. "I can only just hear thee.... I don't understand either.... We are certainly not dreaming.... Oh, it was just that important?... Well, go on, tell me.... Ha! Thou art a fool, hush up."

When the footsteps began again, Degora stepped out into the hall, curious to find it empty, save for Leanna. You see, dear Reader, Leanna had just then discovered it was possible for her to communicate with the far away Kennedy while awake as well! To others, it merely appeared as though she were talking to herself. The page offered a bashful smile to Kn. Degora and went on her way, giggling. The knight watched the page from behind until she turned a corner and went out of sight.

One night, as they dreamt, Leanna and Kennedy lay beside one another in the cerulean emptiness and stared up, drawing clouds in the sky with dream-powered gestures. They both inched closer to each other with every drawing as they playfully competed to make their own additions to the others' designs. At last, they prevented each other from continuing on by holding tight to each other's hands until, with laughter, they relaxed into a partial embrace, staring again at the mess of clouds they had crafted together.

"Taking it all as one," Kennedy remarked of their creation, "the shape now reminds me of the Pancomis Blossom. Hast thou heard of it?"

Meeting Kennedy's gaze, Leanna shook her head slight and offered an interested eye.

"It is the most beautiful flower I have ever known. It only grows in the Infinite Wood," she went on. "It grows in pairs which tend to each other, each blossom offering nutrients to its other when it has excess, or stretching itself to provide shade when the other is at risk of being too dried by the sun. Both blossoms grow ever closer to one another so that their seeds pass between them with every wind."

Leanna smiled. "That sounds like a lovely way to live a life."

"I think about it every day," Kennedy agreed, and she blushed, looking down at their entwined hands and tracing the lines of Leanna's fingers with the tips of her own. She swallowed. "Dost thou have anything like that in Masor?"

Leanna shifted her palm so that the dream-sanded, petal-soft fingers of her dear friend crosshatched into a purple-brown weave in her tender grasp.

"No, Kennedy. Not in Masor," she said.

Months passed, and Leanna's days continued as normal. An early morning meal with her mother and father, stable work with the sunrise, castle chores before noon, notetaking for the king when he held court, discussions with the king as to the best courses of following action, deciphering letters for the king written in a poor worker's hand, organizing the king's records, adding details where they were missed, avoiding Isolda whose scowl grew darker every time she passed her in the halls, meeting her mother in town from whence they would return to the cave, supper with the little family, then share a nighttime-long dream full of friendship and laughter with Kennedy. Overall, it suited her nicely.

Then came the announcement. There would be no balls or banquets, although they would proclaim it to the kingdom in due time, but they wanted Leanna to be the first to know: Leif and Madrick were to be love-promised. It was not quite marriage, with all the legally and royally binding responsibilities that Leif had no interest in, but in all the ways that mattered to the heart, the two were engaged to be wed. Leanna screamed with glee and pulled them both into a grand embrace. Then, suddenly thinking of the perfect engagement favor, she declared, "I will return before nightfall," and dashed out of the room, leaving Leif and Madrick alone in the chambers that now belonged to them both combined.

She thought of the flower which Kennedy had described and knew it grew not too far from the Masorian castle, just inside the Wood. Once Leanna had determined to retrieve it, no thought of danger could stop her. Besides, she knew best of all that the Woods were in fact peaceful so long as the visitor arrived with kindly intentions. She tossed on her cape and ran out the servants' entrance, through the gardens until she was beyond the bounds of the castle. She looked up to figure in which direction the Sky was hidden by infinite foliage and, in that way discovering South, began again to run.

She had no need to slow until she was some considerable distance into the Wood and needed again to discover her appropriate path. At that time, by chance alone, she had already lost Kn. Degora who failed to follow any further than twenty paces through the forbidden Trees. Leanna continued on her search, blissfully unaware, while the knight skulked breathlessly back to Masor Castle, wondering at the child's incredible speed and stamina, and at her inexplicable comfort in the Infinite Wood. Leanna thought of nothing but her quest for the blossom.

LINES OF IVY No.5

To know of hearts is knowing true the sun,
The way that it can blaze, and burn, and glow,
But knowing hearts in truth tells naught of one,
If she is whom thou wishest true to know.
To touch of hands is touching stuff of life;
The flesh that hides the quivering of bone;
But touching hands does naught to end the strife
Of one who still will wake that morn alone.
The feel of love is feeling in the air,
As ivy soars through cold and windy Sky,
But when a love's not free to give its share
The same doth stretch the length 'tween thee and I.
To be with love is warm and close and real.
To know, for truth, thy touch; what love I'd feel.

CHAPTER XII

Nebulous is Stolen

"It really is to be a beautiful affair," Leanna told her father over a bowl of vegetable stew after a long day of wedding preparations. "The courtyard will be draped in roses, and the central podium dressed in a fine summer satin. By the hour of the vows, the sun should be just behind the tops of the Infinites so that the courtyard is blanketed in the glorious shadow mosaic from the Leaves."

"Thou dost paint a pretty picture," Byrdon said, and Esta merely smiled with a nod, having heard all the same from the countless others who would be helping to set that scene come the wedding day.

"Madrick and Leif have asked that I perform in the ceremony as a member of their inner circle. I hope it's alright that I said yes; I was far too overcome with happiness to hesitate."

Esta's smile grew, but Byrdon furrowed his brow.

"Isn't it odd for a king to request that of a page?" He said. "Such a thing should not be listed among thy duties."

"I would not be there as a servant, but as a friend."

"A servant should never befriend a king. They will only ever be used and discarded, even if it is done kindly for a time." The father allowed his idea of his own wisdom to lay a didactic tone over his speech. Leanna could not stand it.

"Madrick's betrothed is a stablehand! He isn't as you say, Father. I would know."

"Love may blind him to the station of one peasant, but that will not change how he views the rest."

"That's absurd! This is Madrick Oxbien II, King for the Commoner; and he trusts me."

Byrdon scowled, his pretense at wisdom falling away to distaste. "The trust of a king is nothing to be celebrated. It is revoked as quickly as it is given."

"Madrick is not Petrenair. You cannot conflate the two."

"A king is a king."

Esta placed a hand on Byrdon's knee. "Please, dear, this is a happy time in Masor. Whence comes thy distress?"

Byrdon flared his nostrils and sucked in a breath before replying, "Guiomar received an invitation to the wedding." Esta sat back in surprise, and Byrdon continued. "As did Petrenair, and a number of Pavol lords and ladies."

"It was only a courtesy," Leanna explained. "We have not been presuming they would all attend, least of all Guiomar."

"Well, the 'courtesy' was not taken as such, not by the prince."

"How could he be angered by receiving a wedding invitation? We were afraid of offending the Pavols by not inviting them."

"Child, think!" Byrdon said, desperately containing agitation. "The envelopes were not sealed save for a small ribbon, easily undone and retied." Leanna nodded, having tied a great many of them herself. "The peasant messengers who delivered the invitations then, naturally, also read them. So they read of the Good King Madrick of Masor, Crown for the Commoner, who loves his everyperson so much that he would marry one! Word has spread throughout the kingdom, and day after day we receive notes from our lords that entire households under their domains have uprooted in favor of settling across the River to put their taxes in the pocket of a king who will care. And the land of Serenity! Why, the lord there himself has declared that everything south of Lifallen Creek now is loyal to New Masor. Petrenair does nothing, and Guiomar grows in his rage every day. He is certain this has all been a ploy to deplete the morale of Pavoline's civilry."

"But Byrdon, thou knowest such is not the truth," Esta tried.

"It does not matter what I know," he replied. "What Guiomar believes is all I am afforded by my position to consider."

"He will not be attending, will he, Father?"

"Denying the opportunity to look his enemy in the eye? Use thy sense. With his cunning, and the king's interest in shows of friendship, of course they will be attending." Byrdon looked to his daughter with renewed care and fright. "The last thing I would wish is for Guiomar to see thee on the podium with the inner circle."

"He would not know me."

"Precisely. An unknown to him is no one worth sparing."

Leanna looked intently to her soup.

"He would not risk violence so publicly," Esta said.

"That is what concerns me all the more. During such a journey, he would control my every hour. I dread to think what he might ask of me."

Leanna looked up. "If he asked of you evil, you would refuse."

"Child, thou dost underestimate the control a sovereign has over their servant."

"Am I not a servant myself?"

"Not to a wicked man," the father replied.

Esta spoke. "Byrdon, fear not. I too have concerns with Isolda. She will say nothing, but she is far from pleased with the happy circumstances. Nevertheless, we cannot trouble ourselves so with the distasteful qualities of our sovereigns. We hold more knowledge of the greatest danger in this world than any of the royals above us could dream to know." Leanna perked up with interest but retreated into quiet. She understood the importance of the Jewel they kept hidden away, but still burned with mysterious questions, even as simple as its very location, to which she had lost hope of being permitted to know the answers. Her mother continued. "Perhaps the prince shall ask of thee terrible deeds, my love, but they shall be nothing compared to the worst. Whatever they may be, after their completion, thy family will be waiting hither to welcome and absolve thee with open arms. My sole concern is that we stay together. Together we can keep one another safe, no matter the obstacles."

Byrdon smiled, taking Esta's hand, but Leanna turned her gaze down and occupied herself outwardly by stirring her stew. She was not certain she shared her mother's priorities. While she too hated the thought of their separation, it was unclear to her how she might look her father in the eye if he aided in any of Guiomar's evil doings.

In truth, they knew nothing of the lengths to which Guiomar would go to avenge Pavoline. In his mind, not only now was Masor responsible for the death of his mother, but too, with their conniving, peasant-loving king, they were tricking the uneducated villagers into crossing the Gwahanu. He fumed at their unending success in growing ever stronger at Pavoline's expense. He pleaded with his father to retaliate, send forces to reclaim the land below Lifallen at least!, but the tired old man would hear none of it, loathe to perform any but his most essential duties, content to spend the remainder of his time in lost memories of his queen, and, Guiomar thought, imaginations of joyous hours with the son he would never have.

After receiving notice of another cohort of Pavols leaving the kingdom, after more than a month of the same, and the same, and the same, Prince

Guiomar burst forth with impatience upon his father in his apartment, pointing towards him with the most recent billet.

"You are the king! You must put an end to this," he said.

Without pause, Petrenair chuckled and said, "I wish thou couldst recall when thy mother taught me to play lilypads. Never could I manage to win, no matter how she tried to let me. My little tantrums brought the most humble and beauteous smile to her face."

"The villagers, Father. What are you going to do about the deserting villagers?"

"I don't believe I've played it since we lost her. Should we give it a go now? The game board should still be in thy mother's closet."

"Petrenair!" The aging prince was shaking in rage.

The king turned calmly to face him. "Yes, my son?"

"Our kingdom will shrivel into nothing if you do not act. Our farmers are leaving their lands. Soon, we'll have no one to perform the harvest."

"When we visit them for the wedding at the beginning of the season, we can request aid from the Masorians. They will not allow us to starve."

"That damned wedding is the only reason we would require it."

"All the same."

Guiomar uttered a sound of deep distress. "If you are to place us so under their care, you may as well hand them the rule of our kingdom!"

"If the people love them so, then perhaps that is precisely what I should do."

Guiomar stepped back from the king. "You are mad."

"Son, please—"

"You are mad!" The prince stormed out of the chambers, the door crashing shut behind him. At last, the inevitable was all too clear to Guiomar. It was entirely his responsibility now to save the kingdom of Pavoline, and he would not fail it, no matter the cost.

When Spring's final bud had given way to a new Summer's bloom, a small caravan from the castle at Pavoline set off on the long road to Masor. Byrdon bid a long farewell to his loved ones before accompanying his prince on the journey. The gentry and royalty among the party slept often in their carriages, but the servants and drivers slept only every other night when they would set up camp and rest some hours. On their final night of rest before arriving in Masor's citadel, Guiomar waited awake into the twilight, then called to his servant.

"Yes, My Liege?" Byrdon answered upon entering the prince's tent. He stood tired, though at attention. He was unable to deduce the royal's precise emotion. Guiomar seemed in a combined state of somber intensity and repressed, though giddy expectation.

"Tomorrow, at the wedding-eve feast," Guiomar began, "my father intends to make a plea to Masor's crown and vice-crown for aid. His blind allegiance to their friendship would cripple our kingdom in due time, and this I shall not allow. I require of thee a serious task that I would entrust to no other. While the kingdom feasts, I will have thee find every dark crevice of the castle, every secret it holds, and discover where lies the Masorians' greatest weakness. Thou shalt discover my method of revenge," he declared. Byrdon shuddered.

"Your Highness, forgive me to speak plain, but I have not seen my family in a fortnight. I am weary, and not entirely in my best mind. I beg you not to ask of me anything rash that I have not the current capacity to refuse."

"Fool, hast thou ever known me to be rash?" Byrdon couldn't be sure of the most appropriate response, and in his silence, Guiomar went on. "Thou knowest this is no mere request."

The servant sighed. "But I have never undertaken such a task. I would not know whither to begin."

"I myself have not the answer, therein lies my order to thee," Guiomar retorted. "Someplace Masor must have its fragile fault. I need only one thing that can completely destroy them."

Suddenly, at the prince's words and entirely devoid of his own will, Byrdon's mind conjured an image of the all-powerful Jewel that resided in secret so near his own chambers. He masked his remembrance just as soon as the danger of it brushed his consciousness, but that left moment enough for Guiomar to see his solution lay already in his servant's understanding.

"Speak, Byrdon," he commanded.

With meek hesitation, the servant replied, "Speak of what, Sire?"

"Thou knowest well, yet I do not; an entirely unacceptable arrangement."

"I only think of my fear of being caught were I to risk such a task, although I will attempt it regardless, in your service." Byrdon bowed and tried to leave.

"If thou liest again, I shall kill thee hither."

Byrdon froze. "Your Highness—"

"Proceed cautiously,"

So Byrdon proceedeth not.

The prince continued. "Thou wilt not leave this tent until thou hast spoken the truth. If thou speakest untrue, thou wilt not leave this tent at all. And thou knowest I speak only the truth to thee. Thou hast shown great loyalty throughout the years; prove it unquestionably now. Tell me what thou dost know, and thy reward will be grand."

Byrdon thought of his dear Leanna, the danger she may yet face, and he thought of his beloved Esta, her promise of love and absolution singing comfort to the pounding in his ears. His memory lingered on the prince's last words, telling of a grand reward, and he imagined a true home in Pavoline where his family could be secure and cared for, no longer needing to serve any kings. At long last, he spoke.

"I know of a weapon."

"I already have a weapon."

"This one is stronger."

Guiomar's eyes burned in anticipation. "What is it?"

Byrdon hesitated but told himself Esta would understand. "It's a Jewel," he said. "With great power."

The prince drew closer. "Tell me everything."

"I must admit to knowing nothing of its mechanics but, somehow, it gives its possessor ultimate command over the Skies. If you seek one object of absolute destruction, this Jewel would be the answer to your call."

"Thou dost not perchance know whither it resides?" Guiomar said, his cheeks painfully repressing a grin.

"The dangers of this Jewel are no trifle, I would beg you—"

"Dost thou know?" The prince queried with growing intensity.

"Sire, please—"

"Speak, thou fool!"

"Yes!" Byrdon revealed. "I know."

Guiomar's grin broke free of its restraints, and he laughed. "Is it near?"

"I could retrieve it soon enough," Byrdon shakily admitted.

"Go. Bring me this Jewel, and I shall make thee the richest lord in this land."

The poor, exhausted servant, swimming in new dreams of comfort, freedom, and a safe home for his family, took little more than a moment's thought to promise: "Yes, My Liege."

"Go!" Guiomar bellowed, and Byrdon ran off.

He ran towards Masor, fleeing with just sufficient speed so that every regretful thought which occurred to him was left unheard in the dust behind. He reached the city in the dead of night and saw again the moon that had first called him to Esta's side. Surely it would not lead him astray now. Byrdon repressed all feelings of pain and exhaustion, seeking tirelessly for Esta's old well which would lead him homeward. He turned down every corner and walked in full every street, and finally, on his third pass of the primary market road, he saw, with fresh moonlight, a break in the endless stone buildings and, turning into its hidden alley, found the ivy strewn well, bucket line falling downward into the mouth of a cave. He drew up the rope and lowered himself down as Esta had always described.

They were perfect in their sleep; peaceful. The father gazed upon his beloved little family in their cots and thought of the future they may yet have together. He knelt before Esta and placed a light kiss upon her brow, and as he rose, he felt her gentle touch stay his hand.

"Byrdon," she whispered with barely unclosed eyes, "is it thee?"

He smiled and knelt again beside her.

"Wherefore art thou returned so soon? I thought I would see thee in Masor before I saw thee again hither."

At his elongated silence, she found her alertness and looked to him with more love and compassion than he could bear. He could not lie to her.

He told her of Guiomar's designs and his promise of lordship in exchange for the Jewel of Nebulous. Byrdon felt the snake of guilt constrict his innards as he watched Esta's expression sharpen to exude fear and pain.

"Thou spokest of the Jewel to Guiomar?"

"I had no choice. It was on my life." He spoke in whispers, endeavoring not to wake Leanna, whose cot lay but paces away.

"We cannot give Guiomar that power," Esta replied.

"And why? With it, he will do harm only to Masor while Pavoline thrives. Leanna and thee will travel with me to Pavoline where you will live in comfort all your days. This is the only way we may be free."

"Masor is my homeland. I shall not forsake it."

"But thither thou art only a servant. In Pavoline thou couldst be a lady."

Esta grimaced. "What need I of ladyship when I have happiness?"

"This is not happiness, this life. We deserve more than to live underground with our lives dictated by those above."

"I do not wish for more!" Esta stifled a cry. "I wish for thee, and Leanna, alive and well and unchanged. How couldst thou betray us so?" Her voice rose and Leanna stirred, though the child's eyes remained unopened.

Byrdon's voice began to shake. "My dear, please, I do this not to betray thee but to secure thy only wish that we be not parted."

Esta rose from the bed and stood in the center of the chamber gazing around at the life they had built. Her breath quickened with every inhalation, and she spun to Byrdon.

"Thou dost not understand what thou hast done!"

He met her gaze as his heart rate mimicked her own. "I have served at the hand of wickedness for so many years with only the desire to love and protect thee. Of course, I understand the gravity of my actions; I think thou dost not see the gravity of the reward."

"Thy reward will be a close companionship with death and destruction. Thy reward will be our downfall, and to know thou wert the cause!"

"The reward will be my life."

"Not a life with me," Esta declared. He stared to her with disbelief.

"My love, if I do not return to Guiomar with the Jewel, he will certainly have me killed."

"Then do not return to him at all."

"I know his secrets. He will not cease his searching until I am found, and I am dead."

"Then let me protect thee!"

He shook his head decisively. "I cannot ask thy protection from an evil I could avoid bringing upon us." Byrdon stormed past Esta and began digging bags of grain away from the opening that led to the Jewel's chamber, continuing through her wailings and pleas. When at last the bright cerulean light flooded through a clear opening, Byrdon looked a moment to Esta who then seized him, wrapping him in her arms and raining tears onto his chest. Though his heart ached, he thought of the alternative to his success and walked on into the tunnel, leaving a shaken Esta standing behind. Esta turned her gaze to Leanna who, for what the mother knew, lay soundly asleep. She turned again, following Byrdon to the Jewel's dreaded chamber, and Leanna unclosed her eyes.

The girl lay curled in bed, wildly awake, eyes drying from opening so wide. She listened as her mother screamed at volumes yet unreached and her father revealed cowardice yet unshown. She had come from a dream with

Kennedy who must now be worried as to the late disturbance. What could she tell her? A sickness started in Leanna's stomach and her hands grew cold gripping the comforter. She pinched her eyes shut and Dawn's visage appeared before her. She watched him nicker softly. His sight seemed the only calming presence in a newly terrifying world.

"Byrdon, look around thee!" Esta exclaimed, gesturing to the murals on the chamber wall. "The man I love could never condemn our world to such a fate."

"Thy love will absolve me, that was thy oath."

"It matters not the extent of my love. No love can absolve thee of this."

"I have no choice!"

"Leave the Jewel in its place, that is thy choice. We have no way to know the outcome of removing the Jewel from its pedestal."

"I know too well the outcome of failing Guiomar. His rage would endanger us all."

"Better us than all of Masor," Esta declared.

"No!"

"I implore thee! She has stayed free of it all these years; thou cannot risk her this way!"

Byrdon stopped, confused. "Who?"

Esta glanced to the dark antagonist of the murals and thought suddenly to tell him all and purge the fears she had kept hidden for so long, but a wave of distrust overcame her.

"I have to protect her," she said and hurried from the chamber. She emerged from the tunnel and stopped cold in the center of the cavern, seeing her daughter's cot empty with its blanket thrown off the side.

"Leanna!" Esta looked all round the small cavern home but found her daughter nowhere. As Byrdon emerged from the tunnel, Esta turned to him with fright.

"Byrdon, she's gone," and, in a moment, both parents forgot every idea of the Jewel. Each bounded down separate tunnels in search of the child, calling her name, but soon met again in the central cavern, certain their daughter was nowhere within.

"Where could she be?" the father asked.

"Masor, I am certain," Esta shook her head. "We should not have argued so loud."

"We will find her," he said, with a calming hand on her shoulder. Esta wrapped herself in her cape, and the couple set off together now towards

Masor, Esta climbing first up the well then lowering the bucket for Byrdon behind her. He held onto her as he stumbled his final leg out of the basin, and just as he did so the pair caught a glimpse of the dim light from their cavern flickering, then extinguishing into darkness. At once, all the ground below them began to quake, and they leaned onto each other, as well as the stone, to look down and watch below as dirt was upturned and the familiar pathway sped away, new ground erupting in its place. They could all but feel their precious apartment disappear into the northern distance as the magic was sucked out of their home, and the short walk through their perfect caves was elongated into the weeks-long journey of the land above. The lovers stared down their well, unable to believe it.

"What was that?" Esta asked.

Byrdon whispered his response, hardly daring to admit it: "The outcome."

She glared at him. "Tell me it isn't so."

Slowly, Byrdon reached into his pocket and removed a clump of cloth in his fist. As he opened his hand, the cloth fell open and revealed in his palm the Jewel of Nebulous.

"No!" Esta shoved him in his chest.

"Esta, please, thou must understand. Thou must forgive me."

"I must do nothing of the kind. See what thy choices have caused? Our home is gone!" She scowled and pushed past him, striding into the dark empty street, lit only by the moon.

"My dear—"

She faced him, and her countenance of disgust nearly brought the lover to his knees. "Leave me, Byrdon," she said.

"Let me help thee find Leanna," he pleaded.

"I will find her. Thou goest to that prince of thine if thou must."

"But I shall see thee again?"

Esta paused in her grief as she looked to the stars, confounded. Byrdon could not be clear of her answer. All she replied was, "If that Jewel ever comes near my child, I will never forgive thee," then she turned a final time and bounded toward the castle.

"Esta!" He called, but she did not stop. He tried regardless to plead with the back of her hood. "Travel with me to Pavoline after the wedding. I beg thee, my love."

But the cape merely went on into the darkness.

Meanwhile, Leanna had charged into the Masorian stables and, opening the door to Dawn's stall, felt a sudden rush of dread as her knees fell out from beneath her. She knelt beside the resting steed, unfeeling yet with complete terror, knowing for certain what had just then taken place in the caves. Dawn whinnied and brought his nose down to the shaking girl, coaxing Leanna to lift her head. She threw her arms around his neck and cried into his shoulder as he wrapped his chin around her back. It was here she sat, hopelessly trying to clear her mind as she watched her father in visions returning to Guiomar's tent and showing the prince the Jewel of Nebulous. She watched Guiomar stand with eager anticipation and carefully approach the servant, reaching for the powerful gem he held in his hands. Leanna watched the prince take hold of the gem, enclosing it in his grasp. Small, pine-colored vines erupted from the Jewel, wedged out from between his fingers, and took hold in a locked spiral around his wrist. Within moments, a web of vines wound up his forearm and around his hand, holding the Jewel securely between the knuckles atop the prince's fist. He let loose a laugh which mingled in dissonant harmony with the thunder he now forced from the clouds. At this, Leanna's vision ended, and she turned swiftly away from Dawn as her dinner forced itself onto the stable floor.

CHAPTER XIII

A Drought's First Days

Leif found Leanna asleep in the stables beside Dawn the next morning. Her face was flushed, and she was dripping with sweat. Leif attempted to dry their own liquid palms on the side of their trousers before taking Leanna's arm.

"There you are," they said, and she woke in a daze, allowing them to pull her to her feet. "Come inside at once, the heat is too terrible, and your mother is worried sick." When Leif stumbled back into their chambers with Leanna, Madrick and Esta were inside in anxious discussion, fanning themselves with papers. All talk instantly halted upon Leanna's entrance while the mother ran to the child and gratefully kissed the top of her head.

"Never go running off again; never," Esta said, and kissed Leanna's head once more before backing slightly away and resuming the use of her makeshift fan.

"I'm sorry to have frightened everyone," Leanna said, although the guilt she felt was very little when compared to every other feeling that still swam so wildly within her.

The mother turned Leanna toward her and brushed a small curl away from the girl's eye. "I explained to them what happened," she said, "how we two merely had a small spat in our cottage, and the place, in thy mind, was too small to hold the both of us that night." Leanna scowled at the lie. "We're alright now though, are we not? It was just a little nothing."

Leanna desperately wished to scream. Howl. Wail. If not these, then at least to acknowledge the truth of the horrid happenings of which they were all now living through the effects. If it was only the king there with her, then perhaps, in her rage, her familial loyalties would weaken, no longer preventing her from revealing their every terrible secret; yet, there was Esta's anxious stare, her commanding eyes which never failed to remind Leanna of her promises. Now, as was so horridly predicted those years ago, the family was again dependent on the state of the nations above ground, and a war betwixt Masor and Pavoline, especially with the Jewel having been tossed into play, would wreak havoc on their chance at a life together, not to even consider its effects on the whole of their world. But what good was peace if it meant evil was permitted its domination? What did it matter if the family had a chance at life together if her father had turned too horrid to include in it? Did any childhood oaths maintain their relevance now that such a thing had happened? Perhaps hither, in front of Masor's king, was an inopportune time to inquire. Leanna forced the corner of her mouth to flinch into a brief smile and said, "Yes, Mother."

"I am glad that's settled;" Madrick began, "however," the king looked out the window, "We have a larger dilemma."

"The heat," Leanna agreed, with all the resentment her greater comprehension allowed.

"It's absurd!" He exclaimed. "No such temperatures should be upon us this early in the season."

Leif threw their hands up in exasperation. "The heat has only worsened every hour, with no indication of halting its growth. I have never seen anything like it, no matter the time of season. If it continues like this, the local crops won't survive the day!"

"And we don't yet know how much of the kingdom is affected," Madrick added.

"So what do we do?" Leanna asked.

"There is nothing we can do." Esta was stern.

"We must do something!" Leanna replied.

"We have to look out for the food and water," said the king. "If the Sky means to challenge us, those necessities will be our best chance of surviving Its attack."

Leanna nodded. "I will send the crown's word into town to ensure people cover the wells and secure their stores and rations." The page briskly left to her task without a word to her mother.

"I'll see the horses have what they need." Leif took Madrick's hand then, after a worried smile, departed.

"Isolda will just now be waking; I'll see she's informed."

Madrick nodded. "Yes, good. Then, I shall prepare to meet our guests from Pavoline."

With that, the apartment was emptied, left on its own to sizzle in the drying heat.

"Princess?" Esta let herself into the chambers without awaiting an answer to her knock.

"Yes, Esta, good morn." Isolda sat at the edge of her bed, shaking the night's disorder out of her hair and wiping the falling locks away from her neck. "There is actually something I meant to speak about with thee."

"Certainly, Your Highness, but, if you will allow, there is an issue of urgency to address first."

"I am sure it could wait but a moment."

The maid was baffled. "If you insist."

"I do." Isolda stood, pacing toward her vanity. "I heard a whisper that many years ago thou in fact gave birth to a child. Is this correct?"

Esta blinked. "May I ask where you heard this?"

"That matters not. Only know it is a source thou shouldst not contradict lightly. Is it true?"

The maid had far too much on her mind. Simply having the child had been no crime, and how much good was the secret now? "I'm afraid so, Your Majesty," she admitted.

"My goodness." Isolda tied her hair back with a ribbon, staring at Esta through the mirror's reflection. She took a dry kerchief to her brow. "Rumor also says that the child serves hither in our castle, and has for many a year. Being that the options are not vast, I must inquire: Madrick's page, is she thine?"

Esta sighed, patience growing thin. "I'm afraid so, Your Majesty."

The princess turned darkly to the maid. "Whyever didst thou keep it secret?"

Esta had reached her limit with gentility. She shrugged. "I was young, and unpartnered, and had succumbed to one evening's desperation for another's touch. The father was no one to take pride in, some starving poet who lived just outside town, and I could not bring myself to speak of it to one as accomplished as yourself."

Isolda relaxed her intrigue, masking her disappointment, accepting the story which, Esta was pleased to discover, was an entirely reasonable fabrication.

"Very well then. Thou art permitted thy secrets. I only wish I had possessed more of thy trust."

"If anything of the like occurs again, Your Highness, I can swear to confide in you every detail."

Isolda grimaced. "Well, perhaps not." She returned her gaze to the vanity. "Your Majesty, might I now acquaint you then with the other, arguably more important, matter?"

"Oh, yes, do; but first, open that window. It is dreadfully hot."

Esta fought back her vexation as she began to explain.

"Guiomar, Son, by all that is good, how can you don such length of sleeve in these temperatures? And gloves! I do say, a formal occasion is no justification to torture oneself."

The prince smirked, fastening his shirt cuffs, as he and his father stepped into Masor's courtyard. The lines of flowers that had been hung from the surrounding walls and archways were already beginning to dry and their color turn dull, spotted with brown. Madrick came to greet them, attempting his most grand countenance of welcome, and Petrenair halted in awe before the castle steps.

"Ah!" He sighed. "If I were not more aware of time and tragedy, I would think you were the first of your name."

Madrick tousled his hair and pressured himself into a grin. "Thank you, Your Majesty. I do regret how long it has been since we made acquaintance."

Guiomar smiled jovially and proactively offered Madrick his left hand, the one absent a jewel. "My most heartfelt congratulations to you and your stablehand."

Madrick reciprocated the gesture and shook his hand with all politeness. "Gramercy," the young king said.

"I too offer all my most happy regards," Petrenair agreed, overjoyed at his son's new enthusiasm toward pleasantness. "Although, I am becoming afraid my old heart will not allow me to remain in your fine city if this heat remains as it is. I never recall a Masorian summer like the present one. I remember the tall stone structures and the kind friends, but never these temperatures. I would hate to depart so soon and risk offense, but in truth, I fear much longer in this would make my chance of ever returning home quite slim."

Madrick offered an apologetic smile. "I assure you there would be no offense, Your Highness. If we had any indication such a wave like this was near, we would have sent word so you might have avoided the city altogether. As it is, we are just this very hour deciphering the intricacies of what has come upon us and hoping to make some sense of it ourselves, for indeed it is like nothing we have known in the past. So long as you would like to stay, I will see to it your comfort is attended to; yet, I hope you'll understand, my first interest will have to be in seeing to the needs of my people."

"Of course," Guiomar sneered, and Petrenair thanked him graciously for his reasonableness

"Sire," Leanna stepped out of the palace doors, holding one open to remain partly inside.

"Yes? Wait!—" Madrick excitedly moved up a few steps and turned back to his guests. "Allow me to introduce Leanna Page; my greatest friend and advisor."

"A page?" Guiomar asked with repugnant disbelief. Petrenair pinched the back of his son's arm, and Madrick smiled.

"Verily," he said.

Leanna would have glowed at the praise but the sight of Guiomar brought up such hatefulness within her she hardly took notice of the compliment.

"What is it, Leanna?" Madrick asked, returning her to her purpose. She kept her gaze to him, endeavoring to forget the Ranzentines.

"Isolda obtained word from the lagifs," she reported. "The condition is the same all throughout Masor. Only north of the great River do cool breezes blow today."

Petrenair frowned. "How could you know of the whole kingdom in but an hour?"

"The mirrors." Madrick hastily explained, then at a sudden recalled that hitherto the Oxbiens had always averted mention of the magical gifts around their friends from Pavoline, and he attempted to create another answer that would not offend them, but he found he had not the time. "Forgive me, Your Majesties. I must confer with my sister."

"One moment, young Madrick." Petrenair held up a finger to hold the other king to his place on the steps. "If it is true that all of Masor experiences the same heat as the city, and I and my party will continue to suffer it a full week after we begin our leave, I am inclined to make our departure far sooner than could be hoped; perhaps no later than after a brief rest."

Guiomar feigned regret as he nodded in agreement.

"I completely understand," Madrick pronounced, his interest having long moved away from the men before him. "Leanna, wouldst thou show them to a lower apartment where they can rest—it is slightly cooler below" he explained to them, "—and ensure they are brought good refreshment?"

"Yes, Your Highness." Leanna bowed her head dutifully as Madrick thanked her in a small smile and rushed past her to attempt to address the onslaught of disaster. Guiomar and his father met Leanna at the top of the steps and stood strangely before her, unsure how to interact with this servant, friend of the king. She kept her hands behind her and her countenance cold.

She looked Guiomar in the eye. "Might I take your gloves, Sire? I could have them laundered; they must be drenched in perspiration."

The prince glared at her feeling as though she might, yet knowing she could not possibly, know anything about the Jewel. "Just show us the way," he said. She turned on a heel and walked forth, forsaking the nicety to look back and ensure they had followed.

"Byrdon," Guiomar called toward the carriages, and Leanna skipped a step, containing a cry upon hearing the name behind her. She only kept forward as the prince ordered, "Prepare our departure for Pavoline. We shan't be staying long." Only then did Byrdon emerge from behind the cart, giving an unseen gesture of acknowledgment to his prince's command, unable to speak for shame.

Mere moments after the page had left the royal guests to their temporary chambers, Esta caught Leanna in the hall.

"Fetch the Ranzentines," she said. "Local lagifs are present as well; Madrick and Isolda wish to hold a conference."

"Certainly," Leanna said, following a sigh, then she stopped, realizing this was the first moment all day that she had been alone with Esta. "Mother? Father is here."

"I know, dearest," was the reply.

"Will you speak to him?"

"I don't know that we'll have the opportunity," she said frankly and tried to return from whence she came.

"Mother," Leanna stopped her. "What are we going to do?"

There was a moment, the briefest halting of time, where all the world seemed to start collapsing inward upon itself. Esta shook herself from it and returned the commanding power of her stare.

"Get the Ranzentines," the mother said.

The great hall of the throne had been hastily furnished with as much of the grand meeting table as could be currently acquired. In usual times, it was a symmetrical piece, comprised of four long sections that came together in perfect practicality for the discussion of a noble group. The castle possessed many such sectional table parts; however, all but three of them were now stuck in the ballroom on the ground floor below which was set for the night's intended pre-wedding feast and the celebration that was to take place on the morrow. So, today, the table, missing a corner, could sit two people on the end nearest the throne while only one on the end further, and on one long side it could only sit half as many as the other.

As the invited filed inside the room, each took seats nearest to the throne as would they dare. The lagifs in attendance, the five wealthiest in the city, arrived together and prior to anyone else. Lagif Oscar Bisqueth took hold of the opportunity and sat directly beside the right hand of the table's full end. Lagif Lilac Huebert and Lagif Sorjal Fitzcoalint hesitated, standing in the space of the missing far-right corner, while Lagif Tyrene Aquincia and Lagif Rengenisis Volatia III sat opposite Bisqueth, although with a touch more deference to the yet unknown who would be joining them, leaving a seat between themselves and the table's head. Leif was next to arrive, and with them Galen, the city's leading grain and vegetable farmer. Unfastidious regarding placement, Leif sat themself at the strange half-head of the table, farthest from the throne, and Galen took the outer chair beside them. Kn. Grilliot then appeared, followed by the old physician, Albain, and they occupied the two remaining seats between Galen and Lagif Aquincia. None in the party felt particularly inclined to speak to those near them, either in space or station, while the rest of the room was present, and those who truly wished to speak at all were occupied with mental rehearsal of what they would say to the crown, so silence conquered the air while inner thoughts ran apace with worries.

The final entrance, that of the royals, took place with a crash as Madrick pounded upon the grand doors, forcing the tall, dense wood to move apart as swiftly as he meant to enter. Leanna rushed in beside him, Ranzentines in tow, with Isolda coming in last and closing the doors behind them. Petrenair sat beside Bisqueth, and Guiomar sat beside that in the final chair before the table dropped off into nothing. At this, Lagif Huebert and Lagif Fitzcoalint merely decided to remain standing for the duration of the conference. Madrick took his place at the throne-ward head, sharing a corner with Bisqueth, and Leanna sat herself directly next to the king, readying herself to make notated record of the discussion; that is, until she felt the vice-crown's irate breath cross her neck and, looking up, saw Isolda's hand gripping the back of her chair. She rose and reseated herself around the corner in the open place beside Volatia. Isolda sat beside Madrick at the head.

"Many thanks to you all for attending us on such short notice," Isolda began.

The chaos followed in an instant. Lagif Bisqueth started with rushed speech on numerous unsurprising concerns, all of which had been already considered by the present company, but that he spoke of with utmost import and novelty. This sparked a diatribe by Lagif Huebert regarding 'what mattered in actuality,' and a point then from Galen concerning the unlikely practicality of some of Huebert's 'indisputable solutions.' Madrick and Leif exchanged private volumes of thought while Fitzcoalint and Aquincia bemoaned how the heat would serve to worsen the lethargy of the serving population, and Albain firmly reminded them that a pronounced extent of rest would be required in such conditions to bypass the dangers of overexertion. Lagif Volatia inquired, if the condition was to continue, on the possibility of obtaining fresh resources from Pavoline in the event that Masor's crops did not survive, as surely, at this rate, they would not. Prince Guiomar explained that Pavoline could reasonably expect to see an influx of villagers seeking refuge and could not promise to have any excess available to provide. Petrenair made no disagreement. Isolda asked Kn. Grilliot to report on the condition of the city's emergency ration supply, and upon hearing that the tower just outside the castle gardens contained enough to sufficiently feed the kingdom for approximately two months, the table generally calmed. Lagif Huebert remarked that it would not last quite as long with all the peasants who were likely to steal from it, but Kn. Grilliot explained the meticulous ordering of knights who would guard against the same, and she quieted.

Leanna looked up from her notes as the table fell into silence, all seeming to have said their intended piece. The lagifs looked to Isolda; Galen, Albain, and Leif looked to Madrick; and Kn. Grilliot looked between the two. Leanna, however, could not peel her gaze from Guiomar's glove, and the prince perceived the direction of her stare.

Guiomar turned to Madrick. "Are we through?"

"No."

Leanna kept her voice calm while she seethed within. Every gaze stuck to her after her declaration. She took note of no one but Guiomar.

"What is it, page?" Isolda condescended.

Leanna tore her attention from Guiomar to address the vice-crown. "Since early morn, all have spoken of how the Sky is acting entirely out of Its own character, the likes of which none in our world has seen. Has it occurred to no one, then, that this circumstance may in fact have an unnatural cause?"

"Like what?" Madrick queried.

Leanna chose her words with great care. "Something, perhaps, having to do with the magical."

"Ha!" Petrenair laughed. "What fairy hath the power to cause this?"

"Fairies are not the only ones with the ability to harness magic, Your Highness," Leanna told him.

Leif spoke at last. "Do you suggest a human could be responsible?"

"Isn't it possible?" Leanna encouraged them all to wonder. On the whole, they refused.

"Dost thou possess any proof of such an idea?" Lagif Volatia asked.

Leanna's gaze turned instinctively to Guiomar's hand, and he brought both his fists to his waist beneath the table. She met his eyes. A singular brow cocked above his eye, uncertain what more the curious page might dare to say. Rage flared within her, and she thought of precisely how she might let loose the damning words, condemning the wicked prince to the consequences of his guilt, but she remembered her mother's fruitless attempt to warn Isolda of the Ranzentine, her father's hardships in the aftermath of accusing Petrenair's son, and Vice-Crown Isolda's ever-present glare beside her. She remembered her father's words.

A king is a king.

A page is a page, she added.

"Forgive me," she shook her head. "I am sometimes no more than a foolish peasant, seeking answers where there are none to be found."

"Indeed," King Petrenair declared. "Thou wouldst do well to think less on magics, girl." She offered him a polite nod. "We immensely regret Masor's misfortune; yet, as Pavoline cannot do any good for it, I think we should make our departure."

All rose from their places and shifted about, saying their final notes and farewells. As the hall emptied of its guests, King Madrick spoke to Leanna.

"I know it is unreasonable to ask for perfect calm in a time such as this," he said, "but do maintain thy reason, Leanna. I rely on it so." He placed a steadying hand on her shoulder then moved on to converse with Leif.

Leanna looked over her page of notes that lay on the table and fought down the urge to tear it to pieces.

The Pavol traveling party was on their way north only a three-quarter hour later. As the final carriage passed the portcullis, the castle breathed a sigh, grateful to be relieved of its extraneous inhabitants who had only served to crowd the ever-thickening air. Several moments later there was a flash of lightning in the cloudless Sky, and a crash of thunder rang out from behind the castle. Shortly thereafter came the sound of many servants hollering to anyone who would hear: "Fire! Fire! The wheat tower is aflame! The rations are burning! Fire! Fire!"

It took the remainder of the afternoon and half the water in the wells to douse it. The sun was behind the Infinites before they were done, but if anyone had been in the courtyard they still would not have seen the way the shadows drew beauties on the walls for a heavy veil of smoke from the flames had draped over the whole of Masor city and, in the absence of wind, it lingered. Only half the grain had been salvageable, but only half of that remained in the tower by the time evening fell. The remainder had gone missing in the chaos.

Madrick and Leif, Isolda, Esta, and Leanna were alone in the ballroom by the time of the feast. No one else any longer being expected, this place of intended joy had become the only solace for quiet solemnity the group could find, hither protected both from extraneous bother and the stench of smoke. They sat scattered between the spoils of seats at the tables, Madrick and Leif beside each other at the front of the room where they would have been intended.

"We are not to have a wedding tomorrow, are we?" Madrick asked sadly.

"No," Leif said.

The young king dropped his head into his hands and released an ironic chortle. "Perhaps a toast tonight then," he said. He reached for a bottle of wine, but Leif stopped him with a gentle hand.

"Please, my love. No."

Madrick took Leif's hand in place of the bottle and nodded, willing himself not to cry. Seeing this touched Isolda more deeply than she could ever expect. For this one moment, she thought it possible that the stablehand might be an appropriate match for her brother, even one to be glad of.

"We could marry you now," she offered, and the company looked to her in surprise. "I know this is not quite the inner circle you had in mind, but perhaps we three could suffice in its stead?"

Isolda, Esta, and Leanna looked to the couple, the last two indicating their perfect pleasure to comply. Leif turned to Madrick.

"Why wait?" They whispered, and, despite himself, the king smiled with deep joy. The full company rose and pushed all the furniture to the sides of the room. After the rearrangement, Leif remained at one end of the hall and Madrick the other, while the last three formed a large circle in the center. Leanna, Esta, and Isolda combined their voices in a light rendition of the beloved Masorian wedding melody, and the king and the stablehand walked toward the center, smiling to each other all the while. The couple stepped inside the inner circle and took each other's hands. Changing speaker line by line, the members of the circle all spoke through Masor's traditional wedding ceremony, and, where appropriate, Leanna added lines of her own, forcing the room to work to contain its laughter. When they had finished, Madrick and Leif each spoke their vows, swearing to remain committed to the constant endeavor of supporting the other in everything, and making the other know they are loved. Upon the vow's completion, those of the circle threw up their hands and sang out, "You are wed!"

Madrick and Leif forgot the heat, pulling one another close and diving into the most perfect kiss of love. For one moment, in that one place, everything was right in all the world.

But, my dear Reader, such moments can never last, not in stories like these.

CHAPTER XIV

∽

Byrdon, The Father

The days that followed offered no relief from the dry heat in Masor, and it was becoming clear that a drought was settling over the land. Atop it all, those in and around the city were learning to abstain from treading outdoors if possible in order to lessen the inhalation of the air, which was filthy with heavy smoke that refused to dissipate. The conditions continued on a full fortnight, then another. Before long, villagers who had but recently migrated to the outlying land of Masor were retreating to their Pavol homeland where, at least, there was food enough to eat and cool air to walk in. Many in the northern cities of Agoshany and Ritahest began to make the migration to Lake Masor in hopes of surviving off its natural reserves, but before even arriving most were informed by the inhabitants of Norkeif and Northlake—as these then began journeying toward Pavoline—that such volumes of the lake were evaporating in the heat that all which remained was too saturated with lake matter to be potable. Pavoline, with its happy Skies and new tax-paying villagers, saw a wave of great health—greater than many a year past—while Masor fell into its deepest moral and economic depression. After the first week, Isolda closed the castle gates to hungry beggars and reserved the remaining grain store for rationing to royals and knights necessary to governmental functions. Madrick took to starving himself so he might give out his meals to local villagers, but he soon fell ill and was unable to maintain the charity. Even Leif could not prevent him from eventually returning to his drink as his source of political passion was depleted and the state of the kingdom became only more dire. Leanna wished to encourage him toward something, anything, but even she fell prey to the great haze of inaction that settled upon the citadel as more and more it seemed there was nothing anyone could do to ease the catastrophe.

On the other end of the world, a light mist showered down on the courtyard at Pavoline castle. Byrdon noted a cool breeze late one morn and thought of the hardships his dear Esta and Leanna would be facing in the same moment. He had not expected any correspondence from them, but it was agony to have seen none, nonetheless. Guiomar had not raised the subject of Byrdon's reward for his great act of loyalty, and as of yet Byrdon had hesitated to remind the prince, fearful of appearing impatient; however, impatient he was, and today, a full month after leaving Masor to their doom, the man's reserve of the virtue was entirely spent. He would discuss it, Byrdon decided, over the prince's breakfast.

"A lordship!" Guiomar scoffed, nearly choking on a fresh grape. "And how would I offer that to thee?"

Byrdon fell firmly stoic. "That was your promise, Your Majesty."

"I merely meant thou wouldst have my gratitude," said the prince, returning focus to his meal.

"How am I meant to feed my family with your gratitude?"

"Thou hast family?"

The father steamed. "Yes, Your Highness."

The prince's features stretched to intake the curious fact, then swiftly relaxed into relative disinterest. "Surely they are well, as are all in Pavoline now. What need thee of a title?"

Byrdon stumbled over the facts of his situation, then resorted to pure principle. "The promise of it is the entire reason I brought you the weapon. It is what I am owed!"

Guiomar frowned. "I thought thy loyalty brought me my Jewel."

The servant let out a slow, controlled breath. "Yes, Sire, all the same."

"Rest, fool." The prince returned to his meal. "Thou hast heard my apologies for the misunderstanding. Couldst thou have any other meaningless oaths to disturb my meal with? Byrdon?"

But the servant had already stormed out the chamber doors. Without thinking, Byrdon found himself in the throne room, kneeling before a startled King Petrenair.

"I beg your forgiveness at my intrusion, Your Highness, but I have a grave confession to set forth before you," quoth he, and the king sat back to allow it. "One month past, just outside Masor, Prince Guiomar asked my assistance in acquiring a method to destroy the Oxbiens. To my deepest regret, I remembered a Jewel that gave one the power to command the Skies. I acquired it for him, at his demand, and he now dispatches its power daily to wreak havoc on the Masorian people."

The king stood from his throne, towering over the kneeling servant. "This is the second of such base accusations thou hast made against my son. Is it a jest to thee? Tell me why I should not have thee executed hither?"

"I would not risk my life on an inaccuracy, My Liege. I swear it is the truth."

Petrenair stepped nearer and stood high above the kneeling man. "What house dost thou imagine thyself to serve? We are Ranzentines! None of my name would dare trifle with such powers."

"Then your son should be revoked of your name," quoth he. If he were wiser, Byrdon might have cowered before the king, but on this day he could not. "Prince Guiomar is not the Ranzentine you would have him be, and with this fact I know you are well acquainted. He is undiluted wickedness, Your Highness, and so long as you are intent to be blind to it, you are no better than he."

"I could have thee broken; beheaded; burned."

"Or, once, you could take the word of an honest man! I have spent too long cowering under the pretense that your son contains some quality worth redemption, but I can stand it no longer. I swear, whether by desertion or death, I shall serve him not one more day."

The king maintained an unwavering stare at the servant, absorbing the intensity of his genuine oaths, and it brought a flickering remembrance to his mind of the odd Masorian page who had seemed, for a moment, so certain that the destruction of her home had been formed by human will.

"If thou art deceiving me—"

"I am beyond deception," Byrdon swore. "The jewel is secured to the prince's hand with a gauntlet of vines which he hides beneath his sleeve. He wears it day and night. I implore you, Your Highness, check his arm. You will see it in truth resides there."

And then he remembered the gloves. Petrenair bounded from the room, Byrdon scrambling to his feet to follow closely behind, neither of them speaking a word of their endless thoughts, the king at last pounding upon the entrance to Guiomar's chambers, and discovering instantly upon his opening them that the servant had spoken true.

"Byrdon, thither thou art," the prince barked. "What happened to the remainder of breakfast?" No one replied. "What is this?" he asked his father.

"Son, what is that on your hand?" the king spoke low.

Guiomar looked instantly to Byrdon with a snarl and pulled his palm into his sleeve. He then looked to his father with an attempt at innocence. "I found it amongst Mother's old things."

"A foolish lie," Petrenair hissed. "I remember thy mother too well. She had nothing of the kind. Does Byrdon speak the truth? Hast thou so doomed our friends in Masor?" A cry crept into Petrenair's throat.

"Masor will never be our friend, Father."

"O! But the magics of the River and Sky, they thou shalt take as thy fellows." The king flung his arm wildly, stepping back and forth in furious indecision. "Thou darest call me mad?"

Guiomar was still. "The magics are not to be feared, Father, they are to be controlled."

"They are to be left untouched!"

"I disagree."

"O! Thou art still a fool; worse!" The king turned to the servant who had remained steadfast in the hall. "Byrdon, take the ring box from the dresser and bring it hither. Son, thou shalt place the Jewel within, and relinquish all use of it." Petrenair spoke without breaking his stare at the prince. Byrdon hastened to obey the order of the king, but when pushing past Guiomar, the prince extended his heel and toppled the servant to the ground. Petrenair thrust his own heel into the prince, forcing him to stumble into the casement beside his bed. As the prince regained his footing, his father strode toward him, the king's right hand taking up an iron poker as he passed the mantle and placing the point of it at the prince's throat. "Give me the Jewel, or I shall confine thee in the dungeon to rot with the rats."

Byrdon had now remembered his purpose and brought the small, decorative box to the king who held it open expectantly.

Guiomar's icy stare bore into Petrenair's soul as he tore the Jewel from his fist and placed it in the container. Byrdon marveled at the vines which now withered off the prince's arm, but he refocused his attention at the snapping of the box's lid. Jewel contained and in hand, Petrenair turned from his son, threw the poker in the hearth, and started towards the door.

"King, what shall you have me do?" Byrdon stood at attention, full of a passion for his position he had not felt in many a year.

The king looked at him with complete apathy, verging on a hint of disgust. "Thou? His accomplice? I have nothing left for thee."

"But, Sire—"

"Enough!" Upon seeing the shock in the servant's countenance, Petrenair began to soften, but it only turned his apathy to grief. "I beg thee, Byrdon. Thou hast caused me enough pain. I do not wish to see thee more."

The king bristled off down the hall to engross himself in deep deliberation.

Byrdon, disbelieving, started to follow the king but was halted by Guiomar's call who remained in the casement. The servant, recoiling, returned and faced the prince.

"Close the door, Byrdon."

Byrdon's arm followed the instruction, and his feet pointed him again in the direction of Prince Guiomar. In the next breath, Byrdon found himself pinned to the wood, Guiomar's hand securely around his throat.

"Thou hast betrayed me," Guiomar snarled.

Struggling for breath, Byrdon managed, "Following you, I have betrayed my family, and I have betrayed my world. At last, betraying you, I have done right."

"Thou shouldst have ensured that family of thine said their final farewells to thee." A grin crept onto Guiomar's lips as he tightened his hold on the servant's neck.

"They know of thee," Byrdon croaked.

Guiomar loosened his grip.

"My family knows everything you have done. They know well of the Jewel. Their silence is to preserve my safety. If you kill me, you will never become king."

"Where are they?" Guiomar demanded.

Byrdon laughed. "Nowhere you would find them."

Guiomar threw Byrdon to the floor with a thundering shout. Byrdon nursed his bruised neck, and smiled. Considering carefully, Guiomar stood with the still of death, his rising and falling breast the only sign of life beside his raging eyes. Then, jolting to motion, he took hold of Byrdon by the arm and charged him to the dungeon below the castle. Tossing the servant to the floor of an empty cell and locking the door behind, Guiomar looked dead into Byrdon's eyes and swore, "Thou wilt not see the light of day until thy familial traitors are made known to me."

Contented, Byrdon replied, "Then I shall nevermore see the light of day," and watched as the prince fumed away, leaving the simple serving man to a newfound peace.

CHAPTER XV

Guiomar, The King

The little, one-room cottage Esta had left behind in Masor had remained exactly the way she left it. Still, now, all these years later, it had never felt so small. Leanna insisted her mother sleep in the lone little bed, and the child herself used a bundle of blankets to craft a place for her own repose in the opposite corner. Tonight, Leanna slept restlessly, avoiding dreams, same as she had the past thirty nights since losing her home in the cave. In those thirty days, everything Leanna had built in Masor had crumbled into dust. Her work in the castle had been relegated to the stables as King Madrick, in an ever-worsening depression, had entirely succumbed again to his drink. Lief had insisted they themself take over any of Leanna's tasks that would put her in direct contact with Madrick, for the king was in no shape to be giving orders to a servant, much less a youthful one. Leanna had done all she could to maintain the aid programs she had helped Madrick develop for the commoners, but the need was so great and the resources so little that the aid turned to naught but apologies. This night, she felt a tugging at her mind and knew Kennedy wished for her, same as she had the past thirty nights in which she had kept her dreams solitary. Leanna missed Kennedy dearly, but the shame of her father's betrayal encroached upon her heart and prevented her from letting her friend into her mind. Still, tonight, Kennedy pulled so strongly that Leanna gave in, stepping into the endless sky of their shared dreamscape.

"Leanna!" Kennedy gleamed, then glowered. "Why hast thou ignored me so?"

Finally, the weight of every calamity was fully felt upon the dreamer's heart, and Leanna fell into Kennedy's arms, bursting into tears. She told her of all that had come to pass, raging at the world for its unkindness and bemoaning the uncertain future. The Alquorians of course knew of the drought their neighbor faced, but Kennedy assured Leanna that the Woods as yet had remained entirely unaffected. Leanna spoke of her father, how beloved he was to her, and how disgusted she felt to watch him hand Guiomar the Jewel. Kennedy was naturally shocked at the events and undertook every manageable effort to console Leanna. Among these efforts, she reminded Leanna the extent of her father's love.

"Thou shouldst speak to him, hear the tale from his own understanding."

"How would I travel to Pavoline now?"

Kennedy smiled. "Thou needn't travel an inch," she suggested. "Go to his dreams."

"I have never shared a dream with another," Leanna realized. "Besides you."

"Thou shouldst try."

Leanna looked down, afraid. "What if he is corrupted? What if he is not the loving father I remember?"

"No amount of corruption could lessen his adoration of thee," the fairy said. "His actions have no excuse, but seek to understand them and he may in time be worthy of forgiveness."

Kennedy took Leanna's hand and the young women gazed into each other's eyes and remained there a time as they sometimes did when words were no longer needed to communicate their care. Leanna tightened her grasp around the palm of her dearest friend and felt the authenticity of the sensation give way to the lesser reality of the immaterial vision. She sighed.

"One day," they promised each other.

"Tonight, my father," Leanna said, and Kennedy nodded.

The dreamer closed her eyes and, at her thought, Kennedy faded away, and she heard the voice of her father behind her.

"I knew I would see thee again," he said.

Leanna looked to him solemnly, saying nothing, so he spoke in her stead. He apologized profusely, named himself king of all fools, and detailed his latest actions that now had earned him permanent residency in the dungeons of Pavoline. Upon hearing of her father's danger and bravery, the anger in Leanna melted away. She flew to him and threw her arms around his neck. He pulled her close.

"I love thee dearly," he said, and she responded in kind.

"Leanna, I beg thee, keep thyself safe. I have no faith that Guiomar will cease his villainy here, and he knows now to weed out my kin to hide his secrets."

"I am as safe as anyone in Masor now," she lamented, "which is to say very little. Although now that Guiomar no longer controls the Jewel, perhaps there is hope for the kingdom yet."

"All I care now is that he does not discover thee."

"I will be cautious," she assured him.

"Good." He smiled sadly. "That said, dear one, hear an old wretch's plea: Do not allow anyone who claims to be wise, be them Crown, tutor, or parent, ever persuade thee away from acting, always, in the manner thou knowest to be right."

Leanna nodded and leaned in for another embrace before waking into another merciless Masorian morn.

Some days passed and Petrenair had yet to arrive at a perfect conclusion to the problem of his son. On this day, he was tired of stewing in his own helpless thoughts and at last approached the prince in his chambers, where he had ordered him to be confined until further notice. A guard unclosed the door to allow the king entrance, then pulled it shut again behind him. Petrenair stood in the doorway, looking at the prince who sat childishly atop the face of his desk at the far end of the room, gazing out the window beyond.

"Might I join you for a time?" the father asked.

Guiomar made no motion, and Petrenair sat on the foot of the bed.

"I am going to speak to you of your mother."

The prince slowly pointed his eyes toward his father.

"I shall not offer continued speeches of her goodness and gentility, for this I know you have heard of, likely beyond the point of the appreciation. I wish to tell you now of her politics, an area in which I so often fail to credit her to the extent that is due. In my arrogance, I tend to forget that it was she who, in our youth, first suggested I connect with the Oxbiens. 'What a world this could be,' she would say, 'if only all those who ruled it made a point to be the best of friends.' So we did." Petrenair smiled in remembrance. "It was the loveliest time of all our lives. But then, you say, they murdered her, and for this you must ever be engrossed in a quest for vengeance upon them."

"I know you don't believe it, Father. That doesn't mean it isn't true."

"Very well." Petrenair halted him. "Let us suppose today that you are correct in your accusations. In actuality, my son, we may never know the true story; so today, your truth may rise above the rest."

Guiomar skeptically turned his full attention to the king.

"If, as you say, Madrick Oxbien I and his dear Fionella, indirectly, though with purpose and malice, murdered my Helena, I too would wish all evil upon them. I would wish that they drown in as many tears as I have cried since that day, but as it is, they are no longer here to wish evil upon. The Wood took its own vengeance upon them, and I would accept that in placement of my own. Now, there is Masor afresh, with a new set of Oxbiens, younger than yourself, who have done no wrong to us, nor to any in Pavoline. Thus, as your mother would say, our duty to befriend begins anew. Do you understand, Guiomar?"

The prince remained stoic, a slight scowl in the corner of his eye.

"Wherefore would you wreak havoc on an entire kingdom that has done you no wrong? You must realize, I am certain, you are the sole cause of numerous deaths, the starving of thousands. Do you take pleasure in their grief?"

"I care not for their grief," Guiomar explained. "I care only for the prosperousness of Pavoline. If one cannot rise without the existence of the other, so be it. That is our duty to our kingdom."

The father shook his head in disbelief. "Wherever did you gather such a philosophy?"

"Tell me this, Father. The tales held in our record hall of your extraordinary success in extending your command to the society of River Dwellers on the eastern sands of the Gwahanu, are they true?"

Petrenair sighed and dropped his head low. "Yes, my son."

"And those telling of your recovery of the Serenity Orchard when it was overtaken by a rebellion of fairy lovers?"

"Yes."

"Your conquering of The Lonely Valley; your settling of Brutivan?"

"Yes! Yes, Son, all of it is true, but I was a different kind of king then. When your mother was dying, I had to assume her qualities as my own if the kingdom was going to have any balance."

"You changed, King Petrenair. You were once a mighty king, far from the man who now refuses to send even a single knight to reclaim Lifallen Creek, forsaking all your strength out of 'friendship' for the people of Masor. If not for your maddening dedication to this politics of friendship, none of their damage to us would have been possible."

Petrenair lost himself in memories and conclusions as they slowly brought him to a new clarity. He looked to his son, afresh with despair.

"Is it I that you despise, and not the Oxbiens?" he asked.

"One and the same."

The king found himself again, pushing pain aside to make way for determination. "You must realize, Guiomar, it is not from weakness that I do not enact the same wreckage of my youth. It is from wisdom. Violent actions can never lead a people to peace."

"It is not peace I seek, Father, but prosperity. This is something that violence is particularly suited to achieve."

Petrenair sat straighter, his countenance twisted in perplexity. "I believe I understand you at last, my son. It only pains me that I failed to impress upon you your mother's dreams."

"I dream of a glorious destiny for Pavoline," Guiomar reiterated. "I regret that our visions of such a concept do not align."

The king nodded. "As do I, my son. As do I."

Petrenair leaned on his knees to make himself stand and moved to the door, knocking so the guard outside would unlock it.

"Are you to release me, then, Father, now that you understand?"

The door opened and Petrenair stood before it, moving only his eyes to pronounce his decision. He spoke with deep sadness, but perfect acceptance.

"Now that I understand you, Guiomar, I will see to it that you never become king."

The prince's eyes widened in rage but his shock paralyzed him as he watched his father exit and have the door once again secured with a sturdy lock.

"A messenger is come from Pavoline."

Esta woke Leanna in the night and they rushed to the castle, noting a number of the lagifs in town hurrying to do the same. They arrived in the throne room with just time enough to see Pavoline's message-bearer hand an envelope, royally sealed, to Princess Isolda who sat upon the throne. Beside it, on the floor, reclined an exhausted king, inebriating himself to recover from the effects of the same on the previous eve, only a few hours prior. The vice-crown accepted the billet and read it aloud for the gathered court. All expected renewed sympathies, given their nation's elongated malady, and an offer of generous support. All other than Leanna, that is, who remembered her father and thought King Petrenair might have something far more damning he meant to reveal. Isolda began:

"My dear Masorian friends:

"I write to you with portentous tidings. First, I will unequivocally state my disappointment at the state of Masor's skies, and assure you, if there is any type of traditional aid you would request from us, it would be gladly given. I sincerely hope this generosity will serve to soften the news I must relate to you next.

"It has been long understood between our families the immense strength of our friendship. It has also been long conceded between us that the warmth of our alliance was not felt in the mind of my son, Prince Guiomar. I have come to learn, with terrible regret, that the current condition of Masor is not in fact due to the natural ebbs and flows of nature as we had all so reasonably deduced; instead, it was brought about, and intentionally maintained, by the malice of my son who utilized an unassuming weapon with despicable power which, I have been informed by he who retrieved it for the prince, is called The Jewel of Nebulous."

Isolda paused and allowed her gaze to flicker over the court as they whispered to one another in wild shock and confusion. For the briefest moment, she met eyes with Leanna. Then she continued to read.

"The moment I was made aware of this, I forced the prince to relinquish the Jewel and confined him perpetually to his chambers. I have the gem locked away whither it can nevermore charm an otherwise harmless soul into the temptations of desolation. If its effects remain active on your kingdom by the time you receive this note, I rue the fact that I myself know not how to reverse them. Under my instruction, numerous attempts have been made to rid the world of this power, but as of yet, the Jewel has resisted destruction. On understanding that your wretched condition remains, I would continue these efforts and pray their success would return the beautiful Masorian summer to what I remember from all those years ago. If not, I am terribly sorry.

"Please be assured, I have made up my mind to revoke my son's birthright to the throne. I will find some other wise pavol youth to take my place and resign myself to being the last of my name to rule over the kingdom of Pavoline. I ask of you no mercy for Prince Guiomar, nor forgiveness on the level of the heart. The servant who, against what would have been my wishes, discovered the weapon and provided it to the prince is currently imprisoned in my dungeons and, if you wish it, is yours to reprimand as you please. However, I do ask for you to show mercy to myself, and refrain from taking vengeance on a son whose old father may not survive the grief of his loss after so many years of weeping on the grave of a lost wife. I shall take great pains to ensure the friendship of our kingdoms' rulers may remain so that we might have a continuance of peace. I beg of you to do the same.

"Ever yours,

"King Petrenair Ranzentine, last of his line, Ruler of Pavoline."

The court stood still. Isolda saw only the letter, her eyes adhered to the page as she read its brief post-script, reread its earlier passages, and considered every implication. The gentry, the knights, the servants, and the king, saw only Isolda, each of them frozen in eerie anticipation of her pronouncement. She stood.

"It says here thou art the swiftest messenger in the land," Isolda spoke low and with care.

"Yes, Your Highness," the courier replied.

"Then fly. Fly faster than thou ever hast, and tell thy king to prepare for war."

Shaken, the messenger nodded and began to flee from the room.

"Hold," Madrick objected. "With what aim, Isolda? Has Petrenair not done as much for our interests as we could hope for?"

"That old king has done as much as he is capable, but I regret that those efforts are far from sufficient. Kn. Grilliot,—" As she began to address her knights, the pavol messenger dashed out through the grand entrance. "—You will prepare as many fighters as we can spare and march to Pavoline this very dawn. Capture the prince and, out of respect for Petrenair, take him alive out of the capital, then drown him in the Gwahanu. Above all, do not return until you have retrieved this Jewel of Nebulous. If necessary, take the castle with it."

Kn. Grilliot brushed off the sweat from his brow with growing haste, a grin rising to his countenance at the promise of action. With a brief obeisance, he swore, "Yes, Your Highness," then hurried to his mission.

The vice-crown addressed the court. "We shall take hold of the Jewel and utilize it—as the foolish king across the River would never dare—to force our Sky to return to its benevolent ways. If we are prevented from this, then we shall instead take the lands in the north, placing ourselves where now sit the people of Pavoline, and sending them into the blistering heat they sent to loom over the South. In either event, I swear to it, the grandeur of Masor shall be returned."

The gentry cheered, the remaining knights beat their armor, and the servants—most of them—gave great thanks for the promise of better days before the court was dismissed and the hall was emptied. Madrick and Isolda remained at the front of the room while Leanna, having asked her mother to depart without her, stood before the doors, closing them from the inside. She turned to the throne.

"You cannot do this to Pavoline," she said. Madrick gave her a curious glance. Isolda scoffed. "What art thou to tell me what I can and cannot do?"

"I am a child of this world who does not wish to see it ravaged by senseless war." Leanna strode firmly toward the center of the hall, and Isolda took a step forward in confrontation, equal in her strength of will.

"Senseless! Dost thou wish then that our kingdom withers under the power of another? Wouldst thou that we perish?"

"No, but neither do I wish the perishment of Pavoline! For more than a fortnight, people have in fact begun to whisper that the heat might be slowly lifting. Surely, we now hold the reason why! Perhaps we need only have patience."

"I will not patiently await the knowledge that I have doomed my kingdom, certainly not on the witless plea of a soft-hearted page."

Leanna filled her chest, standing tall. "The Crown respects my opinion."

"Not this half of it," Isolda rejoined.

The king groaned. "What if she is right, Isolda? She was before…"

"Quiet, Madrick." She snapped to face her brother, then added, "What would you know in your condition?"

The page again stole her attention, treading forward until she was just before the platform of the throne. "I will not allow you to do this. Our knights are now the only well-fed among us and with the mission of vengeance, in the sudden absence of the oppressive air, they will have no instinct to refrain from complete obliteration of every Pavol person in the citadel. It isn't right!"

"Thou shouldst not care so for a people who are not thine own," Isolda warned.

"How can you care so little?"

"I hold interest in all of our world, sufficient to allow me to make decisions that work towards the betterment of Masor. Thou couldst not dream to have such wisdom. Do not question thy queen again."

"You are not the queen; you are the princess!" Leanna roared.

Isolda swiftly raised an arm and struck her across the cheek.

Madrick caught Leanna's gaze as she returned to face forward and gave her nothing more than a mere countenance of sad surrender. He shook his head and took a sip from his flask.

"Leave, page," Isolda commanded, "before I lose my temper."

Leanna glared at her then stormed out of the hall. Upon arriving home, she ignored Esta and instantly began to put together a small pack of consumables and took up her canteen.

"Wherever art thou headed now?" Esta asked as Leanna wordlessly returned towards the door.

"I am going to stop the destruction of Pavoline."

Leanna opened the door and meant to exit, but Esta rushed to her and slammed the entryway closed.

"I will not have thee go to that place."

"By birthright, Pavoline is my home as much as Masor," Leanna declared. "I shall not forsake it."

Esta vigorously shook her head. "There is nothing that can be done, not by one of us."

"I have power beyond my station, and if it shall not be recognized by the monarchs of Masor, I can at least utilize it to retrieve the Jewel. The Masorian knights can then seek me for their prize instead of spilling blood in the castle of my father."

"No, Leanna, no. Thou mustn't."

"I will not be persuaded away from this."

"This is no persuasion. I directly forbid it!"

"Do you wish Father to be killed?! Or do you expect the knights to spare him?" Leanna asked, dripping with facetiousness.

"Thy father doomed himself when he took the Jewel. I cannot express to thee, or even completely explain to myself, the ways in which that has broken, and hardened, my heart, but I will not lose thee to his mistakes."

"And I will not lose him to yours. Let me go, mother."

Esta's palm flew over her mouth as she stifled the weeping that threatened to steal through her. "Thou cannot, not ever, go near that Jewel. Child, please."

"I will do what I must."

Leanna forced her way through the door and started off, while Esta fell to the floor of the cottage and wept.

As she stepped onto the main road, Leanna brought a vision of Pavoline to her mind. She could see the shaded gardens, growing vibrantly under a cool mist. She could see the streams and the green fields and the wheat. She determined, if she could manage it for the weeks-long journey, she would not rest a single moment until she reached it.

As days went on, Leanna surprised herself with how little she felt she needed to pull rations from her pack and, in fact, when it was finally emptied, she gave it no serious thought and continued on. Likewise, in her determination, she pulled herself ever on through the heat, evading the need for sleep, finding she could decently maintain her senses without it. She despised herself once again for shutting Kennedy out, but she could not now imagine sharing her cluttered mind with another. She strode on steadily, through day and night, marching ahead of the Masorian forces, and even, eventually, ahead of the messenger who ran back to his king with news of war, down the long trading road that she knew, if faithfully followed, would lead her straight to the citadel of Pavoline.

She stopped only once, pausing at the Gwahanu River where the road became a small bridge. Stepping onto the ancient planks of sturdy, maintained wood, she was nearly brought to tears by the fresh, cool air that welcomed her into the new kingdom. She turned and looked out at the great Gwahanu which she had only yet known in stories and wondered what it would be like to live at Its edge. Not far off, she could see the sands of the River Dwellers and their huts built beside the water. The construction style was the same on the sands in Pavoline as it was in Masor and she realized these two peoples must be the only in all the world who had frequent communication, even friendship, across the River. She smiled, grateful to have witnessed it; then, again, marched off on her quest.

As she neared the city, she thought of the castle at Pavoline and willed her mind to travel there in visions. She explored its halls and hidden corners, memorizing the unfamiliar architecture and the positioning of the rooms. Seeing the dungeon, her father still trapped within, she spoke to him as he slept to ascertain the location of the Jewel.

The vault, she heard through her father's unconscious. *The king keeps the keys.*

She discovered, in mental exploration, where this vault lay, hidden below the castle, opposite to the dungeon, and further found in the king's chambers where the keys to it were stowed away in the night.

Finally reaching the citadel, Leanna entered a little inn whither she waited out the remainder of the day, then, when night fell, made her way to the castle. She discovered an unattended servants' entrance and, smiling, remembering her youth, entered unseen through the small door. Creeping on, she used her powers to evade the sight of the guards and swiftly stole through the halls until she approached the central chambers of the king. All was silent within, and she risked pressing open the door. Indeed, Petrenair slept, so she stepped inside and closed the door silently behind her. Knowing already the object of her search, she strode directly to the stand beside the king's bed and pulled open the compartment which held the keys. She retrieved them easily enough, but when she moved to reclose the drawer, it refused her. She pushed again, beginning to panic, realizing it had stuck in its place. With the application of all her force, it flew shut with a bang, instantly rousing the king. He saw her immediately and she dashed from the apartment, charging down the hall with her greatest speed, hearing the bellows of the king fading behind her ('Guards! Intruder!'), not daring to stop until she reached her destination.

Prince Guiomar too was awoken by the commotion and before long realized the knights posted to guard his chambers—which lay at the far end of a wing—had deserted in favor of aiding their fellows. He gave no hesitation before storming to the hearth, taking hold of the iron poker, and forcing it through the lock, wrenching himself free. He tossed the iron behind him and stepped into the open hall.

"The vault!" He distantly heard his father's voice in distress, calling repeatedly, "The wretch took the keys to the vault!"

Guiomar smiled.

When Leanna at last, having outrun her chasers, let herself into the strongroom, she halted in the entryway, instantly laying eyes upon a small wooden box. In her visions, she had not been able to locate the Jewel amidst Pavoline's other treasures, but she now could sense its presence so strongly that there was no question in her of whither it hid. She paced halfway towards it and was then paralyzed in apprehension. Her mother returned to her mind with those desperate pleas that Leanna not go near the brutal weapon. She had come all this way. What would it be for if she could not retrieve the Jewel? And yet, in the same, what good would it be if simply taking the Jewel in hand, even enclosed safely away in its case, were to entirely undo her, as she felt certain now it inescapably would. Her indecision kept her rooted, eyes unwavering, so much so that she did not perceive the prince's entrance into the vault until he knocked her to the ground and out of his path.

Returned to herself, Leanna grasped at the prince's legs to prevent him from his obvious intention, but her efforts were insufficient. Taking up the object of his desire, he strode past her again, kicking her to the wall, grinning at his reunion with the Jewel of Nebulous as he paced toward the exit. Leanna, in contrast, was reunited with the greatest of terror as she observed again, now in reality, the Jewel wrapping its growing vines around Guiomar's hand. They met eyes upon hearing approaching footsteps and remained locked in a stare as they listened to voices beyond.

"Wait!" The nearby footsteps halted as a farther voice called out. "Forget the thief, there are worse tidings. As we speak, knights of Masor are marching on Pavoline. Ready yourself, they have already reached the eastern plains."

Prince and page were deadly still, waiting until all they could hear was the pounding inside their own chests, then Guiomar sped out at a run into the cleared halls, taking several sudden turns to evade any followers. Leanna ran after him as best she could, tripping over newly regretful and uncertain steps, at length finding herself helplessly outside the castle, atop the stairs of the grand entryway in the courtyard. As she stood, surveying the empty scene, King Petrenair appeared from the shadows of the court and marched toward her.

"Thou thief! What hast thou taken?"

Leanna was far too shaken already to be further disturbed by being discovered by the king. She spoke to him as an ally. "I have nothing, Your Majesty. The prince; he took the weapon. He escaped."

Petrenair had not so much as a moment to rage before Guiomar came galloping across the cobblestones and disappeared through the massive gates, which were hurriedly opened just in time by the standing guard in response to his prince's order.

"The knights," Leanna realized. "He rides to the plains!"

"One man against an entire army? Even he is not so mad."

Leanna shook her head, fearing the worst. "He is not merely a man. Not when he has the Jewel."

She forgot the king and sped away, running at blinding speeds, nearly keeping pace with the horse's gallop, such that she was present, though breathless, to witness the prince dismount on a great sloped field which overlooked the approaching Masorian front. Masor's knights were now only a hundred meters away. Dark clouds flooded the night sky and, at the cinching of Guiomar's fist, lightning rained upon the knights in blow after merciless blow. The thunder was deafening. Leanna looked on in dismay, slowly stepping closer to the horror, watching as every knight was struck and fell dead upon the ground.

The scream of a king in fear is a little-known sound but too well remembered once heard, and the bellows of King Petrenair on this day, as he dismounted his own steed before the scene, would have been remembered above them all, if only any other than the iniquitous prince and the poor page had been there to witness it. All the king's dread, his terror, his grief, and his guilt were put on display before him as his only son stood smiling before a field of burning bodies.

"What have you done?" Petrenair cried as the thunder faded.

Guiomar turned and paced toward the king. Prideful, he pronounced, "I have done what you no longer could, Father. I have done what is necessary to protect Pavoline."

The king shook his head, backing away, his countenance twisting in horror as he now grew to detest the sight of his son's eyes.

Prince Guiomar took in the hatred in his father's stare and every lonely childhood hour of grief coursed through him in the form of old memories, wishing he could connect with one of his parents after having caused the death of the other, failing to bring any pride to his father's heart, going mad with anguish on account of his principles, refusing to succumb to the practices of his newly cowardly king, knowing for certain of his destiny, being certain his father would thank him once it was achieved, seeing now the connection he yearned for would never be made, and he was filled with an unadulterated hatred of his own. His fist closed tightly once more, and the Sky was split with a violent bolt, a blinding flash, that struck the father and, after all his long years, finally ended the reign of King Petrenair Ranzentine. Guiomar paused but a moment, expressionless, then mounted his steed, riding down the plain to the fallen knights, taking up one of their spears, and, returning to the king, pierced the weapon through the dead man's heart. It was only then he looked up and saw Leanna. She was staring at him from mere paces away.

"You killed him." She gasped for air between phrases. "Your own father; your king!"

"Certainly not." Guiomar observed his father's blood trickle down the gentle slope of the hill. "A tragic casualty of war," he declared, "taken only moments before the merciful Sky came to avenge us."

"I saw everything. The kingdom will be made to know, I will see to it."

"Thee? Art thou not the page of King Madrick; clearly an enemy sent to infiltrate the castle ahead of the attack? None in Pavoline would listen to thy words."

Leanna desperately sought to trap him in reason. "They will believe of your villainy. The kingdom knows you are no longer the heir to the throne!"

"Do they?" Guiomar smirked, and Leanna shuddered, now in question.

"They must," she hoped.

"Father himself explained to me in private that he was waiting to make the pronouncement of my change in title, or, for that matter, of my 'wrongdoings', until he had found a suitable heir to replace me." Leanna groaned with despair. "Yes, it is dreadfully unfortunate he did not live to fulfill his intentions." Guiomar looked down and knelt beside his father, closing the corpse's eyes and taking up the crown that had fallen behind the king's head. He stood and placed it grandly atop his own. At Leanna's distress, he smiled.

"Go," he said. "Run back to thy royals and report to them with certainty: the drought has only begun."

Guiomar, the King of Pavoline, lifted himself again onto his horse, took up the reins of the second steed, and rode with perfect calm back into the citadel, leaving Leanna alone on the field, shivering in the night.

CHAPTER XVI

The Aldorian Waterfall

"How could I have been so foolish!" Leanna paced circles around Kennedy in their dreamscape as she mercilessly hounded herself for the events in Pavoline. "I was told I was specifically forbidden; why could I not have simply obeyed my mother? She could see into what madness I had fallen, and yet I pressed on." It had been over a week past the double fortnight it took Leanna to pursue her fruitless undertaking since Kennedy had shared a dream with her, for until now, after returning to Masor, Leanna had still resisted sleep, sitting up, staring all through the nights, taking herself to wakeful vision after vision of the destruction across her world that she had worsened. Seeing her now, Kennedy could only be silent as she observed Leanna's hatred of her own actions. "I thought myself so mighty," she said. "What, in truth, could I ever have done? I have no warrior training, no skill! These powers; I fear they mean to destroy me."

Leanna stood, giving her eyes at last to Kennedy, pausing briefly for a breath, and received a countenance of great care and concern, but even her beloved friend was too much in shock to yet have words that might console her. Leanna began to speak on, but did so now slowly, choosing her words with caution. "The vision of Guiomar first donning the Jewel was so deeply unnerving, and the thought of Isolda taking it on was no improvement, such that, if it could be helped no other way, I was near determined to take it on myself in their place. That alone should have dissuaded me. Couldst thou imagine? Me, colluding with so wicked a power. For weeks, during the journey, the vague idea of it did not so much as concern me in the slightest. Worse, when I stood there directly in its presence, knowing it without even seeing it, I had the horrible realization that, all this time, all this magic swirling around my life, it had all been the Jewel. It had been reaching for me. The Jewel wants me. This weapon, this object of evil, I could swear has intention, and it desires me to be its wielder! How abhorrent a thing might

I be?" Kennedy rushed to her side and placed a stable, sure, comforting hand on her arm. With the most stern countenance and the slightest shake of her head, she conveyed enough to prevent Leanna's collapse into tears. "I was too terribly afraid," Leanna went on, "if I took the Jewel in hand, even enclosed within its box, I would succumb to its call; so, after throwing the castle into disarray, in the only moment of consequence, I did nothing, and the Jewel has fallen again to Guiomar, now King!, three-quarter of all Masor's knights have perished, and the Sky is only more dreadful above Masor than before."

"Such an intention as thine can never be faulted. Thou meant to protect the lives of the countless," Kennedy reminded her.

"Instead I may as well have murdered them myself."

"No." Dark violet sparked off Kennedy's wings in a brief flash. "That was Guiomar's doing. Guiomar alone."

"Guiomar would not have escaped his chambers if I had not infiltrated the castle."

"And thou wouldst not have infiltrated the castle if Isolda had not decided, against thy pleas, to begin a needless war! Leanna, if thou wishest to despise thyself for these actions, I will not pretend they were free of irresponsibility and shortsightedness, but such are small delinquencies when set beside the true crimes."

"And what of the Jewel?" Leanna asked. "What am I to do if it means to corrupt me?"

Kennedy shook her head with a sad but certain smile. "Thou art good, Leanna. There is nothing of evil that can change that."

Leanna wished so to accept these words as truth but before she was entirely convinced, Kennedy faded away, awakening, returning to her faraway land. The dreamer fell to her knees upon the face of her endless sky and curled so that the palms of her hands pressed upon her eyes, swaying and aching for some method of redemption to reveal itself. Her eyes strained against the pressure which, in waking times, would have brought an array of speckles to the darkness, but now, as she pressed only further, she fell helplessly into a new dream.

A great blue heron flew up from her perch on a river rock as a stream flowing through the Infinite Wood picked up momentary speed. Her grand wings spread and took her from the Forest floor to the Treetops within seconds where she again found stillness on a branch. Hither, however, a great horned owl stood in a stealthy stalk, and when his prey had found an ignorant peace, he pounced and clawed at her wings. The heron darted away but was not swift enough to avoid injury. With one wing now clipped, she fell to the Forest floor and, upon dropping to it, pushed herself up onto her tall legs and ran, disregarding the pain. The owl maintained a rapid pursuit, but just as the heron looked back to her predator and thought she might have reached her end, a sudden wind blew harsh and swept the owl away. Startled, the heron stopped and searched for the source of the lucky wind, but none presented themselves. She walked on, tending to her wing as she followed a familiar path. At length, once passing through a particular density of foliage, she arrived at the edge of a pool, a graceful fall trickling into it from a wooded precipice above. Slowly, the heron waded into the water, first only feet, then breast, then finally sank all her feathered body into the water, up until the middle of her long neck. The water around her rippled and glowed, and even her small inexpressive eyes exuded a sense of peace as she lifted her beak to the Treetops. Stepping back to more shallow waters, the great heron again spread her beauteous wings, now each as powerful as the other, and flew off, returning to her rock.

Leanna awoke with the heron's image in her eye and relief in the corner of her smile, pleased at the bird's recovery. Reorienting herself to the darkness of the morning in her mother's Masor cottage, she wondered if the dream was only that, a pleasing distraction from her distress, or something more. She closed again her eyes and was returned to the picture of the waterfall, cascading gracefully to the reflective pool below. In the pool swam schools of mature fish, each older than any being had a right to be. Leanna unclosed her eyes and lost the image, but its memory sang a name into her ears, *The Aldorian Waterfall*, and she knew asudden not only of its reality but its precise location in the Wood far to the North beside the western border of Pavoline. She wondered if there was a way in which this far away pool was the answer to her plea for redemption, if there was some pragmatic way it could be utilized to aid the kingdom, but concluded it was not to be. Perhaps it was only that the heron in need had called her to the vision. Thinking so made her evermore thankful for the wind that could be of assistance when she could be of naught. Lying in her bedding a moment more, Leanna sent good wishes to the heron and thought for certain she felt the sentiments of *thank you* arrive in response. She was grateful the drought was at least contained in Masor's borders.

Leanna sighed and readied herself for another day. Having long trained herself to awaken before dawn—and before her mother—the truehearted daughter carried out her newly established routine of removing a plate from the cupboard, washing it with a small reserve of soapy water they had maintained in the home, and placing it out to dry as though it had recently been eaten upon. It might have deceived Esta the first time or two that the child had consumed at least a parcel, but by now it was merely a tacit agreement between the two that the mother would eat from their small supply, and the daughter would supposedly munch on some of the king's breakfast. This became especially plausible as, in his state of intensifying depression, infinitely worsened after (as the castle understood) his friend and page brought about their unthinkable defeat on the plains of Pavoline, the king had been unwilling to eat even a morsel for near a week since Leanna's return. She tried to put his disappointment in her out of her mind, along with her new reality that those who used to exchange friendly greetings with her in the castle halls now averted their gaze and hurried away. She kept mostly to herself, serving her duties as page as best she could.

Fastening a kerchief around her nose and mouth to protect against the indefatigable layer of smoke that refused to lift from the city, Leanna glanced quickly to her sleeping mother, then snuck out the cottage door into the hot, dry, vexatious air of the thirsting Masor dawn. An ashen Sky overlooked the city and the air was unnervingly still. Out of habit, Leanna stopped by the central well of Masor citadel on her way to the castle stables but, as she'd come to expect, not a drop was to be found within. She continued on toward the back of the castle, walking through what had been hedges of yellow roses and now housed naught but browning, fragile petals that cracked and fell from their stem at the slightest provocation.

Seeing Leif working at the stables, she decided to turn toward her other duties. She had yet to speak with them since returning from Pavoline, and was too afraid of their reproach to risk interaction although she knew they must be hurting. With Madrick resisting any gentleness or aid, Leif had returned to sleeping in their own apartment in the city. Leanna knew it would be good of her to speak with them, express sympathy at least. Perhaps she would gather the courage on the morrow.

She approached the castle and stopped at the sight of a well-dressed lagif exiting the palace from the servants' door at the back, carrying a sack of grain like none that had been released to any in the kingdom save knights and royals for several weeks. Squinting in curiosity, she approached him.

"Good morn, my lagif. May I ask your business at the castle?"

He hesitated, held his parcel closer, then straightened and announced with pride, "Well, surely those who can pay for the food ought to have it."

"Have you stolen it?" Leanna asked, appalled.

"No, indeed! I have been rewarded by the vice-crown for my loyalty to this kingdom."

Keeping a curious fury at bay, the servant inquired, "Does the princess give out a great many of these rewards?" The lagif simply huffed and stormed away, as the storm in Leanna grew all the stronger.

The sturdy doors to Princess Isolda's chambers were near downed by the girl's assault on their hinges, and Isolda—still in nightdress—lurched to attention at their sound.

"Do you know your people starve?" Leanna stood steadfast and bore daggers into the princess with her stare.

"Out, page. This instant."

"If there is food to be spared, wherefore do you not provide it to the hungry?"

Isolda snarled at the insolence. "Thou, of all, hast no place of righteousness to stand upon, and thou dost dare to speak so?"

"My own errors have no relevance to your wrongs, Isolda. Your crimes remain unchanged."

"Out. I want thee out! Remove thyself from this castle and never return."

Leanna shook her head. "The king will not stand for this," and she barged out the princess's chambers, hurrying down the hall.

She entered the king's apartment and found him languishing in a stupor, laying atop the puckered mass of comforter on his bed. His eyes were open, but he did not see.

"Sire," she began.

"Leave me, Leanna. I do not need thee now," Madrick said, staring solemnly ahead.

Keeping her nerve, Leanna answered, "But your people need you, My King." His silence told her to cease, but she continued nonetheless. "You cannot hide away while your peasant folk starve."

"We are all starving, Leanna, in more ways than one, and there is nothing to be done of it now. Guiomar controls our Skies, and we have no force to fight him with."

"But Isolda has rations for those who will pay. Peasants starve, while the gentry survive."

At this the king was curious. "Dost thou mean the royal rations?"

"There is more than she informed us of, My Liege. I am beginning to think she secretly maintained what was thought lost in the tower fire."

"I see," he said. "I should have expected so."

Leanna waited for his next order, but none came.

"We must act, Your Highness," she said.

"Then thou may act!" He bellowed. "Such is a talent of thine, of late."

Leanna winced. "Please believe, Sire, I despise myself for recent events sufficiently for the both of us, but dwelling on it will not help the people."

"I no longer have care for such things."

"It cannot be that you have lost all your passion," she demanded.

He held back a rageful sob. "I am full of fatigue, Leanna. My very mind feels ill, and I have done naught but ingest liquor since it began so that I might forget and dream of better times. My own love can no longer bear to look at me. I am in no state to be a king."

A remembrance of the injured bird from her dream came again to Leanna's mind and she knew at once that the vision had in fact been the answer to her midnight pleas. She sought out a reason the king might accompany her to the place.

"If you cannot be King entire, might it be in you at least to aid one wretched friend?"

He sighed. "No, Leanna. Leave me."

"But I am dreadfully thirsty."

"Yes—" he scoffed, "—as are we all. There is no fresh water in Masor."

"No—" she agreed, "—but there is fresh water in the Infinite Wood."

The king froze, investigating Leanna's sincerity, then reminded her, "There are fairies there as well."

She smirked. "Would you rather then that I go alone?"

"I forbid thee to travel there."

Her smile grew. "And if I disobey?"

"Thou wilt die in the Wood."

"I do not believe so. I am not afraid of fairies."

"Thou art a fool."

"Perhaps."

He paused pensively, then shook with disbelief. "It is out of the question!"

"Alas," she sighed. "I must then request an extended leave to venture it on my own. No knowing when I'll return."

"Tell me thou dost jest."

"Do I appear in jest, Your Highness?"

He studied her. "Damn," he said, realizing she was entirely serious. "I cannot very well let thee from my sight then look thy mother in the eye after thy death. Ready my armor and my best sword. I shall ready my largest flask. If we go to the Infinite Wood, we go prepared."

In half a moment, the servant had rushed from the chamber to make all the preparations. King Madrick fell back on his bed and stared at his canopy. Fear crept into his throat and, rising again, he washed it down with wine. It would be fitting, he supposed, if he died in the Woods. It would at least be suited to the tradition of his name.

Madrick halted upon his first step into the Infinite Wood. If there had been any uncertainty around the drought's magical nature, this first step swept it away, for the air at once was clear and had the touch of fresh dew, so unlike the heavy aridity that remained just a step behind in the kingdom. Forgetting himself, the king reached out and placed a hand upon the massive trunk of an infinite Tree and was overcome with the energy of the Wood. He let his eyelids fall at the peace. Unclosing them again, he saw Leanna kindly smile, watching his emotion, and he urgently returned his hand to his sword and a prideful glare to his countenance.

"You needn't be fearful, Your Highness," Leanna said.

"I'll decide that." He took a swallow from his flask. "Come, let us find thy water, then we may leave this place."

"Indeed, Your Highness…" she trailed off in hesitation.

"What is it?" He growled.

"Only, our destination," she explained, "is a waterfall and pool that I have heard tales of. The place exists outside the western bound Pavoline. It will take several weeks to reach it and return."

He laughed, presuming she spoke in jest. She did not. "West of Pavoline? Surely there is water nearer."

"None potable for humans, Your Highness," she claimed. "Stories say the waterfall refines the liquid from the Wood's various streams and transforms it to something remarkable. It is our only hope."

"That is absurd. I have never heard of any such thing."

"It is all peasant talk, Your Highness. You wouldn't have heard it."

"By the River and Sky, dost thou sincerely expect I shall follow thee for weeks on end while we blindly tramp through the Infinite Wood on an impossible task?"

She stood tall and raised her chin. "I intend to travel there, Your Highness. Whether or not you accompany me is entirely your choice."

He gaped at her, astonished. "Leanna, we left without notice."

"Not so! I explained everything to my mother." In truth, she had not, but she intended to that very night when they made camp.

The king flustered his speech, amazed, then settled on the objection: "We brought with us no food!"

"Oh, forgive me, Sire, I thought you had forsaken food. Moreover, there is hardly any in the kingdom reserved for one of my station." She shrugged contentedly. "We shall live off the Wood, and dare I say be far more comfortable doing so than were we walking through the kingdom."

Madrick blinked for a long moment, then threw up his arms, his dissenting energy being entirely spent. "So be it," he said, and he followed the page further under the cover of the infinite Trees.

The odd pair walked on in silence, the girl skipping ahead, balancing on unearthed roots or large rocks, and the king keeping a frantic, watching eye, with hand to sheath, ready to slash at any pair of wings which crossed their path. When hour after hour passed with no confrontation, he began to fall again into his rigid despondency. He made all attempts to shield his spirit from appreciating the wonder of the Wood, but certain breathtaking images he could not implore his mind to successfully disregard. He had maintained a downcast glare as they climbed an incline, closing his view to all but the needles and downed leaves which blanked the ground, but, when they reached a summit, they came to face a clearing of wildflowers like none the king had yet seen. Stopping asudden at the grandeur, he noted how otherworldly it seemed. He thought of the rose bushes of the castle garden in better times, so carefully kept. This meadow kept itself a beauty, with none to prevent the golden buttercup from intermingling with the tall violet lupines, or the small white yarrow blossoms from gracing the ground beneath. If there was fairy magic hither, for but a moment, Madrick was glad of it, but he denied the thought, certain no wicked creature could have a hand in such splendor.

He turned now from the meadow to recover his mind but lost it once more to feeling upon finding two Trees bending apart and leaving view of all Masor between them. He could see little of the citadel save for the towers of the castle peeking above the smoke, but he looked now to the outlying towns and saw that upon those rolling hills the smoke began to clear. From so far and high, he could not see the suffering thither and near forgot it. The amber hills appeared to glisten in the sun, and the villages, all connected by interweaving paths, stood so still and quiet the king could imagine they were even at peace.

Leanna waited with indefatigable patience for the king to breathe in the sight. Gazing over his shoulder to the branches above, Leanna saw now a shrunken fairy warrior camouflaged in the verdant brush. Her eyes darted to the king, then to the soldier who stalked the potential predator from the Leaves.

Pray, do not be seen, Warrior. Leanna directed her thought at the soldier who started, searched the ground, then locked eyes with the girl. *No harm will be done to the Wood, you have my oath.*

Whether assured at her message or merely befogged by its method of deliverance, the fairy warrior let them alone, flying off.

Leanna looked again to the king.

"Shall we continue, Sire?" She asked.

He paused, then uttered, "They will all die. Won't they, Leanna?"

With a sharp breath, she replied, "Not if we can help them, Your Highness."

"I can help no one."

"You are helping me."

"Thou revoked my choice in the matter!" Leanna laughed, admitting the truth of it. "But regardless, thou art different. Thou knowest I am no king."

Leanna squinted her disapproval but released it with a smirk. "Well, not a good one, perhaps," she said. Madrick laughed and turned to face her.

"Whence comes thy spirit? Thou must be starved."

Maintaining her saddened smile, she implored, "Come, King. Let us go on."

He nodded, "Yes. On."

They continued two full fortnights, then half another, until they reached the top of a new hill and, beginning to trod some steps down, suddenly heard the ambient rush of a steady rapid. Despite himself, King Madrick all but cried for joy and continued on to follow Leanna with alacrity as she picked up an eager pace. Gleeful now, each, the king and page allowed the downward slope to make them fly as they ran until reaching level ground, the water now roaring in their ears though they could see nothing of its source. Leanna then led the king through a curtain of ivy vines, and they both froze in breathtaking wonder at the sight they now beheld. Madrick saw only the waterfall's shine and the glory of white sparkles from the sun intermingling with a likeness of the viridescent canopy of the Trees above, all painted with light on the pool beneath the gracefully falling torrent. Leanna saw all the king did and more, recognizing precisely where the injured heron had entered the pool in her vision and recovered its flight. As the king continued to stare in awe, Leanna returned to the ivy curtain and plucked the largest leaf from the vine.

"Take this, Sire. It will help you drink," she said, handing him the leaf.

He shook his head with furrowed brow. "We journeyed hither for thee, Leanna. Worry not, I have my flask."

She continued to hold out the ivy to him. "I will not drink before the king," she declared.

He looked at the girl's steady countenance and could not find it within him to oppose her. Gazing upon the leaf of ivy, he accepted it into his grasp and saw more life in its veins than he had felt in himself for some time. At Leanna's repeated encouragement, he at last knelt before the pool and cupped the leaf beneath the water's surface. Raising it now to his lips, he sipped at the magic drink. Instantly upon a swallow, his expression grew wide and breast full of air as he felt every hint of pain, every drunken ache, every inch of despondency, fade away, at last seeing life again true. His eyes fell upon Leanna who stood staring expectantly.

"What is this place?" He asked.

She smiled. "Only a waterfall, My Liege."

The king studied her, making all attempts to decipher how the young page might have led him safely to a magical pool in the Infinite Wood, but failing in all efforts.

"All I thought I knew of thee, of late, is all uncertainty. I see naught but a mystery before me."

Leanna became grave and spoke in earnest. "See no mystery, Sire. See but a poor friend, and a loyal servant to Masor, both in desperate need of a king."

Madrick stood, holding the ivy leaf which now sparkled with mystical droplets of water.

"Wilt thou not drink?" He inquired.

"I will drink in our home when the drought is ended," she replied.

"Yes. As will all." King and servant, a glint of hope returned to each eye, both let loose a smile. "Go, Leanna. Start up the hill. I shall follow thee."

Leanna gazed once more around the home of the Aldorian Waterfall, then, nodding to the king, passed through the ivy vines. Now in solitude, King Madrick glowed, grateful again to find himself, spirit intact, returned to his bodily encasement. He removed his flask from its holding, only a drop of the liquor left inside, and spilled the remainder into the pool, watching it dissolve and disappear. Kneeling again, he placed the flask within the water and watched the ripples dance amongst the Leaves' reflection until the vessel was filled and the ripples ceased. Closing its lid, he returned the flask to its place and looked now to the ivy leaf he still held in the opposite hand. He thought to toss it away but found himself now unable. Instead, he placed the leaf under his chainmail, directly above his heart.

They managed their return far more swiftly than the outgoing journey and, in three simple weeks, they were returned. Upon arriving at the castle, Leanna hurried off to complete the grossly overdue chores she had forgone for the excursion. Madrick, instead, strolled pensively around the grounds, and even into town, before restoring himself to his chambers. When Leanna, at length, completed her duties late that eve, she approached him to ensure all was well and to see if there was anything else he might require before she left for home. She asked from the entryway, finding him at his desk, and held the door ajar.

"Yes, all is quite well, but do come in a moment, Leanna."

She did, turning to softly close the door behind her. Facing the king, she now saw he held a small decorative vial—translucent night-blue glass with silver embellishments—which was filled with a clear liquid and fastened to the end of a lengthy necklace chain.

"I filled my flask with water from the pool," he explained, "and took the vial from dear Albain's offices. I know not precisely what power it holds, but I thought: it was offered to me in my darkest hour only due to thy goodwill; so, in thy darkest hour, I would like my gratitude to be what offers it to thee, Leanna. Please, take it." He eagerly held out the vial of magic water to the page.

"Thank you, Your Highness," she said, accepting the gift.

"And," the king continued, a slight smirk pulling at the corners of his lips, "if thou art to continue bursting in upon an already angry Princess Isolda, I would suggest thou wearest the vial of healing water often."

Leanna laughed. "I shall wear it always," she swore.

"Good."

The youth looked to him with some kind of anticipatory curiosity and, guessing its cause but wishing not to speak of it, Madrick merely gave a small smile and offered a nod to indicate the page could be excused, but she could never be dismissed so simply.

"Have you seen them since we returned, Your Highness?"

"Not yet, Leanna."

"Wherefore?"

The king sighed. "There are issues of state that must occupy my entire mind and I wish not to bother them with thought of it."

"They love you."

"I have given them no cause for it of late."

"Leif will always love you, Sire."

Madrick dropped his brow into his palm and pressed upon his temples, willing his eyes to remain dry. "I have acted monstrously, reverted to everything I swore to never again be. I know that Leif's love is stronger than my shame, but until I feel worthy of a gift like that from one so good as they, I cannot allow myself to lean upon it. I must serve my people, and once I have done so I may tend to my own heart."

She paused a breath, unblinking. "Tomorrow, then?"

Madrick scoffed. "There is work to be done tomorrow."

"Then the day following?"

"Leanna—"

"The third day, then, surely? Sire, you must not let three whole days pass before addressing the pain between your hearts."

He sighed once more. "Very well, Leanna. Three days hence, I will speak to them."

"Good."

She began to start out the door, looking once more to the vial he had given her. "This cannot be nearly all from the flask, Sire," she said, turning back to him. "May I ask what you did with the rest?"

He shrugged sadly. "I poured the remainder down the well in town. It is empty now, but perhaps if the water returns it shall do for the villagers all it did for me."

"I think, so diluted, it is unlikely to have such an effect," she said with regret.

"I know. Still, a king must dream."

"Indeed." Leanna beamed. "You are a good king, Madrick Oxbien, and a good man. I have always known so."

Madrick looked to her, speechless from his vast emotion. He did all he could to express his gratefulness without a word. The serving girl understood well. She slid the chain around her neck, bowed, and slipped out the door. Madrick sat there, pensive, at his writing desk, then, lurching to action, stole some parchment from his drawer and took immediately to writing. Upon completion, he near upset his chair as he bounded from the chamber towards the home of the royal scribe. In his urgency, he forgot apologies for the hour and handed Margot Clark the scribbled page directly upon her opening the door.

"Scribe, copy this, and send one to every lagif of Masor before dawn."

"Every lagif! Sire, are you certain?"

"Most definitely. They must be informed."

"Of what, Your Majesty?" Margot examined the page before her but looked up to Madrick's swift and impassioned response.

"Their king has returned."

CHAPTER XVII

Love and Loyalty

"What is this, Madrick?"

Princess Isolda stormed into the throne room where King Madrick sat in his rightful royal seat the next morning.

"My apologies, Isolda, did Clark not write it clearly?"

Isolda sighed. "Brother, you cannot simply... take power."

"Why not? You did," he replied.

"That was an entirely separate circumstance."

"Yes," he rejoined. "One which has now been entirely resolved."

The princess was confounded. "What brought this on?" She asked. "Surely you had no sudden awakening. Last I saw you could hardly stand; or, at least, you had no interest in doing so."

He paused before revealing, "Leanna inspired me."

Isolda laughed furiously, then scowled. "That insolent page. What hath she done?"

"She opened my eyes to the truth. You have made a mockery of your position, Isolda, and I have come to set it right."

"Do not insult me, brother," Isolda growled. "I have done more to tend to this entire kingdom than thou hast done tending to thy own little bedchamber."

"I quite resent that. I have done a great deal for our people."

"You made some peasants feel important for a time. That is hardly a great deal."

Madrick stood from the throne, beginning to see his sister anew. After all this time, did she still think so little of him? "Isolda, how can you speak so cruelly about my achievements? I brought our nation a level of happiness I am not certain it had ever seen before."

"None of that would have been possible if I had not taken up your duties while you were wasting away with wine."

He nodded. "I appreciate your diligence, Masor is indeed better for it, but that does not delegitimize my later accomplishments, nor your improper priorities."

"My priorities?" She laughed. "With the exception of a brief period of years, your greatest priority has been seeing your flask is filled."

"That may be true, but—"

"You can find no objection to my claim, Brother, you know I am right."

He looked at her, astonished, taking a moment to think. Finally, he asked, "Why did you never help me?"

She paused, then shook her head. "Help you? I was occupied helping the kingdom."

"We have advisors and lagifs and servants to whom you delegated everything. If you had so desired, there was plenty of time in which you might have helped a member of your own family. Do you understand that I have been ill?"

"You were not ill, Madrick, you were drunk. The fault for that lies entirely with you."

"Yes, and I take responsibility for all I have done, but the fact remains that in order to change I needed assistance. I needed loving aid from someone who cared. Before Leif and Leanna, no one so much as offered that; least of all, you."

Isolda scoffed, flustered. "What was I meant to do? Should I have allowed the kingdom to perish while I nursed you?"

"No." He strode toward her, a saddened anger fueling his stride. "You could have helped me be a king. You had so much knowledge and understanding where I had so little, but my heart was good. Most of all, it is my passion for our people that has healed me. You could have helped me find that. You could have given me tasks, required me to make decisions. You could have taught me about leadership and shown me what it was that I was missing; instead, you simply took it all away from me. You left me with nothing."

"You did not want it, brother."

"I did not want any responsibility; I hardly wanted life at all." A cry crept into his throat. "Was that any reason to push me toward throwing it away?"

Isolda fell silent. A touch of apology entered her eye, and she looked down. "Perhaps I indeed have not been good to you, Brother." She met his gaze. "I am glad that, eventually, somebody was."

"Thank you."

"Nevertheless," she continued, "I have worked dreadfully hard to earn my right to lead this kingdom. I will not allow that right to be trampled upon."

His brow wrinkled in confusion. "Isolda, you do not have the right to lead the kingdom. That right is bestowed upon the oldest. That right is mine."

"But you relinquished it."

"I relinquished the duties, not the title and right. I am reclaiming what is mine."

Isolda's heart ran faster. "The lagifs will not follow you. In all matters of consequence, I am their queen, and they are quite pleased with it that way."

Madrick chuckled. "You believe the lagifs of Masor, every one of them the eldest of their line, would be pleased to allow you to do away with our ancient heirship laws so you could circumvent the order of our birth?"

"I would be doing no such thing. The law will still stand, we will simply deem it irrelevant for our circumstances."

"The law applies to the crown, Isolda. Do you mean to challenge the law? I assure you, there is no other way in which you can retake the power that belongs to me."

Isolda turned away and paced the room. When she spun back toward him, she stopped and looked down her nose at her sibling. "You disappear for weeks, probably squandering the last drink the nation has, then suddenly return with a grand declaration because of the meager suggestion of a servant. How is anyone meant to trust this 'passion' of yours will not once again prove temporary?"

Madrick deflated, dropping his gaze. "As much as I will work to prevent it, my leadership may very well be interrupted again by my weaknesses. Still, I am not encumbered with them now. I have found hope again, and I refuse to allow it to go to waste." He paced back toward the throne.

"Then I am afraid we have reached an impasse, for I will not so easily walk away from everything I have built."

Madrick sat in his grand seat and, leaning forward, casually rested his chin on his fists. "Explain yourself to me, Isolda, for I am truly bewildered. Do you not see that peace can only come about when, at large, people are content? If you continue to disregard the greatest portion of our people, then they will never be content, and we will never have peace. Why are you so intent to fight against my governing style?"

"Because it is not peace and contentment that I seek, Brother, but prosperity and grand historical notability. That is what my governing style is particularly suited to achieve."

Madrick rose off his knees and sat tall. "Then you truly care nothing for the lives of our people?"

"I care for our kingdom. I care for our name and our royal posterity. Is that not enough?"

"No, Isolda. It isn't." He sat back, relaxing into the throne. "If you wish to challenge me, so be it. I suppose, with the lagifs soon arriving, now is as good a time as any. Shall we tell them together how you mean to enact a coup and throw our nation even further into disarray?"

The princess clenched her fists and clamped her lips together as they twisted in contempt.

The king continued. "Unless those are the lengths to which you are willing to go, Sister, then I am the crown, and you are the vice-crown, and there is nothing to be done to change it. Do you wish to see how many of our respectable lagifs will support you in a baseless insurrection?"

"Don't be absurd."

"Very well, then. I am Crown. When the local lagifs arrive, and the others watch from their glass, I expect to see you treat me as such."

Isolda did all in her power to bury her contempt under a complying silence. She slowly strode back to stand beside her brother's throne, vowing to hold her tongue until she could discover the fragile fault which would bring down his witless reign permanently.

Just then they began to hear voices clamoring outside the hall; shortly thereafter, Leanna came stumbling into the room.

"Your Majesty"—and seeing Isolda—"Vice-Crown. They've arrived."

At a wave of Madrick's hand, the grand doors were unclosed. A torrent of lagifs spilled into the room and the mirror to the side glowed bright and vivid with sudden use. All quickly fell silent at the unusual sight of Madrick on, what they thought to be, Isolda's throne.

"My grand Masorians," Madrick began, rising to stand tall before them. "You will have received my note, and so I will not bore you with speeches of why I have gathered you here today. The length of it is this: You, gentry, are not all that holds value in the Masor population. In this time—dire for all—it is ever vital that the gentry, peasants, and royals together are able to collaborate so that we might lose as little from our numbers as life will allow.

I have come to understand you, lagifs, have found assistance in Isolda's castle despite otherwise our civilry having to fend for themselves. Even we here in the castle, I admit, have eaten better than most in these times. I will change that. The entirety of our resources in Masor shall now be fully accounted for, and distributed equally to all." Murmurs began to accumulate in the listeners, but Madrick continued, silencing them. "Save your thoughts, I will offer time for them. Now, only understand that this afternoon, assessors will begin arriving in the towns and villages, determining what is had and what is needed. I expect you, our noble lagifs, to cooperate best of all."

Lagif Oscar Bisqueth stepped forward from the crowd with a request, now, to speak. King Madrick allowed it.

"Forgive me, dear King, say again. Surely a lagif might receive more than a peasant."

"Why is that, Bisqueth? Will they eat more than a farmer?" Madrick asked.

"Perhaps not, Sire, but..." Bisqueth floundered, then found his pride. "Well, we are gentry!"

"Indeed, and as the gentry I trust you will respect your king's decree. You asked that I say again, so I shall: All in the kingdom shall receive equal, including you, myself, and all others—" Madrick looked now to Leanna with the sudden thought, "except peasants with larger families, perhaps they should receive more—" Leanna shrugged and nodded while the lagifs groaned. "Regardless," the king continued, "none will have luxury, but all will fill their plates; at least, so long as there is anything to provide."

Lagif Lilac Huebert stepped forth and exclaimed, "The gentry are not meant to live like peasants, Your Highness. We can pay for the extra rations!"

"What good will gold do for a kingdom that starves?" Madrick rejoined. He returned to sit in his chair. "I have made my decree, and it shall be carried out as such. Consider this session adjourned."

The lagifs all looked to Isolda, but the princess simply shook her head in helpless disdain. Before any could begin their disgruntled shuffle toward the door, Kn. Degora entered the hall, leading in a strong older peasant who held a bucket.

"Your Highness," Kn. Degora began addressing the throne, then looked from it to Isolda, then back to Madrick, making all attempts to hide that she was shaken. "This woman would not be halted at the gate. She requests an urgent word with you," then added, "King."

"This is highly irregular, Kn. Degora," Isolda began. "These lagifs have no time—"

"I wish to hear her," Madrick interrupted. "Come forth."

The woman began a procession through the throne room, walking down an aisle created in the space left by the lagifs who parted to the sides. The difference between them was clear with a glance to their footwear alone. The woman's dusty sandals were a stark contrast to the heeled boots and embroidered patterns of the wealthier feet around her. Nonetheless, to see the confidence in the woman's eye, one would never suppose she thought herself less than any of her fellow Masorians.

She kneeled before the king, placing down her enclosed bucket, then stood again.

"What hast thou brought to us?" King Madrick asked.

"Water," the woman replied. A sound of envy erupted from every throat in the chamber. She continued. "I regret this here is all I managed to carry, Your Highnesses, but the information I can provide will wet many more a parched tongue than one more bucket carried on my old back."

Degora, without order, stepped before the woman and lifted the lid from the container to see inside.

"It is water indeed," she gawked. "Water, Your Highness!"

"Miraculous!" said the king. "Whither hast thou acquired it?"

"Keep naught in concealment," Isolda added.

"I meant never to conceal a thing;" the woman began, "however, seems so I've done it without that intent. Mine is one of the families that lives on the sands of the River. Me, my children, my ancestors, we've all lived off the River since long before any Oxbien e'er thought to call the land 'Masor.' As it is, Sires, we hadn't known such a terrible drought had been hurting people down South, or for certain at the castle! 'Course would've said something earlier but was no one coming round to tell the River Dwellers things had changed. Sure, rain hasn't been in, tide's been low, and the heat—well, something dreadful odd about the heat—but we and our northern friends across the bridge have been living off the River all the same."

"Your crops, have they grown?" The king asked.

"Not ours, but, just across the River grain grows a plenty, and them that tends it have been more than generous."

All in the room stood silent a moment as the court heard the news.

"Is it enough to feed the kingdom?" Madrick urged.

"Might not be so much for a whole kingdom to get particu'ly comfortable over, but enough to keep it living, that's for certain."

"Ha!" Laughed the king. "This is brilliant."

"Might I inquire?" Isolda began, a jealous eye to the king. He hid a distrustful glare, but he nodded and she continued, "If you all had gone such time unaware of the extremity of our conditions, what, prithee, brought it at last to attention?"

"You won't believe the tale, Your Majesty, but I swear it came to me in a dream."

"A dream?" Madrick asked, interest piqued.

"Just so, Your Highness. I remember it more vivid than anything, though a week ago now it was. The voice of some girl, the likes of which I swear I never heard, jolted me from a dream about—well, that's beside our purpose here—but I started seeing these scenes of Masor; villages, farms, towns, hither city!, like I was a cloud flying over it all, except I couldn't've been since there were none. Everything was so dry, not a drop in the wells—you know how it is—and the smoke. All that smoke, the sun burning red behind it. This voice, this girl, she told me how she'd seen the Gwahanu and knew I could help the whole kingdom if only I knew the truth. Woke up straight then, I did, and I bounded out to the nearest village, asked how things were, and heard again all that I'd just been told while I was asleep! Was right then I hurried back for a bucket then hurried here. Been walking all week, I have."

"Unusual," Isolda declared.

Leanna looked down to hide her pride.

Madrick felt the same as Isolda, this being now his second recent meeting with inexplicable magic, but all the same, "Why worry on that now?" he said. "There is sustenance at the Gwahanu enough to save our people, and surely we shall make good use of it."

An anxious breath, so long held, now released throughout the chamber as all accepted the good fortune. The king asked the woman her name.

"Lucinda Stone, Your Highness," she said proudly.

"Lucinda, the crown is grateful to thee," Madrick pronounced. "Prithee, rest today here in the castle. We shall gather a force that will return with thee to the River at dawn tomorrow and carry the resources to every person in our land."

"Thank you," Lucinda said. "Thank you, Your Highness."

The king went on. "I hereby place my page, Leanna, as the head of this force. Leanna, thou hast a greater understanding of the townspeople in need. I want thee at the forefront. Thou shalt choose thy knights from those who remain and accompany them to the River. But now, wilt thou please show Lucinda to a chamber where she may rest."

"It will be an honor, Your Majesty. Thank you for your trust." Leanna bowed, and Madrick smiled. "Come, Lucinda," she said. "Follow me. You have my greatest esteem for making the journey here."

Lucinda stared in amazement at the young girl whose voice was so familiar. She burned to ask, but at the page's knowing smile, Lucinda simply mirrored the countenance and followed Leanna out of the throne room.

The court was filtered from the chamber until King Madrick and Princess Isolda stood alone inside.

"Madrick," Isolda began sternly, then started once more with an attempt at gentility. "Brother, wherefore would you appoint your servant to charge this mission when you have a sister—a vice-crown—far more qualified and willing?"

"I made myself clear," said the king. "She hath a better understanding of the people."

"But I am the princess, Madrick, she is a page! Moreover, she has so recently been the cause of our intensified destruction. How can you reward her so?"

Madrick thought solemnly, then responded with genuine truth. "She brought me life again when no one else could. Despite her recent error, grave as it was, she is wise, and she means well."

"What could she have done that could have such an effect?"

He smiled, unwilling to let Isolda twist the true memory. "She said I was a good king," he replied simply.

Isolda scoffed. "She blinds you, Madrick. That page will be the downfall of your reign."

He smirked and raised a brow, standing and beginning to walk out of the room, stopping beside her on his path. "I may be able to say the same of you, Isolda," he warned, then, pleased with himself, left the chambers. Isolda stalked out behind him, fuming, and halted before Kn. Degora who had remained to guard the royals in the hall.

"Degora," she said with quiet fervor. "I need something against her, something damning."

The knight sighed. "I have followed her for months, My Liege, and discovered nothing beside that the servant is the daughter of another servant. Perhaps there is nothing more to find."

"What of when she went into the Woods?"

"Many a young Masorian has done the same, and it has come to nothing since. The page may be more simple than you imagine."

"You would deny me?" The princess's eyes burned into the knight.

Startled, she replied, "Never, Your Majesty."

"Go," Isolda demanded. "Find something, anything, and be quick about it."

"I will do what I can."

"Do more," she ordered, then stormed off down the hall.

As the first rays of light brushed low against the horizon and the color of early evening Sky began to impede upon that of the noon, Leanna sighed in relief, the final preparations now being set for the next day's expedition. In the excitement of the hour, she had suppressed her anxieties around leading such an important mission and now, when they were allowed to settle, she realized just how breathless they had made her. She stood now on the steps outside the main castle entryway and watched as the knights she had been directing now scurried out of the courtyard to pack their essentials. The sun beheld her from an even level, hovering just above the citadel wall, nearing scarlet in its vicious blaze. She watched it in return, daring its rays to harm her, and it seemed to acquiesce, sinking slight. The slightest hint of a cool wind blew through the courtyard and Leanna, marveling at the moving air, fell to relax in her solitude upon the steps.

Her thoughts then turned to Kennedy. Leanna realized now they had not shared a dream these last several nights, and she wondered how Kennedy might be occupying herself. The thought was due to no happenstance, for Kennedy in that moment wished dearly to speak to Leanna and, sensing so, the latter opened their channel for mental communications.

Leanna? Kennedy's voice rang through clear, and its sound brought a smile to Leanna's lips, as well as a warm flush to her cheeks.

Looking out towards the Sky, Leanna answered, "I am here, Kennedy."

Leanna, I must see thee. She sounded urgent.

"Art thou well? We can dream tonight as soon as—"

No, the fairy interrupted, *not a dream, my friend. Please. Come to me. Meet me in the Woods tonight.*

Leanna explained to her all that had gone on that day and the importance of her preparedness to leave for the Gwahanu at dawn.

Kennedy was sympathetic but begged again.

Something has happened to me, Leanna. I am not harmed; still, I am frightened.

Without further question, Leanna decided, "I will come. Whither will I find thee?"

Shall we meet in the Forest of Lufian? It is still remembered for the Oxbien's death; no fairy would wander there now, and Masorians never traverse that far into the Wood. We will be alone.

"Lufian?" Leanna confirmed, brow raised at the thought.

Kennedy replied shyly, *If it seems suitable to thee.*

Leanna beamed. "I think no place should suit our meeting more."

Neither of them could see the other smile, but both felt the glow of their feeling. They set out at once.

After weaving behind townhomes and between shopfronts, Leanna stopped just before entering the Wood, searching the space behind her, ensuring herself she was foolish to feel anyone might be following her. Casting aside doubt, she walked amidst the Infinites and picked up speed, continuing faster until she found herself running, and did not stop for even a breath before standing at last beneath the magical canopy of the Forest of Lufian. It was not long before she saw a bright iridescent glow reflect off the Trees before her. She turned behind her to see the source.

"Kennedy," she gasped. "Is it thee?"

"It is, Leanna," the fairy replied.

"Thy wings!" Indeed, the violet complexion of the young fairy was no longer matched by wings of her hue, nor had they but a simple lavender shine. Leanna gazed in awe at her dear companion whose wings had mystically transformed into articles of such splendor with every color shining from within them. Anchoring the sight was Kennedy's fine countenance that Leanna had only beheld behind the veil of visions for so many years, and at last she spoke the only words that appeared to her mind. "Thou art a beauty," she said.

Kennedy turned away from the kindness. "Think the sight of me not lovely, for my greatest fear is now forever attached to my back."

Leanna stepped nearer. "I don't understand. What happened?"

"Dost thou possibly recall, long ago, I might have spoken to thee about how the heir to the always unmarried, always childless Queen of Alquoria is chosen?"

"Isn't it that the magic within the Anwansi Pool somehow designates someone itself?"

"Yes, and dost thou perchance recall how it makes its choice known?"

Leanna thought a moment then gasped in remembrance. "The wings of white!"

Kennedy nodded, fearful to even say it aloud. "Anwansi has chosen me to be its queen. A queen, Leanna! What am I to do as Queen?"

The human smiled. "All thou wert meant to! This is glorious. Why dost thou fear?" Leanna asked.

"I am disliked," Kennedy began. "I am a menace to the traditions of Alquoria. At only sixteen, I have thoroughly succeeded in turning away any esteem the Elders might have had for me. I have made good friends of warriors and commoners, but the royals at large shun me. If ever a queen was to be locked away from her people, deep underneath the pool, never to see the sun, I would be she! What am I to do in a prison, Leanna?"

The human rushed to the fairy's side and stroked her arms, speaking with a soft touch to her firm tone. "Thou wouldst wait but a moment until I could arrive and rescue thee," she said. "There is nothing in this land capable of stifling thy purpose, nothing that could silence thy voice. It is thy spirit that always empowered mine. There is nothing in this world I would not do for thee, and if ever thou art at risk of forgetting that, I shall remind thee, my love."

A silence fell between the two as they held one another. Their chests rose and fell at the mercy of their accelerating breaths, and their gazes hovered between the eyes and the quivering lips of the young woman before them. Kennedy looked shyly to the ground.

"How is it that between the two of us we manage to find all the trouble?" Her wings lost a touch of their light as she spoke. "Thou art despised by thy princess as I am by the Elders." Leanna chuckled in agreement. "If only thy father had not surrendered the Jewel to Guiomar, we might have faced only one complication at a time."

Leanna looked to Kennedy and gently raised her chin so they met eyes.

"I am not so afraid of trouble," she said. "Not when thou art beside me."

Kennedy sighed, the corners of her lips finding their warmest smile.

"I love thee, Leanna," she said.

In an instant of the fullest connection, every truth they held was shared between their minds, and with not a single moment more left wasted apart, they were then wrapped in the embrace of passion. Each one's lips parted to become ever more attached to that of the other and they drew their waists together, arms tightly encircling one another, as every color spark rained down on them from Kennedy's wings in a shower of excitement and care.

The Trees of Lufian smiled.

But Kn. Degora, concealed behind overgrown roots, wrinkled her nose and turned away from the treacherous page who fraternized with fairies and who had familial ties to the Jewel that had caused the terrible state of their kingdom. All that had perplexed the castle about the young Masorian who would go to such lengths to defend the people of Pavoline now fell into perfect clarity. Surely, it was more than sufficient to eliminate any of the page's influence over the king.

Late that night, once the two lovers had—at great length—persuaded themselves to part, Leanna snuck through the door of the small cottage she shared with her mother only to find, upon entering, that she stood in the little house alone. She lit a candle and discovered a small parchment with a few words, though none written in her mother's hand.

Come to the castle, she read.

With wrinkled brow, Leanna diligently extinguished the flame, walked out the door, and headed straight to the palace. Kn. Degora waited on the castle steps, unmoving, as though carved from their very stone. Leanna entered the courtyard at a brisk pace, slowing now as Degora started towards her.

"Have you seen my mother, Degora? She is not at home."

Kn. Degora said nothing, but secured Leanna by the arm and led her inside.

"What is this?" Leanna asked as she was pulled up the steps. She received no answer but knew better than to struggle against the knight.

Shortly thereafter, they entered the throne room, the several candelabras only shining a dim light on the scene. King Madrick sat solemn on the throne. Princess Isolda stood proud beside him, and—Leanna was astonished, then vexed, to see—Esta knelt in drying tears at Isolda's feet. Isolda glanced to Madrick, but he would not raise his gaze from the ivy leaf he examined in his hand. Degora shoved Leanna's shoulder to make her kneel. Once on the hard floor, Leanna glared at Isolda, and the princess glared in return. Isolda never broke her gaze with the page as she spoke.

"Kn. Degora, report again your finding for the court."

She did:

"Leanna Page was found conspiring with a fairy royal—"

"Conspiring?" Leanna interrupted.

"I saw thee tonight," the knight snarled.

Leanna's eyes widened in shock, then wrinkled in rage, finally simmering into a stoic understanding. "You have misconstrued the meeting, knight."

The king shook his lowered head, scowling in fury. "Why should we believe thee, with your actions in Pavoline, and now this? Fairies!" An alarmed silence followed his rageful question.

Leanna looked to him with sincerity, bemused that his trust could dissipate so suddenly. "I wish you well, Madrick. Same for all Masor." When she managed to win Madrick's glance, Isolda stole it away.

"All she says is a lie, Brother. What loyal servant has once been smiling to their kingdom's enemy?"

"The fairies are not your enemy," Leanna tried.

"They took my parents from me," the king reminded her.

"They didn't."

"Cease thy lies!" He bellowed. "I have told thee of them all these years. How hast thou maintained thy delusions?"

"I know the truth of them, Your Highness, I always have." Leanna's heart raced. "It is you who are mistaken. Guiomar Ranzentine is the enemy of the Oxbiens, not the fairies. It is he who brought on this drought, it is he who—"

Isolda interrupted, prodding. "Yes, and who offered him the power to ravage us so?"

Leanna, bewildered at Isolda's accusatory tone, stared to the princess until remembering Kennedy's words about her father and the Jewel—the same words Kn. Degora would have heard. Her gaze fell to her mother who responded with naught but apologetic helplessness. The young page collected her breaths, then looked back to the royalty before her.

"My father erred in an effort to support us."

Isolda turned to the king, "A father loyal to Pavoline, might we recall," then returned to Leanna. "One who has intentionally doomed our kingdom. Didst thou make any effort to stop him? Didst thou think to inform us? We might have undone it while we had the Ranzentines in our castle."

"I tried to warn you, Your Highness! You would not hear of it. What else could I have done?"

"Thy warnings might have been more explicit. We might have sought the proof!" The princess screeched.

"I would have had to relay my knowledge, and my reason for it, thither before Guiomar. He would have murdered my father in the next instant."

"That is not the concern of Masor," Isolda replied.

Leanna remained stern. "I shall not apologize for protecting my father's life when all he has done in all his days has been to protect mine."

Isolda clicked her tongue. "Thou art a traitor, dangerously disloyal to our kingdom."

Leanna shook her head, astounded, seeking to defend herself. "I helped return the health of our king, did I not?"

Isolda scowled, and Madrick felt the knife of betrayal fall deeper in his chest. Wounded, he asked, "With what magic, Leanna? I persuaded myself those stories of the waterfall might have come from within Masor so I did not have reason to distrust thee, but it is impossible. I know of no magic that does not have root in the world of fairies. Art thou so intertwined with them that they share with thee their magical secrets?"

Leanna sighed. No effective lie occurred to her, and she knew to refuse him an answer was to imply her guilt. She thought of Kennedy, fighting proudly through the disapproval of the royals, and knew at once her only path forward was through the truth. She looked straight to the king.

"There were no stories about the pool, Your Highness," she began. "Knowledge of it came to me in a vision. In the same manner, I have communed with my father as he sits trapped in the cells of Pavoline, kept locked away by Guiomar to unearth my mother and I who know his secrets. In mystic dreams, I have met with the same beauteous fairy I did tonight near nightly since my youth; and, it was that same magic—born embedded within me—that permitted my thoughts to carry into the dreams of Lucinda Stone."

Madrick stood, stunned, and Isolda stared at the page in awe.

Leanna continued. "Your Highness, in truth, I do not know what I am, but I know I am part of Masor; and part of Pavoline; and, in equal share, part of the fairies, whether somehow in body, or in spirit and love alone. I have no loyalty to any of the human monarchs in our world that could cause me to revoke that love."

Madrick crushed the ivy leaf he held in his seething fist.

"If—" Leanna went on. "If you have such hatred of them that you will not see beyond it to the truth, then you must let your hatred fall upon me in its path.

I will no longer pretend to favor your delusions—My King."

"Dungeon," Madrick croaked, leaving no space for Isolda to demand the same. Leanna raised a prideful chin, hiding the ache in her heart. Madrick looked to the knight expectantly. "This instant, Kn. Degora. Remove this traitor from my sight."

"Yes, Your Highness." Degora secured Leanna's arms behind her and muscled her around toward the door.

"Wait!" Leanna pleaded.

"I have no heart left for thee, page," the king declared.

Though his words came at her like daggers, she shook her head. "Not for me. I beg you, find sympathy for my mother." Esta cried at her daughter's strength. "She hath done no wrong in all her life but fall into a love that left the world inexplicably with me. Do not hold her responsible for my crimes."

"She shan't be employed in the castle!" Isolda scoffed.

Madrick nodded, "But we shall not pursue her beyond that. Esta, thou hast my word. Thou art not welcome here, but thou art free." He turned back to Leanna. "Now go." He waved at Kn. Degora who continued to march Leanna from the chamber. She had one final glance to her mother before the grand doors were shut between them.

From a small, wide-eyed trespasser, to servant, to traitor, Leanna walked back through her memories of the Masorian castle, shoved now down halls and stairwells she had never yet seen where the tapestries ended, windows became scarce, and a few meager ensconced torches were all that attempted to shed light on the dark stone walls. At last, at Kn. Degora's direction, she walked into her own cell and watched with dread as the bars closed in around her.

CHAPTER XVIII

Friends, Enemies

After Leanna was marched from the throne room, Madrick stood painfully still while Isolda ordered Esta to get hence, and the distressed mother flew from the room. Once Esta had gone, Isolda turned to Madrick and expressed her assumption that, given the night's discovery, he must intend to rescind his recent proclamations.

"No," he said. "All I spoke to the lagifs remains true, Isolda. Whatever the knights collect at the Gwahanu will be allocated equally to all no matter their rank, only now the force will be led by Kn. Pouray instead of..." his voice trailed off but the princess knew well of whom he spoke. Madrick returned to his seat on the throne and rested his eyes on a tired palm while Isolda berated him with a multitude of reasons why he was a fool to disregard the gentry, not to mention the insult it was to let her own royal skills go unutilized. Although it may have felt otherwise to the princess, Madrick truly had been paying her an ear until now when he felt a strange, though painless, sensation at his temple as though something were pulling on his mind.

Madrick, he heard, and he jolted his gaze to his sister.

She looked to him expectantly. "Madrick, are you listening?"

He said nothing, and as Isolda's lips began again to move he heard instead entirely separate words from a distinctly separate voice.

My Liege, please. I must speak with you. You cannot leave me in here, I despise confinement.

Madrick held up a hand to Isolda, entreating silence, as he rose from his chair and strode to a corner of the chamber.

"Leanna?" he said.

"The page again. What of her?" Isolda inquired.

You do hear me, Madrick.

"Quiet Isolda, she speaketh to me." He felt his brow.

"You can hear her? In your head?" The princess walked round the king as though expecting to find Leanna in his ear. He turned from her.

"Speak not to me with thy magic, traitor," Madrick growled.

Then hear me in the cells and I shall have no need. In all these years, I have earned that at least.

Strong as he struggled against it, the king could not help hearing the voice of a troubled friend.

"Come, Isolda," he said, and he started toward the dungeon.

When Leanna saw the two royals approach, she stood and placed a hand on the bars of her cell.

"King." Then in a lower, quite unhappy register, she added, "Princess." Isolda crossed her arms and stood beside her brother.

"What is this, Leanna?" Madrick scowled.

"You must know, Sire, that I am not such a danger to the public that I must be hidden away. If you hate me so, banish me, but lock me not behind bars."

The king endeavored to speak, but Isolda answered in his place. "The concern is not how thou might harm some peasant, but how the diffusion of thy knowledge and ideas might harm the Crown."

"Foolhardy!" Leanna laughed. "There is nothing in my mind that cannot reach beyond confinement."

"Can it reach beyond death?" Isolda asked.

"We have not discussed such things," Madrick broke in.

Leanna quieted, watching intently as the royals turned to one another.

The princess was evidently decided. "Brother, for what other cause would we have detained the traitor if not to hold her for an execution?"

Madrick's brow grew tight, and his breath unsteady. "I had not considered it."

"You still care for the child," Isolda realized with disdain. "You are of no mind to be deciding upon the necessary verdicts."

Images flashed before Leanna's vision of her father in his cell in Pavoline. Guiomar was approaching with the glint of expectation in his eye. Leanna shook herself back to her own place, her own cell.

"I am of perfect mind, Isolda, and I wish us to not be hasty in this matter."

"There is no matter, Madrick. Our law is clear on the sentence for treachery, and you have recently reminded us both about the importance of the crown abiding by its own laws."

"Perhaps a trial—"

Guiomar's voice rang in Leanna's ear, speaking to Byrdon. "Tell me what thou knowest of the fairies of the Wood."

Leanna watched her father raise a daring chin. "A respectable Pavol hath no knowledge of them at all, Sire," he said.

"Thou art no respectable Pavol."

"A trial would reveal nothing we have not already tonight been acquainted with," Isolda said. "The same decision falls upon us."

"Upon me, Isolda," Madrick said.

Byrdon: "Why, King, would you desire it?"

Guiomar smiled.

Madrick: "What if there were some manner in which we could make use of her abilities, same as we do the mystical glass?"

"There would be no way of assuring she did not use them against us!"

"We do not, in truth, understand her full intentions."

Guiomar's smile widened and voice whispered low: "Knowledge of my intentions is for myself alone, and then for my knights as soon as I can provide greater intelligence of my desired target."

Byrdon: "I have no reason to help you."

"Thou dost know of them then."

"If I did?"

"What if it meant thy freedom?"

Isolda: "'An opportunity for redemption'!? Brother, be reasonable."

Leanna realized she was hearing two conversations at once, and she was missing things.

"She is the reason I am a king, Isolda, even if it was done through treachery."

"Absurd. You are a king because you are the first-born of the Oxbiens."

"You should know best of all it is not so simple."

Byrdon: "Do you truly swear it?"

"On my honor as a king."

"And everything I know of you; you'll free me despite it?"

"With the understanding, of course, if it is revealed, I no longer have reason to allow thee to live." After a nod from his prisoner, King Guiomar asked, "Is our bargain struck?"

"Very well."

"Good. A scribe will record thy knowledge throughout the night, and I shall make arrangements for thy release in the morning."

Madrick, conceding: "Perhaps it would be right for me to give you this choice, Isolda. I fear, despite it all, my care for her remains." The king glanced to his page, but her eyes were unseeing, lost in the horror of her visions from Pavoline.

"That is wise, Brother. Of course, the execution order shall require your seal." Having left the cells, Guiomar turned to the knight standing guard.

The king of Masor looked down in pain at Isolda's words, then nodded, turning away from the cage.

Guiomar: "At first light, after the scribe completes his task, take the prisoner to the western bastion and toss him off the side into the Forest of Beasts. Just ensure that he dies."

"No!" Leanna screamed, returning from her visions in a paroxysm of distress.

"Silence, page. Thy fate is sealed," Isolda declared.

"I must go to Pavoline."

"Ha!" the princess exclaimed in victory. "So the traitor doth confess."

Leanna fumed at the plain miscontrual. "This is out of no loyalty to the wicked king." She turned her plea to Madrick. "I have just seen it now; he is going to kill my father."

Madrick gave her half a gaze, confounded and unwillingly sympathetic.

"As would we," Isolda rejoined, "If we controlled his custody."

Gripping the bars of her cell, Leanna kept her gaze to Madrick. "Please, Sire." She turned her eyes down regretfully. "It is my own doing that brought Guiomar to his current dominion. I cannot now see him take a life so dear to me, not after all our family has endured, not after all I have witnessed already."

"Then don't watch," Isolda said, and she turned, ushering her brother out of the dungeons.

"He is going to invade the Wood!" The royals stopped and turned to her with skeptical curiosity. "He said as much, I saw it now. One day, if he decides to use the Jewel against it, he even may succeed. If you cannot bring yourselves to care that an entire people might be destroyed in his quest, at the least have concern that Guiomar's influence could grow so vast."

"How would thou saving thy father prevent this?" the king asked.

"My father and I know every crime which that king means to keep from his people. More even than you, Oxbiens." Isolda raised a brow, but kept silent. "If I could only prevent him from destroying us, we might reveal all. Pavoline would rebel against him."

The princess shook her head, reasoning, "There is no knowing who might rise in his place. Such an event may bring Masor only more destruction."

Madrick flinched in disagreement. "Could it bring more destruction than Guiomar Ranzentine?"

"We cannot be certain! If Pavoline did rebel, some uneducated peasant might take the throne."

"That would be more terrible to you than our current circumstances?"

Isolda scoffed. "I will not deign to diplomacy with some rebel commoner who has no right to the throne."

Madrick was astonished. "No matter," he said, "as you are only vice-crown I shall see to it you would have no need."

She grew grave. "Do not be silly, Brother."

"If there is opportunity, at so little risk to ourselves, to remove Guiomar from power, we have every responsibility to allow the attempt. In the name of King Petrenair, at least!"

"You are speaking of freeing a traitor."

"I am speaking of freeing the world."

"I forbid this, Madrick."

"As Crown, I disagree." He strode to a fixture on the dungeon wall and took up from it the keys to the cells.

"No," Isolda tried. "No!"

But the king was resolute. He unlocked the cage and held the swinging bars aside for Leanna as she ran out between the royals and down to the end of hall.

"Leanna!" Madrick called, and she stopped, turning to him with a hint of gratitude, expecting the spark of friendship to be reignited in his eyes. She was dispirited then to see the sorrow they instead beheld. "Death upon thy return," he told her.

She absorbed the sentence with a weight on her chest that nearly downed her, but, with all strength and stoicism, she took a sharp inhale, straightened, nodded, and flew from the dungeon. The Oxbiens exchanged neither word nor glance as they themselves exited and retired into their own chambers, sinking into their own thoughts.

The heart-aching page, with now no such employment, thought little on the particulars of whither her feet took her, only that they led away from the castle, and swiftly. More swiftly, in truth, than was perfectly possible. If she was to save her father, it would be imperative that she manage a journey in a single night that it was unheard of to complete in under a fortnight. Then she thought of the caves. Since they no longer held their magic from the Jewel, the time to travel them would be the same as the road above, but there would be no hills or turns or well-intentioned villagers to slow her. She had surprised herself with her speed before, perhaps, with her every mightiest effort, incessantly maintained, she could bring herself to her destination in time. She forced the impossibility of it out of her mind. It was her only choice.

She started down the large market road, turning off where she knew the secret entrance to be hidden. Stopping before the well, pulse running wild, she examined the thick ivy that had grown in every crevice of its stones. Despite the terrible inconvenience of the occasion, she had to confess it was rather beautiful in the moonlight.

Having at last managed to pry the bucket free and having taken it to the bottom of the cave, Leanna began to run. The caves were nothing but darkness and Leanna implored her mind to lose all its sense of space and pain as she ran like never a human dared try run before. Her legs wailed and a sharpness in her side began to shriek, but she paid it no heed. She gave all her thought to the darkness; or so she tried. In all of her years, the life she knew lay consistently on fragile footing. To be found as a child had caused upheaval enough, but now, more, she had been found out. What was left for her to do? Whither was she to go?

Pavoline. Nowhere else was of any consequence. If she could only save her father, and then the world, from Guiomar's control, perhaps her family might all be whole again. They could leave the royals behind, maybe join the River Dwellers at the Gwahanu straight. They could live in peace. They could be happy. It was the only future she could conjure where her life maintained any of its former normality.

If she could only stop the king...

After what might have been moments or hours, Leanna fell to her knees, her wrists painfully finding the dirt of the floor. She stared into the darkness and watched as images of the Pavoline castle intermingled with those Masor, flashing between royals, friends and enemies all the same, and wondered how any of them, in truth, might be capable of bringing about a lasting wellness to the world; if, even, they would ever make an honest attempt.

In the caves, Leanna grasped the vial of water from the Aldorian Pool she still wore on the long chain hidden beneath her shirt, remembering what goodness, even if small, some kings could indeed be capable of. Perhaps, if she succeeded now, she might regain the trust of the one who had been her friend.

Leanna raised her gaze, remaining in the dirt, and suddenly discovered a slight, dim, flickering glow pulsing all around her. With a sigh, she realized she could see through it the outlines of cots and pots and bookshelves, the furnishing of the cavern of her early youth, and she understood suddenly that she had already come to be directly under the Gwahanu. She wondered now whether she had managed the impossible speed, or if the long caves had managed—without the source of their magic—to shorten themselves in her aid. Not stopping to question it now, she implored any magic the caves could hold to help her fly, and she started off again, indeed at a speed closer to flying than she had ever imagined. Her boots remained plodding on the ground, but Leanna was certain she felt the wind at her back.

At last, she emerged from behind the thicket that hid the Pavoline entrance to the caves, and she looked for a brief moment at the Infinites who were beginning to be silhouetted against the rising sun. She continued on now, running through the unfamiliar streets of Pavoline, vaguely remembering the wide path lined with the merchants opening their shops which would lead her to the castle. As she ran, she kept half a mind trained on her father as the knight unlocked his cell and began to lead him out of the dungeon.

"Would you care for a pair of fairy-wings, girl?" The croaky voice of a merchant jolted her from her steady path. She looked, appalled, at the small green wings, pale from death, that the old woman held out in her path. "A secret import from Masor. Some may hate you for wearing such a charm, but it is said it will bring you strength!"

Leanna meant to curse her in disgust but the merchant's poor, large eyes halted her spiteful tongue. She settled simply to confirm the path to the castle, and the woman pointed in the direction she had been headed. Thankful, Leanna disguised her contempt in a smile and continued on.

She stopped short just steps before the gate that would bring her into the courtyard of the palace.

"Dost thou mean to enter?" A guard queried, but she merely stood gawking at the wood, her countenance full of anguish and disbelief. She watched now in visions as her father fell from the castle tower, the knight's poignard falling with him, the blade pierced fatally through her father's heart. She watched as the light in his eyes flickered out, and his body crashed into the forest below. The image of it was seared into her memory. Awakening from her daze, she pounded her heel into the center of the gate, and, with the aid of a sudden wind, the doors crashed open. She stormed inside.

"Guiomar! Whither art thou? Murderer, face thy crimes!"

The guard who had spoken to her before hurried now to her side, warning, "Hast thou gone mad? He is the king."

"He is a plague on this land," she replied, and several servants and merchants began to gather and observe, chattering to one another in amazement. The guard said nothing; he only stood at attention and faced the steps of the palace entrance as King Guiomar walked out upon the landing, having heard the commotion. Leanna looked him directly in the eye.

"This king hath no right to the throne!" she said. "Petrenair himself revoked it upon discovering the consequences of his son's wickedness." Gasps and whispers rippled through the crowd, now joined by a handful of wary knights. "If only the good king hadn't been murdered—by his own son!—perhaps his plans to appoint a separate successor might have been carried out."

"She lieth! Who is this menace?" Guiomar demanded of his knights, feigning innocence so well as ignorance. They all shook their heads, unknowing. "Seize her," he commanded. The girl remained strong against the now familiar sensation of knights restraining her biceps. She suddenly felt her journey's end might be coming near, and it brought her an unexpected calm.

"Do away with me, Your Highness, but you can never do away with the truth. Mine is not the first father you have killed, and yours was not the first king."

"Take her away. Her senses have evidently taken their leave."

Leanna allowed herself to be guided below the castle, beaming at the image she left in her wake of a distrustful people looking unsure at their fuming king.

She was tossed once more into a dark cell, shivering at the touch of the stones, cold and damp, unlike those of the previous eve which had been dried and warmed by the heat of Masor. She heard the king's footsteps booming down the dungeon corridor.

"Thee," Guiomar snarled, instantly having recognized Leanna, the page with the curious ability to always be where she should not.

"I am grieving my father this day. Let me be." She disregarded his approach, closing her eyes, sitting with pride upon the ground.

"Let thee be?!" Guiomar laughed and spun away before returning to face his prisoner. "Byrdon's child, a Masorian? Still, I should have guessed it," he snarled. "Who else would spin wild accusations of murder in front of my people? But hast thou not been in Masor—how couldst thou have known so instantly of his death?"

Leanna remained with unopened eyes, saying nothing.

Guiomar brought his snarl nearer and wrapped his right hand around a bar of the cell, growling, "Dost thou think lowly pages can deny me my reign?"

A glint of the sunrise shone through a crack in the dungeon stones and reflected off the Jewel of Nebulous as it sat atop the king's fingers. The light fell upon Leanna's eye, persuading them to open. She stared at the gem in contempt, every inch of her burning to take the Jewel from him so she might crush the object of wickedness beneath her heel. The pounding of her heart compelled her to obey her instincts and she stood, taking a step toward the bars, but Guiomar stepped back, the Jewel then moving out of reach as the king attempted to mask his being startled by the actions of a measly servant. Leanna tore her gaze from the Jewel and gave it menacingly to the king as he cautiously spoke on, quiet enough that none of the guards in the hall could understand the words.

"My comfort in this," he said, "is I am privileged to watch as you realize all your precious truth-saying will come to nothing." Guiomar kept his gaze in contact with Leanna's eyes and, shocked at the terror he felt taking in the strength of her stare, he forced himself to goad her further. "I have won, and I will continue to do so evermore."

"Not against the Infinite Wood."

He worked to suppress his stupefaction at her knowledge of his plots and made certain not to let on that he was bewildered, returning to the volume of pride. "I am not afraid of the Trees. I will bring new honor to the Ranzentine name!"

"Thou shalt be remembered for nothing but shame."

The guards shivered to hear this young girl speak so. Guiomar burned.

"I am the king! Thou shalt speak to me with respect."

"Thou dost not deserve the respect of a rat, and thou art even less likely to receive it from me."

"Who dost thou think thyself to be, page?"

All resignation fled from her, the intensity of furious purpose flooding her spirit. "I am the one who shall stop you, Guiomar Ranzentine."

He felt clearly, as did she, the air between them shift as the two came to level with one another as adversaries. The king tried to lower her again, allowing his breath to drip into her resolute countenance. "With what?" he mocked. "Thou hast nothing."

"Perhaps," she retorted, maintaining her place. "I pledge your ruin even so."

Guiomar stepped back, astounded, and turned jovially to one of his knights. "She fighteth with me! Do you hear her?" The guard nodded, unsure. "Ha," the king remarked, shaking his head. "I shall have the executioner prepare to burn her at dusk." He returned a final time to Leanna, holding himself to his confidence despite the surety in her own eyes. "We shall make a show of it," he promised, then bounded away, the royal emerald train of his cloak fluttering behind him. Leanna watched him go, unwilling to allow him to be free from her stare so long as she was able to maintain it.

When he was entirely out of view, she turned her eyes to the floor and at last allowed the weight of all the present events to bring her to her knees.

"Kennedy." She closed her eyes and fought through tears. "Kennedy. *Kennedy, please.*"

Drifting into overdue sleep, she opened her eyes to see Kennedy walk into their usual dreamscape and was grateful she had not yet awoken.

"Hast thou been crying, Leanna?" the fairy said.

The prisoner found herself unable to determine any appropriate words. As she thought on what she might say to explain her circumstances, the stones and bars of her cell began to appear around them with the image distorted under a dreamlike sheen as though all the objects around the two dreamers lay just beyond a wall of water.

"A dungeon?!" Kennedy cried. "But I was with thee only hours ago! Hath Isolda put thee here?"

Leanna shook her head. "Madrick had locked me away, but—"

"Madrick? But he adores thee."

Leanna sighed. So much had changed so suddenly.

"No matter," the fairy continued. "I shall gather my warrior friends. Masor can never hold thee."

"I am not in Masor," the prisoner breathed.

Kennedy furrowed her brow. "Whither art thou?"

"Pavoline."

"Pavoline! How?"

Leanna dropped her head and pressed against her eyes in exhaustion. "Please, Kennedy, it is too much. I am to be executed at dusk."

The royal purple hands of the fairy took in those of the trembling page. "Nothing can take thee from me. My friends and I shall be to Pavoline in mere hours." She smiled to add, "Thou art fortunate to be arrested on a day when our schooling is recessed."

The prisoner let loose a small laugh. "Art thou certain it is safe?"

Kennedy nodded. "Guiomar may have a bolt-spear, but he does not have twenty. He does not concern me."

Leanna was not comforted. "He does have the Jewel of Nebulous."

"Then we shall ensure he never knows of our presence. When the moon rises, they shall arrive to execute an empty cell. Thou wilt be safe, and we will be together."

At this, Leanna smiled. "Thank you."

"My heart offers me no choice," Kennedy said, and they brought their lips together gently.

CHAPTER XIX

Another Home

Leanna had known fairy warriors. Indeed, she spent part of her life with them. Still, never once had she had the opportunity to observe them perform their work. It was only late afternoon, and yet she was near certain she had fallen into another dream when, sitting in the center of her cell, she saw a score of green wisps of light flutter into the dungeon and each find a place, hidden, in its every crevice. The guards blinked and looked round, but settled back into their posts, unsure. Looking directly ahead of her now, Leanna found a shrunken pair of wings glowing blue, and a young peasant fairy she would come to know as Nientz gesturing for her attention. She gave it, and the fairy brought her hand over her nose and mouth and motioned for Leanna to do the same. The prisoner raised a curious eyebrow, but brought her kerchief up, shielding her breath.

She watched now as Nientz removed half-opaque spheres from her satchel. The spheres were, in truth, of considerable size, but appeared to Leanna as small marbles in the miniature fairy's hand which now glowed as Nientz deployed them, placing them on the ground and rolling one each to a guard in the hall. The opaque quality of the spheres had been due to a thick fog held within them, and they now turned entirely translucent as the fog escaped, filling the air around the guards and persuading them all into a sudden slumber. Leanna smiled with amazed respect upon hearing a satisfied chortle escape from Nientz.

After a brief hesitation during which the mist settled upon the dungeon which now had no conscious human save Leanna, the tall, verdant, winged warriors began enlarging themselves and emerging from their concealments. The score of them circled round the barred wall of her cell and she saw now, as they did of her, that they shared the same state of youth. While most all the fairies gawked at the human object of their mission, still sitting, amazed, on the ground, one came forward and aimed a steady bolt-spear at the lock of her cage. The prisoner shielded herself from the coming detonation, but none came. Instead, the warrior sent a careful set of minute lightning sparks into the locking mechanism and inaudibly unclosed the cell door as though it had never been locked at all. This warrior, a tall, broad-shouldered girl with a knot of thin, chartreuse hair pulled neatly to the nape of her neck, maintained a cold stoicism as she swung the door wide and stood away from the opening. A shiver of concern struck Leanna with the worry that her rescue was, to some, an unwelcome assignment by the queen's heir, but all anxieties melted from her consciousness when Kennedy, wearing a magnificent smile, stepped from behind the warriors, into view. Leanna mirrored her countenance and accepted her now outstretched hand to raise her from the floor. An active stillness hovered over the assembly as its leader and purpose stood gazing at each other, apparently each in renewed awe of the other's loveliness. The warrior with chartreuse hair signaled impatience with a cough, and, at the sound, Kennedy regained her urgency.

A variety of gestures from the Alquorian heir sent the fairies into a ready airborne formation. Expecting her confusion, Kennedy took Leanna by the hand and, offering her a knowing wink, set off into the air, wrapping her arms around Leanna's waist and holding her tight, maintaining a position of safety in the center of the fleet. Nientz remained close behind them as they were encircled by the formation of flying warriors. The human girl, this being her first time traveling through the air, lost all sense of danger and let loose numerous exclamations of glee. She felt Kennedy's silent laughter against her back and returned her attention to their purpose. They now soared through the halls of Pavoline, taking the paths unhaunted by servants and guards on a route the warriors had scouted upon their arrival, flying past bedchambers and armories, leaving the stairway to the dungeon far behind. Flying silently, the warriors were undiscovered, and thus unchallenged, for much of the escape, but as they neared the grand entrance, turning into the decorated antechamber that sat before the open courtyard, the stationed knights saw them clearly and readied for battle, calling to their fellows for assistance. The chamber was soon flooded with knights donning the emerald-green crest of the Ranzentines and holding their swords and shields aloft, ready to strike. Despite knowing naught of the technique, Leanna thought to wrench free of Kennedy's grasp and aid in the battle for her escape, but even as the thought occurred to her, she was made instantly aware the extent to which her exertion was unneeded.

Two by two, the verdant fairies displayed their valor, peeling off the edges of their ever-symmetrical formation and performing their battle-dance with carefully rehearsed spontaneity. Each knight that tried their hand, leaping up to meet their flying foe or thrusting an aptly aimed poignard towards a heart or wing, was met with perpetual disappointment as, in response, they encountered a faultless deflection and lightning attack from the fairy's spear. Leanna noted, however, as she watched the Pavol knights fall upon the ground, that all in the end were left unaided or unconscious, yet too left constitutionally unharmed. When the last number of knights standing began a retreat, the fairy warriors all pointed their spears to the grand oak entryway and, with a magnificent flash, sent the double doors flying to the limits of their hinges, leaving ample space for the party to exit with smooth celerity into the open air.

Leanna saw the stake that had been readied for her execution in the center of the yard, now to go unburnt, and, in relief, she let loose a celebratory laugh, spreading her arms wide as she soared with Kennedy in the path of the warriors high above the castle and toward the Wood. Kennedy spun so her wings faced the ground and the whole of Leanna's weight fell into her embrace as together they looked up to the clouds, floating ever nearer to the Sky. The party entire began to relax and, as they flew peacefully on their way, Kennedy sang one of her poems into Leanna's ear.

SKETCH OUR SOULS

Whence may we turn when our river runs dry—
When all we feel is hurt?
We search the earth from East to West and find
No solace in the dirt.

Rivers may gleam and they glide on the land,
Yet they remain confined.
We are the ones with no limits except
The limits of the mind.

Holding each star and each rain that doth pour,
Lamenting not the weight,
The Sky doth not fall, only grows and expands,
Directing us to fate.

Destiny vast with such dreams that do stir,
I marvel at us now.
Rivers alone cannot hold what we are,
So Skyward must we plough.

Clouds swirl within us and mist sprays around,
So never could we dry.
Never beholden to borders unjust,
We sketch our souls through Sky.

They remained in their airborne embrace for some time, Kennedy instinctually blazing the trail towards Anwansi with Nientz and the warriors in tow, and Leanna watching the Sky gracefully darken above her with not a care of their current direction, noting the stars that began to welcome her into another night, feeling at last safe and free. At length, they began to be surrounded by branches and greenery, and Kennedy whispered in Leanna's ear, "Art thou ready?" She knew not what for, but Leanna nodded assent and grasped onto Kennedy's arms as they tightened around her. The fairy spun round again and, in concert with the rest around them, made a steep dive into the depths of the Infinite Woods, leaving trails of green, blue, and purple-white sparks intermingling with Leaves in their wake.

When the group's feet touched ground, all looked curiously to Leanna to see how the human had fared in the vicious descent through the Infinites. She met their eyes with an ecstatic smile, and quickly fell into favor with the adventurous bunch.

"Great gramercy to you all," she said, and received only humble nods as the troop began to amble across the Forest floor towards their home. She turned to Kennedy. "I cannot thank thee enough," she said.

Nientz hurried up beside her. "We were told a spectacular being had been jailed unjustly by Guiomar of Pavoline, and required no further persuading."

Leanna smiled to her but then grew worried at a scoff from the chartreuse-haired warrior some paces ahead. With a sigh, Nientz corrected herself.

"Most of us required no further persuading."

Kennedy offered Leanna a look of assurance and explained, "That is only Phidia. She is kind, but despises defying decrees initially, even when they are wrong. Her spite is not aimed at thee; it falls on I tonight and shall disintegrate with the sun."

Leanna turned sharply to Kennedy. "What decree hath hither been defied?"

"Oh, none, truly! Only a little order from the Elders not to rescue thee."

Nientz chuckled at Kennedy's confidence and Leanna looked to the laughing fairy, alarmed. Nientz nodded and confirmed Kennedy's words.

"The Elders ordered such and still thou didst charge a score of warriors to accompany thee?"

"Peace, Leanna," the royal fairy urged. "Thy life was at stake, and we have all defied the Elders for far less. All my friends here are underage as we are and can be deployed by no royal command. Despite their varying levels of enthusiasm on this occasion, all are hither of their own accord and all are allies who shall guard one another, with strength or wit, from the Elder's disapproval." Those walking near who heard Kennedy's speech turned round and offered nods of affirmation, save Phidia who remained forward yet still slight could be seen agreeing.

"I do wish you had required rescuing in Masor, Leanna," Nientz said. "I so wished to catch a glimpse of just one of the infamously lost mirrors."

"Lost?" Leanna inquired, remembering the mystical glass. "I had been told they were gifted."

"Oh they were! All but one," she explained, launching into her favorite story. "After the Oxbien finally conceded his defeat to the Wood, he accepted the mirrors as a token of the fairies' interest in peaceable allyship with Masor, especially strong due to false word of our monstrousness spreading so vast in Pavoline. Naturally, one was maintained at Anwansi to keep open the method of contact. It was utilized only once to invite Emmrand Oxbien into the castle whither his prideful rage at the defeat overtook him and he bludgeoned the mirror to shards. More, he murdered Xelasker Bean, their only creator! No one has attempted their reinvention from fear the Masorians would make wicked use of such a direct connection to Anwansi, so I have only ever read of them in histories."

Leanna scoffed, shaking her head at thought of the false Masorian account of the tale. She looked to Nientz who had returned to trotting cheerfully beside her, navy curls bouncing about an azure countenance. "How came you to be among us? Are you a warrior?"

Nientz released another of her chuckles. "No, I am blue through-and-through, and with it have no interest to fight."

"She does not give herself due credit," Kennedy assured. "She herself is a creator, just as Xelasker was. Those sleeping-spheres used on the guards are her own invention. You may be no warrior, Nientz, but any queen would be a fool to ban your brilliance from the battlefield."

"Thank you, Kennedy," Nientz blushed, small hints of purple revealing themselves on her cheeks.

"Thank you!" said Leanna, and Nientz nodded to assure her it was welcome. "I admit," Leanna went on, "I marvel at the benign effectiveness of the fairy weaponry. In all the human kingdoms, the bolt-spear is thought of as naught but an instrument of death, a firm case against the fairies in the eyes of many."

At this, Phidia spoke at last. "The bolt-spear is naught but a weapon when utilized with inexperience and anger, but with training and grace it is a tool of protection and honor."

Nientz whispered to Leanna. "She memorized that from the rule book."

"That is how you know it is correct, Nientz," Phidia rejoined at the jest. Subsequent laughter abated as minds traveled to remembrances of the bolt-spear's recent history in human hands, and Leanna's mind followed that thought to the most recent atrocity the owner of those hands ordered upon her own father.

"I imagine many a weapon might be benevolent when in the hands of one other than Guiomar Ranzentine," Kennedy conjectured, but Leanna was too lost in grief to hear it.

At length, they reached the point of a promontory and peered over its edge to see that the inhabitants of the Anwansi pool below were sheltered and unobserving. Then, with caution and in turns, each fairy fluttered to and from projecting branches, Kennedy carrying Leanna among them, until they floated down the lengthy descent beside the smooth hollow's walls, landing softly on the piers. All waved their salutations and repeated thanks as warriors, peasant, and royal alike departed to their assigned sections of the watery city. Kennedy brought Leanna carefully around the water's edge to its opposite side where they snuck behind the waterfall and into the royal caves. When at last they reached Kennedy's apartment undetected, they fell upon the bed in relief and giggled in their successful plot.

"Surely I shall be discovered tomorrow," Leanna whispered.

"By then, what are they to do of it?" Kennedy smiled.

"There is still the underpool."

"Queen Okalani would never allow it. Thou art safe, Leanna, I assure thee." She gave her a small kiss, and they both relaxed into the other's embrace, allowing their eyes to close. Kennedy opened hers again, gazing upon the dark brown countenance of her human beloved, sensing the sadness within. She brushed soft fingers against Leanna's cheek until she reopened her eyes.

"Thou hast still not told me all that happened last night."

Leanna felt the loss and betrayal begin to encroach completely upon her, but she temporarily forced them to the side. "Tonight," she promised. "I'll explain everything under the peace of sleep."

Kennedy smiled. "So we are still to dream together?"

Leanna nodded. "I must first briefly dream with another, but then, as in every night to come, I shall be thine."

They kissed once more, and fell into a deep slumber.

CHAPTER XX

Maddening Truth

While King Madrick Oxbien II lay recumbent on his bed, his unconscious kept him from restful repose as it fluttered from one of his kingdom's disasters to another. His stomach churned as he hunched his shoulders inward and jolted his posture to the right, seeing thither, before dreaming eyes, vast fields of burnt wheat disintegrating beneath a red sun. Turning from the sight, he spun to the left and the visions followed thence, bringing the king to stare down a village well whose dry walls had long begun collecting dust. At last, in a paroxysm of discomfort, he sprawled his heel to the foot of his bed and forced both shoulders back into the mattress, raising his chin to the ceiling. His dreams now displayed the sharp silhouette of his baleful neighbor king standing above him, an ensanguined luster hovering around the malignant figure which stood framed entirely by a blood-red Sky. Madrick near woke from fright, but he remained in the dream to observe as the hue of the Sky was slowly infiltrated by a touch of purple. It was then periwinkle, and then blue, and during the change the figure silhouetted before the light was altered as well from the menacing, broad-shouldered, frame of Guiomar Ranzentine, to a shorter frame, touched by youth, which held out a merciful hand. A calm began to overtake the king and he accepted the silhouette's hand, using the aid to stand and enter, for his first time, the cerulean dreamscape so often frequented by his new companion.

"Leanna," he said.

"Hello, My Liege."

"What dost thou wish of me now?"

To say aloud, Leanna finally accepted the tears that now streamed down her cheeks. "My father is dead," she said.

Madrick hid his sympathy behind his anger. "Already?" he asked, and she nodded. "Didst thou know when he was to be executed?" She nodded once more. "Then there was never hope of saving him!"

"I was nearly there. I was at the castle. I was thither! And yet I was not there where it could make any difference." She took a breath and wiped the tears away. "Guiomar had me behind bars again, now on the charge of calumny against the king. I was to be executed, but the fairies rescued me and stole me away."

He stood aghast. "It has been only a day, that is impossible."

"What do you know of what is possible, King?" she retorted, and he fell into silence.

"I am sorry," Madrick said at last.

Leanna nodded. "As am I."

Fairies, Madrick thought, shaking his head. "Thou sworest I would never see thee more."

"I said so if you wished it, and, if you wish it, it can be so still. This is naught but a dream, and I do naught to keep you hither, wake up if you in truth despise me so."

Sparks of fury flamed, then vanished, in Madrick's eye, and, with a sigh, his visage fell to melancholy and fatigue.

"Wherefore didst thou pretend such loyalty?"

"'Twas no pretend, Your Highness!" Leanna avowed.

"Thou dost consort with fairies! The murderers, who forced me to be king before my time, that is who thou choosest as thy playfellow."

"There is so much you do not understand."

Madrick scoffed. "Do not pretend such wisdom. Thou art nothing but a servant, and a child."

She grimaced. "You sound like the princess. She never did care for me."

He looked to her a moment and considered. Speaking softly, with only awe, he replied, "Maybe she knew what you really were."

Leanna's eyes grew wide. "I am simply a servant."

"Leanna Page," he sighed. "You are walking in the dreams of a king. I shall no more pretend to know what you are, but I can say with certainty that it is not, nor has it ever been, a simple servant."

"You must know I would never betray you, Madrick."

"How could I know?"

She hesitated, the distrust in the king's eyes straining a resolution, but Madrick spoke on and recalled her to her purpose.

"Why hast thou come to me, Leanna?"

Finding her strength of heart, she answered, "The time is long overdue for you to learn the truth."

"The truth?"

"Yes. I was sworn by my parents to keep it hidden so we might continue as a family, but now—" She left it unsaid, and painfully went on. "Your hatred of the fairies has to end."

"If thou dost attempt some trick—"

"This is no deception! For once, open thy sense to reality." With the king shocked into silence, she went on. "Your parents were taken by no fairy's hand, but by the same hand that extinguished all hope my family might be reunited."

The king could not believe it. "Their wounds were clearly from a magical weapon."

"Yes, a bolt-spear, stolen from a warrior, and wielded at the time by Guiomar Ranzentine, now King of Pavoline."

Madrick stared into the eyes of his friend, the servant, the part-fairy, the traitor, or the wrongly accused, unsure now what to believe. Could the figure of his recent nightmares be the cause of his longer grief? It would make the kingdom's conflict no longer one of politics but one of deep prejudice and vengeance. It would require a retaliation, one they could not now endure after their defeat, unless, if she spoke true, Leanna's gifts—perhaps even her friends in the Fairy Nation—could be turned to their advantage. Could a weakened Masor defeat the forces of Pavoline, even with the Jewel in play, if they also had magic as an ally? It was all far too absurd.

"It cannot possibly be true," he said.

"I can show you, Madrick," Leanna replied, and instantly the dream-sky began to close in around them, revealing soon a misty reflection of the stones and draperies of a royal bedchamber: the apartment of Guiomar Ranzentine. At a sign from Leanna, the king turned to the corner behind Guiomar's writing desk and, thither, in blazing glory, was a spear whose head was a translucent blue and sparked like a contained lightning storm. Madrick could feel at once that this was indeed the weapon that ripped his parents from the world.

He sat up in bed, wide eyes staring in the darkness and his nightclothes sticking to him with sweat. Hatred like he had never known encroached his heart and forced his hand as he tore the covers away and bolted from the apartment, screaming to every knight in the hall, waking the entire castle. He found himself fuming in the throne room and looked up at length to see Princess

Isolda rush hurriedly into the grand chamber, pulling her robes around her. She halted in the doorway at the sight of her brother, the King, in wrinkled, wet nightclothes, leaning against the throne, while the knights and servants kept to the walls. Madrick clenched his fist around the chair's arm to maintain his uprightness, and his crazed eyes turned red around the lids.

"We must to war," he croaked.

Isolda straightened her spine with a curious expression and spoke steadily. "Calm yourself, Brother. What hath occurred this night?"

"I have seen it, the object of our parents' destruction, the magic spear that struck their hearts; it lies in the chambers of that murderer, of Guiomar. Guiomar was the destroyer, no fairy!" He trod to her, imploring her belief with temperament as much as with words.

Murmurs filled the edges of the hall, but all kept their voices low so they might hear the calm response of the vice-crown.

"How could this be, Madrick?" She asked.

"We know of his wickedness. He hath extinguished his own father as well, Masor's only Pavol friend! Must thy mind stretch so to see it?"

The princess shook her head. "I speak not of Guiomar—nor do I inherently offer the beast any doubt—but I concern over you. How could you have seen the weapon?"

Madrick forgot any hesitation of delicacy. "Leanna hath displayed the image to my sleeping eye. The page was right! The fairies are our enemies only in that we have made them so through unjust accusation and persecution. Leanna was right. Leanna hath been right all along."

"Enough!" Isolda roared, the name of the treasonous page ringing hard on her royal ears. "Hear yourself, Brother. You are king, and all this you do on the word of a traitor."

"She is no betrayer. It is we who have betrayed a loyal friend of the court, a friend who hath shown us the truth at last!"

Princess Isolda stepped back from her brother who raged so as she had never yet observed. Her sight drifted to the throne that rested centrally across the room, then fell back upon the maddened glare of her brother, the same glare that all in the hall could well see.

"What action do you wish Masor to take, King?"

"Pavoline is now led by a monster," he began. "Leanna's father has been killed, and the child herself, after reaching Pavoline, only narrowly escaped his deathly grasp, so hopes that they might turn his people against their mendacious king are for naught.—" Isolda was certain now her brother had lost his wits, but she did not wish to further aggravate the king. Not tonight. "—Masor has suffered under his destruction enough to believe his own people are no longer safe in their own state, so long as it is ruled by this Ranzentine. It is our royal obligation to take it from him."

Maintaining a cool demeanor despite her shock, Isolda inquired, "You mean to overtake Pavoline?"

"I mean to remove its king," Madrick affirmed.

She gazed around at the inhabitants of the castle who still stood watch. She let out a worried breath. "Considering all the factors, Madrick, this is a risk in which we are obliged to confer with the gentry. Might you resist your war-orders until we may hold court in the morn?"

Madrick paused in confusion, having not thought for an instant of involving the nobles. "Do you wish Guiomar to go unpunished, Isolda? Our parents, unavenged, is that your wish?"

She scoffed. "Brother, think yourself not so dauntless. A foolish attack shall do naught but bring further ruin to our state, the same one our parents raised us to protect. I wish only to fulfill their dreams for us."

Deflating, he sighed with a slight nod. "Very well."

"Rest, dear Brother," the princess softened. "Sleep now, at least until dawn, and I shall arrange for the court to convene." She placed a thoughtful hand upon his shoulder. "We shall find our path. Madrick II and Isolda shan't be the Oxbiens to bring ruin on our family name; I will ensure it."

He nodded once more, finding a faintness replace his calming rage. At Isolda's direction, Kn. Degora offered her arm to Madrick and led him back to his chambers, where he returned to his troubled repose.

Despite the official order naming none of the cause for the gentry's session in the castle, word of the king's panic in the night had spread sufficiently from the guards to the locals lagifs to the lagifs afar who all convened thus the following morn, and who were increasingly anxious to hear the royal's remarks. As the early sun seeped through the window-glass of the throne room, it fell upon the crowd of lagifs whispering to one another, and conferring with their fellows in the mystical glass, who now descended into silence as the grand doors were unclosed and King Madrick entered, in fresh royal raiment, donning the Masorian royal-purple cape with the Oxbien's crest embroidered in gold upon the shoulder. Isolda followed in a gown of deep violet, silver trim shining from its edge. They marched to the throne, and each stood equal before it.

"Noble lagifs of Masor," the king began, stepping in front of Isolda. He spoke on, with honor and strength, recounting the last two days' events, disclosing royal wrongdoing on account of the fairies' accusation, revealing all he now understood of Guiomar's crimes and from whence he received the knowledge. The speech was deliberate and methodical. His argument for Masor's occupation of Pavoline was artfully woven and well-planned during the many hours before dawn he spent awake in his bed. It might have had a dramatic effect on another audience, but the gentry this day could only take heed of the princess behind the king who maintained throughout his speech a demeanor of sympathetic condescension and disbelief, contrasting too sharply with the king's furious control.

"This is a time of great need for us all," he continued, nearing his conclusion. "The people of Masor—noble, peasant, and royal alike—yearn for the sustenance of body and spirit that this wicked sun, aiming down on us from Guiomar's hand, hath decreed we must omit from our lives. With the resources from the Gwahanu, Masor will begin to remember its strength, but the tyranny of Guiomar Ranzentine must be ended for our world within these Woods to reach again a peaceful day. While meager, indeed, Masor does still maintain its forces, and with aid from the inhabitants of the Infinite Wood, we have a chance. Lagifs of Masor, as tradition states, a movement of this magnitude ought to have your support, and I ask it of you now. Might we have your acclamations to proceed?"

The court was noiseless. Few even dared take a breath. All gentry eyes turned to Isolda and, confounded, Madrick followed them, looking with full contempt upon the sight of the proud princess beside him. She stepped forth and more directly before the throne, compelling the king to step to the side.

"My concern, dear Brother, is the vehicle from which these asseverations were originally portrayed to you. A fairy-type magic, and one unique to a traitor who, moreover, saith she hath traveled the length of our entire world in a single night! I fear she tells you lies."

Murmurings in the chamber seconded the princess's words, and shook the control Madrick kept over his countenance.

"Magic is a friend to her. Why are we to presume time presents its same limitations to her that it does to us? Leanna is worthy of our doubts in her favor. She hath long been a trustworthy ally."

"Or hath she consorted with fairies since her youth to infiltrate the deepest heart of our castle so that they may pursue a larger goal?"

"That is absurd," Madrick snapped. "What goal of theirs might there be?"

"Consider it, Brother," quoth the princess. "The fairies hold dominance over all the Wood, an infinite territory. All that stands between them and complete control is our own kingdom and that of Pavoline." Isolda began to smile, her speech quickening, as she discovered what she now presumed to be the truth. "The fairies most clearly are using Leanna to manipulate us, turning the two kingdoms against one another. Of course the imposter-page spoke of Guiomar's high crimes to our name; she wants you enraged and vengeful, just as you now are! To attack Pavoline as you suggest is precisely what they wish of us, and I shall not permit it to take place."

"You are wrong, Isolda," protested the king. "I saw the weapon, and my very spirit recognized it."

"You saw an illusion," she corrected.

"I saw truth! Wherefore dost thou insist on perceiving lies?"

As Madrick's anger grew, Isolda inhaled and arched her back, staring down her nose at her brother-king. She spoke with uncanny composure, clearly projected for all the court to hear.

"It is not I who persists in untruths, Brother. I fear now more certainly what I suspected in the night when I saw you fearful, enraged; crazed. The mystic traitor, Leanna Page, hath obstructed your very means of comprehension. You are a danger to Masor, a puppet with strings held firmly by one who would steal our crown and see the very human race meet its end."

Madrick emphatically shook his head. "It isn't so!" he said, then, in near whispers, "Isolda, you know it is not so."

She remained steadfast. "You are pure of heart and intention, my dear brother, but a canker of delusion hath overcome your senses in what I fear may be an irredeemable fashion."

"Thou seek'st the throne!" Madrick vociferated. He turned aghast to the lagifs before him, a three-fourths agreement amongst them enough to declare him unfit to lead the kingdom, and felt for certain they were all against him. Twisting round again to Isolda, he scowled. "Leanna is certainly no traitor when set beside the likes of thee."

"I suggest merely what is best for Masor," Isolda said.

"No!" Madrick howled. "Thou wilt not remove me from my throne, not now!"

"That is not for you to decide, Brother."

"This is madness! The gentry wish thee for their queen, they will decide on what is best for their riches, not what is best for the kingdom!"

"Nevertheless, they will decide," the princess declared.

Madrick lunged toward his perfidious sister and, at an instinctive signal from Isolda, was caught in the grip of two knights who restrained him by the arms, leaving the king panting, chin hanging below his shoulders, eyes trained on the princess.

Isolda suppressed a scoff. "Brother, you make the choice inevitable." She turned tall to the crowd. "Lagifs of Masor, who will you have as your monarch? The son, whose madness multiplies in each moment; or the daughter of sense, the Oxbien of consistent honor?"

Without respite for thought, a chant clamored through the throne room, a unanimous acclamation: "Long live the queen!"

She smiled.

Madrick squinted toward her in disgust. "Thou wouldst be the greatest shame of Mother and Father's eye," he growled.

Isolda knelt to meet her brother's gaze. "I do regret the necessity of this occasion," she said. Pausing her speech, she rose and placed two graceful fingers to the brim of the king's crown, lifting the diadem from his head and placing it atop her own. Then similarly, though with considerably more necessary force, she retrieved the ring engraved with their royal seal from his finger. "Perhaps one day, Brother, thou wilt realize thy wrongs, and come, in time, to forgive me."

Lifting himself up, Madrick took a deep breath, and shot spit upon the queen's cheek.

Isolda nearly bruised herself with the force of her hand as it wiped away her brother's saliva. She turned to the knights who held him.

"Take him to his chambers and see that he remaineth thither."

"Wait, Sister, please—"

"When he is secured, find Leif and see them escorted across the River."

"No!" Madrick bellowed, but Isolda paid him no heed, continuing her instruction to the knights.

"The stablehand is surely as entwined with the traitor as is their beloved. For the safety of Masor, I order them banished from the land."

Nothing could subdue Madrick's tears. "No. Please, Isolda, have mercy," he sobbed.

"Above all, ensure close guard is kept on my brother's door. He would endanger us all if he were to escape."

"Yes, Queen," said the closer knight, with a grand obeisance. The other nodded and both exited the throne room, forcing the struggling former king through a newly formed aisle in the crowd. All watched in silence as the former king's pleas and vociferations faded into the hall beyond, but when the door was closed behind them, an exuberant sigh was shared betwixt the gentry and their new monarch, Queen Isolda.

"Fear not," she assured them, her voice rising as the people cheered. "Neither fairies, nor maddened kings—be it Madrick or Guiomar Ranzentine—shall have their way on our land. I make now a solemn oath to you all that Masor will be what it once was, and we shall only grow stronger through the years!"

CHAPTER XXI

An Alliance

Satisfied, the gentry filtered from the throne room and Queen Isolda returned to her own apartment, continuing to wear her crown despite her solitude. Instantly upon entrance, she sat before her writing desk and began to pen a letter to King Guiomar of Pavoline. The foolish man had played with Masor's half of their Skies long enough, and now there were more important matters than squabbling over the past. Leanna Page was certain to lead the fairies in an attack, one even mighty knights—so long as of the human variety—would be troubled to win; more, they yet had no way of knowing whether the fairies did not have some method of evading the power of the Jewel of Nebulous. If the two kingdoms were to maintain either of their sovereignty, it was necessary they overcome their disagreements and provide each other aid. Isolda had little trust, and complete dislike, already, of Pavoline's recently crowned king, and she knew he thought no kindlier of her. If they had any opportunity to ally their forces, the attempt could not be made, she knew, through any number of written messages. She wrote so in the letter, and implored that the two new royals could meet, speaking personally and alone.

The queen fondled the ring of the royal seal between her fingertips, familiarizing herself with the sense of its power, feeling grateful to have finally acquired it in full. Returning herself to her task, she used the seal to finish the letter and called for Blythe, the new maidservant who had eagerly accepted Esta's position when it was made available. Isolda, startling as the officious maid entered her chambers before she finished her call, passed Blythe the parchment and ordered that she carry it personally to Guiomar. The maid's usual alacrity was dampened a moment in personal fear, but was renewed swiftly by her desire to fulfill every extent of her still novel employment. Isolda was all too pleased to see her set off on the month-long journey to Pavoline castle and back.

Guiomar received the note from a quivering Blythe at the end of the second week. She had been brought to him at sword point as he reclined on a silver chaise in a moment of silent anguish—one of many the king had sat through since learning of the infuriating page's fairy-aided escape from his dungeon. If not for this late occurrence, he more likely would have laughed at Isolda's request and sent her messenger back with naught. As it was, the new knowledge that the girl, Leanna Page, had troubled Masor same as she had now troubled him was enough to spark a sufficient level of his curiosity and concern. He penned a note in response, inviting Isolda, who must be starved, he noted, to dine with him in Pavoline on any day hence she was able to arrive. Blythe sighed, relieved, once Guiomar handed her the billet and sent her off, but too quickly once arriving home in Masor she was sent again to Pavoline by her queen who, in spite, wrote a scathing response, assuring Guiomar she would not deign to set foot on Pavol soil, much less dine with its wicked king. She insisted he, as a show of good faith, meet in the Masorian throne room at his earliest convenience.

It was half a year of traveling to and fro, delivering correspondence betwixt the hateful monarchs, before Blythe at last completed her final journey to Masor, conveying just a few lines from Guiomar which confirmed his participation in meeting at the only place the two could agree upon: the small bridge at the Gwahanu straight.

On the set date of the meeting, one week following the receipt of the final letter, all Masor knights and servants harvesting at the River, by command of the queen, ceased their work and joined the River dwellers in vacating the open riverside, stealing into their homes as they watched the royal retinues approach from afar. The Masor carriage, first, halted several meters before the bridge, then Pavoline's followed suit upon arrival. When each was stationary, attendants unclosed the royal carriage doors and each monarch stepped out upon the dirt path and began a proud stride towards the bridge. Guiomar wore inconsequential robes with short sleeves designed for comfortable practicality as opposed to decoration, but he adorned himself with his lavish crown and, most notably, the Jewel of Nebulous, creating as formidable an appearance as ever. Aligned thus in intimidation, Isolda strode now in flexible trousers with her abdomen and breast protected by a sturdy, though royally embellished, warrior's plate. A sword hung by her belt and from her shoulders proudly waved the purple-gold cloak of the Oxbiens.

"I thought this was to be a friendly encounter, Isolda," Guiomar began when at last the two stopped before one another on the bridge.

Isolda looked meaningfully to the Jewel on his hand, then returned her gaze directly to his eyes. "You have your weapons, Guiomar, and I have mine."

"Alright," he nodded, smirking slightly in competitive respect. "Then let us begin. Tell me what you know of the page."

"Before we negotiate the future, let us settle the present," Isolda responded. "The drought must end, Guiomar, along with your control of our skies."

Any aforementioned gaiety now fell from Guiomar's countenance.

"The pain of this drought is what you filthy Masorians deserve," he snarled.

She sighed with impatience. "Wherefore?"

"You are the reason my mother is dead!"

"That is not the case, but say it were so, you are now ever more so directly the reason mine is the same," she rejoined, and she beamed at Guiomar's gaping surprise. "Is it not the case?" she asked, offering plainly false doubt.

Guiomar said nothing, confirming his guilt.

"I should strike thee dead now, thou murderous fiend," Isolda continued, "but not a soul would be done well by such a deed. Even from your own deranged perspective, you and I stand on even footing, King of Pavoline. Let us treat each other in a manner which reflects that."

Guiomar dropped his sight to the Jewel of Nebulous and brushed his opposite fingers against the gem. He nodded, and clouds at once began to fill the Masor sky, accompanying a cool wind which blew through Isolda's hair. She turned towards her kingdom and, in the distance, could see rain begin to fall. Satisfied, she returned to Guiomar expectantly. He pouted, then pulled the Jewel from his fingers and placed it in the pocket of his robes.

"Gramercy." The queen spoke without a touch of gratitude.

"How did you come to know it was I all those years ago? Was it the page?"

Isolda smiled, pleased with herself. "I have known the truth of it all these years, Guiomar. A fairy came to my maid the night we dined in your castle, and she reported to me the truth she heard. Unlike you, however, I would never act on the word of a servant, and certainly not one speaking on behalf of a fairy."

"So, Leanna doesn't know of it?"

"Oh, the maid was her mother, I am certain she has always known.—" Isolda paused in realization. "Ha! Thinking back to that night, I suppose we can now conclude how the odd couple of parents encountered one another." She returned to her prior thoughts. "More recently, however, the page spoke to my brother in his dreams and brought him to an image of your chambers. A fairy spear rested in the corner, confirming prior accusations."

"Incredible," said the king.

"Her powers are indeed to be marveled."

Guiomar turned cautiously curious. "Why are you not seeking retaliation against me?"

"You are atrocious, Guiomar, but powerful. To be frank, I have found I am the same, only with far more tact. I always thought we might help each other one day, and now such a day has come."

He began a suspecting smile. "This is the second occasion I am now only privy to you, without your brother. He is the king, no? Hath he again fallen ill?"

Isolda calmly gestured in the negative. "He is far from ill; indeed, my brother sees too clearly now for his own good. Nevertheless, he knows nothing of delicacy, nor of politics. In short, Masor no longer recognizes a king, or even vice-crown. There is only I: its queen."

Guiomar made a grand obeisance, jesting in spirit, but avowing true respect to her persistence. "Welcome to sovereignty."

The queen rolled her eyes and returned to the matter at hand. "Leanna may have spoken true of your guilt, but I am certain she does so through no loyalty to Masor."

"I had her in my dungeon before I received your first letter. She escaped, rescued by fairy warriors. If she is not among you in Masor, I can only imagine she remained with the winged ones in the Woods. I can confirm she is no friend to her own race."

"So she did make the journey," Isolda accepted.

"What do you know of it?"

"She traveled from my castle to yours in under a night."

Guiomar was amazed at the confirmation of it, but was unsurprised. "Yes, I suppose that in fact makes a great deal of sense now."

Isolda clicked her tongue. "I should have put a poignard in her when I had the chance."

"You had the chance?"

"Oh, indeed. She resided in my dungeon for a moment before visiting yours. She persuaded Madrick to banish her to Pavoline so she could prevent you from killing her father. I hear she was unsuccessful, same as she could not prevent you killing your own."

Guiomar took a sharp breath and looked round to ensure his guard was still far enough off to have heard nothing. "I want her found," he growled back to Isolda. "I want her gone from this world."

Nodding knowingly, Isolda responded, "As do I, Guiomar. The fairies may be an adversary, but for all their mystery, they are old and known to us. That Page is something new. I wish only for Masor to be as it was when I was ruling over it these many years. That girl, her influence on Madrick, that is my only complication."

"There we differ significantly, Isolda. I have no grand memories of the past I wish to renew. As I always have, I wish Pavoline to be more. I wish to expand." He smiled as he thought of his dreams.

"Yes," she recalled, then queried, "In which direction?"

"All of them," his eyes gleamed.

"I can certainly support any attempts to force the fairies farther from our lands, but surely you do not expect to expand in every direction. Nothing south of the Gwahanu, be it Wood or plain, may ever belong to Pavoline."

"Wherefore?"

"Because I will share no greater portion of a border with the likes of yourself."

"Come, ally. Are you unaware? All borders are flexible." He smiled.

She did not reflect his demeanor. "Not this one," she commanded.

"We shall see."

"No! Fool of a king, we meet today to discuss how we might collaborate, not compete. Do not throw yourself into old habits."

"Could you stop me?"

"I already today have spoken simple words that gave you cause to look over your shoulder. Imagine what might be done to you if I shared what I know with all your kingdom. You are beholden to people other than yourself, Your Highness, despite what you may wish. I know your secrets, same as Leanna does, and I can be as great a danger to you as she, so give me not the cause."

He scowled. "I do not wish you anywhere in my kingdom."

"Nor do I wish you in mine, or any for that matter raised with Pavoline's superstitions." A spark of inspiration lit up Isolda's eye. "So let us prevent it," she continued. "You say borders are flexible; let us make ours fixed. Along the Gwahanu we shall raise a steep wall of stone, your Pavol masons building on your land from the East, and we Masorians building our half from the West. If either manages to overtake part of the Wood, we shall extend the wall directly east or west, never encroaching to the North or South. Construction would begin at the Wood and continue on towards this bridge through which we may maintain correspondence towards our mutual end of securing Leanna Page until such time as she is found and destroyed. On that day, the wall may be sealed, and no Masorian need ever lay future eyes on a Pavol."

"A wall?"

"Do you object?"

"You imagine it is wise to destroy the riverside?"

"We will be destroying nothing. We will be building upon it, improving it. Imagine the shade, and the security. Imagine nevermore having to worry that one of the 'filthy Masorians' you so despise might so much as touch a blade of grass in Pavoline."

Guiomar stood silent, intrigued and considering. At last, he discovered he had no complaints. "So it shall be," he agreed.

Isolda reached out a solemn hand which Guiomar took in his own. They remained in the handshake for time enough to investigate one another's eyes, making certain they were trusted to keep their word.

"If ever again you utilize that Jewel to harm Masor, I shall ensure you are offed your throne," Isolda affirmed.

"Naturally," Guiomar nodded.

Releasing hands, they made loose decisions regarding strategy for collectively attacking the fairies in the search for Leanna, agreeing each to send regular messengers to the Gwahanu bridge to more quickly concretize the schemes in writing at a later date. When their plans were settled, each monarch strode backward a number of distrustful steps toward their own carriage, then, with a final nod, they turned, marching off to execute their designs.

CHAPTER XXII

The Wingless One

On Leanna's first morn in the nation of Alquoria, she awoke to a glint of azure luminescence falling upon her eye. She hesitantly unclosed the lids and released an unconsciously held breath at the remembrance of her comparatively peaceful environs. Kennedy's royal cavern apartment was windowless, as were all in the caves of the Anwansi castle, but in place of a casement to Leanna's left was a pattern of encrusted gems so artfully placed as to filter Anwansi's magical glow through their varied hues and giving the effect of a magnificent sepulcher's window of stained glass, waking itself with the rising sun. Past the footboard of the bed, Leanna now took notice of Kennedy's writing desk, a large but practical instrument which furnished every student's chamber. Looking to the corner of the desk, Leanna wondered curiously at a handful of small branches cleanly placed inside a goblet, but then remembered what Kennedy had remarked to her about the marvelous wooden quills which held and dispersed the ink from their center thanks to the skillful magic of the fairy scientists. Another example, she had said, of why the blue Zils—misnamed 'common'—who upheld such professions should be regarded equally as highly as any other.

Completing a scan of the chamber, Leanna noticed its rough, earthen walls, their rounded shape leaving a viewer incapable of neatly distinguishing one wall from the next. Leanna smiled, as the cavern apartment suddenly gave her the feeling of home. She turned her gaze to the chamber's entrance and instead found Kennedy's open eyes glittering kindly toward her own.

"Good morning, my love," Kennedy whispered.

Seeing her, Leanna's heart was too full for words. She brought Kennedy close and kissed her long and gently. They lay there for a time with nuzzled brows. Then, Kennedy flew up from the bed and playfully pulled her reluctant beloved into the day.

The instant they exited Kennedy's apartment, the odd pair was discovered by an instructor hurrying to her morning class. Instructor Emmer jolted in shock at the sight of a human in, not only Alquoria's capitol, but Anwansi's very castle! Her shock subdued into fury at the sight of Kennedy—the royal pain and heir—holding the human's hand.

"Kennedy!" Emmer shouted. "By every Elders' decree, get this menace from our walls."

"This is no menace, but a dear friend, to Anwansi and to me." Kennedy calmly rejoined. "Argue it not, Instructor, for I shall discuss the matter with none but the queen herself."

Emmer's purple cheeks blazed a deep red and her wings stiffened downward into daggers.

"You wish to place a human before our fairy queen?"

Kennedy offered a smirk, and sparks of certainty flew from her prismatically white wings.

"Your delinquency has gone too far; this is a matter for the Elders. Follow me thence at once," Emmer declared, spinning round and storming down the hall. Kennedy gave Leanna a cue to follow and the two girls started down the hall slowly, Leanna from hesitation, Kennedy from lack of concern. At the first turn, the instructor went off to the right while Kennedy took Leanna down the slight leftward bend in the path they currently followed. Leanna turned and saw that the instructor, deep in private rehearsal for her coming speech to the Elders, had not taken note of their separate direction.

The fairy heir guided Leanna towards a pair of grand doors made of carved stone which Leanna was now too aware must lead to a royal throne room. Kennedy stopped before them and took Leanna's hand.

"Thou needest not fear her, Leanna."

"There are many I should have not needed to fear," Leanna said, still staring at the closed entryway.

"Look at me," Kennedy replied, and Leanna suffered herself to turn towards the other's steadfast countenance. "No harm can come near while I protect thee, and I shall never cease to protect thee."

After a moment of silent agreement, the two turned towards the royal chamber. Kennedy knocked, introducing herself, and they were ushered into the throne room, Leanna walking in behind Kennedy's large wings.

Queen Okalani was in discussion with Head Instructor Citsaloch, but turned from him and fluttered from her throne at the sight of Kennedy.

"Dear Heir, it has been some time since you visited me. How dost thou fare?"

"I fare quite well, Your Majesty; however, I'm afraid I come with a request." Kennedy stepped aside to reveal Leanna and, at the sight of her, the instructor gasped.

"A human!" He exclaimed.

"Indeed," Okalani replied, offering a stern glance to the instructor before returning a look of sincerity to Kennedy. "This would not be the same Leanna Page you were forbidden from rescuing yesterday, would she?"

"She is a dear friend to me. Dearer than I dare say," Kennedy explained.

"This is an outrage," remarked the instructor.

Okalani sighed. "Kennedy, you know our law does not permit humans at Anwansi."

"I request an exception," she stated firmly.

"An exception!" The instructor flared. Okalani took a sharp breath.

"Leave us," she commanded him. "Leave us, all," she added, more gently, to the guards. "I wish to speak to these two alone."

The guarding warriors bowed and took their leave, but the instructor approached the queen.

"If I may, Your Majesty, the Elders already begin to concern—"

"You may not. Leave us."

Recovering swiftly from the interruption, he congeed and followed the guards from the chamber. When the doors were secured, Okalani turned to Kennedy.

"Unlike numerous decrees we have discussed, young one, the law disallowing humans among us was one truly created for our security, which, as queen, is my prime responsibility—and mine alone—so long as I live."

"I know, Your Majesty," Kennedy said, "but I beg you to trust that as Anwansi's heir, I accept that duty with pride and ask of you nothing now that I would not do the same as queen myself."

Okalani nodded. "Then tell me everything."

Leanna listened and watched each royal with astute observation as Kennedy related what she knew of Leanna's story, which was indeed all, beginning with their own childhood in the caves. By her demeanor, it was evident the queen had puzzled out the identity of Kennedy's parents, and that both present parties were aware of such fact, but neither once spoke their names. I imagine, dear Reader, as Leanna heard her tale now for the first time, she must have suffered herself a small laugh, though darkened by the new loss of a precious character, as she thought, if she had not lived it, she might have liked to hear the story as a child. When Kennedy's telling at last approached your present page, dear Reader, she looked to Leanna with care, and then to Okalani with hope. When both were a moment silent, Leanna dispelled her saddened remembrances, and, straightening, spoke her first words to the queen.

"My loyalties have been often questioned, Your Majesty," she said, "by none so often as myself of late; but I assure you, I wish harm to no one, least of all the fairies who have been my only source of true companionship and trust."

"That is greatly appreciated, Leanna," Okalani began, "and please accept my awe and sympathies for how much has already taken place in thy short life." She sighed, taking on a tone of gravity. "The fact remains that the Elders will not agree to provide charitable asylum to one of the humankind, despite thy good nature."

"It needn't be from mere charity, Your Highness!" Leanna's desperation was thinly veiled behind her eagerness. "I could be of service, if you would allow it. War is headed hither. Guiomar of Pavoline intends to invade the Wood. I am young, and there is much still for me to learn of even myself, but I know I am capable of learning the military plans of Pavoline from the moment they are first spoken of to the knights—perhaps, with practice, even from the moment they are conceived in the mind of the king! With my powers and your warriors' skill combined, the Woods will be ever unconquerable. If I am permitted to stay, I will not take such kindness for granted. I will be indebted and ever in your service."

Okalani sat back in consideration. "Thou dost suggest, then, a type of military exemption?"

Leanna shrugged. "Sure," she said.

The queen suppressed a dubious grin. "That, then, would be entirely under my domain." She rose and strode, in a grand stately manner, to stand before Leanna. "Furthermore, it is my royal opinion that, with thine abilities, any monarch well of mind would be a fool to dispel thee." Kennedy smiled and Okalani offered her a conspiratorial wink before returning genuinely to the anxious human. "I shall not err in that way as did thy previous two, and, with the presently made case, I am certain I could subdue the objections of the Elders. Welcome to Alquoria, Leanna."

Relief blew through Kennedy and Leanna alike as both said, "Thank you, Your Majesty," and the queen smiled.

"I, for one, shall be glad to have thee among us, as I am sure Kennedy, and all who adore her, will as well. Evander!" She called to a guard who had stepped outside. He returned, standing at attention, holding one of the chamber doors ajar. "Leanna is a welcome guest among us. Please see she is escorted safely to Kennedy's apartment." Looking again to Leanna, she requested, "If I could have a private word with the heir…"

Leanna bowed. "Of course, Your Majesty, thank you. Thank you." After a kindly nod from the queen, and a brief grasp of Kennedy's hand, Leanna turned from the chamber and followed Evander back through the maze of the castle.

Kennedy stood before the queen and simply smiled. Okalani's countenance became somber.

"Forgive me, young one, if I have misconstrued what appears to me as clarity, but it seems to me that your feelings for this human are not exclusively ones of childhood friendship, and that the grander sentiments felt are shared between you."

The young fairy's smile refused to fade. "I will not deny it, Your Highness."

Okalani nodded. "I presume you are aware that, due to the manner in which Anwansi appoints its speakers, the tradition of the Queens of Alquoria has been to deny any extension of her family, to never take on love. There may be no ordinance preventing it, but it has never been done."

Kennedy's countenance stiffened, but, in her confidence, she refused to allow its gaiety to fall. "Yes, Your Highness. I have been acquainted with this through my readings."

"May I inquire on what you predict will be the length of this affair?"

At this, Kennedy allowed her countenance to become gravely sincere. "There is nothing in this world, nor any amount of time," she swore, "that would cause me to sacrifice the love of Leanna Page."

The queen looked down and let out a great breath, embracing her new understanding. She nodded and restored her forward gaze. "Very well, young one, I will not attempt to dissuade you. Only be warned that this, in all likelihood, shall become a new source of strife for you in itself. Do be cautious."

"Me?" Kennedy's smile returned. "I always exert the utmost caution in everything, Your Highness, haven't you seen?"

Okalani laughed and shook her head, dismissing the proud youth to return to her day.

A year passed by, and events transpired much as was predicted during that first meeting with the queen. Leanna and Kennedy did little to naught in the way of concealing their affections, and it caused great ripples in the Anwansian gossip circles. Their companionship already would have been regarded by all as equally unacceptable as were one of the Kesk warriors to fall in love with a Zil, but then to add to the circumstances Kennedy's heirship!, it was simply unheard of. The widespread recognition of its novelty was accompanied by an equally wide range of opinions on its righteousness. Of the many who thought against it, few were so bold as to say anything that might risk their standing with the queen or her heir, and Leanna successfully developed the confidence to care little about their smaller, snide remarks. Alternatively, Kennedy's friends, who were soon to be counted among Leanna's, such as Nientz, Phidia, Amicus, and all those who aided in Leanna's escape from Pavoline, gave the matter of their relationship little thought beside what was required to tease them with lighthearted rhymes; or, so they let on to Leanna and Kennedy. Their many remaining thoughts on the issue surrounded the manner in which they would defend their defiant friends if anyone would speak up against them or dare to wish them ill. Given how many warriors were counted among these, many who would have been willing to speak ill of the queen's heir, or her partner in life and love, still held their tongue.

As anticipated, the Elders immediately took great issue with Leanna's presence in their nation's capital, and they demanded that Okalani conference with them to explain, and ultimately reverse, her decision on the subject, inviting her into the Gwahanu Rotunda for them to speak. This back-most chamber of the Alquorian castle-caves had a transparent dome for ceiling and walls which allowed one to watch as the water-life in the Gwahanu River swam past, above, and all around, gloriously lit by Anwansi's mystical glow. This magnificent sight was reserved for a small few. Only the seven Elders who met there daily in their half-circle of thrones, and those they specifically called to sit before them, were ever permitted to enter the Rotunda.

On this day, they had called upon Queen Okalani, and she was led into the Rotunda, standing tall only some paces away from the entrance. Chief Elder Salvatore offered her a seat in the lone chair that sat before the Elders' thrones, but she politely declined, remaining in her place throughout the ultimately short conference. Although Leanna was well-informed of the Rotunda's restrictive exclusivity, naught had the power that day to prevent the girl from barging into the chamber to warn the queen of an imminent attack from Pavoline's forces, without glance or apology to the Elders who sat horrified at the brown, wingless girl before them. The queen darted out of the chamber to organize her warriors, and their later defense was victorious in forcing the Pavol knights to retreat. Despite the Elders' disgust and concern, none could argue after that successful day that Leanna's otherwise elusive intelligence was of little consequence. With Leanna's aid, their capital, and all of the Infinite Wood, was increasingly secure, and that alone persuaded the Elders to suffer her presence.

Chief Elder Salvatore chose the path of willful forgetfulness, acting whenever possible as though Leanna simply did not exist, leaving, as usual, all military affairs to the queen. Five of the others followed his lead; however, the seventh among them, Elder Cassius, held firmly to his view that Leanna's presence in their nation was so great a threat to their way of life that any protection she offered from external sources—ones that had never, in all the centuries, successfully encroached upon the Wood—was vastly outweighed by the damage she would inflict from the interior.

"Consider it seriously, Queen," he demanded, standing in the throne room during his twelfth audience with Queen Okalani on the matter, a weekly occurrence that was clear to continue so long as Leanna remained among them. "The girl is a distraction to Anwansi's heir. Putting aside a moment their differing species and color—itself a vital blow to the deep culture of our nation—the idea of a Fairy Queen with a love affair—it is unthinkable! No queen of past—or present, Okalani—hath taken up an emotional partnership. Indeed, no royally-born fairy would be so selfish as to insert themselves between Anwansi and its queen. THAT is the relationship Heir Kennedy ought to be fostering. Leanna Page careth not for Anwansi, nor at all for Alquoria. You know yourself the duties of the queen, they are not to be trifled with!" He paused then, in Okalani's silence, added, "If you would teach your licentious heir restraint, perhaps she herself could settle the matter favorably."

Okalani forcefully lowered a brow that had been involuntarily raised during his diatribe, and her wings twitched in an effort to remain still and sparkless. She sighed.

"As I have relayed to you before, Cassius, Kennedy is, firstly, performing outstandingly in all her preparative studies to be queen, certainly with more success than I in my first year of being heir. Second, Leanna is a valuable asset to our nation that I will continuously fight to retain. More, the girl hath a good heart; I have seen it." Okalani smirked. "I believe Kennedy hath done well for herself." Then with a graver sincerity, she remarked, "If they choose to remain together—perhaps even marry—I believe Leanna's presence will only improve Kennedy's execution of her queenly duties."

"She cannot intend to marry the human," quoth the Elder. "It could never be allowed, on this I know every Elder would agree."

"What if, one day, such was her wish?" Okalani inquired.

Cassius held down sparks of fury. "A Nachov may marry none but others of her kind. That is our law."

Okalani shrugged. "Perhaps it needn't always be."

Deep violet sparks flew from behind Cassius, and Okalani flattened her wings to lean against the back of her throne, patiently listening to his continued vociferation.

As the year passed its six-month, Pavoline's knights were eventually joined by Masor's as both kingdoms now sought to take custody of their neighboring sections of the Infinite Wood. As she'd avowed, Leanna spent hours each day in deep meditation, honing her talents, and grew to such skill as to observe at will through the very eyes of Guiomar and Isolda as they planned their every military operation. She watched their hands as they wrote out instructions to their knights. She put herself in their seat and watched their strategy meetings. Fairy warriors, with Leanna's preemptive word, would grow impatient waiting in place for the human knights to launch their various so-thought surprise attacks. Despite a year of either kingdom failing to conquer territory, the two monarchs refused to relinquish the desire to expand, and, having deduced what must be the cause of their current failure, they increasingly focused their strategic energy toward the locating and destroying of Leanna Page. They sent lone knights into the Wood with arrows, hoping to discover her hideaway and assassinate her from afar, but even these attempts were easily anticipated and met with a fairy warrior who turned the knight away long before they found the Anwansi Pool.

Leanna fought herself over whether to report that the monarchs were targeting her specifically, terrified that if the Elders found out they would take it as cause to expel her. While she wavered in silence, expecting to be confronted on the issue, she soon realized that no one was questioning the human monarch's motives or designs. Alquorians at large understood that the humans wanted the Wood, and so assumed that their every movement, whether large or small, worked simply toward that same base intention. No one beside Leanna noticed the change in Isolda and Guiomar's immediate target, and she found some peace in keeping that piece of intelligence to herself.

Her watchful eye on the human kingdoms naturally offered Leanna full intelligence of the wall that began to be erected between them. From her meditations, she often observed the masons at work on either side of the Gwahanu and thought on her long ties of ancestors who called each kingdom, respectively, their own. Watching the placement of the stones felt to Leanna as though each were placed directly upon her own heart. She would routinely dream with her mother, who had relocated to a small village just southwest of Pavoline's Tradetown, not far from where Lief had resettled, after her expulsion from the Masor castle. In conversation, she and Leanna would every now and then comment on the injury the wall struck against the spirit of their familial philosophy, but the thought of it too swiftly gave birth to thought of he who no longer resided in the northern kingdom and was hurriedly put aside to converse on other matters. Esta was naturally horrified at the alliance between Isolda and Guiomar, but she was grateful at least it meant her friends in Masor would no longer suffer under the drought.

Leanna at first looked in upon Madrick occasionally as he remained confined in his chambers, but she did not speak to him. He was retaining his health and strength of will despite his circumstances, spending his hours writing endless letters to Lief, although knowing they would never be sent. Leanna could not help but feel partly to blame for his circumstances and was sure the sight of her could only trouble him. He was unhappy, but he was safe and well. Once she was confident he would remain so, she let him fade from her thoughts.

Being that the wall had no effect on the operation of Alquoria, she made no report of it and kept private from the fairy-folk around her the deep grief she felt at the separation of the human kingdoms—a grief she felt incapable of coherently verbalizing now that she lived not among them. Warriors who patrolled around the Gwahanu quickly came to know of the wall on their own, and soon all were aware of its construction as well as equally conscious of Leanna's sorrowful silence on the matter. Only to Kennedy did she once let loose her tears.

On all other matters, Leanna came to be quite content. With secured safety, the lives of all on the Anwansi Pool largely grew in joyfulness, and Leanna became increasingly beloved by her new friends. Still, being that she had no predefined place in their system of status, fairies of all colors and aptitudes were equal in their uncertainty as to how to approach the strange human who walked among them. The Elders invisibly sent whispers amongst the fairies which spoke of Leanna, placing her most with the warriors but declaring her nothing more than a tool for military strategizing and encouraging even the commoners to think themselves above her. Many acquiesced to the rumors and shunned Leanna in the marketplace, but others began, little by little, to recognize the goodness in her humanity and welcome her into their lives, following the example of Heir Kennedy in closing their ears to the disdain of those around them. One of the carpenters, being among the kinder, built Leanna a ladder so that she could enter and exit the hollow unaided. Even a few royally-born fairies—especially those who had grown with Kennedy as a school-mate—became wont to, now and again, converse kindly with the wingless one. In time, the human girl developed a circle of friends which, although meager, was diverse as the nation itself.

Contrariwise, with every heart won to her favor, Elder Cassius made it known that he despised her a whole heart's-worth more for soiling their people's minds, and, though they said less of it, it was understood the Elders at large felt much the same as he and would welcome the day when it might be practical to expel Leanna from their grounds. So went on, in growing ferocity, a war of hearts as fairies of every color began to unite either in favor or in contempt of the wingless one among them, but the girl herself heard little of the latter's vociferations against her as, whenever they came about, she would hear Kennedy's words of love sing in her ear and know in her own heart that all would come to a happy end.

Most of Leanna's days were spent, as told, in service to Queen Okalani, but now came a day when the girl broke the trend, with Okalani's allowance, trading a day of service for a day of fun. Nientz had crafted an aerodynamic disc from clay and enhanced its flight power with magic so that, in sport, it might be tossed betwixt friends and soar great distances, showering rainbow-tinted sparks as it traveled; then, it would aid in its own retrieval, flying back to its most recent sender at a thought command, a feature inspired by Leanna's telepathic connections. So that they might test the new device, Nientz invited Leanna, along with Innogen—an artistic fairy, with artificially verdant locks mixed among her naturally ocean-blue, wavelike hair, who craved sport as deeply as any fairy born for battle—and Phidia—who, with now such distance from Leanna's unlawful rescue, had long regained her good spirits—to spend the day deep in the Woods at the infamous meadow all fairylings steal to sometimes in childhood to be free of their guardians' eyes. All three had eagerly accepted the invitation.

"A valiant attempt, Leanna!" Phidia bellowed from the air, laughing at the human's hopeless effort of jumping to the disc as it flew several feet above her outstretched hand.

"A level playing field might even my odds," Leanna retorted with a smirk. Nientz and Innogen chuckled, each themselves hovering at various altitudes above the ground.

"You have your skills. I have mine," Phidia said.

"Admit, at least, yours are more relevant to the current occasion," Leanna responded.

Phidia shrugged, lowering to Leanna's level and staring in her eyes. Utilizing her abilities to know the fairy's intention, Leanna tossed her hand behind her, holding Phidia's gaze as she intercepted the disc on its trajectory to Phidia just before it smashed into the back of her head. Phidia offered her a jovial nod of respect on the successful catch.

"Another well-crafted feature artfully tested," Innogen said to Nientz as the latter caught Leanna's throw. All laughed a moment as the game continued. Nientz threw next to Innogen, who threw to Phidia, who flew higher again in jest but tossed the disc downward toward Leanna who easily caught it with a thankful nod. In a shift of habit, Leanna turned diagonally to Innogen and threw the disc with all her strength on an upward course. Innogen floated up to adjust, but a wind came in and propelled the disc downward. She dove toward it as it passed beneath her, merely resulting in an airborne somersault, the disc soaring by into the Trees. Sympathetic joviality sifted through them, and focus turned to Leanna who could retrieve the disc.

With a smile and a nod, she accepted the duty and—adopting the peaceful essence of her familiar meditative state—closed her eyes and lifted her lids to the sun, opening her mind to all the world and calling the disc to return. Upon unclosing her eyes, her breath caught in her throat and her pulse began to race as she took in a new sight: no longer her meadow environs, but the burning eyes of Guiomar Ranzentine blazing in wicked glee just before her, any more features invisible in the surrounding utter darkness. Birdsong faded away as all sounds yielded to the Pavol king's triumphant bellows. In an effort to evade it all, Leanna reshut her eyes and shielded them in the crook of her arm. The king faded and birdsong returned as the flying disc bounced off Leanna's forearm and fell unceremoniously to the ground.

Lowering her arm and looking to her friends, Leanna could see their concern, but the attention of all four was then pulled to the Sky where dark storm clouds hastily gathered above them. The wind grew stronger, and the three fairies dropped into the grass to steady themselves. Leaves flew from the surrounding Trees. Petals were ripped from wildflowers and blown into the raging air. Innogen, Nientz, and Phidia fought the wind to congregate in the center of the meadow. Although they called for her to join them, Leanna was unable to coerce her feet to make the journey. Something in the storm seemed to speak to her, warning that she dare not face it in any manner but alone.

A thunderous crack sounded from the Forest. Leanna watched her friends' alarm with her eyes and, in visions, saw above her as an enormous branch, large and long itself as an average forest tree, fell from the nearest Infinite and made a rapid plummet towards precisely where she stood. Losing her footing to a gust of wind, Leanna fell to the ground and rolled aside, remaining on her back and looking beside her now toward whither she had been with marvelous relief to see the branch on the ground and the flowers that had been crushed in her place.

Another crack, and the Tree standing beside the first lost a heavy limb, again on a trajectory towards Leanna. She thought to roll further aside, but a third, now deafening, crack was sounded and halted Leanna in place. Another branch, lower than the other now in descent, broke from farther and on the opposite side from Leanna of the first that had fallen, and pointed towards her with its outstretched arm falling in a cross with the one above. As wind pushed against her ears, Leanna felt as though it wished her to remain still and, as she watched the branches fall down to her, she obeyed. This third branch fell faster than the second and it landed across the first, halting in place, inclined above Leanna, as the last completed its descent, landing on the other's raised body, its forward half remaining off the ground and directly in line with Leanna's upward gaze. There was a moment of stillness. Leanna caught her breath. The middle branch then began to quake, and she rolled closer to the first, which lay flat beside her, in time for the former to snap and vault towards the ground. The top branch that might have crushed Leanna if not for the middle's intervention, now rolled down the new decline of the broken trunk, finding stillness once tangled in the other's extraneous branches, and, at last, there was quiet. The wind softened, clouds dispersed, and Leanna lay still, staring at the protective tree above her, and beyond it to the bluing Sky.

Her friends flew towards her, but, seeing that she was unharmed, landed several paces back and waited for her to emerge. When at last she crawled out from beneath the fallen branches and began to pick out the leaves that had tangled themselves in her hair, she was eagerly embraced by Nientz, gripped kindly on the shoulder by Innogen, and offered one of Phidia's grateful nods. She gave them all small smiles but lost the countenance when her thoughts overtook her. Shock, they said it was, and followed her lead, returning to the Anwansi Pool in virtual silence.

CHAPTER XXIII

Defending Love

For some time, Leanna thought of the storm every day, every hour. She imagined Guiomar must have sent it with the Jewel of Nebulous, but in order to do so, in that moment, he must have known her location. If he could trace it on a map, surely his armies would have descended on the meadow, but he knew nothing so precisely. So, how had he found her? And would he be able to find her again?

Stormless month by stormless month went by until at last it had been a stormless year. A year passed again without significant incident beyond the occasionally wondrous military success, and all at Anwansi nearly forgot about the sudden storm or Leanna's remarkable fortune within it. Even Leanna, at last feeling securely hidden from her enemy's eyes, largely allowed it to pass from her mind. Still, when thought of it did occur to her, she shuddered with trepidation, desperate to persuade herself that the storm was an end, or somehow a coincidence, anything other than a beginning.

Kennedy, in the meanwhile, had entered her final and most tiresome season of schooling: an imperious cultural history curriculum consisting of private sessions in the Elder's Gwahanu Rotunda, reserved strictly for the queen's heir when she came of age. The longevity and frequency of these sessions were determined by the Elders based on the heir's progress and rate of retention, beginning with a single, multi-hour session on the eve of each new moon.

Prior to the introductory session, Okalani called Kennedy to the throne room for a word.

"Good day, my heir. It pleases me to see you well," she said as Kennedy entered.

"Well as I can be," Kennedy replied, bowing slight. "I shall admit an anxiety I feel regarding tomorrow's meeting with the Elders."

The queen nodded somberly. "It is this I have asked you hither to speak of."

"I welcome any word of wisdom, although I have been well informed it is forbidden for us to discuss the matter in depth. 'A destructive breach of protocol,' I believe Cassius said it would be."

Okalani laughed. "I would believe that as well."

"Might I take it then we are to dispense with protocol?"

"Not entirely, young one." Okalani sighed, remembering. "It has been such time since my own installment of the same you are now to undergo that I cannot be certain the details would do you any good. Instead, there is a separate tradition which I shall continue with you today, one of which the Elders have no awareness."

A spark flew from Kennedy's wings as she attempted to suppress a smile at the thought, and Okalani mirrored the cunning countenance which she had come to so admire.

"You hold all my rapt attention, Your Highness," Kennedy assured her. Okalani stepped from her throne and began to pace as she recalled years past.

"I did not have such a candor with my predecessor as you have with me; for, regrettably, I had not given my instructors the cause to march me before her so often as have you. So it was that we had not been so much as introduced until I was gifted Anwansi's wings, and even then we had very infrequent contact. It was the time when the Great Winds had been attacking, for the first several years at least, and she had neither the time—nor interest, it seemed—in advising me in the duties of our role. Such responsibility, she had told me, was in the Elder's domain, and they were quite keen to take it up. I would not say I truly knew her, not even by the day she died when I took her place, and I entirely expected my relationship with my own heir to be the same. Thankfully, you were far too persistently disobedient to allow me to be similarly neglectful." The two shared another smile before Okalani continued on. "I had one meaningful conversation with my Queen Rosaline, the same I then came to understand she had had with her Queen Alyssa, which was the same she had had with hers, and the same until the beginning. Through these discourses between queen and queen and queen, a story has survived, one which the Elders of ago would rather have obliterated. I know the story must be truth, for I believe only truth is so important to have survived in this whispered fashion for all these ages.

"It is said to have begun with the First Queen. At the time, the entirety of the Woods around the World Within was populated by our kind, all hues living and loving with one another. There were villages and tribes and small states, all with unique knowledge and history which has been lost. It isn't known precisely when the first Elders banded, for so many of the details have been washed away, but they came together—these various old Nachovy men from different places in the Woods—to declare a single nation of our people to be governed under their decided laws. They convinced enough others to fight for their state and Alquoria began to be established. It was then, in response to this movement, that Anwansi chose its first queen, and that queen went on to rebel against the new Elder's nation which sought to divide the people into classes."

"But—" Kennedy shook her head. "—we were told the Elders created themselves to rein in the wildness of an already active queen. Do you tell me they have lied so blatantly all this time?"

"I would not say anyone has lied, for they all believe they speak truth."

"But they are wrong."

"I believe so, yes."

"Has queen after queen told the Elders what is right?" Kennedy's heart began to pound, and her brow furrowed in anger.

"Many of us have tried, young one, including myself, but they do not wish to hear it and we have nothing to prove it with."

"Perhaps if—"

"Wait, Kennedy, allow me to complete the tale. You have yet to hear of what matters the most."

"Tell me," Kennedy demanded.

"As you know, a great war broke out between those who supported the First Elders and those who supported the First Queen, although they since have named it a matter of peaceful order overcoming ruthless riot. They have told us that those Elders invited the First Queen to truce negotiations in their ancient Rotunda and that through these talks they came to an understanding, building the structures of Alquoria as we know them today and relocating the remaining fairy population to our Anwansi Pool for ease of looking after. It is in the memory of these peace talks that the Elders maintain the tradition of their lectures with the heir. Similarly, it is with memory of the truth that queen after queen has secretly counseled her heir prior to these sessions.

"You see, Kennedy, the First Elders made no invitation to the First Queen but rather captured her and held her in the Rotunda with force until she would submit to their plan of governance. This aspect of the truth is indeed one of which even today's Elders are aware, and they hold great respect for the maintenance of that tradition. I beg you, young one, do not aggravate them in these sessions, despite how assuredly they shall aggravate you. If you can manage it, speak not a single word and let it all be done with so you might live out the rest of your heirship unbothered until the time arrives for you to take the throne.

"With that warning provided, I ask of you now something new, not typically asked in one of these queen's counsels. You see, the last piece of the hidden story is that, the day before receiving her new wings, the First Queen was gifted a dream from the Gwahanu—a vision of our creation. We have all been told for so long, even she, the First!, that fairies were created in phases, first the Zils, then Kesks, then Nachovy, each to further appease a yet unsatisfied River, but it is not true. In her dream, queens have told, the River taught our first predecessor how it created us all as one kind, each differing hue and different spirit merely a natural variation on a single form, none lesser than another, creating us all at once in perfect balance with one another. Only later when we fought and spun new tales and made new words for ourselves did we begin believing the Gwahanu would have separated us so. Unifying the harmony of our kind's many different songs is the singular mission Anwansi gives to its queen. You understood this from the start, but I give you this knowledge now so it can guard your heart in this final test of courage before you. You must not submit to the Elders, Kennedy, as I did, and all those before me. If anyone is to bring about a change in the way we live, I know it shall be you, young one. Hold true to yourself, you must promise me. Do you swear it?"

Kennedy sternly took herself to her knee and bowed, declaring, "By the River and Sky, I do."

She utilized Okalani's advice of silence for over half a year, enduring seven speechless sessions in the Rotunda, each of the Elders in turns lecturing on the history of the fairies, Anwansi's first queen, her recklessness, the formation of the first group of Elders, and the necessity of their purpose in maintaining order. Kennedy would nod and smile, but her high spirits and countenance of interest were maintained solely through focusing on the trout and otter who swam amongst the riverweed outside the dome. Still, she could not help but hear the Elders remark with complete sincerity on the inherent violence of the Kesks who must be kept in check, or the lesser intelligence of the Zils who must be provided for but not taken great heed of. It required every effort for Kennedy not to scoff at their suggestion that Nachovy fairies of their own color were the necessary leaders due to their inherent talent for compassion.

"I begin to despise my own kind!" She told Leanna after returning from a particularly agitating session. "Wherefore had I to be born like this? Fairies of my visage have only the wicked wish for power, and they care not for what harm it brings. Am I to be as horrid as they by the end of this?"

Leanna shook her head. "It is impossible, my love. Thou dost not truthfully believe such a sentiment can be so easily showered upon all of a certain kind. Think of Amicus, if thy own goodness cannot persuade thee. Perhaps an aptitude for leadership is neither good nor evil. Think of power as but the tool; what thou makest with it defines thy worth. Thou wilt make good as Queen, for thou art the incarnate of goodness herself. It cannot be denied."

Despite Leanna's encouragement, Kennedy grew increasingly irritable over these months, angering at every reminder of the harm caused by the Elders forcing their traditional lies onto their people. Without herself among them to challenge instruction, fairylings were once again playing in separate coteries, no color interacting with another; Zils were continuously delegated to agricultural work and craftship, withheld from official honor or recognition for their varied skills; even some among the Nachovy—those less eager to perform instructional or administrative duties in government, regardless of its accompanying status—were largely prevented from integrating with the rest of society to pursue what alternative interests they may hold. Most personal to Kennedy was the children she saw, however rare, who were torn from differently visaged parents in the destruction of families who stood too great a danger to the institutional myths to be allowed to prevail. More, Kennedy would now and then pass Stoman or Alizren in a hall of warriors, repeatedly devastated at their inability to look their royal daughter in the eye, lest her unlawful childhood be more largely discovered.

To worsen matters, the monarchs of Masor and Pavoline had begun to grow toward a cold cordiality, enacting a synchronous ceasefire in their war against the Wood. While the warriors relaxed, Leanna grew ever more vigilant. All the thoughts and communications of Isolda and Guiomar seemed to surround the construction of the wall—each side now almost a quarter complete—but Leanna was certain the tranquility was temporary and dreaded the idea that she had missed one relevant thought, or let slip some small billet, that explained the altered behavior. Despite her concern, from the Elders' perspective she was losing her usefulness, and in each session with them Kennedy could see their pool of patience for the strange human's presence in their capital was running dry.

It was Kennedy's eighth session in the Gwahanu Rotunda when the fragile peace betwixt she and the Elders was broken.

"As our queen," Chief Elder Salvatore began, "it shall fall upon you to encourage the maintenance of these vital traditions we have hither detailed. Your childhood, beginning with years whose content is still unknown to our court, was greatly dissimilar to one we would have wished for our queen. As a result, you have continued to fraternize with those so dearly unlike yourself, whether they be blue, green, or brown,"—Elder Cassius snarled at the reference to Leanna, but Elder Salvatore continued—"and, in your youth, we have allowed it, but you now approach your twentieth year. It is time you wholly accept your place and remove the tarnish you have begotten for your position. We demand you leave these childish relationships behind, and sever your contact with those who do not deserve the friendship of a fairy queen," he said.

Kennedy said no.

"That is unwise," warned Cassius.

"Wreak havoc upon me, then. Revoke my crown!" She rejoined. "How shall it seem to your people that you would deny the will of Anwansi? Even those foolish—or selfish—enough to believe what you have hither endeavored to 'teach' me, maintain an ultimate respect for the strength of the Gwahanu and our very hollow. If it came to the eight of us, my wings would place me above each of you."

"We have no intention to revoke your claim to the crown," quoth Elder Arbor, sitting second from the left and speaking for the others who still cringed at the heir's words. "We only mean to persuade the mind which that crown shall be sat upon."

"On this matter, it cannot be done," Kennedy assured them.

"You do not understand," Chief Elder Salvatore continued. "This purpose is the sole objective of our session today, and we shall not be finished until it is achieved."

Kennedy thought of the guards who secured the only entrance to the Rotunda, and she anxiously sat taller upon her chair.

Late that night, Leanna sat alone on the half-empty bed which, on a usual night by this hour, she shared with Kennedy. She sent her a concerned thought but received no response. Hesitant to intrude upon a private session with the Elders, Leanna lay recumbent on her pillow and coerced herself into an anxious repose. When she awoke similarly alone early the following morning, the glow from the gems being dim but indicating the passage of a sufficiently troubling number of hours, she instantly sat up, pinched her eyes shut, and sought the world for her love. Opening her eyes, and looking though Kennedy's, she now saw the beauteous reverse-aquarium of the Gwahanu Rotunda and the semicircle of thrones each holding a tired yet composed Elder. She could feel the heir's heart pound as Elder Salvatore said, "Forget them, Kennedy. Join us!" Leanna moved to watch through his perspective and at last brought Kennedy into view.

Wet, thick riverweeds had sprung up from the ground and wound themselves around her limbs, securing her to the seat. Her head hung low and wings drooped around shoulders which rose and fell with each heavy breath. Leanna watched as Kennedy slowly lifted her gaze.

"No," the heir said again, and Cassius—the one Elder designated to carry a bolt-spear—shot a spark at the ground near Kennedy's feet. The vines which held her lit up with the lightning and she seized, every vein in her wings igniting in pain. When the current was gone, the paroxysm left Kennedy stooped and contracted, the light in her wings having grown visibly dim.

Leanna, horrified, was stunned into stillness until, at last, she pulled her consciousness to its true surroundings and bounded out of their apartment, charging through the castle halls and around bends until she ran into the hold of Warrior Evander who now prevented her from banging down the Rotunda door. Struggling now with both the guards, she sent out a plea to Okalani, and the queen flew into the hall after but a moment, ordering that the guards release Leanna. Already apologetic at their task, the warriors swiftly obeyed the queen. The four then charged into the rotunda, Okalani at their lead.

Chief Elder Salvatore rose from his throne in dismay.

"Queen Okalani, remove yourself from the chamber at once!" he barked.

"And that human..." Cassius snarled.

"No, Salvatore," the queen declared, looking to her heir bound senseless in the Elders' chair. "How could you mean to continue this?"

"If we must discuss this, let it be in private," Elder Raply said, glaring towards Leanna and the warriors from his seat on the far right.

"No more closed doors! There has been far enough pain."

"Calm, Queen," quoth Elder Arbor. "We do no worse with she than we have with any other who have denied us. We would have done the same with you if you had not been more wise."

"I remember only too well what was threatened in my time here," she groaned. "My single regret is that, then, and since, I have not had the strength to forbid it being ever enacted again, but I have the strength now. Evander," she ordered the warrior. "Break these vines and take Kennedy to the healers at once." Evander did so with celerity, and Leanna watched with a quaking heart as he lifted Kennedy, unconscious, from the seat, and flew from the chamber. Leanna yearned to follow but could not leave Okalani to face the Elders unsupported.

"Order her return, Okalani. Our work with the heir remains unfinished," said Salvatore.

"Any work of the kind you speak is, from here on forth, forever finished," she declared.

"You have not the authority," Cassius condescended.

"I speak for Anwansi!" The queen boomed. "It has been ever disregarded that Anwansi's choice reflects the heart of our people, but their voice has been silenced long enough. I care not for your delegations of authority. Hither, you have mercilessly tortured the young heir to our nation's throne, all in the name of prejudiced ordinances that bring only further grief and separation."

"You speak of what maintains our way of life," quoth Arbor.

"Yes! A way of life that suits only you. Anwansi shall tolerate no more of it."

"Shall we ask the people what they believe? I am certain a great many disagree with you, Queen," quoth Cassius.

"That great many believe what you have told them. Another great many have learned to think for themselves," rejoined the queen.

"You would break our nation into pieces," Raply warned.

"No, I mean to rejoin us where we have been long broken," Okalani said, new hope encircling her heart.

"There would be chaos," Salvatore declared.

Okalani shook her head. "I wish for the stability of our people, as do you. I know you fear for your place in our nation, but understand, I believe you, Elders, are a necessary element in the stability I speak of. I implore you, let us—you and I—come together against these ways we have too long endured, put in place by Elders of a different time. You must know it is right. This needn't divide us."

"Absurd!" Elder Cassius began, but as he took a great inhale to continue his lamentations, the aged Elder Oorweg spoke from his place to the left of Salvatore.

"Perhaps it is time we consider what Anwansi has been trying to make us hear for many years," he said, earning a fiery glare from the Chief Elder before the same made a grinding turn to again face the queen.

"If we refuse?" Salvatore inquired.

Okalani looked to him with regretful surety. "I have the trust of our famously trained warriors. Give me not the cause to utilize it."

Late that day, after signing new ordinances, drafting their individual opinions, and calling for all able fairies to assemble, the Elders stood on the rainbow bridge before the Gwahanu waterfall as Chief Elder Salvatore read out the new order: in summary, all ordinances restricting activities on the basis of a fairy's color were to be disbanded. Warriors could be of any hue. Friendships would be allowed between fairylings of any colors. The odd child born with a countenance different from that of their parents could now be raised by those who had birthed them.

Many on the pool erupted into cheers and applause. Some, feeling with the majority of Elders, were displeased and grumbled away into private laments. Most, however, were merely struck confounded. Life was changing, and not all were certain what that would entail. On the whole, fairies returned that night to the same bed they had awoken in that morn, but something in every room felt shifted. Despite their differing thoughts, all went to sleep fascinated by what the next day would bring.

For Leanna, it brought a day of sitting beside Kennedy as she lay on her bed in the Healing House, embracing and conversing with Stoman and Alizren who were now able to stand openly by their daughter's side. Several of Leanna and Kennedy's warrior friends stood guard in the halls, ensuring none of those angered by the former day's changes to their nation's law could emerge into Kennedy's chamber and wreak more havoc on the two lovers than was already done. Kennedy's parents had warrior duties to attend to most of the day, but whenever possible they would visit the Healing House to see Leanna and Kennedy, both of whom they still lovingly considered their little girls.

The next day brought much the same, as did many days and weeks to follow. In that time, those who had been shocked into fury at the new ordinances began to lessen their show of it, and the sentiments of those who had cheered at the announcement began to win sufficient favor in the public court. Although she had soon awoke, it took time for Kennedy to regain her full faculties, and then still she required further care to see that her wings returned to their former strength. Throughout, the healers also tended to the spiraling burns that wrapped her shins and forearms where the vines had gripped her. Leanna often implored Kennedy to drink her vial filled with the magic of the Aldorian Waterfall which Leanna still, as promised, wore daily underneath her tunic, but Kennedy did not wish to consume the precious gift that was meant for Leanna alone. Leanna reminded her they could simply refill it, but Kennedy vehemently refused, explaining that the location of the mythic Aldorian Pool remained unknown to anyone beside Leanna—for fairies had heard legend of its mention but none had yet discovered it, and surely Madrick would not be capable of finding it a second time on his own—thus the place remained unpillaged, and she wished not to alter that. She assured Leanna, on the word of her healers, that she would be well in time.

On a day when Kennedy rested, Leanna left the Healing House in hopes that the fresh Forest air might ease her mind. After climbing the long rope ladder that had been graciously attached to the cliffside in her aid, she entered the Trees of the Infinite Wood and allowed destination to fall aside, walking whithersoever her feet desired. In her wandering, she strode haphazardly toward the border of the kingdoms and now came across an immense structure of rough, gray stone. Each stone stretched just beyond the width of her shoulders and was as tall as two of her hands. She counted at least a score of them spanning the structure's width and, when searching for where the stack ended in height, she lost it among the branches of the Trees.

Leanna walked beside it, running her fingers against the rock, and used her visions to look into the stones and see the interior of the structure. She found nothing but darkness, with stone after stone placed in the highest density of formations. She stopped, knowing around the structure's corner that Masor began only a few paces beyond, and she rested a palm on the massive wall—still only one-fourth constructed—which she had so often seen from afar in her visions and meditations. Being so near it now, she felt a new sadness come upon her, feeling sympathy for the wall itself. What it must be, she thought, to be created in the image of enmity, to have no purpose but to divide, no fate but to watch people see you and only wonder what further sight you prevented them from.

Creeping around the corner of the wall, Leanna now saw a singular vine, encircled in ivy, scaling the stones. Curiosity struck her as she placed a hand around the thick, sturdy vine, and she was then gripped with determination. She reached her hand high above her and leaped, grasping the vine and allowing it to hold her as she steadied her feet against the wall. Then Leanna climbed, glaring upward toward her destination, placing one hand above the other, moving faster, and faster, goading the wall to attempt to prevent her from reaching its peak, never daring to cease lest the fatigue in her arms overcome her. Even the vine's end only pushed her to grab hold of a nearby Tree branch, the sibling branches of which she continued to climb until, at last, she saw the summit. She inched out to the edge of a branch and, allowing herself to drop, fell upon the top of the wall.

    She remained kneeling there for some time, gazing upon the stone beneath her, attempting to catch a breath that insisted on running, both from exertion and, in equal parts, excitement and fear. She lifted her gaze and saw the pattern of stones she stood upon stretch out into the horizon, taking up all her sight except what her periphery could detect of the surrounding countryside. Finally standing, she walked some paces forward, lifting her chest and letting her shoulders down as she confidently strode upon the border of the two kingdoms. Stepping to the wall's edge on her left, she peered over it and found the Gwahanu River raging directly beneath. Looking up, all of Masor was laid bare before her. The outlying villages which she had never had the opportunity to enter were closer than they had ever been, and still indefinitely out of reach. Nearer, just on the opposite riverbed, she could make out the unique rocky landscape that housed the abandoned ruins of the ancient city of Pavoline that the Oxbiens of Masor had overtaken all those centuries ago. At this she turned to her right, taking in the villages of Pavoline's current kingdom. Massive plains of grain were scattered with homes and vegetable gardens, a web of tawny dirt paths tethering one to the next, all connecting to the same central road which ran from the Gwahanu straight to the Pavoline castle. Leanna looked again to her left, knowing an identical path could be followed from thence to the citadel of Masor. Laying aside some differences in architecture and landscape, each kingdom seemed, from her present vantage, to be so much alike, that it felt strange to think of them as two when—as was evident to her now—they so easily could have been one.

    She sighed and ambled back toward the Infinite Wood, hopping along, playing with the cracks in the stone. When she was again under the shade of the Treetops, she turned back toward the kingdoms and sat upon their wall, relaxing into her meditative position. She closed her eyes and saw, in greater detail, every inch of Masor and Pavoline. She saw the seamstresses mending their neighbors' clothes, jewelers taking their wares to their citadel markets, and children gamboling amongst them, here being lifted by their parent so they could pick an apple from a tall tree, and here accepting a sweet tart from a village baker. Although Leanna knew which sight was from which kingdom, it hardly mattered to her now as all the World Within the Wood flooded at once into her mind.

The images vanished, and the eyes of Guiomar Ranzentine assailed Leanna's vision in their place. His maniacal laugh began in her ears.

I have found thee, she heard him say.

Her magical vision faded and her sight returned to find the environing Sky had darkened and strong winds were circling the clouds. Leanna pinched her eyes against the wind but remained steadfast, watching as the darkness ahead gathered speed. Directly above the Gwahanu, the clouds began to twist into a point, traveling downward and ever closer to where she sat. Leanna took her hands from her knees and placed them upon the wall, leaning forward to steady herself against the wind, scowling at the tornado as it touched the top of the wall and began to race in her direction. As she had been in the storm those years before, Leanna was confounded to feel a certain consciousness seep into her from the winds. There was no question now that Guiomar had sent the storm using the Jewel of Nebulous, but how was it that Guiomar's storm—sent with the certain intention of ending her life—could offer her the simultaneous suggestion that she need only to remain still to remain safe? The Jewel wanted her, she recalled. It seemed, then, it wanted her alive. With her mouth set hard in defiance, she held her place against the storm.

"Leanna!" came a call from the Trees. Leanna gasped, startled out of her conviction, and turned round to see the purple sparks of Amicus fluttering amidst the winds.

"Go back!" she called to them, reaching behind her in a gesture of warning and falling onto her forearm. Despite her calls, Amicus flew towards her, determined they could save her from the approaching storm. Leanna watched helplessly as the tornado leaped over her and picked up Amicus in its winds, hurtling them in spirals through the Trees.

"Release them!" Leanna pleaded, and in the following instant Amicus was flung from the storm and into the nearest Tree, wings and bones fractured on impact, left to fall powerless through the branches and down to the ground.

Leanna thought of Kennedy's healer and sent her a call for aid, then she jumped into the Tree she had climbed and began her descent.

When the healer arrived, she found Leanna halfway down the vine and flew her the remainder of the way to the Forest floor where Leanna brought her to Amicus, who lay in pain, recumbent against the bottom of a Tree. At Leanna's own encouragement, the healer left her behind, carrying Amicus back to the Anwansi Healing House. Leanna watched them until they were out of sight and then looked tempestuously up at the Sky, but the winds had dissipated, and the tornado was gone. With a final glance, promising challenge to the wall, Leanna stumbled her way back to Anwansi.

The next day, Kennedy and Leanna sat by Amicus' bed in the Healing House.

"I was patrolling the Woods. I wanted to see if I could be a warrior," they explained. "I'd be permitted now if the queen wished to accept me in her forces, but I suppose I would be hopeless."

"Amicus, if you had not put yourself in Leanna's way, she might have been killed. You saved a life! That alone puts you in the ranks of our best warriors." Kennedy took Leanna's hand, and Leanna smiled, nodding for Amicus' sake, hiding what she knew to be true, and Amicus thanked her with an uncertain grin. Shortly thereafter, Leanna begged their forgiveness and took her leave, justifying her departure with a need to detail the incident to Queen Okalani. Though she did intend to speak with the queen, she feared to disclose the discussion's true purpose in the public space.

Leanna arrived at the throne room, and Okalani happily bid her enter. At Leanna's involuntary glance toward the guards, the queen motioned for their exit. The guards congeed, taking their leave.

"Thou dost seem troubled, Leanna," the queen said. "I have heard tell of thine ordeal, and I am sorry for it, but I sense there is something further clouding thy mind. Do Kennedy and Amicus continue to improve?"

Leanna nodded. "Kennedy is doing well, and Amicus shall so in time. I come to you now for my own sake, if I may."

"Certainly!" said the queen. "Do go on."

Leanna took a breath. "I have heard that the Jewel of Nebulous is present in the old legends of Alquoria. Could you tell me its story?"

The queen sat back. "I fear the legend tells of little more than the Jewel's mere existence, and of its power," Okalani began. "Until it was unearthed by thine own parents, there was no certainty that stories of it were even true."

"But what do the stories say?" Leanna urged.

"Well, they speak of a deep envy the Gwahanu River felt for the Sky, with all Its varied abilities and colors. Legend suggests that the River wished for the power to control the Sky, same as the Sky had always held charge over the visage of the River, ever reflecting Itself upon the other's surface. If tales speak truth, then the Gwahanu reached into the lowest depths of Itself to forge the Jewel and soon regretted it, thus hiding it away where it could never be found."

"It is malevolent, then," Leanna said.

"It seemeth so," the queen agreed. "Thou hast spoken thyself of the grief it brought to the lands before the human monarchs allied. Tell me, Leanna, wherefore dost thou inquire of it?"

Leanna looked to the floor. "I have not been entirely forthcoming, Your Highness. Guiomar and Isolda did not only send forces to the Wood for the purposes of expansion, but—perhaps more so in the last of them—they sought specifically my destruction, understanding my abilities and wishing to exterminate them from the world."

"My goodness, Leanna! Whyever didst thou hide such a circumstance? I might have assigned thee a closer guard."

"I did not wish to be any more trouble than I was already, Your Majesty; still, I confess that the idea has caused me particular distress of late."

"Of late? Do they not appear to have abandoned their aim?"

"I fear the traditional attacks having ceased merely tells us their strategy has shifted."

Okalani's eyes grew wide with understanding. "The storms."

"Yes, Your Majesty."

"Then we must be ever cautious to keep thee where vicious winds cannot reach."

"That is not my chief concern, Your Highness." Leanna looked down again.

"What is it, young one?"

She hesitated, finding the appropriate words. "The Jewel's storm heeded my word." Okalani's countenance made her puzzlement evident, so Leanna specified, "I asked the storm to release Amicus from its grasp, and it obeyed me. I am certain."

"I see," the queen remarked.

Although her voice felt near shattered, Leanna asked her deepest query, one whose answer she had been conscious of dreading for longer than she dared admit:

"Why would an instrument of evil answer to me?"

Leanna could see in the queen an utter absence of certainty, but Okalani hastened to hide it. At the queen's request, Leanna consented to be examined, and the royal fairy flew from her throne, placing her palms upon Leanna's back. Leanna could see the chamber grow brighter as Okalani's wings glowed at the absorption of energy caused by her touch. The queen then removed her hands, and Leanna spun to face her, seeing Okalani unable to hide her expression of amazement with sufficient swiftness.

"There is great power within you, Leanna," Okalani began, slowly deciding upon her careful words. "The immense magic of the Gwahanu swims freely in your veins. It is the same magic utilized by the fairies, but we are mere conductors of it. You are a source. The small magic held in a fairy's wings permits us to live a hundred, a hundred twenty years. You might survive through several centuries, young one." Leanna's eyes widened and brow furrowed at the prospect, as well as the queen's new deference to her. "If anything was created directly through the magic of the Gwahanu," the queen went on, "you are certain to be counted among them. Perhaps the Jewel knows this, and it wishes to combine its power with yours, taking you for its controller."

"Me?" Leanna said. "With the power to hurl lightning, muster storms, create droughts! I could never take control of such a thing."

"The wishes of such elemental magic as this can be incredibly difficult to defy," Okalani confessed.

"No." Leanna cried, stepping back from a silent, sympathetic queen. "No! I shall never wield the Jewel of Nebulous!" She ran from the throne room, leaving Okalani bewildered in her wake. As she ran, throwing aside the stone doors of the hall, she failed to notice Elder Cassius who had stepped aside and out of her path, having just heard all that had gone on within. He stepped into view from the doorframe, and Okalani caught his glare as the chamber door shut in front of him.

Leanna spoke neither of the Jewel, nor her meeting with Okalani, to anyone for the waxing and waning of many moons. She tried to smile for Kennedy and insist all was well, but beneath the false pleasantries, Leanna's spirit was crumbling. She could no longer glimpse her own reflection in the pool without imagining the terror which could befall the world at her own hand. Kennedy looked at her every day with such adoration. Leanna could not imagine anyone being able to maintain that if they knew what she really was, and she neither wished to break Kennedy's heart with the truth, nor of course to break her own by having to watch Kennedy's looks of adoration turn to horrified disgust.

With the ceasefire of the kingdoms making her unneeded in the planning of defense, Leanna knew only too well that the Elders would be seeking her removal, and she felt their glares upon her during every entrance and exit from the palace caves. She decided to forgo even imagining the diatribes Queen Okalani was enduring in defense of her. The Queen made many attempts to speak with the powerful wingless one, hoping to help her find some comfort, but Leanna refused and evaded her every sympathy. If she could simply avoid looking in the queen's eyes, or in her own, Leanna could nearly pretend nothing had changed at all.

As Kennedy shadowed the queen for further instruction, Leanna, to fill her days, began participating in what she could of the warriors' training, a now more colorful display, proving soon rather adept in the skills of combat and defense. When training took to the Skies, Leanna would aid the carpenters with village repairs or tend to the citadel fruit gardens; she would act as Nientz's assistant as the inventor worked on new creations, and she would picnic in the Treetops with Kennedy when both were unoccupied and whistle along with the birdsong; however, every cloud Leanna saw in the Sky colored her increasingly morose until she was unable to pretend to Kennedy that there was naught upsetting her.

They sat in the Forest meadow on a cloudless day in Spring when Leanna confessed to Kennedy all she had experienced in the storm and all that had been said betwixt herself and the queen.

"I fear I shall become a monster, and one that shall refuse to die!" She concluded.

"Never say so of thyself," Kennedy commanded. "Thou art the farthest from a monster, and the longer thou art in the world the better the world will be for it."

"No, think on it, love: a world where the whims of a near-immortal being controls our Skies. It is not one I would seek to live in."

"Thou needest not acquire the Jewel," Kennedy offered.

"But what if Okalani is right, and it becomes impossible to resist its call? What am I to do with that power?" Leanna's mind began racing as she finally spoke her fears aloud.

Kennedy attempted to calm her. "Was it not thee who said power is but a tool? If such a day was to come, would not thou still be the arbiter of how such power was wielded?"

Leanna shook her head. "The Jewel hath its own intentions, and the murals our mothers have spoken of on its cavern depict nothing of goodness in its desired wielder. Perhaps the Jewel itself would be capable of persuading its supposed master toward malignancy; consider, then, my natural abilities in addition. I can walk in people's dreams! What if I am induced to misuse such powers? The world would be helpless against me! I would become the ultimate—"

"Thou art not a monster," Kennedy repeated. "And thou shalt never become one. It is impossible." Kennedy smiled and Leanna turned away, unsure. The fairy became stern. "Think not a moment more on this, Leanna. We shall always protect each other. That has been our oath. The Jewel will never reach thy hand, not while I might hold it in its place."

Leanna faced her with a sad smile. "If I am to survive centuries beyond thee, how am I to bear the years?"

"I shall deliver my love into the years that succeed me. As long as thou dost live, I shall be in thy heart."

They kissed, and when they held back, brow touching brow, Kennedy whispered softly to Leanna's ear.

"Marry me?" she asked.

The next year was filled with gaiety and jubilation, despite the recurrences of certain irritations and strife. Much of the Alquorian population sought to aid in preparations for the wedding, but another many of the fairies sought to prevent it, the Elders at their forefront. The Elders, united in purpose, reminded Kennedy that royal-born fairies were never married without the Elders as their officiants, and not a single Elder would dream of officiating such an atrocity as this marriage would be. This matter did not concern Kennedy in the slightest, as she had no intentions of having the Elders in her wedding; however, Elder Oorweg, having been the least vocal of all, at last, broke form with his fellows and requested to be part of the ceremony. At this, much of the population's resistance fell away, and, with the support of the queen and an Elder combined, the remaining court had little power to forbid the event from taking place. The preparations went on in full force, fairies from every part of Anwansi coming together to glorify the celebration. Throughout the year, Elder Cassius continued his pontifications ("a fairy queen to marry—And with a human!"), but most no longer paid him any heed, least of all Queen Okalani who was perhaps the most enraptured of all by the engagement. Leanna and Kennedy happily left the preparations to Amicus who had insisted upon taking the lead of decorating the Anwansi marketplace for the grand affair.

They were to have the traditional Anwansi wedding, always an exuberant occasion for all in the community. Merchants would fold up their shops, and the floating cottages would be pushed aside to create a sizable, rounded amphitheater adjoining the Gwahanu fall and its rainbow bridge. Six lengths of wooden deck would be placed in radial symmetry around a circle composed of planks decorated with colorful flowers, this central place being the location of the Inner Circle.

For the marriages of warriors or royal fairies, the Elders would traditionally compose the Inner Circle, but "common" fairies, for whom the Elders would not deign to officiate, would make the request of their dearest family and friends to act as their Inner Circle, and the ceremony would continue on, in all else, the same. The remaining guests—forming an outer circle—would hover over the water between the outstretched, radial docks and offer their brightest glow to the starlit occasion, leaving the surplus population of the capital to watch happily from the casements of their adjoining cottages, atop the rainbow bridge, or from perches amidst the roots of the cliffside Trees.

Now, on the night of Leanna and Kennedy's nuptials, all was set for the beautiful occasion. The docks were in place and guests were gathered around. Forming their chosen Inner Circle stood Nientz, Phidia, Innogen, Amicus, Queen Okalani, Elder Oorweg, and Stoman and Alizren. It was the first Inner Circle in Alquorian history to be multi-hued, and even many who had been against the marriage could not help but smile at the sight.

The soft, sylvan singing began as the two lovers appeared at their alternate sides of the dock. The members of the Inner Circle stepped back so the beloved might gaze upon each other as they walked; and so they did, Leanna sighing in her good fortune, seeing Kennedy's vibrant violet tresses falling around her shoulders, Kennedy smiling at Leanna's exquisite gown— designed by Amicus and ornamented with pale turquoise and lavender sashes around the bodice—Leanna awing Kennedy with her dashing, forest-green cape flowing in her wake, three-parted to frame her glowing wings, and

Kennedy sighing, stupefied by the beauteous eyes which looked back at her, surrounded by tight curls elegantly lifted together with shining, silver pins. Kennedy's tear; Leanna's smile; her sparking wings, and her eager heart; Kennedy taking Leanna's left hand, and Leanna taking Kennedy's right as, together, they stepped into their endearing circle.

Kennedy and Leanna looked round to their friends and loved ones, all of whom returned to them with smiles and restrained tears as they swelled with emotion. Okalani took in a staggering breath, preparing to begin the circle of remarks, then swiftly released it in laughter, wiping aside a tear. She began again, taking in a deep breath, but suddenly the attention of all present was taken up to the Sky as thunder began to rumble in the clouds which now gathered above. Leanna pulled sharply away from Kennedy's hands, now seeing the eyes of Guiomar Ranzentine flash amidst the lightning which developed over her head. She watched, feeling as though the passing of time slowed to a steady pulse, as a bolt erupted, splintering the air, carving a path directly toward her. She tried to shield herself but looked not away as the lightning twisted and turned in its descent, now straying from its intention, falling asudden on the chest of Queen Okalani. Even with the dissipating clouds, the darkness which followed the flash was nearly insurmountable; still, in the fainter glow, no one could miss the body of their queen who, darkened, lay dead at their feet.

CHAPTER XXIV

The Woodbound Players

"See what thou hast brought upon us!" Elder Cassius stormed into the wedding circle in a paroxysm of indefatigable remonstrance, and all those around listened intently. "Thou villain; base, caitiff demon! It is not unknown, thine antagonism with the king of Pavoline, nor how he makes use of the Nebulous Jewel. This attack was meant for thee! Thou hidest among us and bring only strife."

"Speak not to her so; this is not her doing," Kennedy said, and turned a pleading look to Leanna to defend her innocence.

"He is right," Leanna said, now lifting her terrorful eyes from the body of Queen Okalani. Cassius ceased his shouts, looking to Leanna anew.

"Say not so, my love," Kennedy begged, but Leanna motioned for her silence.

"Guiomar doth strive for my death," quoth she, "and his only recourse is the utilization of the Jewel, but I shall never die by its hand. Despite Guiomar's intentions, the weapon refuses to kill me. I realize only now how I have survived it thrice." She looked at the Sky, remembering, and was horror-struck by her new understanding. She turned to the only eyes which might give her comfort. "Kennedy, I was merely frightened—and it spared me!" Leanna gazed upon Kennedy's grave visage that, so recently, had shone with such glee, and she regretted her next words before she spoke them. "So long as I remain hither, the storms above us shall never cease." Kennedy shook her head in plea, but Leanna went on. "I cannot stay. I cannot watch more be harmed where I was meant to be destroyed."

"No, thou cannot leave," Kennedy said, a sob shaking the stability of her voice. "Whither art thou to go?"

Leanna turned from her a moment. "Please, inquire not on what thou knowest I have no answer for."

"I meant thee to be safe here." Kennedy took Leanna's hand, and Leanna gripped it tightly.

"So I was! But it is now thy safety I must care for, and to do so I cannot be by thy side." She thought a moment, then added, "I can be by no one's side."

Kennedy again took on her stern, determined countenance. "Thou art no monster," she said, but Leanna pulled away.

"I feel it calling for me, Kennedy. The Jewel of Nebulous is mine, or it wishes to be, and I fear, as time waxes on, it will take every part of my heart to deny it."

"Thy heart?"

They each gazed upon the gaze of the other, feeling a fracture deep within. Leanna nodded, and tears called out to be released from her eyes, but she denied them.

"For the world now, Kennedy, and all my dear friends," she looked to those around, "I cannot be among you."

"Then wherever thou dost go, I shall go with thee."

"No!" Elder Oorweg interjected, rising from having knelt before the fallen royal, and the sentiment was echoed throughout the crowd. "Okalani hath gone from us, Kennedy. You are now our queen."

As the realization came upon her, she looked out at the fairies of Alquoria, and they began to crowd in around her, whispering words of consolation and awe. She turned back to find Leanna's eyes, but the wingless one had run off and disappeared amidst the crowd.

In their bedchamber, Leanna pulled on her trousers and tightened her belt around her tunic. She took up her wedding gown, holding it before her, memorizing every stitch of the enchanting evening it was born from, then draped the gown gently over her place in Kennedy's bed. On her pillow now lay the vial Madrick had gifted her, holding the enchanted liquid from the Aldorian Waterfall. Again taking up the familiar piece, she tossed the chain around her neck and tucked the vial beneath her collar. Then, without daring to glance at any more of the place, she walked out of the apartment and into the labyrinth of castle caves, all now just as known to her as the halls of the Masor castle had become those several years ago.

"Leanna," a voice called from behind.

She turned to face him and sighed. "Elder Cassius, I shall no longer be the cause of your troubles, and I shall ask you for no forgiveness over the tragedy of tonight."

"A good thing too, for none was to be given." Leanna curiously noticed a slight affable tone about him, as though he meant the words more kindly than they implied. His countenance offered her sincerity without anger. "Thou hast displayed great honor tonight, and I thank thee for it."

Shocked, Leanna knew not how to reply. He continued.

"Think me not 'friend,' for I shall never be so, but—here." He held out his hand, opening it to reveal a bolt-spear, shrunken for the use of a fairy in miniature. "It retains its power despite its size. I believe thou hast been trained in its use?" She nodded. "May it offer thee protection from what the world might have in store."

"Gramercy," Leanna said, otherwise speechless, as she accepted the boon and tucked it within her belt.

"After thy choice tonight, if, by a twist of fate, we meet again, I may not wholly regret it," he confessed.

She could not help but let loose a short laugh. "Same to you, Cassius," she said. He nodded and Leanna smiled as, newly allied, they parted ways.

The chaos that had broken out on the Anwansi Pool made her precaution gratuitous; still, Leanna took care to remain, when at all possible, out of sight, following close to the cliffside and running her fingers across its smooth surface as she approached her little ladder. She reached its peak and stepped out into the Wood. Then, turning back, with a heavy heart, she stooped to the ropes securing the ladder to surrounding Trees and loosed them, allowing the ladder to fall. In its descent, it tumbled off the side of the walkway and sunk beneath the surface of the pool. Leanna stood, staring at the ripples. Her gaze then shifted up, and she took in all of the watery city, another of her homes she was to leave behind. She watched as several of the older warriors lifted Queen Okalani's body to their shoulders and carried her into the castle cave. An emptiness now washed over Leanna's mind as she shut out the world entire and willed an eerie silence to overcome her previously all-hearing consciousness. Only what her small ears could convey would be heard in her mind; all else, she determined, was to be silenced. She took a great inhale and allowed it to stammer out of her chest before she pivoted to the North and, with lethargic paces, strode into the Infinite Wood.

She walked in darkness, and light, and darkness again, she could not say for how long, allowing hours and days and weeks all to become the same, the light inside her ever darkening. She gave no care to whither she walked, so long as she remained alone. She did not stop when she came to The Dead Lands of Pavoline. She did not stop when she paced through Brutivan, or when a person of the town asked if she needed aid. She did not stop when amoral sandstorms blinded her in the desert, and she did not stop when she stepped again between Infinite Trees, walking ever westward, leaving behind the World Within the Woods, and moving ever further into the infinities of the Woods themselves. As time passed, weeks, perhaps months, she found more ease in maintaining a clear mind as the pressures of thought she had learned to absorb from the world began to fade into the distance. She began to return to herself and realized, with a slight smile, that she was dreadfully tired. When at last, one night, she could walk no longer, she brought herself to the Forest floor and allowed herself to find repose, recumbent within the crook of a large, sturdy Tree.

She awoke before she might have preferred. Was it the light? Or was it—she winced again, the toe of a sturdy boot entering her side.

"Ow!" Leanna curled into herself, looking up now wide-eyed to see a gruff visage staring down at her, curiously.

"Thou'rt new here," it said.

"And thee?" she responded, appalled to have discovered anyone in her path.

"Older than I look," The visage smiled, revealing bits of leaf in their teeth, and they offered Leanna a hand. "I called these Woods home for the most of it."

Accepting the hand, she rose to her feet and saw now a whole company of characters standing varying distances away.

"My name is Fantázo Fiala," said the one who'd kicked her, a clear tone of personal pride shining through their rough countenance. "Friends like to call me Táz," they said with a humble shrug, then turned with a grand gesture to introduce the others. Leanna could do naught but marvel as each waved to her upon mention.

"This here's Penny of Ord," Fantázo raised a salute to a woman who was about the same middle age as themself. She leant in comfort against a Tree with a gleam in her eye that meant she knew all the rules yet was unafraid to break them, and she held an oddly long series of scrolls in her belt. "She takes care to see the rest of us do our parts and don't wander off cliffs," Fantázo explained, and they moved on to the next.

"Then there's Dilan-a-Jove," They gestured to a younger man and took on a tone of exaggerated facetiousness. "He's always looking to put himself in the center of the grandest sunbeam." Dilan-a-Jove wore a grand colored cape, worn only over a single shoulder, stitched with intricate designs. This, in combination with his perfectly kempt hair, gave him an appearance only slightly more lavish than all the others whose garbs, Leanna now noticed, were also bright and sumptuous. "But he looks out for the rest of us," Fantázo confessed. "As our tailor, and resident costumer, he ensures the whole of us always shine." On this last word, Fantázo put up their hands beside their hips with fingers spread wide and shimmered them slight.

Dilan-a-Jove scoffed. "I cannot very well appear so marvelous without *some* visual support from the company. It would toss our entire stage picture out of balance."

Fantázo shared a knowing glance with Leanna, or so attempted. She returned only a befuddled awe. In further explanation, the leader went on:

"Next to him there's Gillian Roughhand, our carpenter; good heart in her, but she'll beat thee bruised if thou star'st at her wrong, and that there's Hanker Reed. He might look a bit big and frightful, but the most he aggravates is a little spat now and again with himself when he has trouble mixing the spices for a Forest stew."

"But he's much too hard on himself," Penny of Ord chimed in. "He's brilliant over a pot." The whole of the company agreed, making Hanker blush.

"Then beside him stands the glorious Lady Laborious," Fantázo said, delighting in their turn of phrase. Lady Laborious smiled slight to Leanna then paced toward Dilan-a-Jove, hoping for a new perspective on the odd stranger. Fantázo turned to speak hushed to Leanna. "She is usually perfectly pleasant when we aren't working on a piece, but she does become a bit tiresome once we begin, for once she has a part in her hand there's nothing she'll do in all a day but rehearse her lines with varied alterations in emphasis and pronunciation. Every player tends to have the Lady's part recorded in mind long before they do their own."

Leanna grew increasingly curious, but introductions continued before she could inquire.

"And last of those who dared approach!" They called aloud to encourage those who had stayed further behind to come nearer then, as the rest began to shuffle forward, Fantázo gestured graciously to the last standing nearby. He was a very young man, condensed same in energy as he was in size. "This here's Big Li, our favorite star, even Dilan-a-Jove must admit. Might look like a scrawny thing, but the power in his voice—oh, a song from him could reach the top of the Infinites."

Leanna shook her head and turned to Fantázo. "Forgive me, I believe I may be lost."

"Figured thou must be, this far out in the Woods."

"No, I mean not in location, but in mind."

"Ah, are not we all?" Dilan-a-Jove asked, though he neither expected nor wished for a response. Leanna turned back to the apparent leader beside her.

"Who are all of you?" She asked.

Fantázo took on their grandest smile and threw open their arms in a gesture of ceremony. "We're the Woodbound Players!" they said, and the others cheered.

"A playing company? In the Woods?" Leanna confirmed, and all the many players grinned, wide-eyed. "All of you perform?"

"Each and every one!" The remainder of the company had now approached, so Fantázo gestured to them each in turn. "Here now comes Taut, the weaver; Citron, the painter; Bellum, the tinker; Spark, the fire-tender; Duck, the mender; Slink, the joiner; Dizzy, the wheelwright; and, my personal hero, Quiliss, the scribe. All of them players in their own right when they want to be. Myself, I am the writer." Leanna merely watched in amazement. Fantázo turned to her, jolting her to attention. "And thou art?"

"Me?"

"Indeed!" Fantázo remarked. "'Tis thee who's stumbled into our playing ground; it seems a reasonable query."

"Yes, I suppose so, forgive me. I am Leanna." The company looked to her expectantly, anticipating a complete title. "Oh. Leanna, the—Well, I suppose I'm not much of anything anymore."

"Hast thou come from East or West?" Penny of Ord inquired.

"North or South!" Hanker Reed included enthusiastically.

"Is it possible to have come from so many directions when one is so far from the World Within the Woods?" Leanna responded.

Several players groaned in disappointment and whispered to each other. "Another Withiner," Duck, the mender, assured the group.

"Are there those from without?" asked Leanna with new fascination.

"Well, however are we to know such a thing now that thou cannot provide any information on the idea?" said Lady Laborious.

Leanna's brow only wrinkled more deeply.

"Calm, all, please." Fantázo implored. They spoke to Leanna: "Dost thou have a home, my friend?" Leanna thought to respond in the positive but, upon consideration, merely shook her head. The leader offered a sad smile and appeared to understand. "Then count thyself a player," they said.

Leanna stepped back in vigorous decline. "I have done no such thing in all my life."

"Thou hast never played?" asked Dizzy, the wheelwright, astounded.

"Is it so odd?" Leanna asked.

"I would hope everyone might have played as a child in the least," Dizzy explained.

"That, I have, but it is not the same. I mean that I have never performed upon a stage."

"We have no stage!" Slink, the joiner, assured her.

"But I know nothing of the art," Leanna resisted.

"That can be swiftly altered," said Quiliss, the scribe.

"You could never be assured of any quality," she tried.

Penny of Ord shrugged. "Then perhaps thou shan't be cast in a role."

"Still, thou shalt be among us," Gillian Roughhand gave her a nod.

"Our meal-pot will be thine!" Hanker offered.

"And thy clothing soon entirely new," Dilan-a-Jove declared.

"Our camp can be thy home, if thou wilt have it," Fantázo finished.

Leanna gazed upon the many novel visages before her, each, in their way, thrilling at the prospect of welcoming her into their fold. It had been so very long since she last interacted with others and, in a moment of weakening constitution, she forgot her vow of solitude. She lifted her shoulders nearly to her ears before speaking aloud her entirely mad conclusion.

"Very well!" She smiled.

She was thereupon surrounded by the company and showered with chatter and friendly inquiries as she followed them back to their camp.

That evening, she sat amongst the players in their nightly circle around the fire, Spark sitting especially near to it with pokers and a pile of cut branches, and Hanker standing above the raised pot, filling and dispersing bowls of stew.

"Tell me true, new one," Hanker began, taking another bowl in hand. "Dost thou enjoy an extra spot of licarga root?"

She shrugged. "I'm afraid I haven't heard of it."

"Ah! Of course. I sometimes forget the limitations of a withiner's palete. The root reminds one of garlic, except it has a touch of undying spice that erupts on the roof of one's mouth near the throat." Leanna only smiled, confounded, and Hanker brushed off the inquiry, coming to his own conclusion. "I shall give it thee, and if thou likest it not I shall give thee none tomorrow."

At last receiving a bowl and devouring a spoonful, Leanna gasped and exclaimed "This is magnificent!" while aiming her awe at the now beaming Hanker.

"The inner bark adds to the meatiness," he explained, "and it's the Infinite Herb which gives it that everlasting savor."

"Each one of these stews is like a new fire," said Spark. "No two are quite the same, but in all the years never has one failed to amaze." The company nodded with various mumbled affirmations in between swallows.

"For how many years have you all resided hither?" Leanna asked.

All eyes drifted to Penny of Ord, as though she was the only among them who could have possibly kept record; however, upon feeling the many gazes and looking up from her bowl, she shrugged.

"Impossible to say, really," she said. "Although, with the quantity of scripts we've begun, prepared, and archived, I think it must have been now over a century."

"A century! Then there have been many a generation of Woodbound Players?"

"Oh no," Fantázo said, for in this remembrance they required no record keeper. "We each met in Tradetown of Pavoline. It was not until working with one another for several a year that we decided to migrate to the Wood."

"Decided—Ha! Were expelled, more like," Quiliss said.

"Never legally," Penny of Ord clarified.

"We were chased from the town!" Lady Laborious exclaimed.

"There would certainly be no performing if we were to ever return," said Dilan-a-Jove.

"The people took a bit of offense to a play we had put up," Fantázo explained.

"Said as though thou wert not the writer of the piece, Táz," Big Li chimed in. "That was thine own fault, that was."

"'Twas thee, Li, whose voice carried the offense to their ears. Thou art as much to blame as they," said Duck, the mender.

"'Twas I who decorated the offensive scenery! Forget not my blame as well," Citron, the painter, implored.

"Nor mine, for 'twas I that built what he painted," said Slink.

"And 'twas I that designed what she built!" Gillian added.

"Well, 'twas I who built the costumes!" said Taut, the weaver.

Dilan-a-Jove scoffed. "Darling, the costuming was the one aspect of our performance the public didn't abhor."

"That cannot be said for certain," Taut pouted. "We never read a single review."

"The pitchforks were review enough for me," said Bellum, the tinker. 'Twas she who played the second lead.

"Pardon," Leanna broke in. "Do you all mean to say you lived entire lives in Pavoline before now residing a century in the Wood?"

The players looked to one another with little nods.

"The sound of it seems in the realm of correct," Fantázo said.

"But it isn't possible!" Leanna exclaimed.

"It isn't?" Fantázo furrowed their brow and then seemed to remember. "Oh, no, I suppose it wouldn't be. Alas, it really is impossible to say."

Leanna laughed as the players returned to their soup, entirely unconcerned with their previous subject of discourse. Infinite queries fought to break free from Leanna's imagination, but the most curious now won against the rest.

"Players, what is it that gave you cause to wonder whether I might be from without the Wood?" She turned to Fantázo now, following the gazes of the others. "Hast thou discovered an end to them?"

"No," they said, "But I did once reach the mist."

"The mist?"

They nodded and leant forward, whispering to conceal their words from the Trees. "Walk far enough into the Wood, and one day thou wilt reach a sudden great density of mist. When I discovered it, the sun was shining so, even through the Trees, that I was able to vaguely make out my own form reflected on the vapor. The Trees went on forever beyond it, but they appeared so alike to those I had passed that it was not truly certain whether those I saw now were ahead, or merely reflections of what was behind. I reached out—" Fantázo demonstrated now with a quivering hand. "I reached out and sank just the very tips of my fingers into the surface of the mist, and in a fraction of the briefest moment, I saw everything." They paused, remembering.

"Everything?" Leanna asked, encouraging them on, and they snapped back into their tale.

"Everything! Not of what was at the time, but everything that had been before it; before me! Before all of us. I saw of a time when there were kingdoms of which I never knew tale; languages—several!—of which I had never heard; and world maps, far from the likes of ours. There was food I would never have imagined (much less eaten), but there were also beauteous landscapes, such sights, the likes of which I thought could never be. There was magic like none that we've known of, and violence like none that we've known of, and destruction, and goodness, and hate, and love. So much love, and yet never enough, since the beginning of time. All this, see, I saw with my fingertips!"

"High as a kite, they were," Hanker laughed, and Fantázo confessed as such in a small grin.

"Still," they went on. "It was in that moment I knew there would be no returning to Pavoline, nor moving our practice to Masor. The Woods needed us to tell their stories, and to question every answer that had been hitherto decided upon. No one is better suited to such a task than a company of theatrical players. 'Philosophy's Art,' we call our work; for, what is philosophy beside posing impossible questions, debating the answers between a variety of minds, and preserving the discourse for posterity to consider and speak anew? Before this time, we had been merely fellows with a common pastime, but after we understood our duty. Henceforth, we were the Woodbound Players!, ever in search of that which resides beyond what we can yet imagine." Fantázo finished with a grand smile as the rest of the company cheered and howled with great pride. Leanna mirrored their glee.

"I wonder if I could see it," she thought aloud.

"The mist is a mighty journey out from here," Hanker told her. "Think not of attempting it tonight."

"No," Leanna laughed. "I need not travel a single step." She closed her eyes, sitting back against the large, felled branch behind her, and those sitting atop it leaned forward over their stew to observe her. She opened her mind to seek the world but, remembering the Jewel, closed it again, sitting up and reopening her eyes with terror. She looked to the Sky, fearing wrath, but none came. She waited, and even after moments all was still. Cautiously, she closed her eyes once more and sought with care, first thinking of Kennedy, then Esta, then even the dreaded Jewel, but every vision was hazy and indeterminate, every sound indistinguishable. She began to laugh, marveling at the mysterious Wood that could dampen her power, grateful and frightful all the same. She wept and laughed all at once, finally free to let in the world around her without danger. When she began to return to her sense of the present, the players all looked to her, frozen in countenances of varying concern and bemusement.

"Thou hast a story, hasn't thee?" Fantázo asked.

"I'm afraid so," Leanna confessed.

They smiled, Fantázo and all the players alike.

"We do love a story," the company said at once.

Leanna smiled with a soft sigh, and, at their eager behest, began to tell her tale.

CHAPTER XXV

Philosophy's Art

At first light of the next morn, all in the camp awoke to the clang and clash of plate against pot and stirred to face the dew-damp fire-pit whereupon whose stacked stones stood Fantázo with grand intention.

"I have composed anew!" They bellowed, throwing their pot and plate aside to display their newest pages. In an instant, the haze of sleep was washed away, and each of the players bounded to their feet, prattling atop one another's jabber, inquiring and guessing as to what the subject of their newest work might be.

"No, no, none of that," Fantázo responded to their speculations. "This new drama shall be the Story of Leanna Page!"

"Mine?" Leanna asked, amazed, now at last rising from her bed of leaves.

"Indeed!" Fantázo sang. "Why, it's marvelous! And I believe I've outlined it swimmingly into the dramatic form and shall detail it with poignant speeches, fitted to the scintillating magic, thrilling romance, and dangerous adventure which shall fill its every beat, if I may be less than humble."

"How shall it begin?" Dizzy, the wheelwright, called to them, eager to hear the story anew from a new mind.

Fantázo took on a low, active stance of mystery and intimidation, painting the scene in the air with their decisive gestures. They spoke: "It begins in the Cave of Nebulous whence two lovers had begun and concluded their courtship; concluded, for the power of their own hearts frightened them so that they sabotaged their intentions by each reporting back to their monarchs of the vicious weapon they had found within the cavern. But! their efforts were for naught, for they had already bound themselves in story evermore, for between them they had made a child. Thus—in this first scene I have writ here—when the king and queen of warring nations each arrive armed in the cave, the servants do all they might to persuade them not to fight and, most urgently, to let the Jewel remain in its place (it stands directly upstage center), one of them ever with her hand around the growing babe within her. At the servants' behest, the monarchs pretend peace, but as they begin to make retreats, the king lunges forth, retrieves the Jewel, and charges away to his own kingdom, and hither the story truly begins. As the child grows, she travels to the opposite kingdom every other season, not to be fully parted from either parent, and by the time she comes of age she hath served in both castles all her life, is aware of their every secret, and at last—in a final battle—rises up!, stealing the Jewel from the wicked king and *destroying* it."

Fantázo's intensity on their final words made clear they spoke of the end, and the players lurched into applause and cheers. Eyes turned to Leanna who was amused, yet puzzled.

"Lovely, truly," she said. "However, both the Jewel and I resided in the cave until I was an older child, and I never resided in Pavoline."

"Art thou certain?" Fantázo said, straightening and pulling their notes up to their eyes to study them. "I was sure thou hadst said thou wert the tiniest thing when the Jewel was stolen and that thou hadst traveled to Pavoline multiple times."

"Yes; however—"

"Ah!" Fantázo smiled. "Well, there it is then."

Leanna caught the gaze of Quiliss who shook his head sympathetically, indicating wordlessly that hers was an argument not to be won. She laughed.

"Very well, my friend. Have it thine own way."

"Splendid!" Fantázo leapt from the podium of the fire-pit and was instantly surrounded by players who gave over their every inquiry and idea.

Dear Reader, I interrupt briefly to have you know that, while for our purposes the playwright has comically misinterpreted the events for their dramatization, the version Fantázo Fiala has just told us is, in truth, as common a way to tell the tale as any other, including ours at present. Different Elenvian cultures tell the tale in different ways, with different beginnings, different middles, and different ends, each to the teller's own differing purpose. I have hither chosen to echo the telling that was conveyed to me before all others and which I find most appealing to my own heart. Furthermore, supposing the legend is made of truth, our current volumes contain what I find to be the most plausible of the tale's variations. Now, forgive my intrusion, we continue forthwith.

Following the announcement of the new work, the players set out to their tasks at once, spending their time in their well-practiced manners of play preparation, with Penny of Ord overseeing all to ensure the proper timeline was maintained in each aspect of the project. Taut and Dilan-a-Jove spoke of costuming and began to weave and tailor to their ends. Slink and Bellum, under the direction of Gillian Roughhand, began constructing the inner wall of a cavern and the majestic pedestal which would stand at its center. Gillian herself spent hour upon hour crafting wooden headpieces for the Crowns, carving in such detail, determined to make her fellows swear that the pieces were made of jewels. Citron was under constant consultation and was frequently out exploring the Woods to discover alterior methods of mixing paint that might yield particularly magical results. Fantázo completed their work on the script, each night reading a new part to the company around the fire to receive their compliments and critiques, reviewing, rewriting, and writing anew with each new day. When the final script was complete, Quiliss transcribed each players' part to their own separate book, beginning with that which would go to Lady Laborious, having learned long ago not to force from her any avoidable impatience. The Lady took it upon herself to mentor Leanna in the ways of performance, primarily opting for the method of instructing by example, Leanna then spending her days reading the player's cues and observing her in the habitual task of her namesake. Despite the ineffectiveness of her tutor, Leanna could not mind in the slightest. In reality, she spent these days observing the camp entire, cherishing the view. The care for one another, the dedication to one another, the serious and the silly each seamlessly stirred into a Forest stew. The recreation of her past, ever more similar to reality as the artists detailed their work, somehow stripped the memories of their horror, turning them into stories with meaning and resolution, no longer something that required turning out of mind for fear a glimpse would break her apart. Here, now, Leanna looked directly at every setting and costume of her tale, recalling in detail what the players' script did not contain, and thought perhaps that, for what had been given her, she had lived her life well. She, as with all others in the camp, was cheerfully anticipating the performance.

Once, unable to sleep for happy excitement, Leanna decided to take advantage of the light of a full moon and explore the Woods. Having walked long enough, she eventually came upon the wall of mist Fantázo had described on Leanna's first night with them. She sat on the ground some paces away from it and swayed with the music of the nightbirds while watching the moonlight reflect off the curiously visible air. As she sat and watched and listened and swayed, visions began to come to her from beyond the mist. It was all just as Fantázo had said, only she saw it with infinitely more clarity. It was like an entirely different world out there, and yet it so reminded her of the world she left behind that it began to darken her spirits. She rose and turned away, running back to the camp of the players and rejoicing again in the lightness of their company which was just now rising to a morning meal. Hanker gave her a smile with a bowl of breakfast stew, and they all soon set their minds back to their craft.

It really is impossible to say how long this all continued. Even Penny of Ord, although she ensured no element of the production fell far behind the rest, kept no record of the days as they passed. For the work that was completed, it seems highly unlikely the time that went by was less than many weeks, and with the free unlimited hours granted by the Woods, it seems entirely plausible the preparations could have continued for months, or even several a year. It is certain the players would suppose some years had passed, for this was indeed the most extravagant production they had ever put up in the Woods. With the play's true subject among them, none could prevent themselves approaching her with inquires and clarifications as to the style and manner in which something might have been constructed, ever endeavoring to bring the recreation more near to the history, often times breaking down a nearly finished piece in order to start again in accordance with a new idea. Yes, it was years, they would say. I suppose we may as well believe them.

It was some time in the midst of all this, towards the end of whatever period of time we can agree has hither been spent, that Leanna had a dream. 'Twas no vision, nor communication, nor even was it—as she was accustomed to—the type of dream wherein one is aware they are a dreamer. No, 'twas none of that; 'twas merely a dream, and, in so being, it confounded her. She spoke of it to Fantázo the following morn when they inquired privately as to her unusually silent demeanor.

"A dream?" They asked, soon nodding in—what appeared to be—deep understanding. "I had one of those myself," they explained, somberly. "Say nothing of it to Hanker, but I'll confess to thee, in the dream, I was eating bread and jam. Oh, I do miss it terribly now and again. Thou dost realize we have all eaten nothing but stew since we arrived in the Wood that millennium ago?"

Leanna was now all too aware, and, after a small laugh, she smiled in sympathy.

"I'm afraid the dream I have had this night was worse," she said.

"Worse!" Fantázo exclaimed. "My goodness. Wouldst thou care to tell it? Mine ear is thine."

The dreamer nodded, with brief hesitation, then began to speak. "In the dream, I had wishes unlike any from my waking life; or, more truthfully, I had one wish, one I have wished to never wish." She paused before confessing, "I wanted the Jewel. Táz, I sought the Jewel! Yet, I felt nothing of evil, nor wanted anything of domination or destruction. I thought nothing on anything of the sort, I only wanted the Jewel itself. I would find it—in the dream—nearly take it in my hands, and I would feel such relief, but the Jewel would then be swept away in winds and, devastated, I would begin the search anew. This continued time and time again until at last, once, nothing swept it away, and I took the Jewel in hand. I held it! Then I awoke."

Mirth had fallen away, and Fantázo studied her, deep in consideration. "What dost thou think of the Jewel now?" They asked, and Leanna shrugged as though it were unimportant.

"No differently than before. I knew the Jewel had methods of persuasion, only I never thought it could infiltrate my thoughts so directly. It frightened me, slight, that is all."

A moment passed, then a thought sparked behind Fantázo's eyes. "Excuse me, Leanna, I must confer with Quiliss." They were away in the following breath, and Leanna laughed, having now become much accustomed to the sporadic life of the players.

That evening, as Big Li collected the bowls now emptied of stew, setting them aside for washing (the best method of being useful he had been able to find beyond his talent for song and speech), Fantázo and Quiliss—who as yet had been absent from the supper—approached the company, heavy bundles of new pages in hand.

"I finished it," Fantázo said, but without their usual pomp. There seemed a gravity about them that none, beside Quiliss, could determine the reason for.

"But thou finished it some time ago," Lady Laborious recalled, holding her part in hand.

Fantázo shook their head. "I thought I had, but at the time I had not truly known what play the Woods had needed me to compose. I discovered it this morning, and now I have finished it."

Quiliss took the pages from the writer, offered half to Penny, and together they distributed the parts to their corresponding players. Fantázo remained holding one final part in hand, and they held it out to Leanna.

"Thou shalt read the role of Queen Okalani," they said, and Leanna accepted it curiously, not understanding. "It shall be good for thee," Fantázo explained, and they smiled, winking slight to ensure her all would be well. They turned and spoke to all the players. "If we could, let us read it aloud tonight around our perfect fire. Let the tale come alive!" They sat beside Penny of Ord who now held the only complete script. The players readied themselves, and Penny embarked upon the first words, reading the notes that sketched the script's first moments.

Lady Laborious became Isolda, opening the script with a ferocious speech, declaring dominance over her kingdom and over the world, as Guiomar (portrayed by Dilan-a-Jove) now barged in from the opposite side of the cave. Behind each royal stood Esta or Byrdon (Taut and Gillian, respectively) begging for peace.

Leanna watched the players move artfully through the script, Big Li taking on her own persona, traveling between kingdoms scene-to-scene. Now, in one such journey, the script began to stray from its last edition. In a speech from the bridge at the Gwahanu strait, where once the character of Leanna swore everlasting enmity to the Jewel whose chamber she stood several leagues directly above, now she (Leanna in truth) heard her recent dream echoed through Big Li's sturdy and purposeful cadence, speaking of standing above the Jewel's home, not angered at being so near but instead saddened by being so far. The Jewel was meant for her, Big Li spoke of in Leanna's voice; surely, it could not be wicked for her to desire it.

The scene which followed had Big Li and Gillian, speaking as Leanna and her father, as she confessed her inclination to take the Jewel from the vault of Pavoline in which it was kept and combine herself with its power, certain such would be the only way to maintain its security. Byrdon (Gillian) lamented in great vociferations on the malicious heart which dared remove it from its prior chamber at the start, and assured her only one of evil would consider such a thought in earnest, imploring her to put it out of her mind.

"Exeunt Byrdon," Penny read, "and enter Kennedy, in a dream."

Leanna's heart began to race as she turned eagerly toward Bellum who spoke Kennedy's words to Big Li, assuring the character of Leanna that there could be nothing evil within her, but her father's words had already pierced too deep. Big Li stood in the passion of it, bellowing to the Treetops Leanna's speech of self-loathing, ending as she forcefully awakens, sending Kennedy away, and herself dashing from the scene.

The last scene into the next took her once again from Pavoline into Masor whither she halted in the central market, slandering the crown with all her might, spewing vicious untruths to the public until guards swept her away and locked her deep below the castle. Kennedy found her again in a dream and listened in pain as Leanna explained her purpose, intentionally forcing her own arrest in Masor so she might be ever incapable of reaching the Jewel. Bars were a necessity, she said, because her weak will would never keep her from taking up the weapon; she had no such strength.

Bellum glanced up from her script only briefly as Big Li spoke to see Leanna staring toward him, entranced in anxiety. Thankful, she took her next line, earning Leanna's instantly shifting attention, to speak in Kennedy's voice the gracious gift of a kinder solution:

"Let me rescue thee, Leanna, and same I shall rescue the Jewel from the grasp of Guiomar. I shall take you both to Queen Okalani in the Fairy Nation and thou shalt watch as she destroys the weapon, as surely she hath the power to do. Thou shalt be free, Leanna; truly free."

With tears, Big Li spoke Leanna's acceptance of her beloved's proposition, and Penny introduced the next scene.

There was silence.

"This is thy part, Leanna," Penny prompted.

"Oh!" Leanna turned to her script to find Okalani's words, and, between each of her lines, looked urgently again to Big Li to see her own character's reply.

Okalani (Leanna): "What have you brought to me, young heir?"

Kennedy (Bellum): "On the ground between us, I now place before you a weapon of legend. Thither it lays, the Jewel of Nebulous. She whose hand I now hold is known as Leanna Page, and it is she who, in its wickedness, the Jewel most calls to, causing her much pain and strife. We ask of you now a great service. Might you destroy the Jewel, and save both Leanna and the world from its power?"

Okalani (Leanna): "You were right to bring this to me, Kennedy, thank you. I would like a word alone with the page, if you would step outside."

Penny: "Exeunt Kennedy."

Leanna (Big Li): "Is it possible? Can you vanquish it?"
Okalani (Leanna): "I can, but I will not."
Leanna (Big Li): "Wherefore!? I beg you, Queen, I have not the strength to resist its call!"
Okalani (Leanna): "Then—"
Leanna paused as she saw the Queen's next words and flashed her glare to Fantázo who merely nodded, gravely. With chest pounding, Leanna returned to the page.
Okalani (Leanna): "Then do not resist the call."
Leanna (Big Li): "That is madness. It is wicked. I would be wicked!"
Okalani (Leanna): "The calling within you may not be villainous as you believe it to be."
Leanna (Big Li): "How can it be anything but evil to yearn for such power?"
Okalani (Leanna): "To yearn for power is indeed to yearn for what may bring great evil to the world; but, it is also to yearn for what may bring great goodness. Until you take the power upon yourself, it is impossible to know which you shall become."
Leanna (Big Li): "Then I shall not take it upon myself. The risk is too great."
Okalani (Leanna): "Is there no risk in denying it? Who shall wield the power in your stead?"
Leanna (Big Li): "No one! You can destroy it!"
Okalani (Leanna): "I can destroy the Jewel, but Power shall always remain. Who wields it over your world now?"
Leanna (Big Li): "The royals."
Okalani (Leanna): "And do they wield it well?"
Leanna (Big Li): "No."
Okalani (Leanna): "Might you wield it better?"
Leanna (Big Li): "I couldn't possibly."
Okalani (Leanna): "Wherefore?"
Leanna (Big Li): "I am no one. Who am I to hold such sway over the world?"
Okalani (Leanna): "Who are they who hold it now? Who am I? We are No One of a different kind. This Jewel seems to think you are someone of great import. I think you should hear it."
Leanna (Big Li): "What if I am wicked?"
Okalani (Leanna): "I believe you are good."
Leanna (Big Li): "You said it was impossible to know for certain."

Okalani (Leanna): "I did not say 'I know.' I said, 'I believe.' Can you do that? Can you believe that you are good?"

Leanna (Big Li): "But I do not. I feel such anger and envy. Surely there is a base chamber of my heart, and I wish never to see it."

Okalani (Leanna): "Leanna, to find what is truly good within us, we must face what is evil with open eyes. So, you are angry, you are envious. See it, feel it, then rise above it. Use it to understand what you wish not to be, and decide instead to become all the goodness you wish for the world."

Having completed her final line, Leanna held the page tightly to her chest and watched Big Li, desperate to see what he would do in her part. For a moment, she hoped he would say, 'Very well, perhaps you are right.' Still, when he did precisely so, flames rose up in a raging tempest within her, and she fought through it to remain silent, giving attention to Penny who spoke on.

"Leanna lowers to the Jewel," Penny read, "and takes it up, securing it to her hand. She falls to kneeling and raises her arms to the Sky. Thunder cracks, then the clouds begin to disperse, and the sun shines down upon the stage."

Silence.

"What happens next?" Leanna implored, urging Fantázo to continue.

"That is the end of the play," they replied.

"But there is more to the story."

The writer's eyes widened. "Indeed," they said, smiling.

"So what is it?" Leanna was firm.

"It has yet to be written."

"Surely thou hast some idea."

Fantázo shook their head. "It is not my place to guess at that. Not for this story."

"Why didst thou write this?" Leanna cried.

"It is a good tale. I think it deserves being told."

"It is not the truth."

"It is part of the truth."

"It cannot end this way!"

Fantázo flinched back. "What—the play? I think it is a splendid end to the play. To thy life? No, I concur, this could not be the ending to thy life, for I am certain it would only be the beginning."

"Dost thou wish me to leave? Is that why thou hast written this?"

"No!" they exclaimed with utmost sincerity. "Thy company has been a joy, and I dread the thought of thy departure; but this, here, is not thy life, Leanna Page, however much thou might wish it, and I am too fond of a good story to let thine go wasted."

Leanna turned her gaze away, facing the Treetops, and held back a tear of anguish. When she was certain the tear would not fall, she returned to the writer.

"What if I am torn apart by the weight of it all?" she asked.

Fantázo returned one of their confident smiles. "Then thou shalt return to us, swifter than the wind, and we shall help thee be whole again."

Slowly, with steadfast fear and yet growing acceptance, Leanna nodded. "Do you promise it?" she asked the company. "All of you? I may return at any time, in any year, and you will be here? I need you to promise." Her glance fell on Fantázo's smile.

"Always, and into eternity," they said, and the others offered many similar assurances.

"I shall hold thee to that," she said to the writer, a glimmer of the players' mirth reinfecting her spirit.

"I hope thou dost," Fantázo responded.

Leanna stepped out of the circle and toward her sleeping place in the leaves where she kept her few belongings.

Hanker called to her. "Thou shan't leave this very instant! Sleep, and walk in the light."

Unwrapping her bundled cape for the first time in who-knows-how-many years, she held now her gifts from Madrick and Cassius which had been stored within. She sighed.

"I fear I may have stayed too long already."

Hanker, and several likeminded players, looked to Fantázo to convince her to delay her journey, but the writer merely nodded, understanding she would do what she must. Leanna tucked the necklace vial into her newer, more colorful, brightly decorated tunic, and slid the miniature bolt-spear into a new pocket of her old trousers which had been embellished with designs that partnered with the new top. She returned toward the circle holding her old, more drab, tunic and cape. Dilan-a-Jove turned to her and spoke severely but with great care.

"Burn them, dear. They shan't fit any ensemble that is suited to thee."

Leanna laughed with a shake of her head, but, with the permission of Spark, assented, tossing the old garb into the flames. She watched them burn, then lifted her gaze to Fantázo Fiala.

"I do not promise to wield the Jewel," she said, "but if I do and I am not torn apart but instead I do something marvelous, wilt thou write about me?"

"On my life, I swear I shall."

"I would look forward to reading it," she told them.

"As would I," they replied.

She turned from the fire and left the circle. A few paces out, she returned her gaze to the players once more, and they gasped, smiled, and broke into their merry laughter, hearing her telepathy for the first time as, speechless, she thanked them. At last contented, Leanna smiled, and strode off into the Wood, heading straight for the World Within.

CHAPTER XXVI

One Last Mural

When she was near enough once more, Leanna began again to be able to see, in her visions, the World Within the Woods. She used the night as an excuse to delay her fears and, settling onto a pile of leaves, she slept dreamlessly. As the dawning sun pierced her eyelids the next day, Leanna took her forearm to her brow and wiped away the morning's dew. Now unclosing her eyes, she found a sudden stillness and stared before her. There, in a stream of sunlight which filtered through the Trees, stood a magnificent blue heron. Her neck was elongated and chin lifted proud until, turning, she looked to Leanna. The two gazed at one another, breathing in synchronicity, neither daring to move lest the moment be squandered. Between them hung a sense of knowing that neither would claim to fully understand, but Leanna trusted it so that, in an instant, she decided whichever way this heron next flew, that would be the path she would follow. As if understanding its task, the heron bent her legs, lifted her grand wings, and propelled herself through the air, flying in the direction of the Pavoline castle. Leanna smirked at the sly bird, accepting her determined path.

 She jumped to her feet and ran after the heron, leaping over Tree roots and dashing between wild berry bushes, laughing in her play. She halted and caught her breath, watching as the heron flew out of sight. Leanna remained there a moment, gazing at the Sky, and suddenly wondered what it would be like to change Its mood at her will. Whisking her gaze down and away, she looked at the vibrant shrubbery around her and took new note of the Forest's fruit. She picked at it and nibbled on huckleberry and caraway as she continued on toward the kingdom. Having not yet decided upon any definite objective, she subdued any fear of her future and allowed it to melt away, becoming filled instead by a new amazement and curiosity about her present. Eventually, she found herself in the Forest of Beasts, just within the border of Pavoline. The place was said to be deadly; still, the smaller stature of the trees allowed for so much light to fall upon the wooded ground that even Leanna's few sightings of bears and boa constrictors did naught to build up any fear within her.

The citadel showed itself to her at last, and, with the refreshing crisp air of a new day filling her breast, Leanna strode steadily into the marketplace, entering the flow of civilry, expecting to go unrecognized throughout the thick crowd. As she continued on at an amble, she caught the sideways glance, and even the pointed finger, of more than a few passersby until, thinking it best to pull aside, she turned into a small alley between buildings and leaned against one of the sandstone walls. Seeing now directly across to the opposite side of the alley, she discovered with dismay the cause for her mild celebrity. Pasted to the stone was a parchment with a portrait of Leanna's likeness, along with a declaration announcing a reward for her head, signed with the oath of King Guiomar of Pavoline and Queen Isolda of Masor. She had no time to consider any of the implications, for a clamoring came from behind and she stepped out from the secluded passage, seeing several Pavol knights gesturing, and now shouting, for her capture. She leaned back against the inner wall and sighed. Then she began to run.

Daring not to examine her surroundings, or consider heavily her direction, Leanna barreled down little-known paths toward the only location in Pavoline she thought might bring her seclusion and safety. Winding around the back of the citadel, she discovered the wooded entrance to the mysterious caves of her youth and leapt within, plastering herself to the cold, clay wall as the knights charged past the exterior thicket, searching for her up ahead.

Once again entreating her breath to calm, Leanna looked all around the opening of the cave, then, satisfied no knights remained near, relaxed the back of her head upon the wall. Lifting it again, with furrowed brow, she turned to her right, spying deeper into the caves whence, indeed, she now saw a faint, pulsing, azure glow in the distance, and could just discern the shadows of her childhood apartment within it. Curious at it being so near, she took several paces toward it and stopped as the glow of the hollow grew brighter at her every step. Amazed, she walked on, quickening her pace with every step that she took, heart beating in sync with the pulsing glow of the cave. Within moments, she stood again in that hollow of years past, but the light then extinguished, plunging the apartment into darkness, total except for the far corner of the hollow in which a thin column of light emerged from a small tunneling entryway. Leanna flew to it, leaping over the bags of wheat that lay scattered on the floor below. She dove into the small tunnel, traveling through its turns, and at last took her first steps inside the antechamber of the Jewel of Nebulous.

She instantly despised her own heart for its feeling of wonderment at the chamber's beauty, for though the majesty of the Gwahanu swam gloriously upon the walls, so too did the infamous murals lay their horror bare upon them. She saw, as had her mother, the first image of the untouched Jewel upon its pedestal and the peaceful tree with all four seasons in its branches. She saw, beside the tree, the lightning cutting across the wall, directing her gaze to the next panel with the Jewel loosed and adorned by a wicked silhouette with raging eyes. She saw the red sun, and she saw how this villain directed its fiery rays upon a burning wood. She saw the massive wave erupting and cascading upon a helpless village, and the knights, peasants, and children who lay dead in its wake. She saw the moon high above them withering into dust. She came to the final panel, still shrouded by the thick basalt that covered the wall, and stepped in front of it, placing the central pedestal behind her at her heel. With utmost disdain, she bore her glare into the stone and demanded it reveal to her its final, greatest horror.

The earth began to shake. Leanna placed a steadying hand on the empty pedestal behind her but refused to fall. She stood steadfast as the towering basalt started to crack and splinter, shutting her eyes and turning away at the dust, until all was stillness and silence. She reopened her eyes, looking down at the debris which surrounded her until, gripping the pedestal harder still, she lifted her glare to look upon the last of the murals. Leanna's countenance of contempt softened into astonishment. In the mural before her there was a sun, but no drought. Water, but no flood. There was green grass and wildflowers, wheat and vegetable gardens in full bloom. Atop it all was the Jewel, shining more brightly here in its goodness than it did in any depiction of its evil. Still, however, it failed to return to its pedestal. It was cradled in the palms of another silhouetted adorner whose eyes displayed a stunning brightness, exuding balance and peace.

Leanna's brow wrinkled in confusion, and she spun to the former images which had given her—and her mother—such fear. Again, looking upon them now, she quivered. Turning back to the final mural, she began to weep, furious at the Gwahanu for not having revealed it sooner. Never had the Jewel of

Nebulous been a name thought of with any kindness, but might Fantázo have been right? Might she think altered of the gem now without considering herself a heinous beast? She remembered the horrid drought in Masor, and the knights struck down by one prince's envious lightning. She thought of the tornado that mutilated her friend. She thought of the misaimed murder of Queen Okalani. Could anything with such an evil history, one day, bring true goodness to the world? Perhaps the possibility of this goodness would have all the sooner caused the Jewel's power to wreak havoc on the world, commanded by a weak hand. Perhaps this is why the mural was hidden, to not provide false hope to a base spirit. Did the River then, in truth, trust the spirit of Leanna Page to wield the power well? She leaned upon the pedestal and slid her back against it, dropping to the floor. Her gaze stayed trained upon this last image, and she remained, sitting thither, until the fall of night.

At length, she fell into her dreamscape and opened her eyes to find her mother sitting in front of her, older now than Leanna remembered.

Leanna worked to hide her surprise. It had been so long since she had shared a dream with anyone else's mind and, in truth, she had come to appreciate the privacy. Esta must have been reaching for her to have appeared there in the same moment as did Leanna. It was almost as though the mother had been waiting in the dreamscape, just in case.

"So, thou dost live!" the mother said. "My dear, I have missed thee so."

Esta dove into an embrace, pulling her daughter into her arms. Leanna remembered then how unlike reality a sensation in a dream truly felt. The depth and texture was all missing, but the love was there. Leanna kissed her mother on the cheek.

"And I, you, mother. Forgive me."

"Whither hast thou been all these years?"

"Years..." Leanna thought, realizing the time.

"Yes! I thought I lost thee."

"I am sorry."

Esta wanted to further lament the time, scorn Leanna for the lack of contact, but something in her child's quiet, melancholy eyes put her beyond reprimand. Esta looked around and saw the dream-blurred chamber of the Jewel.

"I never imagined I'd again see these walls," quoth the mother. "But when hast thou to dream us hither?"

"I am hither now."

"Wherefore?" Esta exclaimed, and Leanna explained briefly whither she had disappeared to those years past, why she had now returned, and the events of her intended wedding to Kennedy which set her off in the first. Esta lost all her anger and fell into grief. "My dear—" She wanted to offer words of wisdom, or something that might be a balm to her child's pain, but all she could muster was, "I am so sorry, my dear child."

Leanna shrugged. "It is not thy doing."

"Isn't it?" Esta began. "If I had but not entered this chamber, if I had not spoken of the Jewel to thy father—"

"It is not thy doing," Leanna repeated, and Esta fell silent.

After a moment, the mother queried, "Thou entered Pavoline this morn? Why hast thou remained hither so long?"

Leanna gestured behind Esta to the newest mural.

"My goodness," quoth the mother, turning round, sitting now beside Leanna and remaining fixed there as the first had. In their silence, Leanna now thought of Kennedy, and then thither the fairy stood. Due to the illusion of dreams, it felt now as though she had been standing beside them in the chamber all along.

"Leanna!" She cried, then halted her exclamations in disappointment. "This is but a dream. Is it only another of my usual dreams?"

"No, Kennedy. It is I."

The fairy hardly dared to believe.

Leanna met her gaze and held it for a long moment. "I swear it, my love. I have returned."

Kennedy dropped to Leanna to lay endless kisses upon her, and she did so until Esta coughed slightly, making the mother's presence known. Kennedy bashfully sat back on her heels and took Leanna's hand. Smiling politely, she said, "Greetings, Esta. A joy to see you as well."

Leanna wrapped Kennedy's hand in both of her own. "Forgive me for leaving as I did, but I could not bear a farewell."

"We needn't have had a farewell, for thy magic, Leanna."

The dreamer shook her head. "I was too far away, in more ways than one."

"I don't understand. I assumed thou must have died to leave me waiting so long with nothing."

"In a way, perhaps I did. I had to. I did not know how to go on. But I am returned now. Can you forgive me?"

Kennedy looked to their hands, entwined once more, then turned her gaze to the dreamer. "I never thought I'd see thee again. I shall always love thee, Leanna."

Leanna sighed, looking down, and, at Kennedy's curious eye, Esta took up the task of relating all she'd been told, including pointing the newcomer towards the peaceful mural. Kennedy's visage widened in awe, but she withheld any opinion, turning to Leanna.

"What dost thou wish to do?"

"It is mine to take, I know that now," Leanna said, "but I still fear it so."

"This is one benign image beside several of villainy," Esta reminded her. "To maintain that state of peace may require strength of heart beyond anyone's capacity."

"Leanna's is the purest heart I know," Kennedy declared.

"Hast thou seen thine?" Leanna asked, half in jest. Kennedy scoffed, and Leanna turned to sincerity. "Kennedy, it was thee who taught me to seek adventure. Thee who helped me first see the beauty of the world. It was thy courage which instructed me how to fight for what is good. My love, if my heart is pure, it is because of thee! How would I be meant to remain so when thou art inevitably gone from the world?"

"Thou dost not offer thyself due credit for thy worth, Leanna. Caring for me may blind thee to certain faults of mine, but, in thine absence, I often sought furiously for faults within thee and came up with little to naught. Thou hast strength in thee beyond imagining."

Leanna looked up to the mural. "See her, Kennedy. She is alone. I do not want to be alone."

Kennedy held more tightly to Leanna's hand and smiled with a new idea. "Then return to me."

Leanna met her eyes with deep sadness. "I think I must take up the Jewel."

"No!" Esta cried, but Leanna pushed on.

"It was made for me, mother—or I for it, I suppose. Though wielding it doth frighten me, indeed, I am frightened more so by thought of it being wielded by another. For myself I fear weariness, solitude, even madness; but for the world, at another's hand, I fear destruction and worldly grief." Leanna nearly laughed now in realization, explaining, "The River wishes for peace, that is why it calls me to the Jewel! I cannot abandon it."

"Why need it be wielded at all?" Esta tried. "Thou couldst obey the River without so endangering thyself by simply returning it to its pedestal."

Leanna shook her head. "Someone is certain to again discover these chambers; the risk is too great."

Kennedy saw Esta's fear seep into the crevices of her cheeks and, with a thought, turned Leanna toward her.

"Bring it instead to Anwansi," she offered. "We shall hide it within our castle, and it will be guarded."

"If its location were to be rumored it may invite attack."

"No army has had good fortune in such efforts so far." The young queen smirked with pride, but Leanna remained unpleased.

"Kennedy, it does not want to be hidden away. It wants *me*."

"But, love, canst thou in truth want *it*? What life would that leave thee? Please, Leanna, return to me, and we can protect the Jewel together."

It pained Leanna so to deny Kennedy her wish, so she considered it. "Thou art certain it would be safe?"

Kennedy eagerly affirmed it. "I trust our warriors. It shall never be wielded again."

"What if it is then displeased? What if it calls to me still?"

"We shall be together nonetheless! Is that not for what thou dost wish after all this time?"

"Of course, I wish for that," Leanna said.

"Then bring the Jewel to me."

Leanna nodded, slowly. "So it shall be," she conceded.

"Truly?"

"Of course, my love."

"If some happenstance goes awry, thou wilt tell me. Thou wilt not leave me again without a word."

"I swear it. I do."

The fairy's countenance grew bright as she declared, "Then thou shalt return to me swiftly."

Leanna gave her a kind smile, saddened at the thought of the lost years. "With more celerity than a shooting star," she avowed.

Awakening in glee, Kennedy vanished from the dream, her form becoming a light mist which drifted away into the air. Leanna now turned to her mother who remained with a countenance of dread.

"There is something I never told thee, Leanna; nor, thought of myself for some time." Esta paused and Leanna looked to her curiously. "That day, when

I first discovered this chamber, it was not the images that frightened me, horrid though they be, but—and forgive me, but—it was thee."

"Me?"

"Yes. I could feel thee inside me, turning, pushing… reaching. It was though thou wert reaching for the Jewel, as though thou didst wish for it the way thou sayst now that it wishes for thee. It frightens thee, thou dost say, and thou hast now agreed to hide the Jewel away, but I fear thou art reaching for it still. I never want to see thee wear it."

"I shan't. We found another way," Leanna whispered.

"I need thy word," the mother commanded. "Promise me, thou wilt never take on the power of the Jewel."

Leanna remained a moment, stunned into silence. She swallowed her hesitation, then spoke. "So long as I can avoid that day, I shall."

Esta winced and shook her head, disappearing from the dream. Leanna awoke into the true chamber and sat again against the pedestal, staring at the mural above her. She analyzed its every line and seared its colors into her memory. At last, seeing through the earth and knowing the moon had risen high above the castle of Pavoline, she stole away her gaze and left the chamber behind.

CHAPTER XXVII

Nebulous Rises

Emerging from the cave, Leanna wound her way towards the castle, taking care to evade the sight of any—knight or peasant—who walked out in the night. She snuck around to the rear of the fortress and found once more the small, unassuming servants' entrance. Seeing that no one stood by, she hurried to it and, removing the bolt-spear from her pocket, sent its quiet sparks toward the latch, unfastening the lock. Now entering, she was blinded by the darkness within and felt her way to the summit of a staircase until she found an archway leading to a torch-lit hall. Hiding in the darkness of the stairwell, she observed two knights guarding the end of the hall and could only presume many more were stationed throughout the palace, far more fortified now after the intrusion of the fairies those years before. Looking through her mind's eye, she charted the path through the castle to Guiomar's chamber at the edge of the fortress where he presently slept, and she knew there would be no reaching it unseen. She twirled the bolt-spear between her fingertips and, placing her shoulders back and lifting her chest, brazenly stepped out into the hall, stampeding towards the guards. They lifted their swords at the sight of her, but she threw them each a controlled bolt and stunned them to the side. Leanna turned a confident corner, and the knights guarding thither received the same fate. Upon hearing their fellows fall, and the subsequent bellows, more knights came thronging into the halls, but none hindered Leanna's speed. She charged through them, nostrils flared, paces steady, and aim keen. When the halls were such that no direct path though the crowding knights could be seen, Leanna remembered her training with the Warriors of Alquoria and executed their battle-dances with grace and ferocity, tucking beneath the sword of one knight, and leaping over that of another. Her elbow found the chainmail on a knight's side, unprotected by his plate armer. Her fist met the under-chin of the next. She somersaulted beneath several, knocking them to the ground, and sent a bolt between the legs of one who meant to take her as she slid under him before leaping to her feet. A couple took their chance to retreat, and the rest were finished off with blasts from her spear.

Taking her final turn, she released a stunning bolt and quieted the knights who guarded the chamber of King Guiomar Ranzentine. Stooping to them, she removed one of their gloves and placed it within her pocket, then she stood to face the double doors, gazing at the handle that would open them. Closing her eyes and seeing inside, Leanna saw that the king slept soundly. She tucked her bolt-spear away and coaxed the right door open with a light touch, peering in to look upon the king. Leanna slipped into the chamber and closed the door with nimble rapidity upon her entrance, letting no more than a sliver of torchlight into the apartment and for no longer than a swift moment. Still, the light of the moon shone in from the casements and flooded the apartment in copious amounts, plenty to reflect a great shine off the gem that adorned the king's fingers. The Jewel rested there, glittering, wrapped to Guiomar's right hand which recklessly dangled off the side of the bed closer to the door. Leanna remained a moment, fingers still on the door handle behind her, staring at the Jewel of Nebulous, so close to her now, desperately forcing her heart to calm. She took a step into the chamber, and the king's finger twitched. Jolting her eyes up to see he still slept, she pushed forward, at length finding herself before him, before it, and she placed one knee upon the ground to bring her eyes in line with the Jewel. A rush of anxious excitement prickled at her fingertips as she reached her hand up to meet the king's. She might have then ripped the Jewel from his hand and escaped the chamber, but her fingers stopped in the air, remembering she should not touch the gem if she meant not to wear it. She took a moment to slip the glove onto her hand. In the ill-advised moment of pause, the eyes of Guiomar Ranzentine flared open before her, and she jolted back, falling upon the ground as he whisked his hand away and vaulted to the opposite side of the bed.

The king called for his knights, but there was no response. He scowled at the silence, and Leanna smirked, taking her bolt-spear in hand. Despite its size, Guiomar instantly recognized the weapon and retrieved his own bolt-spear which he had mounted upon his wall, firing at Leanna in the same instant she fired a bolt at him. The directed lightning from each spear met in the center of the chamber and exploded in a crash of thunder, Leanna's spear flying from her hand and breaking through the window beside her, falling into the courtyard below. Guiomar simultaneously dropped his sizzling weapon to the chamber floor, and they both watched as the blue spearhead at last revolted against its untrained wielder and lost its glowing spark, the handle burning into a blackened crisp. King and page flashed each other a leery glare then dove toward subsequent fighting tools, Guiomar taking hold of his sword and Leanna grabbing the fire poker beside the hearth. Guiomar rushed to her, slashing his sword, and she blocked his blow with her makeshift blade, her force knocking him back a step. They recovered in the same moment and sent their blades together, iron clashing with steel, he now overpowering her, and she maneuvering to throw him off his footing. Their weapons met several times more, and the sound of it at last brought a loyal knight storming into the chamber, sword held at the ready.

The knight placed his sword at Leanna's back and, keeping her eyes trained on Guiomar to the front, she swung the poker behind, clashing with the knight's blade. She was successful in thrusting the knight's sword hand away, but with his other he grasped the iron she fought with and, in her thwarted attempt to maintain her hold, she was thrown, weaponless, to the wall, her back thrust flat against it. A glint of pride shone in Guiomar's eye as he lifted his sword and rushed to Leanna, driving his sword into her chest, just above her heart, forcing it through until the point stopped at the stone behind her. She gasped, pain rippling through her, panting now into her lower abdomen, careful to maintain stillness above where the blade sat within her. Guiomar began to chortle, holding his right hand upon the hilt.

"This is finished," he declared, leaning his weight toward Leanna and onto the sword, unable to relinquish his victorious sight. Leanna persisted through her pain, offering him a sly grin. He furrowed his brow.

Her glove shot up to his hand and tore the Jewel of Nebulous from his fingers. With a knee to his groin, she kicked him against the bed and used a cautious speed to pry the sword from her chest, endeavoring not to howl against the pain. She threw the bloody blade at the knight who evaded it by stepping in front of the doors. Opposite him, Leanna looked to the window and knew of the steep height at which it stood from the castle courtyard below. Guiomar began to stand, the knight stepped toward her, and, tightening her fist around the Jewel, she hurled herself through the glass. She could hear Guiomar's scream as she descended, but it hardly compared to her own upon her impact with the cobblestone of the ground below. Knights began filtering out into the court. Leanna endeavored to walk, to run, or simply to stand, but her now shattered leg would have none of it. She managed to drag herself to the center of the courtyard towards the open gate, but spotted blackness began to conceal her vision, and Pavol knights now encircled her in every direction, swords held at the ready.

A sense of relief overcame her. She opened her hand and glared at the Jewel which sat, at home, in her gloved palm. It glowed bright under her glance, and she felt its warmth. There would be no reaching Anwansi with the Jewel uncaptured, she could see that clearly now, and too Leanna knew asudden that, even if she did successfully reach Alquoria's capitol with the coveted gem, she herself would never be able to part from it. She looked round at the knights who encircled her, and she twisted the Jewel around to the top of her fingers.

Forgive me, she thought to her mother and Kennedy in the same. *I was made to wield the Jewel. It is time.* She could hear them begin to plead with her, but she shut them out. Now, closing her eyes, she plunged the Jewel deep into the wound above her heart, screaming at the pain, then, keeping her right hand pressed against the profuse outpour of blood, she took up, with her left, the vial of Aldorian water and placed it to her lips, tilting her head back and drinking to the last drop. The empty vial hung around her neck as she came up to her knees and pressed her palms into the floor. She pinched her eyes tighter, feeling every sensation, as the magic coursed through her every vein and brought remedy to her injuries, healing her wounds, and sealing the Jewel of Nebulous inside her.

Her visions brought her once again to the Nebulous chamber, and the images she saw flashed uncontrollably betwixt the first of the murals and the last, Leanna seeing her own visage in place of the anonymous, silhouetted adorners, now the one in peace, and now the one in evil. She shook the vision from her head and regained her sight of the stones lining Pavoline's royal courtyard, comprehending with complete clarity the vastness of her newly acquired power. With the Jewel of Nebulous sitting above her heart and its magic coursing through her, she felt, at long last, complete.

The knights whispered in astonishment as she steadily came to her feet, facing away from the castle. She widened her stance and shot her hand into the air as above them dark clouds began to gather, soon blanketing the Sky and crackling with lightning. Horrified at the power of the young mystical woman, the knights slightly lowered their swords and took some steps away, countenances covered in fear.

Leanna looked up at the massive clouds and grinned. In a sudden pivot to face the grand entryway of the palace, she sliced her arm down to her side and rain began to pour, drenching the knights but leaving Leanna dry. Lightning split the Sky and only thundered all the louder. She now met eyes with Guiomar who stood under the protective covering of the landing of the castle steps. He stood frozen in a furious terror. She remembered the knights of Masor and glared at the king, raising her hand once more to her thundering Sky. A flurry of lightning flashed down into the courtyard and, in its retreat, it left the world unseeable. Lightning flickered again amidst the clouds and shone momentary light on the scene until the thunder quieted and the clouds drifted south, allowing moonlight to flood into the courtyard. Only then did Guiomar see.

Some of his knights seized, the others all unconscious, and the eyes of Leanna Page burned before him with a vengeance. He looked to her, this page, evermore the wielder of Nebulous, and he shuddered, now jumping back as thunder crashed once more and lightning rained over the fields beyond. Fire began to grow, turning the horizon a deep red before clouds returned to rain upon it, beginning to subdue the flames into rising smoke. Leanna paced steadily toward the king, her eyes glowing with the power of the Jewel behind them. She climbed the castle steps and Guiomar fell to his knees before her, paralyzed in awe.

Upon reaching him, Leanna snatched his poignard and held it at his throat.

"Look beyond the walls, Your Majesty. Watch it burn." Even her snarled sentiments seemed to boom like thunder in his ears. "This is what thou hast earned for thy people, King. THIS—the destruction of the peace—is for what thou shalt be remembered."

"So kill me," he dared. "You can finish it. Finish me!"

She raised the poignard high and readied to strike, but king and page both were then frozen in their place, suddenly hurtled into a new type of waking dream.

They stood, weaponless, in Leanna's bright dreamscape, Guiomar looking round in horrified haste.

"Have you done it?" He asked. "Am I gone?"

"No," she snarled. "It seems the River doth not wish it." Finally, she began to soften, remembering herself. "Or, perhaps, in truth, it is that I do not wish it."

He looked to her, at last unabashedly amazed. "How could you not wish my end?"

"Because I would not have you released from the burden of your crimes. Death, I imagine, is nothing so real as this place of my mind; nothing where you can feel. And if anyone deserves to be made to feel, it is you, Guiomar Ranzentine. No, for you, it will not be so simple as death. You have to make remedy."

"Remedy for what?"

"Do not dare look me in the eye and ask such a question."

Guiomar turned his gaze away and sought round him for an escape. There, of course, was none. He returned to her.

"Let me free of this place."

She shook her head. "What are you going to do after today, King?"

Striding up and looking down with a maddened glare into her unshaken, steadfast eyes, he said, "I am going to lead my people how I have always intended."

"With steel, and greed, and prejudice? I will not allow it."

"What will you do of it?"

"What I promised many years ago. I will stop you. You know I can, and you know I will always be watching."

He paced back and turned away, fiercely rubbing the terror from his chin. He remained staring out into the cerulean. "What would you have me do?"

"Fix it."

"Fix it!" He cried, returning his gaze to her. "To what standard?"

"The standard of peace."

"Impossible."

"Peace is always possible," the Nebulous woman assured him.

"I have nothing in me that would allow it. I never learned how to be a peaceful king."

"Yet be so you must," she commanded.

"I do not know how!"

"I can guide you."

"You despise me. Why would you aid me?"

Leanna held back her rage, rising to her own decided measure. "Guiomar, if you shall wish to aid the world, then I shall wish to aid you. Such a matter is too vital to be lost in vengeful remembrances."

They remained now in one another's stare, unspeaking and unmoving, as new voices began to ring in their ears.

Madrick: "Isolda, put that down."

Isolda: "Get back to thy chamber, brother. Where are thy knights?"

Madrick: "I will no more be locked away."

Leif: "Madrick?"

Madrick: "Leif, is it thee? And Esta!"

Esta: "Your Majesty. Leanna! ... Madrick, what is she—"

Madrick: "Isolda, no!"

Thunder cracked and all flashed darkness in the dreamscape. Guiomar's sight returned to his place in the clear night, standing atop the palace steps. He saw now two peasants some distance away, his knights beginning to rise, his royal ally holding the small bolt-spear in hand, her previously imprisoned brother grasping onto the same as it pointed toward the steps, and at last Leanna, having fallen unconscious at his feet. The older peasant woman, who had a striking visual similarity to Leanna, ran to the steps and held the young woman's face. At her cry of relief, it could be seen that Leanna still had breath.

"Madrick, thou fool," Isolda snapped, pulling her arm out of her brother's grasp and tossing the bolt-spear aside. "Thou hast ruined the shot. Look, she lives!"

"I will never allow thee to take her life!" he declared.

"Thou art nothing but trouble," the queen snarled.

"To be trouble to thee is an honor."

Isolda scoffed and pushed her brother aside, pulling her dagger from her belt. She tried to walk to the steps but was stopped asudden by the other peasant's firm hand on her arm.

"Leif, release me at once or die where thou dost stand." Isolda warned.

Madrick pulled the two apart and put himself between them. "Isolda, by the River and Sky, find some sense of tenderness. I beg you, Sister, hear me now as you have not dared to in years."

"It is not a matter of daring, Brother, it is a matter of not wasting my time."

The peasant woman spoke now. "Your Highness, for all we have each endured, please, hear him."

"How is it thou art even here, Esta?" Isolda barked.

"I knew where my child would be."

"So be it. But thee, stablehand?"

"Esta needed a horse," they replied.

Isolda scoffed, laughing further as she paced back toward the center of the courtyard and slipped her dagger away in its place. "Well, then is this not simply the loveliest? The whole family, reunited." She looked to Esta. "Not all, actually. Where might the father be? I thought he of anyone would be in Pavoline."

"Do not be cruel, Isolda," Guiomar said.

"Me? You killed the man!"

The king's countenance was grave. "I know."

Madrick looked to no one but Isolda. "Let us return to Masor and tend to our own people. You can leave this blood-thirst behind."

"It is not blood-thirst, it is strategy. She would ruin us!"

Madrick scowled. "That is only a lie you crafted to make your yearning for power more palatable."

"Is it a lie that she sought my crown? Why else would she have befriended one such as thee?"

"She befriended all, regardless of status," Leif spoke now. "She was the last to ever think of seeking a crown."

Isolda fumed. "She maneuvered behind my back to turn my own brother against me. Madrick, she pushed you toward the throne, and the closer you became, the closer did she."

"If you had not been such a status-minded, riches-hungry ruler, perhaps she would never have bothered. She was nothing but a page in our castle until you made a villain of her."

"She was always more, Madrick, you know that," Esta said.

"She should not have had to be," he replied.

The mother scowled, various remembrances returning to her in a flurry of sorrow. "If you had not held so tightly to your prejudices, perhaps she would have revealed her power to you sooner and all the banishment and strife could have been prevented."

"You mean to blame me?" Madrick asked. "I was a friend to you all those years."

"You were the king, yet you acted a fool."

"Esta, be kind." Leif tried.

"Is it your child on the steps, Leif?!"

"It might as well be!" they rejoined, pulling back in offense. "I cared for Leanna, we both did, you know that. You had every opportunity to speak the truth, Esta, if not to him then to me. You might have told of what dangers were possible, and I would have helped you."

"You spent more time with my daughter than I did, Leif. Was I meant to offer you more of her unprompted? It was a family matter, in which you were not involved."

"Would Leanna agree with that?" Lief asked.

Esta rose and marched to stand before them. "Do not speak of her that way."

"Might we, though?" Madrick asked, holding a hand up for her attention. "You say we were not family, fine, but I loved that child. It matters not if you knew it because I know she did. Still, I have languished in solitary imprisonment for years, all for her sake. She hath these many powers, yet I heard nothing of her for all this time. Did you?"

"Of course, I am her mother."

"And I'm—! I thought she might have said something. She might have sought to know if I were well. If she had known—" He shook his head. "She had to have known."

"I'm sorry, Madrick," Esta told him.

"You had to have known as well, Esta," he realized. "If you knew where to find Leif in Pavoline, then you must have known all. Did you speak of me to her? Did you suggest I might have wished to hear something—anything? If she had only spoken to me, perhaps we might have made a plan. With all her powers, her friends, she might have helped me escape, and we could have gathered the people in our favor. I could have—" He looked to Leif and stifled a cry, forcing his gaze back to Esta in his effort to keep away tears. "We could have lived our lives! Instead, what have we been all this time?"

"We have been waiting," Isolda said, "and now the wait is over." She started back toward Leanna, releasing again her dagger and holding it ready before her, but Madrick blocked her way.

"I will not allow it," he said.

Isolda, impatient, plunged her ready dagger into her brother's side.

"No!" Leif ran to him, catching him in their arms before he hit the stone below. Esta rushed to their side, grievances forgotten.

"Stop her," Madrick breathed as Leif cried over him. "Please."

Isolda took her dagger up the steps, and Guiomar now caught her arm, halting her as he watched the scene below and startling the queen into doing the same.

"Keep your strength," Leif whispered to Madrick.

Madrick chuckled, then winced at the pain it caused. He simply shook his head.

Leif started to cry. "I began to hope we would have our time,"

"As did I." Madrick lifted his arm, forcing himself to bear the aching, and he brought Leif's cheek into his hand.

"Do not leave me when I have just found thee again."

"I am so sorry. If I had spoken sooner, or been more cautious later—"

Leif brought their lips to his, silencing the apology with a kiss. As they parted, only just, Leif whispered, "I shall always love thee, Madrick Oxbien." Then, with the smallest smile, the former Crown of Masor, King for the Commoner, Madrick Oxbien II was gone.

Leif bent over him in agony, and Esta placed a hand on their shoulder.

Guiomar turned to Isolda, astonished. "You killed him. Why?"

"He was in the way." Isolda tried to pull her arm free of the king's grasp, but he held only tighter.

"You are mad," he said.

Her brow pulled into itself in bewilderment. "You killed your own father for no greater offense."

"Yes. We are both mad, Isolda, and it ends today." He pushed her a step away.

She laughed—"You are being silly"—and shook her head. She raised her blood-soaked dagger and started for Leanna once more. Guiomar called to his rising knights.

"Seize the queen at once!" He ordered, and at this Isolda stopped and looked to him aghast, holding her hands high.

"Don't be absurd, Guiomar." She flashed a glare to the approaching knights. "Touch me and die," she told them. The king dismissed them, content the queen would hear him.

"I shall not have you kill her, Isolda."

"I do not understand," she said. "For what other reason have I resided in your castle these several years? I swore I would not leave until she was buried, and now she can be! Do not falter in our purpose now, King."

Guiomar's chest grew tight, ashamed to confess the truth of his changed heart, so he spoke in partial incompletes. "Perhaps she can be of use," he said.

"We shan't ever control her, especially now," Isolda reminded him.

"I no longer wish for her death."

"Then your wishes have strayed from sense! Find the rational course."

"It isn't right."

"What, murder? When has the morality of it strayed you in the past?"

"WE are not right, Isolda!" Guiomar bellowed, banging a fist to his chest and restraining new tears.

The queen stood back, stunned. "The page worked her magic on you, didn't she? She hath troubled your mind."

"No, Isolda," he said softly. "She hath cleared it."

Isolda growled. "I want her destroyed."

"Please. This destruction, this terror in our world, I have been its cause; myself, and this burning rage within. This youth, this page, is the only thing in all the world that may yet help me make recompense. See those who have loved her." He looked to Esta and Leif who still knelt over Madrick's body. "Perhaps I could feel such things as them one day. I shall not see her die."

"You are a fool, Guiomar. I thought you were not so soft-hearted." Isolda raised her dagger once more and began to strike down, but Guiomar caught her arm. Her fiery breath dripped onto him in disgust, and Esta looked up to him now, watching, terrified as he spoke.

"I would that the violence be ended, but understand me, I shall kill you myself in one last vicious act before allowing you to harm Leanna Page."

Esta let go of some of her fear and turned back to Leif who now lifted Madrick to carry him away from the angry scene toward a more loving place to be laid down. The mother, neither wanting to leave Leif to their task alone nor to leave Leanna, now watched as Leif buckled under the weight of their love and their grief and, running to their side, trusted the changed king to protect her child and gave herself as support for Leif, holding their arm and following them from the courtyard. Isolda now tore her arm away from Guiomar with a scoff and paced in bemusement down the steps, watching a moment as her brother was carried out. She turned back to the king in fury. "Is that what you wish for? That is the fate of a king who puts his trust in Leanna Page."

"No, Isolda, that is the fate of a loved one who is doomed from birth by a cold-hearted relation. Let us seek to be better for our newer, younger relations, if for no one else."

"I only seek better for Masor, as you have always known. You have your heir now, and I have mine. What is to prevent this page from obliterating the legacies we meant to ensure? I want nothing of her in my kingdom, and no wall could keep out her kind."

Guiomar looked down to Leanna, in awe and yet fearful of her, even as she slept. He returned to Isolda with a proposition. "What if she was within it?"

"What?"

He nodded, deciding. "The wall is complete save for the short length which is to close it atop the Gwahanu straight. Let her be placed within it," he declared. "We shall cage her and have her carried to the River. The cage shall be dropped in the epicenter of the wall with stones below, stones around, and at last we shall place the final stones above. She will be buried, so you—and your heir—may return to Masor. At length, she may die, or perhaps she shall live on into eternity. Either way, this shall be truly finished."

"None of her powers shall be prevented from affecting us."

"Regardless, that is my only offer. If you wish to challenge it, you challenge me, Isolda."

She squinted, studying him. "She hath changed you, Guiomar."

"Perhaps, in time, she will reach you as well."

Isolda scoffed. "That will never be. But if burying her alive is the only way you will allow us to finish this, then make it so, and do so with haste. Have the cage built quickly, hither around her as she sleeps. Every side of it shall be fastened in place, for it need never open."

Guiomar nodded and set his knights to work, closing off the courtyard to any others who might interfere.

As Leanna slept, the remaining magic from the Aldorian water flooded to her back and healed her where she was last struck. With the complete absence of pain, she was sure, when she saw the sunlight, that she was awaking into a better day. Her eyes unclosed completely and came into focus. It was then that she saw the bars. She jolted up and, in an effort to stand, banged her head against more iron. She held a hand over the pain and scanned the courtyard which now teemed with knights, servants, and masons, all scurrying to their tasks. She studied her cage and discovered it was unopenable. Her gaze now fell on the carriage behind her that was waiting in front of the castle steps, decorated in the banners of Masor. Isolda and Guiomar stood before it, watching her now that she had stirred.

Release me, she commanded them, but they made no sign of having heard. Servants now took up the palanquin that held her, and she begged them to stop, to aid her, to free her! but they pretended they could not hear and completed their task of placing her atop a wagon that faced toward the courtyard entry. She sought her mind for Kennedy and whispered to her an apology, but, after all the years, she could not bring herself to ask again for a dangerous rescue and even wondered now if an escape from these particular bars was possible. In her anger and grief, Kennedy said nothing in response. Leanna put aside that particular heartache and now glared once more to the royals. Suddenly afeared, she saw that there would be no altering the course they had put her on. She caught a distasteful glance from a passing knight and endeavored, in her pride, to now face her unknown fate with stoic strength. She crossed her legs in front of her and sat tall, resuming the meditative stance that once had brought her peace of mind, although merely pretended at the peace now as the fear and fury of her capture pounded within her. Finally, she held Guiomar's gaze with a threatening gravity, then took a deep breath and closed her eyes.

"Fear her not," Isolda whispered to the king. "She shall now be hidden, as good as gone from this world, evermore and into eternity."

Guiomar did not stir nor remove his gaze from the dreamer he had caged. His countenance merely softened from anguish into awe. "No, Isolda," he now replied. "In truth, I do not believe she shall." He turned away without a glance to the queen and stepped into his own carriage behind that from Masor, leaving Isolda alone to settle into her torment.

At the end of a week, the cavalcade—half colored in the fashion of Pavoline and half in that of Masor—completed its journey down the main road, arriving now at the Gwahanu strait. Esta and Leif, being prevented from returning to the courtyard, had quickly managed to loosen the tongue of one who explained to them the royals' intention and, with ever increasing grief, had decided to follow in the path of the procession. They had each filled small packs in their homes then followed the train by foot together, staying some distance from the royals but arriving at the strait with the lot of them. The Masorian carriages continued across the bridge then stopped once fully in the land of Masor. Isolda and Guiomar emerged from their respective carts and stood, each on their own soil, looking on as the masons demolished the old bridge and placed several steel supports into the River, securing the stones atop them and connecting the bottom layers of both kingdoms' halves of the wall.

All present remained there for many days as the stones were built up to just under half the wall's full height. They remained there more days still to see Leanna lifted atop into the center and the stones secured around every face of her cage. Since the courtyard, the young woman had persisted in keeping her eyes unopened, and still now she continued on with them shut, not suffering herself to look any of the builders in the eye as they closed her off from the light. When the sunset of the following week flooded the horizon with deep yellows and reds, and the pink and purple streaks of clouds lay strewn across the Sky, Isolda and Guiomar gave their last collective order, commanding the final stone be placed atop the wall.

The last builders climbed down their ropes and set foot on the ground. They set fire to the ropes and watched them turn to ash, leaving the structure unscalable. No one cheered. All, on either side, simply watched it for a time, unmoving. At length, owls sounded their calls, and the monarchs commanded their now separate cavalcades to return to their respective castles. When Pavoline's carriages had gone, and even after Leif had similarly taken their leave, Esta remained, now completely alone in the vast landscape. She tentatively approached the wall, staring into it, imploring Leanna to speak with her, but the child did not. She could not, not now. As yet, she could not even bring herself to unclose her eyes.

Daylight broke the next morn, and the mother awoke, having slept outside next to the wall, hoping in vain to have met her daughter in a dream. She sat up and marveled at the mountain of stone which stood before her, pernicious now as it fought against the light. Esta began to cry and reached into her satchel for a handkerchief. Instead, she found her old diary hidden away in a forgotten sleeve. She removed it and opened to a page of the distant past, gazing now at the pressed ivy leaf Byrdon had offered her the day that they met. She looked at the leaf and remembered he had told her it might direct them together and ever homeward. Esta wiped away a tear and smiled, presuming that, for so many years, the leaf must have done what he had hoped. She looked again to the wall, and thought that perhaps the leaf could work so again. She took it from its page and stood, walking to the very bottom of the wall, just before the stones turned and crossed the Gwahanu. She hesitated a breath, then knelt to the bottom most stone, placing the leaf upon it.

"May it bring thee home," she whispered.

Esta began to walk off down the road then stopped, gasping between cries as she finally heard the voice of her daughter flood her mind. The mother smiled, hearing for the first time her own child singing the lullaby of her youth.

> *'...The day may come when I must go;*
> *Still, don't despair for even though*
> *They build a wall to keep us 'part,*
> *My love will find thee where thou art.'*

She sent Leanna love enough to last the ages, and the dreamer felt the affection seep through the space and stones. Within her tomb, Leanna's heart began to pound, beating steadily in determined passion, and, although surrounded by impenetrable darkness, the Nebulous Woman unclosed her eyes.

For Elenvia: Publications and Productions is a 501(c)3 charitable arts organization. To support our work, please consider making a tax-deductible donation at ForElenvia.org and spreading the word about us and our projects.

ACKNOWLEDGEMENTS

Great thanks to Carolyn Cooke, Ruby Adamousky, and Allison Pearson for your dedication to and support for the development of this work.

Your encouragement meant everything to me.

www.ingramcontent.com/pod-product-compliance
Lightning Source LLC
LaVergne TN
LVHW091708070526
838199LV00050B/2305